THE POWER

All over the world, women are discovering they have the power. There's Roxy, a white British teenager and the daughter of a gangster. There's Allie, a mixed-race girl who runs away after years of abuse and finds herself at a convent, revered as a goddess. There's Margot, an American mayor and one of the few older women to develop the power. And then Tunde, a young Nigerian man and aspiring journalist who captures early footage of the power in action. With a flick of their fingers, these women can inflict terrible pain — even death. Every man on the planet finds he's lost control. The day of the girls has arrived — but where will it end?

THE POWER

NAOMI ALDERMAN

LARGE
PRINT

First published in Great Britain 2016
by
Viking
an imprint of Penguin Books

First Isis Edition
published 2019
by arrangement with
Penguin Books
Penguin Random House

A catalogue record for this book is available from the British Library.

ISBN 978–1–78541–656–9 (hb)
ISBN 978–1–78541–662–0 (pb)

For Margaret and for Graeme,
who have shown me wonders

The people came to Samuel and said: Place a King over us, to guide us.

And Samuel said to them: This is what a King will do if he reigns over you: he'll take your sons and make them run with his chariots and horses. He'll dispose them however he wants: he'll make them commanders of thousands or captains of fifties, he'll send them to plough, to reap, to forge his weapons and his chariots. He'll take your daughters to make perfume for him, or cook his food or do his baking. He'll take your fields and your vineyards and your olive groves — oh, he'll take the very best of those and give them to his cronies. He'll take much more. A tenth of your grain and your wine — those will go to his favourite aristocrats and faithful servants. Your manservants and your maidservants, your best men, your donkeys — yes, he'll take those for his own use. He'll take one tenth of your flocks and you yourselves will become his slaves. On that day, believe me, you will cry out for relief from this King, the King you asked for, but the Lord will not answer you on that day.

But the people would not listen to Samuel. They said: No. Give us a King over us. So that we can be like all the other nations. Give us a King to guide us and lead us into battle.

When Samuel heard what the people said, he told it to the Lord.

The Lord answered, Give them a King.

1 Samuel 8

The Men Writers Association
New Bevand Square

27th October

Dear Naomi,

I've finished the bloody book. I'm sending it to you, with all its fragments and drawings, in the hope that you'll give me some guidance or at least that I'll finally hear the echo of it as I drop the pebble of this book down the well.

You'll ask me first of all what it *is*. "Not another dry volume of history" was what I promised. Four books in I realize that no general reader can be bothered to wade through endless mounds of evidence, no one cares about the technicalities of dating finds and strata comparison. I've seen audiences' eyes go blank as I try to explain my research. So what I've done here is a sort of hybrid piece, something that I hope will appeal more to ordinary people. Not quite history, not quite a novel. A sort of "novelization" of what archaeologists agree is the most plausible narrative. I've included some illustrations of archaeological finds that I hope are suggestive, but readers can — and I'm sure many will! — skip over them.

I have questions for you. Is it very shocking? Too hard to accept that anything of this sort could ever have been the case, no matter how far back in our history? Is there anything I can do to make it all *seem* more plausible? You know what they say about "truth" and "the appearance of truth" being opposites.

I've put in some terrifically troubling stuff about Mother Eve ... but we all know how these things work! Surely no one will be too distressed ... everyone claims to be an atheist now, anyway. And all the "miracles" really *are* explicable.

Anyway, sorry, I'll shut up now. I don't want to influence you, just read it and tell me what you think. I hope your own book's going well. I can't wait to read it, when it's ready to be seen. Thank you *so much* for this. I am so grateful you could spare the time.

Much love,
Neil

Nonesuch House
Lakevik

Dearest Neil,

Wow! What a treat! I've been flicking through the pages and can't wait to dive in. I see you've included some scenes with male soldiers, male police officers and "boy crime gangs", just as you said you would, you saucy boy! I don't have to tell *you* how much I enjoy that sort of thing. I'm sure you remember. I'm practically on the edge of my seat.

I'm very intrigued to see what you've done with the premise. It'll be a welcome relief from my own book, if

I'm honest. Selim says if the new one's not a masterpiece, he's leaving me for some woman who *can* write. I don't think he has any idea how these offhand remarks make me feel.

Anyway! Looking forward to this! I think I'd rather enjoy this "world run by men" you've been talking about. Surely a kinder, more caring and — dare I say it? — more *sexy* world than the one we live in.

More soon, my dear!

Naomi

The Power
A historical novel

NEIL ADAM ARMON

The shape of power is always the same; it is the shape of a tree. Root to tip, central trunk branching and re-branching, spreading wider in ever-thinner, searching fingers. The shape of power is the outline of a living thing straining outward, sending its fine tendrils a little further, and a little further yet.

This is the shape of rivers leading to the ocean — the trickles to rivulets, the rivulets to streams, the streams to torrents, the great power gathering and gushing, becoming mightier to hurl itself into the great marine might.

It is the shape that lightning forms when it strikes from heaven to earth. The forked tear in the sky becomes a pattern on flesh or on the earth. These same distinctive patterns bloom in a block of acrylic when struck with electricity. We send electric currents down orderly runs of circuits and switches, but the shape that electricity wants to take is of a living thing, a fern, a bare branch. The strike point in the centre, the power seeking outward.

This same shape grows within us, our inward trees of nerves and blood vessels. The central trunk, the pathways dividing and re-dividing. The signals carried from our fingers' ends to the spine to the brain. We are electrical. The power travels within us as it does in nature. My children, nothing has happened here that has not been in accordance with the natural law.

Power travels in the same manner between people; it must be so. People form villages, villages become towns, towns bow the knee to cities and cities to states. Orders travel from the centre to the tips. Results travel from the tips to the centre. The communication is constant. Oceans cannot survive without trickles, nor steadfast tree trunks without budlets, nor the enthroned brain without nerve endings. As above, so below. As on the outskirts, so at the very heart.

It follows that there are two ways for the nature and use of human power to change. One is that an order might issue from the palace, a command unto the people saying "It is thus." But the other, the more certain, the more inevitable, is that those thousand thousand points of light should each send a new message. When the people change, the palace cannot hold.

As it is written: "She cuppeth the lightning in her hand. She commandeth it to strike."

from the Book of Eve, 13–17

Ten years to go

Roxy

The men lock Roxy in the cupboard when they do it. What they don't know is: she's been locked in that cupboard before. When she's naughty, her mum puts her there. Just for a few minutes. Till she calms down. Slowly, over the hours in there, she's worked the lock loose with a fingernail or a paperclip in the screws. She could have taken that lock off any time she wanted. But she didn't, because then her mum would have put a bolt on the outside. It's enough for her to know, sitting in there in the dark, that if she really wanted to she could get out. The knowledge is as good as freedom.

So that's why they think they've locked her in, safe and sound. But she still gets out. That's how she sees it.

The men come at nine thirty in the evening. Roxy was supposed to have gone over to her cousins that night; it had been arranged for weeks, but she'd given her mum lip about not getting her the right tights from Primark, so her mum said, "You're not going, you're staying in." Like Roxy cared about going to her poxy cousins, anyway.

When the blokes kick in the door and see her there, sulking on the sofa next to her mum, one of them goes,

"Fuck, the girl's here." There are two men, one taller with a face like a rat, the other shorter, square-jawed. She doesn't know them.

The short one grabs her mum by the throat; the tall one chases Roxy through the kitchen. She's almost out the back door when he grabs her thigh; she falls forward and he's got her by the waist. She's kicking and shouting, "Fuck off, let me go!" and when he puts a hand over her mouth she bites him so hard she tastes blood. He swears, but he doesn't drop her. He carries her through the living room. The short one's pushed her mum up against the fireplace. Roxy feels it start to build in her then, though she doesn't know what it is. It's just a feeling at her fingers' ends, a prickle in her thumbs.

She starts screaming. Her mum's going, "Don't you hurt my Roxy, don't you fucking hurt her, you don't know what you're into, this is gonna come down on you like fire, you're gonna wish you was never born. Her dad's Bernie Monke, for Christ's sake."

The short one laughs. "We're here with a message for her dad, as it goes."

The tall one bundles Roxy into the cupboard under the stairs so fast she doesn't know it's happening until the dark is around her, and the dusty-sweet smell of the hoover. Her mum starts screaming.

Roxy's breathing fast. She's frightened, but she's got to get to her mum. She turns one of the screws on the lock with her fingernail. There's one, two, three twists, arid it's out. A spark jumps between the metal of the screw and her hand. Static electricity. She's feeling weird. Focused, like she can see with her eyes closed. Bottom screw, one, two, three twists. Her mum's saying, "Please. Please don't. Please. What is this? She's just a kid. She's just a child, for God's sake."

One of the men laughs low. "Didn't look much like a kid to me."

Her mum shrieks then; it sounds like metal in a bad engine.

Roxy tries to work out where the men are in the room. One's with her mum. The other . . . she hears a sound to her left. Her plan is: she'll come out low, get the tall one in the back of the knees, stomp his head, then it's two against one. If they've got guns, they haven't shown them. Roxy's been in fights before. People say things about her. And her mum. And her dad.

One. Two. Three. Her mum screams again, and Roxy pulls the lock off the door and bashes it open as hard as she can.

She's lucky. She's caught the tall man from behind with the door. He stumbles, he topples, she grabs his right foot as it comes up, and he goes down hard on the carpet. There's a crack, and he's bleeding from the nose.

The short man has a knife pressed against her mum's neck. The blade winks at her, silver and smiling.

Her mum's eyes go wide. "Run, Roxy," she says, not more than a whisper, but Roxy hears it like it was inside her head: "Run. Run."

Roxy doesn't run from fights at school. If you do that, they'll never stop saying, "Your mum's a slapper and your dad's a crook. Watch out, Roxy'll nick your book." You've got to stomp them till they beg. You don't run.

Something's happening. The blood is pounding in her ears. A prickling feeling is spreading along her back, over her shoulders, along her collarbone. It's saying: you can do it. It's saying: you're strong.

She jumps over the prone man, groaning and pawing at his face. She's going to grab her mum's hand and get out of here. They just need to be on the street. This can't happen out there, in the middle of the day. They'll find her dad; he'll sort it out. It's only a few steps. They can do it.

Short man kicks Roxy's mum hard in the stomach. She doubles over in pain, falls to her knees. He swishes the knife at Roxy.

Tall man groans. "Tony. Remember. Not the girl."

Short man kicks the other in the face. Once. Twice. Three times.

"Don't. Say. My fucking name."

Tall man goes quiet. His face bubbles with blood. Roxy knows she's in trouble now. Her mum's shouting, "Run! Run!" Roxy feels the thing like pins and needles along her arms. Like needle-pricks of light from her spine to her collarbone, from her throat to her elbows, wrists, to the pads of her fingers. She's glittering, inside.

He reaches for her with one hand, the knife in the other. She gets ready to kick him or punch him but some instinct tells her a new thing. She grabs his wrist. She *twists* something quite deep inside her chest, as if she'd always known how to do it. He tries to wriggle out of her grip, but it's too late.

She cuppeth the lightning in her hand. She commandeth it to strike.

There's a crackling flash and a sound like a paper snapper. She can smell something a bit like a rainstorm and a bit like burning hair. The taste welling under her tongue is of bitter oranges. The short man is on the floor now. He's making a crooning, wordless cry. His hand is clenching and unclenching. There's a long, red scar running up his arm from his wrist. She can see it even under the blond hairs: it's scarlet, patterned like a fern, leaves and tendrils, budlets and branches. Her mum's mouth is open, she's staring, her tears are still falling.

Roxy tugs at her mum's arm, but she's shocked and slow and her mouth is still saying, "Run! Run!" Roxy doesn't know what she's done, but she knows when you're fighting someone stronger than you and they're down, you get out. But her mum doesn't move quickly enough. Before Roxy can get her up the short man is saying, "Oh no, you don't."

He's wary, pulling himself to his feet, limping between them and the door. His one hand hangs dead by his side, but the other's holding that knife. Roxy remembers what it felt like to do the thing, whatever it was she did. She pulls her mum behind her.

"Whatcha got there, girlie?" says the man. Tony. She'll remember his name to tell her dad. "Got a battery?"

"Get out the way," says Roxy. "You want another taste?"

Tony steps back a couple of paces. Eyes her arms. Looks to see if she's got anything behind her back. "You dropped it, dintcha, little girl?"

She remembers the way it felt. The twist, the explosion outward.

She takes a step towards Tony. He stands his ground. She takes another step. He looks to his dead hand. The fingers are still twitching. He shakes his head. "You ain't got nothing."

He motions towards her with the knife. She reaches out, touches the back of his good hand. Does that same *twist*.

Nothing happens.

He starts to laugh. Holds the knife in his teeth. Grabs her two wrists in his one hand.

She tries it again. Nothing. He forces her to her knees.

"Please," says her mum, quite softly. "Please. Please don't."

And then something hits her on the back of the head and she's gone.

When she wakes, the world is sideways. There's the hearth, just like always. Wooden trim around the fireplace. It's pushing into her eye, and her head hurts and her mouth is mushed up into the carpet. There's the taste of blood on her teeth. Something is dripping. She closes her eyes. Opens them again and knows it's been longer than a few minutes. The street outside is quiet. The house is cold. And lopsided. She feels out her body. Her legs are up on a chair. Her face is hanging down, pressed into the carpet and the fireplace. She tries to lever herself up, but it's too much effort, so she wriggles and lets her legs drop to the floor. It hurts when she falls, but at least she's all on one level.

Memory comes back to her in quick flashes. The pain, then the source of the pain, then that thing she did. Then her mum. She pushes herself up slowly, noticing as she does so that her hands are sticky. And something is dripping. The carpet is sodden, thick with a red stain in a wide circle around the fireplace. There's her mum, her head lolling over the arm of the sofa. And there's a paper resting on her chest, with a felt-tip drawing of a primrose.

Roxy is fourteen. She's one of the youngest, and one of the first.

Tunde

Tunde is doing laps in the pool, splashing more than he needs so Enuma will notice him trying not to show that he wants to be noticed. She is flipping through *Today's Woman*; she flicks her eyes back to the magazine every time he looks up, pretending to be intent on reading about Toke Makinwa and her surprise winter-wedding broadcast on her YouTube channel. He can tell Enuma is watching him. He thinks she can tell that he can tell. It is exciting.

Tunde is twenty-one, just out of that period of his life where everything seemed the wrong size, too long or too short, pointing in the wrong direction, unwieldy. Enuma is four years younger but more of a woman than he is a man, demure but not ignorant. Not too shy, either, not in the way she walks or the quick smile that darts across her face when she understands a joke a moment before everyone else. She's visiting Lagos from Ibadan; she's the cousin of a friend of a boy Tunde knows from his photo-journalism class at college. There's been a gang of them hanging out together over the summer. Tunde spotted her the first day she arrived; her secret smile and her jokes that he didn't at first realize were jokes. And the curve of her hip, and the way she fills her T-shirts, yes. It's been quite a thing to arrange to be alone together with Enuma. Tunde's nothing if not determined.

Enuma said early on in the visit that she had never enjoyed the beach: too much sand, too much wind. Swimming pools are better. Tunde waited one, two, three days, then suggested a trip — we could all drive down to Akodo beach, take a picnic, make a day of it. Enuma said she would prefer not to go. Tunde pretended not to notice. The night before the trip, he started to complain of an upset stomach. It's dangerous to swim with a stomach complaint — the cold water might shock your system. You should stay home, Tunde. But I'll miss the trip to the beach. You should not be swimming in the sea. Enuma's staying here; she can bring a doctor if you need one.

One of the girls said, "But you'll be alone together, in this house."

Tunde wished her to be struck dumb in that very moment. "My cousins are coming later," he said.

No one asked which cousins. It had been that kind of hot, lazy summer with people wandering in and out of the big house around the corner from Ikoyi Club.

Enuma acquiesced. Tunde noticed her not protesting. She didn't stroke her friend's back and ask her to stay home from the beach, too. She said nothing when he got up half an hour after the last car left and stretched and said he was feeling much better. She watched him as he jumped from the short springboard into the pool, her quick smile flashing.

He makes a turn under the water. It is neat, his feet barely breaking the surface. He wonders if she saw him do it, but she's not there. He looks around, sees her shapely legs, bare feet padding out of the kitchen. She's carrying a can of Coca Cola.

"Hey," he says, in a mock-lordly tone. "Hey, servant girl, bring me that Coke."

She turns and smiles with wide, limpid eyes. She looks to one side and then the other, and points a finger at her chest as if to say, Who? Me?

God, but he wants her. He doesn't know exactly what to do. There have only been two girls before her and neither of them became "girlfriends". At college they joke about him that he's married to his studies, because he's always so single. He doesn't like it. But he's been waiting for someone he really wanted. She has something. He wants what she has.

He plants his palms on the wet tiles and raises himself out of the water and on to the stone in one graceful movement which he knows shows off the muscles of his shoulders, his chest and collarbone. He has a good feeling. This is going to work.

She sits on a lounger. As he stalks towards her, she digs her nails in under the can's tab, as if she's about to open it.

"Oh no," he says, still smiling. "You know such things are not for the likes of you."

She clutches the Coke to her midriff. It must be cold there against her skin. She says, demurely, "I just want a little taste." She bites her bottom lip.

She must be doing it on purpose. Must be. He is excited. This is going to happen.

He stands over her. "Give it to me."

She holds the can in one hand and rolls it along her neck as if to cool herself. She shakes her head. And then he's on her.

They play-wrestle. He takes care not to really force her. He's sure she's enjoying it as much as he is. Her arm comes up over her head, holding the can, to keep it far away from him. He pushes her arm back a little more, making her gasp and twist backwards. He makes a grab for the can of Coke, and she laughs, low and soft. He likes her laughter.

"Aha, trying to keep that drink from your lord and master," he says. "What a wicked servant girl you are."

And she laughs again and wriggles more. Her breasts push up against the V-neck of her swimming costume. "You'll never have it," she says. "I will defend it with my very life!"

And he thinks: Clever *and* beautiful, may the Lord have mercy upon my soul. She's laughing, and he's laughing. He leans his body weight into her; she's warm underneath him.

"Do you think you can keep it from me?" He lunges again, and she twists to escape him. He makes a grab at her waist.

She puts her hand to his.

There's the scent of orange blossom. A wind gusts up and hurls a few white handfuls of blooms into the swimming pool.

17

There is a feeling in his hand as if some insect has stung him. He looks down to swat it away, and the only thing on his hand is her warm palm.

The sensation grows, steadily and swiftly. At first it is pinpricks in his hand and forearm, then a swarm of buzzing prickles, then it is pain. He is breathing too quickly to be able to make a sound. He cannot move his left arm. His heart is loud in his ears. His chest is tight.

She is still giggling, soft and low. She leans forward and pulls him closer to her. She looks into his eyes, her irises are lined with lights of brown and gold, and her lower lip is moist. He is afraid. He is excited. He realizes that he could not stop her, whatever she wanted to do now. The thought is terrifying. The thought is electrifying. He is achingly hard now, and does not know when that happened. He cannot feel anything at all in his left arm.

She leans in, bubblegum breath, and kisses him softly on the lips. Then she peels away, runs to the pool and dives, in one smooth, practised movement.

He waits for the feeling to come back to his arm. She does her laps in silence, not calling to him or splashing water at him. He feels excited. He feels ashamed. He wants to talk to her, but he is afraid. Maybe he imagined it all. Maybe she will call him a bad name if he asks her what happened.

He walks to the stall on the corner of the street to buy a frozen orange drink so he won't have to say anything to her. When the others come back from the beach, he falls in gladly with plans to visit a further cousin the next day. He wants very much to be distracted and not to be alone. He does not know what happened, nor is there anyone he could discuss it with. When he imagines asking his friend Charles about it, or Isaac, his throat clamps shut. If he said what happened, they would think he was crazy, or weak, or lying. He thinks of the way she laughed at him.

He finds himself searching her face for signs of what happened. What was it? Did she mean to do it? Had she planned, specifically, to hurt or scare him, or was it just an accident, involuntary? Did she even know she'd done it? Or was it not her at all but some lustful malfunction of his own body? The whole thing chews at him. She gives no sign that anything happened. By the last day of the trip she's holding hands with another boy.

There is a shame like rust working its way through his body. He thinks over that afternoon compulsively. In bed at night: her lips, her breasts pressing against the smooth fabric, the outline of her nipples, his absolute vulnerability, the feeling that she could overpower him if she wanted. The thought of it excites him, and he touches himself. He tells himself he is excited by the memory of her body, the smell of her like hibiscus flowers, but he cannot know for certain. The things are tangled together now in his mind: lust and power, desire and fear.

Perhaps it is because he has played the tape of that afternoon over so often in his mind, because he has longed for some forensic evidence, a photograph, or a video, or a sound recording, perhaps that is the reason

19

that he thinks of reaching for his phone first, in the supermarket. Or perhaps some of the things they have been trying to teach them in college — about citizen journalism, about the "nose for the story" — have been sinking in.

He is in Goodies with his friend Isaac a few months after that day with Enuma. They are in the fruit aisle, inhaling the sweet fug of ripe guava, drawn to them from across the store like the tiny flies that settle on the surface of the over-ripe, split-open fruit. Tunde and Isaac are arguing about girls, and what girls like. Tunde is trying to keep his shame buried very far down in his body so his friend will not be able to guess that he has secret knowledge. And then a girl shopping alone gets into an argument with a man. He might be thirty; she is perhaps fifteen or sixteen.

He has been sweet-talking her; Tunde thought at first that the two knew each other. He only realizes his mistake when she says: "Get away from me." The man smiles easily and takes a pace towards her. "A pretty girl like you deserves a compliment."

She leans over, looks down, breathes heavily. She clasps her fingers around the edge of a wooden crate full of mangos. There is a feeling; it prickles the skin. Tunde takes his phone from his pocket, flips on the video. Something is going to happen here that is the same as the thing that happened to him. He wants to own it, to be able to take it home and watch it again and again. He's been thinking about this since the day with Enuma, hoping that something like this might happen.

20

The man says, "Hey, don't turn away from me. Give me a little smile."

She swallows hard and keeps looking down.

The scents in the supermarket become more intense; Tunde can detect in a single inhalation the individual fragrances of the apples and the bell peppers and the sweet oranges.

Isaac whispers, "I think she is going to hit him with a mango."

Canst thou direct the lightning bolts? Or do they say to thee: "Here we are"?

Tunde is recording when she turns around. The screen of his phone fuzzes for a moment when she strikes. Other than that, he gets the whole thing very clearly. There she is, bringing her hand to his arm while he smiles and thinks she is performing mock-fury for his amusement. If you pause the video for a moment at this point, you can see the charge jump. There's the trace of a Lichtenberg figure, swirling and branching like a river along his skin up from wrist to elbow as the capillaries burst.

Tunde follows him with the camera's eye as he falls to the ground, fitting and choking. He swivels to keep her in frame as she runs from the market. There's the noise in the background of people calling for help, saying a girl has poisoned a man. Hit him and poisoned him. Struck him with a needle full of poison. Or, no, there is a snake among the fruit, a viper or puff adder concealed in the piled fruit. And someone says, "*Aje ni girl yen, sha!* That girl was a witch! That is how a witch kills a man."

Tunde's camera turns back to the figure on the floor. The man's heels are drumming the linoleum tiles. There is a pink foam at his lips. His eyes have rolled back. His head is thrashing from side to side. Tunde thought that if he could capture it in the bright window of his phone, then he would no longer feel afraid. But looking at the man coughing up red mucus and crying, he feels the fear travel down his spine like a hot wire. He knows then what he felt by the pool: that Enuma could have killed him if she'd wanted. He keeps the camera trained on the man until the ambulance arrives.

It is this video which, when he puts it online, starts the business of the Day of the Girls.

Margot

"It has to be fake."

"Fox News is saying not."

"Fox News would say whatever makes the most people tune in to Fox News."

"Sure. Still."

"What are these lines coming out of her hands?"

"Electricity."

"But that's just . . . I mean . . ."

"Yeah."

"Where'd it come from?"

"Nigeria, I think. Went up yesterday."

"There are a lot of nut-jobs out there, Daniel. Fakers. Scammers."

"There are more videos. Since this one went out, there have been . . . four or five."

"Faked. People get excited about these things. It's a what-they-call-it — a meme. You heard about that thing Slender Man? Some girls tried to kill their friend as a tribute to him. It. Terrible."

"It's four or five videos every *hour*, Margot."

"Fuck."

"Yup."

"Well, what do you want me to do about it?"

"Close the schools."

"Can you even *imagine* what I'll get from the parents? Can you imagine the millions of *voting parents* and what they'll do if I send all their kids home today?"

"Can you imagine what you'll get from the teachers' unions if one of their membership is injured? Crippled? Killed? Imagine the *liability*."

"*Killed?*"

"Can't be certain."

Margot stares down at her hands, clutching the edge of the desk. She's going to look like an idiot, going along with this. It has to be a stunt for a TV show. She'll be the shit-for-brains, the Mayor who closed the schools of this major metropolitan area because of a fucking *practical joke*. But if she doesn't close them and something happens . . . Daniel will get to be the Governor of this great state, who warned the Mayor, who tried to convince her to do something, but all to no avail. She can practically see the tears running down his cheeks as he gives his interview via live feed from the Governor's Mansion. Fuck.

Daniel checks his phone. "They've announced closures in Iowa and Delaware," he says.

"Fine."

"'Fine' meaning?"

"'Fine' meaning 'fine'. Do it. Fine, I'll close them."

There are four or five days where she barely goes home. She doesn't remember leaving the office, or driving back, or crawling into bed, although she supposes she must have done these things. The phone doesn't stop. She goes to bed clutching it and wakes up holding it. Bobby has the girls so she doesn't need to think about them and, God forgive her, they don't cross her mind.

This thing has broken out across the world and no one knows what the fuck is going on.

To start with, there were confident faces on the TV, spokespeople from the CDC saying it was a virus, not very severe, most of the people recovered fine, and it just *looked* like young girls were electrocuting people with their hands. We all know that's impossible, right, that's crazy — the news anchors laughed so hard they cracked their makeup. Just for fun, they brought in a couple of marine biologists to talk about electric eels and their body pattern. A guy with a beard, a gal with glasses, aquarium fish in a tank — makes for a solid morning segment. Did you know the guy who invented the battery was inspired by looking at the bodies of electric eels? I did not know that, Tom, that is fascinating; I've heard they can fell a horse. You're kidding, I'd never have imagined it. Apparently, a lab in Japan powered their Christmas-tree lights from a tank of electric eels. We can't do that with these girls, now, can we? I would think not, Kristen, I would think not. Although doesn't Christmas seem to come earlier every year? And now the weather on the ones.

Margot and the office of the Mayor take it seriously days before the news desks understand that it's real. They're the ones who get the early reports of fighting in the playgrounds. A strange new kind of fighting which leaves boys — mostly boys, sometimes girls —

breathless and twitching, with scars like unfurling leaves winding up their arms or legs or across the soft flesh of their middles. Their first thought after disease is a new weapon, something these kids are bringing into school, but as the first week trickles into the second they know that's not it.

They latch on to any crazy theory going, not knowing how to tell the plausible from the ridiculous. Late at night, Margot reads a report from a team in Delhi who are the first to discover the strip of striated muscle across the girls' collarbones which they name the *organ of electricity*, or the *skein* for its twisted strands. At the points of the collar are electro-receptors enabling, they theorize, a form of electric echo-location. The buds of the skein have been observed using MRI scans in the collarbones of newborn infant girls. Margot photocopies this report and has it emailed to every school in the state; for days, it's the only good science in a host of garbled interpretation. Even Daniel's momentarily grateful, before he remembers that he hates her.

An Israeli anthropologist suggests that the development of this organ in humans is proof positive of the aquatic-ape hypothesis; that we are naked of hair because we came from the oceans, not the jungle, where once we terrified the deeps like the electric eel, the electric ray. Preachers and televangelists grab the news and squeeze it, finding in the sticky entrails the unmistakable signs of the impending end of days. A fist fight breaks out on a popular news discussion programme between a scientist who demands that the

Electric Girls be investigated surgically and a man of God who believes they are a harbinger of the apocalypse and must not be touched by human hand. There is an argument already about whether this thing was always latent in the human genome and has been reawoken or whether it is a mutation, a terrible deformity.

Just before sleep, Margot thinks of winged ants and how there would be just one day every summer that the house at the lake would swarm with them, thickly upon the ground, clinging to the timber-clad frame, vibrating on the tree trunks, the air so full of ants you thought you might breathe them in. They live underground, those ants, all year long, entirely alone. They grow from their eggs, they eat what — dust and seeds or something — and they wait, and wait. And one day, when the temperature has been just right for the right number of days and when the moisture is just so . . . they all take to the air at once. To find each other. Margot couldn't tell this kind of thought to anyone else. They'd think she'd gone crazy from the stress and, God knows, there are enough people looking to replace her anyway. Still, she lies in bed after a day of dealing with reports of burned kids and kids with seizures and girl gangs fighting and being taken into custody for their own protection and thinks: Why now? Why right now? And she comes up again and again with those ants, biding their time, waiting for the spring.

Three weeks in, she gets a call from Bobby to say that Jocelyn's been caught fighting.

They'd separated the boys from the girls on the fifth day; it seemed obvious, when they worked out the girls were doing it. Already there are parents telling their boys not to go out alone, not to stray too far. "Once you've seen it happen," says a grey-faced woman on TV. "I saw a girl in the park doing that to a boy for no reason, he was bleeding from the eyes. The eyes. Once you've seen that happen, no mom would let her boys out of her sight."

Things couldn't stay closed forever; they reorganized. Boys-only buses took them safely to boys-only schools. They fell into it easily. You only had to see a few videos online for the fear to hit you in the throat.

But for the girls it has not been so simple. You cannot keep them from each other. Some of them are angry and some of them are mean, and now the thing is out in the open some are vying to prove their strength and skill. There have been injuries and accidents; one girl has been struck blind by another. The teachers are afraid. Television pundits are saying: "Lock them all up, maximum security." It is, as far as anyone can tell, all of the girls of about fifteen years old. As near to all as makes no difference. They can't lock them all up, it makes no sense. Still, people are asking for it.

Now Jocelyn's been caught fighting. The press have it before Margot can make her way home to see her daughter. News trucks are setting up on her front lawn when she arrives. Madam Mayor, would you care to comment on the rumours that your daughter has put a boy in the hospital?

No, she would not care to comment.

Bobby is in the living room with Maddy. She's sitting on the couch between his legs, drinking her milk and watching *Powerpuff Girls*. She looks up as her mother comes in, but doesn't move, flicks her eyes back to the TV set. Ten going on fifteen. OK. Margot kisses the top of Maddy's head, even as Maddy tries to look around her, back to the screen. Bobby squeezes Margot's hand.

"Where's Jos?"

"Upstairs."

"And?"

"She's as scared as anyone."

"Yeah."

Margot closes the door of the bedroom softly.

Jocelyn is on her bed, legs stretched out. She's holding Mr Bear. She's a child, just a child.

"I should have called," says Margot, "as soon as it started. I'm sorry."

Jocelyn's near to tears. Margot sits on the bed gently, as if not to tip her full pail over. "Dad says you haven't hurt anyone, not badly."

There's a pause, but Jos doesn't say anything, so Margot just keeps talking. "There were . . . three other girls? I know they started it. That boy should never have been near you. They've been checked out at John Muir. You just gave the kid a scare."

"I know."

All right. Verbal communication. A start.

"Was that the . . . first time you've done it?"

Jocelyn rolls her eyes. She plucks at the comforter with one hand.

"This is brand new to both of us, OK? How long have you been doing it?"

She mutters so low that Margot can barely hear, "Six months."

"Six *months*?"

Mistake. Never express incredulity, never alarm. Jocelyn draws her knees up.

"I'm sorry," says Margot. "It's just . . . it's a surprise, that's all."

Jos frowns. "Plenty of girls started it before I did. It was . . . it was kinda funny . . . when it started, like static electricity."

Static electricity. What was it, you combed your hair and stuck a balloon to it? An activity for bored six-year-olds at birthday parties.

"It was this funny, crazy thing girls were doing. There were secret videos online. How to do tricks with it."

It's this exact moment, yes, when any secret you have from your parents becomes precious. Anything you know that they've never heard of.

"How did you . . . how did you learn to do it?"

Jos says, "I don't know. I just felt I could do it, OK. It's like a sort of . . . *twist*."

"Why didn't you say anything? Why didn't you tell me?"

She looks through the window to the lawn. Beyond the high back fence, men and women with cameras are already gathering.

"I don't know."

Margot remembers trying to talk to her own mother about boys or the stuff that happened at parties. About how far was *too far*, where a boy's hand should stop. She remembers the absolute impossibility of those conversations.

"Show me."

Jos narrows her eyes. "I can't . . . I'd hurt you."

"Have you been practising? Can you control it well enough so you know you wouldn't kill me, or give me a fit?"

Jos takes a deep breath. Puffs her cheeks out. Lets the breath out slowly. "Yes."

Her mother nods. This is the girl she knows: conscientious and serious. Still Jos. "Then show me."

"I can't control it well enough for it not to hurt, OK?"

"How much will it hurt?"

Jos splays her fingers wide, looks at her palms. "Mine comes and goes. Sometimes it's strong, sometimes it's nothing."

Margot presses her lips together. "OK."

Jos extends her hand, then pulls it back. "I don't want to."

There was a time when every crevice of this child's body was Margot's to clean and care for. It is not OK with her not to know her own child's strength. "No more secrets. Show me."

Jos is near to tears. She places her forefinger and her middle finger on her mother's arm. Margot waits to see Jos *do* something; hold her breath, or wrinkle her brow, or show exertion in the muscles of her arm, but there's nothing. Only the pain.

She has read the preliminary reports out of the CDC noting that the power "particularly affects the pain centres of the human brain", meaning that, while it looks like electrocution, it hurts more than it needs to. It is a targeted pulse which sets up a response in the body's pain receptors. Nonetheless, she'd expected it to look like something; to see her flesh crisping and wrinkling, or to watch the arcing current, quick as a snake's bite.

Instead, she smells the scent of wet leaves after a rainstorm. An apple orchard with the windfalls turning to rot, just as it was on her parents' farm.

And then it hurts. From the place on her forearm where Jos is touching her, it starts as a dull bone-ache. The flu, travelling through the muscles and joints. It deepens. Something is cracking her bone, twisting it, bending it, and she wants to tell Jos to stop but she can't open her mouth. It burrows through the bone like it's splintering apart from the inside; she can't stop herself seeing a tumour, a solid, sticky lump bursting out through the marrow of her arm, splitting the ulna and the radius to sharp fragments. She feels sick. She wants to cry out. The pain radiates across her arm and, nauseatingly, through her body. There's not a part of her it hasn't touched now; she feels it echo in her head and down her spine, across her back, around her throat and out, spreading across her collarbone.

The collarbone. It has only been a few seconds, but the moments have elongated. Only pain can bring such attention to the body; this is how Margot notices the answering echo in her chest. Among the forests and mountains of pain, a chiming note along her collarbone. Like answering to like.

It reminds her of something. A game she played when she was a girl. How funny: she hasn't thought of that game in years. She never told anyone about it; she knew she mustn't, although she couldn't say how she knew. In the game, she was a witch, and she could make a ball of light in the palm of her hand. Her brothers played that they were spacemen with plastic ray-guns they'd bought with cereal-packet tokens, but the little game she'd played entirely by herself among the beech trees along the rim of their property was different. In her game, she didn't need a gun, or space-helmet, or lightsaber. In the game Margot played when she was a child, she was enough all by herself.

There is a tingling feeling in her chest and arms and hands. Like a dead arm, waking up. The pain is not gone now, but it is irrelevant. Something else is happening. Instinctively, she digs her hands into Jocelyn's patchwork comforter. She smells the scent of the beech trees, as if she were back beneath their woody protection, their musk of old timber and wet loam.

She sendeth her lightning even unto the ends of the earth.

When she opens her eyes, there is a pattern around each of her hands. Concentric circles, light and dark, light and dark, burned into the comforter where her hands clutched it. And she knows, she felt that *twist*, and she remembers that maybe she has always known it and it has always belonged to her. Hers to cup in her hand. Hers to command to strike.

"Oh God," she says. "Oh God."

Allie

Allie pulls herself up on to the tomb, leans back to look at the name — she always takes a moment to remember them: Hey, how're you doing there, Annabeth MacDuff, loving mother now at rest? — and lights a Marlboro.

Cigarettes being among the four or five thousand pleasures of this world that Mrs Montgomery-Taylor considers abhorrent in the sight of the Lord, just the glowing embers, the inhalation, the stream of smoke from her parted lips would be enough to say: Screw you, Mrs Montgomery-Taylor, screw you and the ladies of the church and Jesus fucking Christ, too. It would have been enough to do it the usual way, impressive enough and a sufficient promise to the boys of things that might come to pass right soon. But Allie doesn't care to light her cigarette the usual way.

Kyle gestures with his chin and says, "Heard a bunch of guys killed a girl in Nebraska last week for doing that."

"For smoking? Harsh."

Hunter says, "Half the kids in school know you can do it."

"So what?"

Hunter says, "Your dad could use you in his factory. Save money on electricity."

"He's not my dad."

She makes the silver flicker at the ends of her fingers again. The boys watch.

As the sun sets, the cemetery comes alive with crickets and frogs calling, waiting for rain. It's been a long, hot summer. The earth yearns for a storm.

Mr Montgomery-Taylor owns a meat-packing company with centres here in Jacksonville, and up in Albany and as far as Statesboro. They call it meat-packing but what they mean by that is meat-producing. Animal-killing. Mr Montgomery-Taylor took Allie to see it when she was younger. He had that stage when he liked to think of himself as a good man educating a little girl in the men's world. It's a sort of pride to her that she watched the whole thing without wincing or looking away or carrying on. Mr Montgomery-Taylor's hand was on her shoulder like a pair of pincers throughout the visit, pointing out to her the pens where the pigs are herded before their encounter with the knife. Pigs are very intelligent animals; if you frighten them, the meat doesn't taste so good. You've got to be careful.

Chickens are not intelligent. They let her watch the chickens being uncrated, white and feather-fluff. The hands pick them up, turn them over to show their snowy behinds and shackle their legs into the conveyor which drags their heads through an electrified water-bath. They squawk and wriggle. One by one, they go rigid, then limp.

"It's a kindness," said Mr Montgomery-Taylor. "They don't know what's hit them."

And he laughs, and his employees laugh too.

Allie noticed that one or two of the chickens had raised their heads. The water hadn't stunned them. They were still awake as they passed along the line; still conscious as they entered the scalding tank.

"Efficient, hygienic and kind," said Mr Montgomery-Taylor.

Allie thought of Mrs Montgomery-Taylor's ecstatic speeches about hell, and about the whirling knives and the scalding water that will consume your whole body, boiling oil and rivers of molten lead.

Allie wanted to run along the line and pop the chickens out of their shackles and set them free, wild and angry. She imagined them coming for Mr Montgomery-Taylor in particular, taking their revenge in beaks and claws. But the voice said to her: This is not the time, daughter. Your moment has not come. The voice has never led her wrong yet, not all the days of her life. So Allie nodded and said: "It's very interesting. Thank you for bringing me."

It wasn't long after her visit to that factory that she noticed this thing she could do. There was no urgency in it; it was like the day she noticed her hair had gotten long. It must have been happening all that time, quietly.

They were at dinner. Allie reached for her fork and a spark jumped from her hand.

The voice said: Do it again. You can make that happen again. Concentrate. She gave a little twist or a flick of something in her chest. There it was, a spark. Good girl, said the voice, but don't show them, this is not for them. Mr Montgomery-Taylor didn't notice, and Mrs Montgomery-Taylor didn't notice. Allie kept her eyes down and her face impassive. The voice said: This is the first of my gifts to you, daughter. Learn to use it.

She practised in her bedroom. She made a spark jump from hand to hand. She made her bedside lamp glow brighter, then dimmer. She burned a tiny hole in a Kleenex; she practised until she could make that hole a pinprick. Smaller. These things demand constant, focused attention. She's good at that. She's never heard of anybody else who can light their cigarettes with it.

The voice said: There will be a day to use this, and on that day you will know what to do.

Usually, she'd let the boys touch her if they wanted. That's what they think they've come to this graveyard for. A hand sliding up the thigh, a cigarette popped from the mouth like a candy, held to one side while there's kissing. Kyle props himself up next to her, puts his hand on her midriff, starts to bunch the fabric of her top. She stops him with a gesture. He smiles.

"Come on now," he says. He tugs her top up a little.

She stings him on the back of his hand. Not a lot. Just enough to give him pause.

He pulls his hand back. Looks at her and, aggrieved, at Hunter. "Hey, what gives?"

She shrugs. "Not in the mood."

Hunter comes to sit on the other side of her. She's sandwiched between them now, both their bodies pressing in on her, bulges in their pants showing their minds.

"That's fine," says Hunter, "but see, you brought us here and we *are* in the mood."

He lays an arm across her midriff, his thumb grazing her breast, his hand large and strong around her. "Come on," he says, "we'll have some fun, just the three of us."

He comes in for a kiss, his mouth opening.

She likes Hunter. He's six foot four; his shoulders are broad and strong. They've had fun together. That's not what she's here for. She has a feeling about today.

She gets him in the armpit. One of her pinpricks, right into the muscle, precise and careful, like a fine-bladed knife up through to his shoulder. She increases it, like making the lamp glow hotter and hotter. Like the knife is made of flame.

"Fuck!" says Hunter and jumps backwards. "Fuck!" He's holding his right hand into his left armpit, massaging it. The left arm is trembling.

Kyle's angry now and pulls her towards him. "What did you make us come all the way out here for then, if you —"

And she gets him at the throat, just under the jaw. Like a metal blade slicing across his voice-box. His mouth falls slackly open. He makes choking sounds. He's still breathing, but he can't speak.

"Fuck you, then!" shouts Hunter. "You don't get a ride home!"

Hunter backs away. Kyle gathers up his school bag, still holding his throat. "Uck! Ou!" he shouts as they walk back to their car.

She waits there for a long time after it gets dark, lying back on the grave of Annabeth MacDuff, loving mother now at rest, lighting cigarette after cigarette with the crackle from her fingertips and smoking them down to the hilt. The noise of the evening rises up around her and she thinks: Come and get me.

She says to the voice: Hey, mom, it's today, right?

The voice says: Sure is, daughter. You ready?

Allie says: Bring it.

She climbs up the trellis to get back into the house. Her shoes are slung around her neck, shoelaces tied together. She digs her toes in, and her fingers hook on and grab. Mrs Montgomery-Taylor saw her once when she was younger scaling a tree, one, two, three, up she went, and said, "Would you look at that, she climbs just like a monkey." She said it like she'd long suspected this would be the case. Like she'd just been waiting to find out.

Allie reaches her bedroom window. She'd left it open just a crack, and she pushes the jamb up, takes her shoes from around her neck and throws them inside. She levers herself through the window. She checks her watch; she's not even late for supper and there'll be nothing for anyone to complain about. She lets out a sort of laugh, low and croaking. And a laugh meets her in return. And she realizes there's someone else in the room. She knows who it is, of course.

Mr Montgomery-Taylor unfolds himself from the easy chair like one of the long-armed machines from his production line. Allie draws breath, but before she can form half a word he's hit her very hard across the mouth, back-handed. Like a tennis swing at the country club. The pop of her jaw is the *thunk* of the ball hitting the racket.

His particular kind of rage has always been very controlled, very quiet. The less he says, the angrier he is. He's drunk, she can smell it, and he's furious, and he mutters: "Saw you. Saw you in the graveyard with those boys. Filthy. Little. Whore." Each word punctuated with a punch, or a slap, or a kick. She doesn't roll into a ball. She doesn't beg him to stop. She knows it only makes it go on longer. He pushes her knees apart. His hand is at his belt. He's going to show her what kind of a little whore she is. As if he hadn't shown her many times in the past.

Mrs Montgomery-Taylor sits downstairs listening to the polka on the radio, drinking sherry, slowly but unceasingly, little sips which couldn't do no one any harm. She doesn't care to see what Mr Montgomery-Taylor does up there in the evenings; at least he's not catting around the neighbourhood, and that girl earned what she's getting. If an interviewer from the *Sun-Times*, taking an interest for some reason in the small doings of this little home, had placed a microphone to her mouth at that moment and said: Mrs Montgomery-Taylor, what do you think your husband is doing to that sixteen-year-old mixed-race girl you took into your house out of Christian charity? What do you think he's doing to make her holler and carry on like that? If she were asked — but who would ever ask? — she'd say: Why, he's giving her a spanking, and it's no more than she deserves. And if the interviewer pressed — What did you mean, then, about his catting around? — Mrs Montgomery-Taylor's mouth would twist a little, as if she'd caught an odour of something unpleasant, and then the smile would return to her face and she'd say, confidentially: You know how men are.

It was some other time, years ago, when Allie was pressed back, head cricked against the headboard, his one hand around her throat like this, that the voice first spoke to her, clearly, right inside her own head. When she thinks on it, she'd been hearing it distantly for a long time. Since before she came to the Montgomery-Taylors'; since she passed from home to home and hand to hand there's been a dim voice far away telling her when to be careful, warning against danger.

The voice had said: You are strong, you will survive this.

And Allie had said, as he tightened his grip on her neck: Mom?

And the voice had said: Sure.

Nothing special has happened today; no one can say she was more provoked than usual. It is only that every day one grows a little, every day something is different, so that in the heaping up of days suddenly a thing that was impossible has become possible. This is how a girl becomes a grown woman. Step by step until it is done. As he plunges, she knows that she could do it. That she has the strength, and perhaps she has had it enough for weeks or months, but only now is she certain. She can do it now and leave no possibility of misfires or reprisals. It seems the simplest thing in the world, like reaching out a hand and flicking off a light switch. She cannot think why she hasn't decided to turn out this old light before.

She says to the voice: It's now, isn't it?

The voice says: You know it.

There is a smell like rain in the room. So that Mr Montgomery-Taylor looks up, thinks that the rain has started at last, that the parched earth is drinking it in great gulps. He thinks it might be coming in through the window, but his heart is gladdened by the thought of rain even as he continues with his business. Allie brings her hands to his temples, left and right. She feels the palms of her mother around her own small fingers. She is glad Mr Montgomery-Taylor is not looking at her but instead out through the window, searching for the non-existent rain.

She maketh a channel for the thunderbolt and setteth a path for the storm.

There is a flash of white light. A flicker of silver across his forehead and around his mouth and his teeth. He spasms and pops out of her. He is juddering and fitting. His jaws are clattering together. He falls to the floor with a loud thump and Allie is afraid that Mrs Montgomery-Taylor might have heard something, but she has the radio turned up loud, so there is no foot on the stair and no voice calling. Allie pulls up her underwear and her jeans. She leans over to watch. There's a red foam at his lips. His spine is curled backwards, his hands held like claws. It looks like he's still breathing. She thinks: I could call someone now, and maybe he'd live. So she puts her palm over his heart and gathers the handful of lightning she has left. She sends it into him right there, in the place where human beings are made of electrical rhythm. And he stops.

She gathers a few things from the room. Money she'd stashed in a spot under the windowsill, a few bucks, enough for now. A battery radio Mrs Montgomery-Taylor had had as a girl and had given her in one of those moments of kindness that serve to cloud over and obscure even the simple purity of suffering. She leaves her phone, because she's heard those things can be traced. She glances at the little ivory Christ impaled on a mahogany cross on the wall at the head of her bed.

Take it, says the voice.

Have I done well? says Allie. Are you proud of me?

Oh so proud, daughter. And you will make me prouder yet. You will do wonders in the world.

Allie thrusts the little crucifix into her duffel bag. She has always known she must never tell anyone about the voice. She's good at keeping secrets.

Allie looks at Mr Montgomery-Taylor one last time before she levers herself out of the window. Perhaps he didn't know what hit him. She hopes he did. She wishes she could have sent him alive into the scalding tank.

44

She thinks, as she drops down from the trellis and crosses the back lawn, that maybe she should have tried to filch a knife from the kitchen before she left. But then she remembers — and the thought makes her laugh — that aside from cutting her dinner she really has no need for a knife, no need at all.

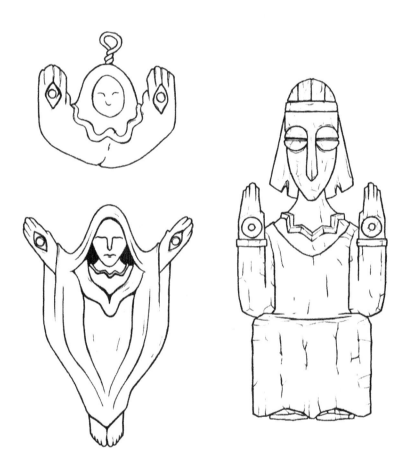

Three images of the Holy Mother, approximately
five hundred years old.
Found in a dig in South Sudan.

Nine years to go

Allie

She walks and hides, hides and walks for eighty-two days. Takes rides where she can, but mostly walks.

To start with, there's not much trouble finding someone willing to give a sixteen-year-old girl a ride, criss-crossing the state, covering her tracks. But as she travels north and as the summer turns to autumn, fewer drivers answer her stuck-out hitching thumb. More of them swerve, panicked, away from her, even though she's not in the highway. One woman makes the sign of the cross as her husband drives on.

Allie bought a sleeping bag early on from Goodwill. It smells but she airs it out every morning and it hasn't rained hard yet. She's been enjoying the journey, though her belly is empty most of the time and her feet are sore. There have been mornings she's woken just past dawn and seen the hard, bright edges of the trees and path drawn fresh by the morning sun and felt the light glittering in her lungs and she's been glad to be there. Once, there was a grey fox that kept pace with her for three days, walking a few arm lengths away, never coming close enough to touch but never drifting too far away either, except to take a rat once, returning with the body soft in her mouth and the blood on her muzzle.

Allie said to the voice: Is she a sign? And the voice said: Oh yes. Keep on trucking, girl.

Allie hasn't been reading the newspapers and she hasn't been listening to her little radio. She doesn't know it, but she's missed the Day of the Girls completely. She doesn't know that that's what's saved her life.

Back in Jacksonville, Mrs Montgomery-Taylor walked upstairs at bedtime, expecting to find her husband in his study reading the paper and the girl suitably chastened on the subject of her misdeeds. In the girl's bedroom, she saw what was to be seen. Allie had left Mr Montgomery-Taylor with his pants around his ankles, his member still partially tumescent, a bloody foam staining the cream rug. Mrs Montgomery-Taylor sat on the rumpled bed for a full half-hour, just looking at Clyde Montgomery-Taylor. She breathed — after a first quick gasp — slowly and evenly. The Lord giveth, she said to the empty room at last, and the Lord taketh away. She pulled Clyde's pants up and remade the bed with fresh linens, being careful to step around him. She thought of propping him up in a chair at his desk and laundering the rug, but although she grieved for the indignity of him there, tonguing the floor, she doubted she had the strength for it. Besides, the story told itself better if he'd been in the girl's room, delivering the catechism.

She summoned the police and, when the men came, sympathetic, at midnight, she gave testimony. To have given a home to the wolf and succour to the rabid dog. She had photographs of Allie. That would have been plenty enough to find her in a few days if, that very night, the calls had not started to this police station, and the one in Albany, and in Statesboro, and on through the country, spreading out, branching and re-branching, the calls lighting up the police stations like a vast and spreading web.

In a town on the coast whose name she never knows, Allie finds a good sleeping place in the scrubby wood that skims the houses; a sheltered bank with a warm, dry place to curl up where the rock is curved under into a lip. She stays there for three days because the voice says: There's something here for you, my girl. Seek and go fetch.

She's tired and hungry all of the time, so that a light-headed feeling has become part of her, pleasant in its way. She can hear the voice more clearly when her muscles are buzzing like this and it's been a while since her last meal; it's tempted her to stop eating in the past, particularly because she's sure the tones of the voice, its low, amused rumble, are the notes of her own mother speaking.

Allie doesn't really remember her mother, although she knows she had one, of course. The world began for her in a bright flash when she was somewhere between three or four. She had been at the mall with someone, because she had a balloon in one hand and a snow cone in the other and the someone — not her mother, she's sure of that, she'd know that — was saying, "Now you must call this lady Aunt Rose, and she will be kind to you."

It was in that moment that she first heard the voice. When she looked up into Aunt Rose's face and the voice said: "Kind". Sure. Uh-huh. I don't think so.

The voice has never steered her wrong since then. Aunt Rose turned out to be a mean old lady who'd call Allie bad names when she had a little to drink and she liked a drink most every day. The voice told Allie what to do; how to pick the right teacher at school and tell the story in such a way that she didn't seem to be saying it artfully at all.

But the lady after Aunt Rose was even worse, and Mrs Montgomery-Taylor was worse than that. Still, the voice has kept her safe from the worst harm all these years. She still has all her fingers and toes, though that's been a near-run thing, and now it's telling her: Stay here. Wait for it.

She walks into town every day and explores every place that's warm and dry and where they don't throw her out. The library. The church. The little, overheated museum of the revolutionary war. And, on the third day, she manages to sneak into the aquarium.

It's off-season. No one's minding the door so hard. And it's only a small place, anyway; five rooms strung together at the end of a line of stores. "Wonders of the Deep!" says the sign outside. Allie waits until the guy on the door has wandered off to get a soda, leaving a "Back in twenty minutes" sign, and she flips open the little wooden door and walks straight in. Because it's warm, really. And because the voice told her to look everywhere. No stone unturned.

She can feel there's something here for her as soon as she walks into the room full of brightly lit tanks with fish of a hundred coloured kinds patrolling the water back and forth. She feels it across her chest, in her collarbone, down to her fingers. There's something here; another girl who can do the thing she can do. No, not a girl. Allie feels out again with that other sense, the one that tingles. She's seen a little bit about it online, other girls saying they can sense if another woman in the room is about to discharge her power. But no one has it like Allie has it. Since she first got her power, she's been able to tell at once if anyone around her had any at all. And there's something here.

She finds it in the last tank but one. A darker tank than the rest, without the coloured, garlanded and fronded fish. It contains long, dark and sinuous creatures waiting at the bottom of the tank, stirring slowly. There's a meter-box to one side of the tank with its needle at zero.

Allie has never seen them before, nor does she know their name.

She puts her hand to the glass.

One of the eels shifts, turns and does something. She can hear it. A fizzing, cracking sound. The needle on the meter jumps.

But Allie doesn't need to know what the box is to know what just happened. This fish made a jolt.

There's a board up on the wall next to the tank. It's so exciting that she has to read it three times, and keep herself under control or her breathing goes fast. These are electric eels. They can do crazy things. They give

53

shocks to their prey under water; yeah, that's right. Allie makes a little arc between her finger and thumb under the table. The eels stir in the tank.

That's not all electric eels can do. They can "remote control" the muscles in their prey by interfering with the electric signals in the brain. They can make those fish swim straight into their mouths if they want to.

Allie stands for a long time with that. She puts her hand back on the glass. She looks at the animals.

That is a mighty power indeed. You would have to have control. Why, but you've always had control, daughter. And you'd have to be skilful. Why, but you can learn those skills.

Allie says in her heart: Mother, where shall I go?

And the voice says: Leave this place and go from here to the place that I shall show you.

The voice always did have a Biblical way with it, just like that.

That night, Allie wants to settle to sleeping, but the voice says: No, go on walking. Keep on. Her stomach is so empty and she feels peculiar, light-headed, troubled in her mind with thoughts of Mr Montgomery-Taylor, as if his lolling tongue were still licking at her ear. She wishes she had a dog.

The voice says: Nearly there, my girl, don't you worry.

And out of the darkness Allie sees a light, illuminating a sign. It says, "Sisters of Mercy Convent. Soup for the homeless and beds for those in need."

The voice says: See, I told you.

54

And all Allie knows after she crosses the threshold is that three women take her up bodily, calling her "child" and "sweet" and exclaiming when they find the crucifix in her bag because this is the proof of what they'd hoped to find in her face. They bring the food to her while she sits up, barely conscious, in a soft, warm bed, and that night not a one of them asked who she was and where she'd come from.

There is very little attention paid to a mixed-race child with no home and no family washed up at a convent on the eastern seaboard in those months. She is not the only girl who beaches on this shore, nor is she the one most in need of counsel. The sisters are glad to find a use for the empty bedrooms — they are living in a building too large for them, built almost one hundred years ago, when the Lord was still calling women by the fistful to His eternal marriage. By the time three months have passed, they have put in bunk beds and tacked up a schedule of classes and Sunday school and given out chores in exchange for meals and comforters and a roof over the head. There has been a great tide in the movement of people, and those old ways have taken precedence again. Girls thrown out on to the street — the nuns will take them in.

Allie likes to get the stories out of the other girls. She becomes a confidante, a pal, to several of them so she can match her tale up to theirs. There's Savannah, who struck her stepbrother across the face so hard, she says, that "spider-webs grew on him, they grew right over his mouth and his nose and even his eyes." Savannah tells this story wide-eyed, chewing her gum enthusiastically. Allie digs her fork into the tough old stewing meat the nuns serve for dinner thrice weekly. She says, "What're you gonna do now?" And Savannah says, "I'm gonna find a doctor will take it out of me. Cut that thing right out." A clue. There are others. Some of the girls were prayed over by parents who thought a demon had possessed them. Some fought with other girls; some are still fighting here. One had done the thing to a boy because he *asked her to*: this story holds much interest for the girls. Could it be that boys like it? Is it possible they want it? Some of them have found internet forums that suggest that this is the case.

There's one girl, Victoria, who showed her mother how to do the thing. Her mother, who, Victoria says as simply as if she were talking about the weather, had been beaten so hard and so often by Victoria's stepdad that she hasn't a tooth left in her head. Victoria woke the power up in her with a touch of her hand and showed her how to use it, and her mother threw her out into the street, calling her a witch. None of them needs an internet forum to understand that. They all nod, and someone passes Victoria the jug of gravy.

In a less chaotic time, there might have been police, or social services, or earnest folk from the school board asking what was going on with these girls. But the authorities are simply grateful that someone is helping them out.

Someone asks Allie what happened to her, and she knows she can't give her real name. She calls herself

Eve and the voice says: Good choice, the first of women; excellent choice.

Eve's story is simple, not interesting enough to be remembered. Eve's from Augusta, and her parents sent her to relatives for two weeks and when she came back they'd moved away, she doesn't know where. She had two younger brothers; her parents were scared for them, she thinks, although she'd never hurt no one. The other girls nod and move on to someone else.

It's not what I've done, Allie thinks to herself, it's what I'm going to do.

And the voice says: It's what Eve's going to do.

And Allie says: Yes.

She likes it in the convent. The nuns, for the most part, are kind, and the company of women is pleasing to Allie. She's not found the company of men has had much to recommend it. The girls have chores, to complete, but when they're done there's the ocean for swimming and the beach for walking, there are swings out back and the singing in chapel is peaceful and quiets all the voices in Allie's head. She finds herself thinking in those quiet times: maybe I could stay here for ever. To dwell in the House of God all the days of my life is my one request.

There is one nun, Sister Maria Ignacia, who particularly draws Allie's attention. She has dark skin like Allie herself, and soft, brown eyes. Sister Maria Ignacia likes to tell stories of the childhood of Jesus and of how his mother, Mary, was always kind to him and taught him to love all living things.

"See," Sister Maria Ignacia says to the girls who gather to listen to her before evensong, "our Lord learned from a woman how to love. And Mary is close to all children. She is close to you now and has brought you to our door."

One evening, after the others have gone, Allie leans her head against Sister Maria Ignacia's knee and says, "Can I live here all my life?"

Sister Maria Ignacia strokes her hair and says, "Oh, you would have to become a nun to stay here. And you might decide you want other things from your life. A husband and children, a job."

Allie thinks, This is always the answer. They never want you to stay for ever. They always say they love you, but they never want you to stay.

And the voice says, very quietly: Daughter, if you want to stay, I can fix that for you.

Allie says to the voice: Are you Mary, the mother?

And the voice says: If you like, my dear. If that's what floats your boat.

Allie says: They never want to keep me, though, do they? I never get to stay.

And the voice says: If you want to stay, you'll have to make this place your own. Think about how to do that. Don't worry, you'll figure it out.

The girls play at fighting, trying out their skills on each other. In the water, on the land, giving each other little jolts and thrills. Allie uses that time to practise, too, although she's more subtle about it. She doesn't want them to know what she's doing, remembering the thing

58

she read about the electric eels. She manages, after a long time, to send out a tiny jolt that will make one of the other girls' arm or leg jump.

"Oh!" says Savannah, as her shoulder flies upward, "I felt someone walk over my grave!"

"Huh," says Victoria, as Allie jangles her brain a little, "I have a headache. I can't . . . I can't think straight."

"Fuck!" shouts Abigail, as her knee buckles. "Got a fucking cramp from the water."

It doesn't take much power to do it, and it doesn't hurt them. They never know it was Allie, like the eels in the tank, her head just above the waterline, her eyes wide and steady.

After a few months, some of the other girls start to talk about moving on from the convent. It's occurred to Allie — or Eve, as she is trying to think of herself, even in private — that some of the others might have secrets, too, might also be hiding here until the heat dies down.

One of the girls, they call her Gordy, because her surname's Gordon, asks Allie to come with her. "We're going to Baltimore," she says. "My mom's family has people there, they'll help us get set up." She shifts her shoulders. "I'd like your company along the way."

Eve has made friends in a way Allie has always found difficult. Eve is kind and quiet and watchful, where Allie was spiky and complicated.

She cannot go back to where she came from and, what, indeed, would there be to return for? But there will be no great hunt for her. She looks different now, anyway, her face longer and leaner, her frame taller. It is that time in life when children start to wear their adult faces. She could walk north to Baltimore, or move on to some other nowhere town and take a job as a waitress. In three years' time, no one back in Jacksonville would know her for certain. Or she could stay here. When Gordy says, "Come away," Allie knows she wants to stay. She is happier here than she has ever been.

She listens at doors and around corners. She has always had this habit. A child in danger must learn to pay more attention to the adults than a child loved and cherished.

That is how she hears the nuns arguing between themselves, and how she learns she might not have the chance to stay at all.

It is Sister Veronica, her face like granite, whose voice Allie hears through the door of their small sitting room.

"Have you seen it?" she is saying. "Have you seen it working?"

"We have all seen it," rumbles the abbess.

"Then how can you doubt what it is?"

"Fairy stories," says Sister Maria Ignacia. "Children's games."

Sister Veronica's voice is so loud it makes the door tremble a little, and Allie takes a pace back.

"Are the Gospels themselves *fairy tales*? Was Our Lord a liar? Do you tell me that there has never been a demon, that when He cast out devils from men He was playing a *game*?"

"No one is saying that, Veronica. No one is doubting the Gospels."

"Have you seen it on the news reports? Have you seen what they do? They have powers that men are not meant to know. From where does this power come? We all know the answer. The Lord told us where these powers come from. We all know."

There is a silence in the room.

Sister Maria Ignacia speaks softly. "I have heard that it is caused by pollution. There was an interesting piece in the newspaper. Pollution in the atmosphere causing certain mutations in the —"

"It is the Devil. The Devil walks abroad and tests the innocent and the guilty, giving powers to the damned, as he has always done."

"Oh no," says Sister Maria Ignacia, "I have seen the good in their faces. They are *children*, we have a duty to care for them."

"You would see good in the face of Satan himself if he arrived at your door with a pitiful story and a hungry belly."

"And would I be wrong to do so? If Satan needed feeding?"

Sister Veronica gives a laugh like a dog's bark.

"Good intentions! Good intentions pave the road to Hell."

The abbess speaks over them all. "We have already asked for guidance to the Diocesan Council. They are praying on it. In the meantime, the Lord told us to suffer the little children."

"Younger girls awaken it in older women. This is the Devil working in the world, passing from hand to hand as Eve passed the apple to Adam."

"We cannot simply throw children out on to the street."

"The Devil will gather them to his bosom."

"Or they will starve," says Sister Maria Ignacia.

Allie thinks it over for a long time. She could move on. But she likes it here.

The voice says: You heard what she said. Eve passed the apple to Adam.

Allie thinks, Maybe she was right to do it. Maybe that's what the world needed. A bit of shaking up. Something new.

The voice says: That's my girl.

Allie thinks, Are you God?

The voice says: Who do you say that I am?

Allie thinks, I know that you speak to me in my hour of need. I know that you have guided me on the true path. Tell me what to do now. Tell me.

The voice says: If the world didn't need shaking up, why would this power have come alive now?

Allie thinks, God is telling the world that there is to be a new order. That the old way is overturned. The old centuries are done. Just as Jesus told the people of Israel that God's desires had changed, the time of the Gospels is over and there must be a new doctrine.

The voice says: There is a need for a prophet in the land.

Allie thinks, But who?

The voice says: Just try it on for size, honey. Remember, if you're going to stay here, you're going to need to own the place so they can't take it from you. The only way you're safe, honeybun, is if you own it.

Roxy

Roxy's seen her dad hit blokes before. She's seen him hit them square in the face, with all his rings on, casual, just as he was turning to leave. She's seen him punch a bloke till his nose was bleeding and he fell to the floor, and Bernie kicked him in the stomach again and again, and when he was finished he wiped his hands on the handkerchief from his back pocket and looked down at the mess of the bloke's face and said, "Don't you fuck with me. Don't you think you can fuck with me."

She's always wanted that.

Her dad's body is a castle for her. A shelter and a weapon. When he puts his arm around her shoulders she feels a mixture of terror and comfort. She's run up the stairs from his fist, screaming. She's seen how he hurts people who want to hurt her.

She's always wanted to have that. It's the only thing worth having.

"You know what's happened, don't you, darling?" says Bernie.

"Fucking Primrose," says Ricky.

Ricky's the oldest of her half-brothers.

Bernie says, "It was a declaration of war, killing your mum, darling. And it's taken us a long time to be sure we can get him. But now we're sure. And we're ready."

There's a look that passes around the room, between Ricky and Terry the middle son, between Terry and Darrell the youngest one. Three sons from his own wife, and then there's Roxy. She knows why she's been living with her granny this past year and not with them. Half in and half out, that's what she is. Not in enough to have over for Sunday lunch but not out enough to leave out of something like this. Something like this involves all of them.

Roxy says, "We should kill him."

Terry laughs.

His dad gives him a look, and the laugh cuts off halfway through a breath. You don't want to mess with Bernie Monke. Not even if you're his full-born son. "She's right," says Bernie. "You're right, Roxy. We should probably kill him. But he's strong and he's got a lot of friends, and we need to go slow and careful. If we do it, we're gonna do it just the once. Knock everything out in one go."

They get her to show them what she can do. She holds back a bit, gives each of them a dead arm in turn. Darrell swears when she touches him, and she feels a bit sorry. Darrell's the only one who's always been nice to her. He brought her an extra chocolate mouse from the sweetshop whenever his dad took him over to her mum's after school.

After she's finished, Bernie rubs his big arm and says, "That all you can do?"

So she shows them. She's seen stuff on the internet.

They follow her out into the garden, where Bernie's wife Barbara has one of them ornamental ponds full of big orange fish swimming around and around each other.

It's cold. Roxy's feet crunch on the frost-crisped grass.

She kneels down and puts the tips of her fingers into the pond.

There's a smell, suddenly, like ripe fruit, sweet and succulent. The smell of high summer. A flicker of light in the dark water. A sound like a hiss and a crackle.

And one by one the fish bob up to the surface of the water.

"Fuck!" says Terry.

"Bloody hell!" says Ricky.

"Mum's going to be pissed off," says Darrell.

Barbara Monke never came to see Roxy, not after her mother died, not after the funeral, nothing. Roxy's glad, for a moment, thinking of her coming back to see all her fish dead.

"I'll deal with your mother," says Bernie. "We can use this, Rox, my girl."

Bernie finds a couple of his blokes who've got daughters about the right age, gets them to show what they can do, too. They do play-fighting. Sparring each against each, or two against one. Bernie watches them in the garden, sparking and flickering. All over the world people are going crazy about this thing, but a few people always look at anything and go, "Where's the profit in this, and where's the advantage?"

One thing's certain after the sparring matches and practice bouts. Roxy's got a lot of it. Not just more than average, more than any of the other girls they can find to practise with her. She learns a few things about radius and reach, about how to make it arc and how it works better on wet skin. She feels proud of how strong she is. She puts everything into that.

She's the strongest one they've found, out of all the girls they've heard of.

That's why, when it comes time, when Bernie's arranged the whole thing and they know just where Primrose is going to be, that's why Roxy comes along, too.

Ricky pulls her into the loo before they leave. "You're a big girl now, right, Rox?"

She nods. She knows about this, kind of.

He pulls a little plastic bag out from his pocket and taps some white powder on to the side of the sink.

"You've seen this before, haven't you?"

"Yeah."

"Ever done it before?"

She shakes her head.

"OK, then."

He shows her how to do it, with a rolled-up fifty from his wallet, and tells her she can keep the note when they're done, perks of the job. She feels very clear and very clean when they've done it. It's not that she's forgotten what happened to her mum. Her anger is still pure and white and electric, but she doesn't feel the sadness of it at all. It's just a thing she heard about once. It's good. She is powerful. She has this whole day in her fingers. She lets a long arc go between the palms of her hands, loud and sparking, a longer arc than she's ever managed before.

"Whoa," says Ricky. "Not in here, all right?"

She brings it down and leaves it glittering around the pads of her fingers. It makes her want to laugh, how much she has and how easy it is to set it loose.

He tips a little bit of the powder into a clean bag and pops it into her jeans pocket. "Just in case you need it. Don't do it unless you get scared, OK? *Don't* do it in the car, for Christ's sake."

She doesn't need it. Everything belongs to her, anyway.

The next few hours are shutter-snaps. Pictures like on her phone. She blinks and there's a picture. Blinks again and there's something else. She looks at her watch and it's 2p.m., looks a moment later and it's half past. She couldn't worry about anything if she tried. It's good.

They've drilled her in the plan. Primrose is going to be there with just two blokes. Weinstein, his mate, has sold him out. Brought him to this warehouse saying he needs to have a meeting. Bernie and his boys will be waiting behind some of the packing cases with the guns. Two of the boys will be outside to close the doors, seal them in. Take them by surprise, let her rip; all done and home in time for tea. Primrose won't expect it.

Roxy's only really coming along because she deserves to see it happen, after what she's been through. And because Bernie's always been a belt-and-braces man, that's how he's survived as long as he has. So she's hiding upstairs in the warehouse with a peep-hole view down through the grating of the upper level, surrounded by boxes. Just in case. She's there, looking down, when Primrose arrives. Shutter open, shutter closed.

When it goes down, it's quick and deadly and a complete cluster-fuck. Bernie and the boys are downstairs, they shout to Weinstein to get out of the way, and Weinstein does this thing, this shrug, like he's trying to say, Hard luck, mate, hard cheese, but he ducks down anyway as Bernie and his sons advance, and that's when Primrose starts smiling. And his blokes come in. So many more of them than Weinstein said he'd have here. Someone's fucking lied. Click goes the shutter.

Primrose is a tall man, thin and pale. There's twenty of his blokes here if there's one. They're firing, scattered around the entrance to the building, using iron half-doors up against the rails for cover. There are just more of them than Bernie's men. Three of them have Terry pinned down behind a single wooden crate. Big, slow Terry with his huge, white, acne-marked forehead, and as Roxy watches he peeps his head out from behind the box. He shouldn't do that, she tries to shout, but nothing comes out.

Primrose aims carefully, taking all the time in the world over it; he's smiling as he does it and then there's a red hole in the middle of Terry's face and he falls forward like a felled tree. Roxy looks at her hands. There are long electrical arcs passing between them, even though she doesn't think she ever told them to do that. She should do something. She feels afraid. She's only fifteen. She pulls the little packet out of her jeans and sniffs up some more of the powder. She sees the energy running along her arms and hands. She thinks, and it's like a voice outside her whispering in her ear: You were made for this.

She's on an iron walkway. It's connected to the metal half-doors downstairs which Primrose's men are using for cover. There's a lot of them down there, touching the iron or leaning against it. She sees what she can do all in a flash and it makes her so excited she can barely sit still. Her one knee starts jiggling. This is it, these are the men who killed her mum, and now she *knows* what to do. She waits until one's resting his fingertips on the rail and one's leaning his head against it and a third's clutching on to a handle to lean down low to fire. One of them gets off a shot that hits Bernie in the side. Roxy breathes out slowly through pursed lips. You've had this coming, she thinks. She lights up the rail. Three of them go down, backs arching, crying out, fitting and gnashing and eyes rolled back. Got you. You asked for it.

And then they spot her. Freeze frame.

There aren't many of them left now. They're evenly matched, maybe Bernie's even got the upper hand, especially cos Primrose is a bit scared now; you can see it on his face. There's thundering steps on the iron

70

stairs, and two blokes try to grab her. One of them leans close to her, cos that's scary to normal kids, to any little girl, and it's just instinct, but she only has to put up a couple of fingers to his temple and let a jolt go across his forehead and he's fallen to the floor, crying bloody tears. The other one grabs her round the waist — don't they know anything? — and she gets his wrist. She's learning it doesn't take much to stop them touching her, and she feels pleased with herself until she looks down and sees Primrose heading out the door that leads to the back of the block.

He's going to get away. Bernie is moaning on the floor, and Terry bleeding from the hole in his head. Terry's gone, just like her mum, she's sure of that, but Primrose is trying to get away. Oh no you're not, you little shit, Roxy thinks. Oh no you're bloody not.

She sprints down the steps, keeping low, and follows Primrose back through the building, along a corridor, through an empty open-plan office. She sees him veering left and she speeds up. If he gets to his car she'll have lost him and he'll come back on them hard and fast; he won't leave any of them alive. She thinks of his men taking her mum by the throat. He ordered this. He made it come true. Her legs pump harder.

He goes down another corridor, into a room — there's a door to the fire-exit stairs and she hears the handle go and she's saying, Fuck fuck fuck, to herself, but when she hurls her body round the corner Primrose is still in that room. The door was locked, wasn't it. He's got hold of a metal bin and he's bashing at the window to break it and she dives down just like they'd practised, slides and aims for his shin. Her one hand grasps his ankle, sweet, bare flesh and she gives it to him.

He doesn't make a sound the first time. He topples to the ground like his knee's given way, even while his arms are still trying to bash the window with that bin so it clangs into the wall. And as he goes down she grabs his wrist and she gives it to him again.

She can tell from the way he screams that no one's done this to him before. It's not the pain, it's the surprise, the horror. She sees the line run up his arm, just like on the bloke in her mum's house, and thinking of that, even remembering it, makes it run stronger and hotter through her. He screams like there are spiders under his skin, like they're biting him inside his flesh.

She eases it off a bit.

"Please," he says. "Please."

He looks at her, makes his swimming eyes focus. "I know you," he says. "You're Monke's kid. Your mum was Christina, wasn't she?"

He's not supposed to say her mum's name. He shouldn't do that. She gets him across the throat and he screams, and then he's saying, "Fuck. Fuck. Fuck."

And then he's gabbling, "I'm sorry about it, I am sorry, it was about your dad but I can help you, you can come and work for me, bright girl like you, strong girl like you, never felt anything like it. Bernie doesn't want you around, I can tell you that. Come and work for me. Tell me what you want. I can get it for you."

Roxy says, "You killed my mum."

He goes, "Your dad killed three of my boys that month."

She goes, "You sent your men and they killed my mum."

And Primrose goes so quiet, so quiet and so still she thinks he's going to start screaming again any second or he's going to launch himself at her teeth first. Then he smiles and shrugs. He says, "I got nothing for you, love, if this is the way it is. But you were never supposed to see it. Newland said you weren't going to be home."

Someone's coming up the stairs. She hears them. Feet, more than one pair, boots on the stairs. Could be her dad's men, could be Primrose's. Could be she'll have to run or there'll be a bullet for her any second.

"I was home, though," Roxy says.

"Please," says Primrose. "Please don't."

And she's back there again, clean and clear and with the crystals exploding in her brain, back in her mum's house. It was just what her mum said, just that. She thinks of her dad with his rings on and his knuckles coming away from a man's mouth dripping blood. This is the only thing worth having. She puts her hand to Primrose's temples. And she kills him.

Tunde

He gets a phone call the day after he puts the video online. It's from CNN, they say. He thinks they're kidding. It's just the kind of thing his friend Charles would do, some stupid joke. He called Tunde once, pretending to be the French ambassador, kept up the snooty accent for ten minutes before he cracked.

The voice on the other end of the line says, "We want the rest of the video. We're happy to pay whatever you're asking."

He says, "What?"

"Is this Tunde? BourdillonBoy97?"

"Yeah?"

"It's CNN calling. We want to buy the rest of the video you put online of the incident in the grocery store. And any others you have."

And he thinks, The rest? The rest? And then he remembers.

"There's only . . . it's only missing a minute or two at the end. Other people came into the shot. I didn't think it was . . ."

"We'll blur the faces. How much are you asking?"

His face is still pillow-mashed and his head hurts. He throws out the first stupid number that comes into his head. Five thousand American dollars.

And they agree so fast that he knows he should have asked for double.

That weekend he prowls the streets and the clubs looking for footage. A fight between two women on the beach at midnight, the electricity lighting up the eager faces of their audience as the women grunt and struggle to grab each other's faces, throats. Tunde gets chiaroscuro shots of their faces twisted with rage, half hidden in shadow. The camera makes him feel powerful; as if he's there but not there. You do what you like, he thinks to himself, but I'm the one who's going to turn it into something. I'll be the one who'll tell the story.

There's a girl and a boy making love in a back alley. She coaxes him with a crackling hand at the small of his back. The boy turns around to see Tunde's camera pointing at him and pauses, and the girl sends a flicker across his face and says, "Don't look at him, look at me." When they're getting close, the girl smiles and lights up the boy's spine and says to Tunde, "Hey, you want some, too?" That's when he notices a second woman watching from further down the alley, and he runs as fast as he can, hearing them laughing behind him. Once he's safely out of the way, he laughs, too. He looks at the footage on the screen. It's sexy. He'd like someone to do that to him, maybe. Maybe.

CNN take those pieces of footage, too. They pay. He looks at the money in his account, thinks, I'm a journalist. This is all it means. I found the news and they paid me for it. His parents say, "When are you going back to school?"

And he says, "I'm taking a semester off. Practical experience." This is his life, starting; he can feel it.

He learns early on not to use his cellphone camera. Three times in the first few weeks a woman touches the camera and the thing goes dead. He buys a boxful of cheap digital cameras from a truck in Alaba Market but he knows he's not going to make the kind of money he wants — the kind of money he knows is out there — from footage he can take in Lagos. He reads internet forums discussing what's happening in Pakistan, in Somalia, in Russia. He can feel the excitement tingling up his spine. This is it. His war, his revolution, his *history*. Right here, hanging off the tree for anyone to pick. Charles and Joseph call him up to see if he wants to go to a party on Friday night, and he laughs and says, "I've got bigger plans, man." He buys a plane ticket.

He arrives in Riyadh on the night of the first great riot. This is his luck; if he'd turned up three weeks before he might have run out of money or enthusiasm too early. He'd've got the same footage as everyone else: women wearing the batula practising their sparks on each other, giggling shyly. More likely, he would have got nothing — those shots were mostly filmed by women. To be a man, filming here, he needed to arrive on the night that they swarmed through the city.

It had been sparked by the death of two girls, about twelve years old. An uncle had found them practising their devilry together; a religious man, he had summoned his friends, and the girls had struggled against their punishment and somehow they had both ended up beaten to death. And the neighbours saw and heard. And — who can say why these things happen on Thursday, when the same events might have gone unremarked on Tuesday? — they fought back. A dozen women turned into a hundred. A hundred into a thousand. The police retreated. The women shouted; some made placards. They understood their strength, all at once.

When Tunde arrives at the airport the security officers at the doors tell him it's not safe to leave, that foreign visitors should stay here in the terminal and take the first flight home. He has to bribe three separate men to sneak out. He pays a cab driver double to take him where the women are gathering, shouting and marching. It is the middle of the day and the man is frightened.

"Go home," he says as Tunde jumps from the cab, and Tunde cannot tell whether he's saying what he's about to do or giving advice.

Three streets away, he spots the tail of the crowd. He has a feeling something will happen here today, something he has not seen before. He is too excited to be afraid. He is going to be the one to record this thing.

He follows behind them, holding his camera close to his body so it won't be too obvious what he's doing.

But still, a couple of the women notice him. They shout at him, first in Arabic and then in English.

"News? CNN? BBC?"

"Yes," he says. "CNN."

They start to laugh, and for a moment he is afraid, but it passes like a wisp of cloud when they shout to one another, "CNN! CNN!" and more women come, holding their thumbs up and smiling into the camera.

"You cannot walk with us, CNN," says one of them, her English a little better than the others'. "There will be no men with us today."

"Oh, but" — Tunde smiles his broad and winning smile — "I'm harmless. You wouldn't hurt me."

The women say, "No. No men, no."

"What do I have to do to convince you to trust me?" says Tunde. "Look, here's my CNN badge. I'm not carrying any weapons." He opens up his jacket, takes it off slowly, swirls it in the air to show both sides.

The women are watching him. The one whose English is better says, "You could be carrying anything."

"What's your name?" he says. "You know mine already. I'm at a disadvantage."

"Noor," she says. "It means the light. We are the ones who bring the light. Now, tell us, what if you have a gun in a holster on your back, or a taser strapped to your calf?"

He looks at her, raises an eyebrow. She has dark, laughing eyes. She's laughing at him.

"Really?" he says.

She nods, smiling.

He unbuttons his shirt slowly. Peels it off his back. There are sparks flying between their fingertips, but he is not afraid.

"No gun taped to my back."

"I see that," she says. "Calf?"

There are maybe thirty women watching this now. Any one of them could kill him with a single blow. In for a penny.

He undoes his jeans. Slips them down. There's a little intake of breath around the crowd of women. He turns in a slow circle.

"No taser," says Tunde, "on my calf."

Noor smiles. Licks her top lip.

"Then you should come with us, CNN. Put your clothes back on and follow."

He pulls his clothes on hastily and stumbles behind them. She reaches for him and takes his left hand.

"In our country, it is forbidden for a man and a woman to hold hands in the street. In our country, a woman is not allowed to drive a car. Women are no good with cars."

She squeezes his hand more tightly. He can feel the crackle of power across her shoulders, like the feeling in the air before a storm. She does not hurt him; not even a flicker of it leaks into him. She pulls him across the empty road to a shopping mall. Outside the entrance, dozens of cars are parked in orderly rows, marked out by red and green and blue flags.

In the upper floors of the mall, Tunde sees some men and women watching. The young women around him laugh and point at them and make a crackle pass between their fingertips. The men flinch. The women stare hungrily. Their eyes are parched for the sight of it.

Noor laughs as she makes Tunde stand well back from the bonnet of a black jeep parked right outside the entrance. Her smile is wide and confident.

"Are you recording?" she says.

"Yes."

"They do not let us drive a car here," she says, "but watch what we can do."

She puts her palm flat on the bonnet. There is a click and it flicks open.

She grins at him. She places her hand just so upon the engine, next to the battery.

The engine kicks on. The car revs. Higher and higher, louder and louder, the motor thudding and screeching, the whole machine trying to escape from her. Noor is laughing as she does it. The noise becomes louder, the sound of an engine in agony, and then a vast, explosive percussion, a great white light out of the engine block, and the whole thing melts, warps down into the tarmac, dripping with oil and hot steel. She grimaces, grabs Tunde's hand and shouts, "Run!" in his ear, and they do, they run across the parking lot, while she's saying, "Look, film it, film it," and he turns back towards the jeep just at the moment that the hot metal hits the fuel line and the whole thing explodes.

It is so loud and hot that for a moment his camera screen goes white, and then black. And when the picture comes back there are young women advancing across the centre of the screen, each of them backed by the fire, each of them walking with the lightning. They

80

are going from car to car, setting the motors revving and the engine blocks burning into a molten heat. Some of them can do it without touching the cars; they send their lines of power out from their bodies and they are all laughing.

Tunde pans up to look at the people watching from the windows, to see what they are doing. There are men trying to drag their women from the glass. And there are women shrugging off their hands. Not bothering to say a word. Watching and watching. Palms pressed against the glass. He knows then that this thing is going to take the world and everything will be different and he is so glad he shouts for joy, whooping with the others among the flames.

In Manfouha, to the west of the city, an elderly Ethiopian woman walks out of a half-built, scaffold-supported building into the street to greet them, her hands held high, calling out something that none of them can understand. Her back is bent, her shoulders hunched forward, her spine humped between her shoulder blades. Noor takes her palm between her two hands, and the older woman watches her like a patient observing a doctor's treatment. Noor puts two fingers to her palm and shows her how to use the thing that must always have been in her, must have been waiting all the years of her life to emerge. This is how it works. The younger women can wake it up in the older ones; but from now on all women will have it.

The older woman starts to cry when the gentle force of it wakes up the lines of her nerves and ligaments. You can see it in her face on the footage when she feels it inside her. She does not have much to give. A tiny spark jumps between her fingertips and Noor's arm. She must be eighty years old, and the tears run down her face as she does it again and again. She holds up her two palms and starts to ululate. The other women take it up and the street is filled with the sound, the city is filled with it; the country — Tunde thinks — must be full of this joyful warning. He is the only man here, the only one filming. This revolution feels like his personal miracle, a thing to overturn the world.

He travels with them through the night and records the things he sees. In the north of the city they see a woman in an upstairs room behind a barred window. She drops a note down through the bars — Tunde cannot get close enough to read it, but there is a ripple through the crowd as the message is passed from person to person. They break down the door and he follows them as they find the man who has been holding her prisoner cowering in a kitchen cupboard. They do not even bother to hurt him; they take the woman with them as they gather and grow. In the campus of the Health Sciences department a man runs towards them, firing an army rifle and shouting in Arabic and English about their offence against their betters. He wounds three of the women in the leg or arm and the others are on him like a tide. There is a sound like eggs frying. When Tunde gets close enough to show what has been done, he is perfectly still, the twisted-vine marks across his face and neck so thick that his features are barely discernible.

At last, near dawn, crowded around by women who show no signs of tiring, Noor takes his hand and leads him to an apartment, a room, a bed. It belongs to a friend of hers, she says, a student. Six people live here. But half the city has fled now and the place is empty. The electricity isn't working. She makes a spark in her hand to find their way, and there, in the flash of her, she takes off his jacket, pulls his shirt over his head. She looks at his body as she did before: open and hungry. She kisses him.

"I have never done this before," she says, and he tells her the same is true for him and he does not feel ashamed.

She puts her palm to his chest. "I am a free woman," she says.

He feels it. It is exhilarating. In the streets there are still shouts and crackles and sporadic sounds of gunfire. Here in a bedroom covered with posters of pop singers and movie stars, their bodies are warm together. She unbuttons his jeans and he steps out of them; she goes carefully; he can feel her skein starting to hum. He is afraid, he is turned on; it is all bundled up together, as it is in his fantasies.

"You are a good man," she says. "You are beautiful."

She runs the back of her hand over the sparse fur of his chest. She lets a tiny crackle go, a prickle at his hair's ends, glowing faintly. It feels good. Every line of his body is coming into focus as she touches him, as if he hadn't really been there at all, before.

He wants to be inside her; his body is already telling him what to do, how to move this thing forward, how to

83

take her arms, how to bring her down on to the bed, how to consummate. But the body has contradictory impulses: fear is as significant as lust, physical pain as strong as desire. He holds himself there, wanting and not-wanting. He lets her set the pace.

It takes a long while, and it is good. She shows him what to do, with his mouth and with his fingers. By the time she is riding him, sweating and calling out, the sun has risen on a new day in Riyadh. And when she loses control as she finishes she sends a jolt through his buttocks and across his pelvis and he barely feels the pain at all, so great is the delight.

Later that afternoon, they send out the men in helicopters and soldiers on the streets, armed with guns and live ammunition. Tunde is there to film it when the women hit back. There are so many of them; they are so numerous and so angry. Several women are killed but this just sharpens the rest, and can any soldier keep on firing for ever, mowing down row after row of women? The women fuse the firing pins inside the barrels, they cook the electronics of the vehicles. They do it happily. "Bliss was it in that dawn to be alive," says Tunde in his voiceover report, because he's been reading about revolution, "but to be young was very heaven".

Twelve days later the government has fallen. There are rumours, never substantiated, about who killed the King; some say it was a member of the family, and some say it was an Israeli assassin, and some whisper that it was one of the maids who had served in the palace loyally for years feeling the power between her fingertips and no longer able to hold it back.

84

By that time, anyway, Tunde is on a plane again. What has happened in Saudi Arabia has been seen across the world, and the thing is happening everywhere all at once now.

Margot

"It's a problem."

"We all know it's a problem."

"Think about it, Margot. I mean, really think about it."

"I am thinking about it."

"We've got no way to know whether *anyone* in this room can do it."

"We know *you* couldn't do it, Daniel."

That gets a laugh. In a room of anxious people, a laugh is a release. It wells up to more than its proper size. It takes a few moments for the twenty-three people gathered around the conference table to settle again. Daniel is upset. He thinks it's a joke about him. He's always wanted just a little bit more than his due.

"Obviously," he says. "Obviously. But we have no way to know. The girls, fine, we're doing what we can with them — God, have you seen the numbers on runaways?"

They've all seen the numbers on runaways.

Daniel presses on. "I'm not talking about the girls. We've got that under control, for the most part. I'm talking about grown women. Teenage girls can wake

86

this thing up in older women. And they can give it to each other. Grown women can do it now, Margot, you've seen that stuff."

"It's very rare."

"We *think* it's very rare. What I'm saying is, we just don't know. It could be you, Stacey. Or you, Marisha. For all we know, Margot, you might be able to do it yourself." He laughs, and that also gets a nervous little ripple.

Margot says, "Sure, Daniel, I could zap you right now. The Governor's office treads on a news cycle you agreed to give to the Mayoralty?" She makes a gesture, splaying her fingers wide. "Pfffzzzt."

"I don't think that's funny, Margot."

But the other people around the table are already laughing.

Daniel says, "We're going to get this test. Bring it in state-wide, all government employees. That includes the Mayor's office, Margot. No arguments. We need to know for sure. You can't have someone employed in government buildings who can do that. It's like walking around with a loaded gun."

It's been a year. There's been footage on the TV of riots in faraway and unstable parts of the world, of women taking whole cities. Daniel's right. The critical thing isn't that fifteen-year-old girls can do it: you could contain that. The thing is that they can wake up this power in some of the older women. It raises questions. How long has this been possible? How did no one know until now?

On the morning shows, they bring in experts on human biology and prehistoric images. This carved image found in Honduras, dating back more than six thousand years, doesn't that look like a woman with lightning coming from her hands to you, Professor? Well, of course, these carvings often represent mythical and symbolic behaviours. But it could be historical, that is, it could represent something that actually happened. It could, maybe. Did you know, in the oldest texts, that the God of the Israelites had a sister, Anath, a teenage girl? Did you know that she was the warrior, that she was invincible, that she spoke with the lightning, that in the oldest texts she killed her own father and took his place? She liked to bathe her feet in the blood of her enemies. The TV anchors laugh uneasily. That doesn't sound like much of a beauty regime, now, does it, Kristen? Certainly does not, Tom. But now, this destroying goddess, do you think those ancient peoples knew something we don't? It's hard to say, of course. And is it possible that this capacity goes back a very long time? You mean, women in the past could do it, too, and we forgot? Seems like a hell of a thing to forget, now, doesn't it? How could it have been forgotten? Well, now, Kristen, if a power like this existed, maybe we bred it out deliberately, maybe we didn't want it around. You'd tell me if you could do something like that, wouldn't you, Kristen? Well, you know, Tom, maybe I'd want to keep a thing like that to myself. The news anchors' eyes meet. Something unspoken passes between them. And now the weather on the ones.

★   ★   ★

The official line for now from the Mayor's office, handed out on photocopied sheets to schools across the major metropolitan area is: abstinence. Just don't do it. It'll pass. We keep the girls separate from the boys. There'll be an injection within a year or two to stop this thing happening and then we'll all go back to normal. It's as upsetting for the girls to use it as it is for their victims. That's the official line.

Late at night in a part of town she knows has no surveillance cameras, Margot parks her car, gets out, puts her palm to a lamp post and gives it everything she's got. She just needs to know what she's got under the hood here; she wants to feel what it *is*. It feels as natural as anything she's ever done, as known and understood as the first time she had sex, as her body saying, Hey, I got this.

All the lights in the road go out: pop, pop, pop. Margot laughs out loud, there in the silent street. She'd be impeached if anyone found out, but then she'd be impeached anyway if anyone knew she could do it at all, so what's the margin? She guns the gas and drives off before the sirens start. She wondered what she'd have done if they'd caught her, and in the asking she knows she has enough left in her skein to stun a man, at least, maybe more — can feel the power sloshing across her collarbone and up and down her arms. The thought makes her laugh again. She finds she's doing that more often now, just laughing. There's a sort of constant ease, as if it's high summer all the time inside her.

It hasn't been this way with Jos. No one knows why; no one's done enough research on the thing even to venture a suggestion. She's getting fluctuations. Some days she's got so much power in her that she trips the house fuse box just turning on a light. Some days she has nothing, not even enough to defend herself if some girl picks a fight with her in the street. There are nasty names now for a girl who can't or won't defend herself. *Blanket*, they call them, and *flat battery*. Those are the least offensive ones. *Gimp. Flick. Nesh. Pzit.* The last, apparently, for the sound of a woman trying to make a spark and failing. For maximum effect, you need a group of girls all innocuously whispering "*pzit*" as you walk past. Young people are still deadly. Jos has been spending more and more time alone, as her friends find new friends with whom they have "more in common".

Margot suggests that Jocelyn could come to stay by herself one weekend. She'll have Jos; Bobby will take Maddy. It's nice for the girls to have a parent all to themselves. Maddy wants to take the bus into town to look at the dinosaurs — she never gets to take the bus any more; it's more of a treat for her now than the museum. Margot's been working so hard. I'll take Jos for mani-pedis, she says. It'll be good for both of us to take a break.

They eat breakfast at the table by the kitchen's glass wall. Jos helps herself to some more stewed plums from the bowl and tops them with yogurt, and Margot says, "You still can't tell anyone."

"Yeah, I know."

"I could lose my job if you tell *anyone*."

"Mom, I *know*. I haven't told Dad and I haven't told Maddy. I haven't told *anyone*. I won't."

"I'm sorry."

Jocelyn smiles. "It's cool."

Margot suddenly remembers how much she would have liked to have a secret to share with her mother. How the yearning for it made even the grubby rituals of elasticated bands for sanitary towels or carefully concealed leg razors seem faintly lovable or even glamorous.

They practise together in the garage in the afternoon, challenging each other, fighting and working up a little sweat. Jos's power gets stronger and easier to control if she works with it. Margot can feel it flickering, feel that it hurts Jos when the power rises up and then suddenly shorts out. There must be some way Jos can learn to control it. There must be girls in her own metropolitan-area's schools who've had to learn to control it themselves and could teach Jos a few tricks.

As for Margot: all she needs to know is that she can keep it under control. They're bringing in testing at work.

"Come on in, Mayor Cleary. Sit down."

The room is small, and there is only one tiny window far up near the ceiling, letting in a thin strip of grey light. When the nurse visits for the annual flu shot, this is the room she uses, or if someone's doing the staff review. There's a table, and three chairs. Behind the table is a woman wearing a bright blue security tag pinned to her lapel. On top of the table is a piece of machinery: it looks like it might be a microscope or a blood-testing apparatus; there are two needles and a focusing window and lenses.

The woman says, "We want you to know, Madam Mayor, that everyone in the building is being tested. You haven't been singled out."

"Even the men?" Margot raises an eyebrow.

"Well, no, not the men."

Margot thinks about that.

"OK. And it's . . . what exactly?"

The woman gives a faint smile: "Madam Mayor, you signed the papers. You know what this is."

She feels her throat constrict. She puts one hand on her hip. "No, actually, I want you to tell me what it is. For the record."

The woman wearing the security tag says, "It's state-wide mandatory testing for the presence of a skein, or the electrostatic power." She starts to read from a card sitting next to the machine. "Please be advised that following a state-wide order from the Governor Daniel Dandon, your continued eligibility for your government position is dependent on your agreement to be tested. A positive test result need not necessarily have any bearing on your future employment. It is possible for a woman to test positive without knowing that she has the capacity to use the electrostatic power. Counselling is available if the results of this test are distressing to you, or to help you consider your options if your current position is no longer suitable."

"What does that mean," says Margot, "no longer suitable? What does it mean?"

The woman purses her lips: "Certain positions involving contact with children and the public have been mandated as unsuitable by the Governor's office."

It's like Margot can see Daniel Dandon, the Governor of this great state, standing behind the woman's chair, laughing.

"*Children and the public?* What does that leave me?"

The woman smiles. "If you haven't experienced the power yet, it's all going to be fine. Nothing to worry about, on with your day."

"It's not fine for everyone."

The woman flicks the switch on the machine. It starts up a gentle hum.

"I'm ready to begin, Madam Mayor."

"What happens if I say no?"

She sighs. "If you say no, I'll have to record it, and the Governor will inform someone in the State Department."

Margot sits down. She thinks, They won't be able to tell I've used it. No one knows. I haven't been lying. She thinks, Shit. She swallows.

"Fine," she says, "I'd like it recorded that I'm making a formal protest about being forced to undergo invasive testing."

"OK," says the woman. "I'll get that written down."

And behind her faint smirk, Margot can see Daniel's face again, laughing. She puts her arm out for the electrodes, thinking that, at least, at least after this is done, even after she's out of a job and there go her political ambitions, at least then she won't have to look at his stupid face any more.

They apply the sticky electrode pads to her wrists, her shoulders, her collarbone. They're looking for electrical activity, the technician explains in a low, droning voice. "You should be perfectly comfortable, ma'am. At worst, you'll experience a slight stinging sensation."

At worst, I'll experience the end of my career, Margot thinks, but says nothing.

It's all very simple. They're going to trigger her autonomic nervous function with a series of low-level electrical impulses. It works on the girl babies in routine tests now being run in hospitals, even though the answer is always the same, because all the girl babies have it now, every single one. Give them an almost imperceptible shock across the skein; the skein will respond automatically with a jolt. Margot can feel her skein is ready, anyway — it's the nerves, the adrenaline.

Remember to look surprised, she says to herself, remember to look afraid and ashamed and taken aback by this brand-new thing.

The machine makes a low, buzzing hum as it starts. Margot is familiar with the schematics. It will begin by giving an entirely imperceptible shock, too low for the senses to register. The skeins of those little baby girls almost always respond at this level, or the next one. The machine has ten settings. The electrical stimulus will increase, level by level. At a certain point, Margot's own aged and unpractised skein will respond, like calling to like. And then they will know. She breathes in, she breathes out. She waits.

At the start, she cannot feel it at all. There is simply the sensation of pressure building. Across her chest, down her spine. She does not feel the first level, or the second level, or the third, as the machine clicks smoothly through its cycle. The dial moves on. Margot feels that it would be pleasant, now, to discharge herself. It is like the feeling, on waking, that one might like to open one's eyes. She resists. It is not difficult.

She breathes in, she breathes out. The woman operating the machine smiles, makes a note on her Xeroxed sheet of boxes. A fourth o in the fourth box. Nearly halfway there. Of course, at some point, it will become impossible, Margot has read it in the literature. She makes a rueful little smile at the technician.

"Are you comfortable?" the woman says.

"I'd be more comfortable with a glass of Scotch," Margot says.

The dial clicks forward. Now it is becoming more difficult. She feels the pricking at the right side of her collarbone and in the palm of her hand. Come on, it says, come on. It is like a pressure holding her arm down now. Uncomfortable. She could so easily throw this heavy, pressing weight off and be free of it. She cannot be seen to sweat, cannot show a struggle.

Margot thinks of what she did when Bobby told her he'd been having an affair. She remembers how her body went hot and cold, how she felt her throat close up. She remembers how he said, "Aren't you going to say anything? Don't you have anything to say about that?" Her mother would scream at her father for leaving the door unlatched when he walked out in the morning, or forgetting his slippers in the middle of the living-room rug. She's never been one of those women, never wanted to be. She used to walk in the cool of the yew trees when she was a child, placing each foot so carefully, pretending that if she took one wrong step the roots would curl up through the earth and grab her. She has always known exactly how to be silent.

The dial clicks on. There is a neat row of eight zeroes on the woman's Xeroxed sheet. Margot had been afraid she would not know what a zero felt like, that the business would be over before it began and she would have no choice. She breathes in and breathes out. It is hard now, very hard, but the difficulty is familiar. Her body wants something, and she is denying it. The itch of it, the pressure of it, is across the front of her torso, down through the muscles of her stomach, into her pelvis, around her buttocks. It is like simply not passing water when your bladder asks you to. It is like holding your breath for a few seconds longer than is entirely comfortable. It's no wonder that the baby girls can't do it. It's a wonder they've found any adult women at all with this thing. Margot feels herself want to discharge, and doesn't. Just doesn't.

The machine clicks on to its tenth setting. It is not impossible, not even nearly. She waits. The humming cuts off. The fans whirr and then are silent. The pen lifts from the graph table. Ten zeroes.

Margot tries to look disappointed. "No dice, huh?"

The technician shrugs.

Margot tucks one foot behind the other ankle as the technician removes the electrodes. "I never thought I had it." She makes her voice crack just a little at the end of the sentence.

Daniel will look at this report. He'll be the one to sign off on it. Cleared, it will say, for government work.

She twitches her shoulders and lets out a little barking laugh.

And there's no reason now not to put her in charge of the programme rolling out this test across the major metropolitan area. Not a reason in the world. She's the one who signs off on the budget for it. Who agrees the informational campaigns explaining that this technology will keep our sons and daughters safe. It's Margot's name, when you come right down to it, on the official documentation saying that this testing equipment will help save lives. She tells herself, as she signs the forms, that it's probably true. Any woman who can't stop herself from discharging under this mild pressure is a danger to herself, a danger, yes, to society.

There are strange movements rising now, not only across the world, but right here in the US of A. You can see it on the internet. Boys dressing as girls to seem more powerful. Girls dressing as boys to shake off the meaning of the power, or to leap on the unsuspecting, wolf in sheep's clothing. The Westboro Baptist Church has seen a sudden influx of crazy new members who think the day of judgement is coming.

The work they're doing right here — trying to keep everything *normal*, to keep people feeling safe and going to their jobs and spending their dollars on weekend recreational activities — this is important work.

Daniel says, "I try, I really try, always to have something positive to say, you know, but I just" — he lets the pages slip from his hand, fall across the table — "your people haven't given me a single thing I can use here."

Arnold, Daniel's budget guy, nods silently, holding his chin in his hand, an awkward, twisted gesture.

"I know it's not your fault," says Daniel. "You're understaffed, under-resourced — we all know you're trying your hardest in difficult circumstances — but this just isn't something we can use."

Margot has read the report from the Mayor's office. It's bold, yes, it suggests a strategy of radical openness about the current state of protection, of treatments, of the potential for any future reversal. (The potential is nil.) Daniel keeps on talking, listing one problem after another, never quite saying, "I'm not brave enough for this," but meaning that every time.

Margot's hands are flat against the underside of the table, palms upward. She feels the fizz building as he speaks. She breathes very slowly and evenly; she knows she can control this, it's the control that gives her pleasure, at first. She thinks of exactly what she would do; as Daniel drones on, she can feel it out quite simply. She has enough power within her to take Daniel's throat in her grip and pinch him out with one blast. She'd have plenty left to deliver Arnold a blow to the temple, knock him cold, at least. It would be easy. It wouldn't take much effort. She could do it quickly enough that there'd be no sound. She could kill them both, right here, in conference room 5(b).

Thinking this, she feels very far from the table, where Daniel's mouth is still flapping open and closed like a goldfish. She is in a high and lofty realm, a place where the lungs fill with ice crystals and everything is very clear and clean. It scarcely matters what is actually happening. She could kill them. That is the profound truth of it. She lets the power tickle at her fingers, scorching the varnish on the underside of the table. She can smell its sweet chemical aroma. Nothing that either of these men says is really of any great significance, because she could kill them in three moves before they stirred in their comfortably padded chairs.

It doesn't matter that she shouldn't, that she never would. What matters is that she could, if she wanted. The power to hurt is a kind of wealth.

She speaks quite suddenly, across Daniel, sharp like the knock at a door. "Don't waste my time with this, Daniel," she says.

He's not her superior. They are equals. He can't fire her. He's talking as if he could.

She says, "You and I both know that no one has an answer yet. If you've got a great idea, let's hear it. Otherwise . . ."

She lets it dangle. Daniel opens his mouth as if to say something and then closes it again. Under her fingertips, on the underside of the table, the varnish is softening, curling, crumbling to fall in soft flakes on to the thick-pile carpet.

"I didn't think so," she says. "Let's work together on this one, OK, buddy? No sense throwing each other to the wolves."

Margot is thinking about her future. You're gonna pump my gas someday, Daniel. I've got big plans.

"Yeah," he says. "Yeah."

She thinks, That is how a man speaks. And that is why.

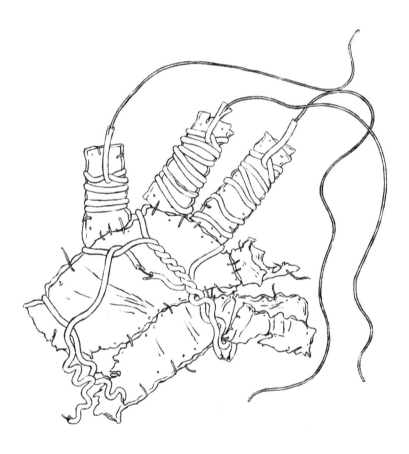

Rudimentary weapon, approximately one thousand years old. The wires are intended to conduct the power. Possibly used in battle or for punishment. Discovered in a gravesite in old Westchester.

Eight years to go

Allie

Not very many miracles are required. Not for the Vatican, not for a group of highly strung teenage girls cooped up together for months and in fear of their lives. You don't need so many miracles. Two is plenty. Three's an abundance.

There is a girl, Luanne. She's very pale, with red hair and a dusting of freckles across her cheeks. She's only fourteen. She arrived three months before and she's a particular friend of Gordy's. They share a bed in the dorm room. For warmth. "It gets awful cold at nights," says Gordy, and Luanne smiles, and the other girls laugh and nudge each other in the ribs.

She's not well, hasn't been since before her power came in. And no doctor can help her. There is a thing that happens to her when she gets excited, or scared, or laughs too much; her eyes roll back in her head and she falls to the ground wherever she is and starts to shake like she'll crack her own back. "You have to just hold her," Gordy says. "Just put your arms around her shoulders and hold her until she wakes. She'll wake by herself, you just have to wait." She often sleeps for an hour or more. Gordy has sat with her, arm around

Luanne's shoulders, in the refectory at midnight or in the gardens at 6 a.m., waiting for her.

Allie has a feeling about Luanne. A tingling sense of something.

She says: Is it this one?

The voice says: I'm thinking so.

One night, there's a lightning storm. It starts way out at sea. The girls watch it with the nuns, standing on the deck at the back of the convent. The clouds are blue-purple, the light is hazy, the lightning strikes one, two, three times on the face of the ocean.

It gives you an itchy feeling in your skein to watch a lightning storm. All the girls are feeling it. Savannah can't help herself. After a few minutes, she lets go an arc into the wood of the deck.

"Stop that," says Sister Veronica. "Stop that at once."

"Veronica," says Sister Maria Ignacia, "she didn't do any harm."

Savannah giggles, lets off another little jolt. It's not that she couldn't stop it if she really tried. It's just that there's something exciting about the storm, something that makes you want to join in.

"No meals for you tomorrow, Savannah," says Sister Veronica. "If you cannot control yourself in the slightest, our charity does not extend to you."

Sister Veronica has already had one girl thrown out who would not stop fighting on the convent grounds. The other nuns have ceded this to her; she can pick and choose those in whom she detects the Devil working.

But "no meals tomorrow" is a harsh sentence. Saturday is meatloaf night.

Luanne tugs on Sister Veronica's sleeve. "Please," she says. "She didn't mean it."

"Don't touch me, girl."

Sister Veronica pulls her arm away, gives Luanne a little shove back.

But the storm has already done something to Luanne. Her head jerks back and to the side in the way they all know. Her mouth opens and closes, but no sound comes out. She falls backwards, smack on to the deck. Gordy runs forward, and Sister Veronica blocks the way with her cane.

"Leave her," says Sister Veronica.

"But, Sister . . ."

"We have done quite enough pandering to this girl. She should not have welcomed the thing into her body and, as she has done, she will have to deal with the consequences."

Luanne is fitting on the deck, slamming the back of her head into the wooden boards. There's blood in the bubbles of saliva at her mouth.

The voice says: Go on, you know what to do.

Allie says, "Sister Veronica, may I try to stop her making a fuss?"

Sister Veronica blinks down at Eve, the quiet and hardworking girl Allie has pretended to be for all these months.

She shrugs. "If you think you can stop this nonsense, Eve, be my guest."

Allie kneels down next to Luanne's body. The other girls look at her like she's a traitor. They all know it's not Luanne's fault — why is Eve pretending she can do anything?

Allie can feel the electricity inside Luanne's body: in her spine and in her neck and inside her head. She can feel the signals going up and down, stuttering, trying to right themselves, confused and out of sync. She can see it, clear as with her own eyes: there's a blockage *here* and *here*, and *this* part just at the base of the skull is mistiming what it's doing. It'd only take a tiny adjustment, an amount of power you wouldn't even feel, the kind of quantity that no one else can fractionate down to, only a tiny thread right *here* to set it right.

Allie cradles Luanne's head in her palm, puts her little finger in the notch at the base of the skull, reaches out with a fine tendril of power and *flicks* at it.

Luanne opens her eyes. Her body stops convulsing all at once.

She blinks.

She says, "What happened?"

And they all know this is never how it goes, that Luanne should have slept for an hour or more, that she might be confused for a week.

Abigail says, "Eve healed you. She touched you, and you were healed."

And this was the first sign, and at this time they came to say: this one is special to the Heavens.

They bring her other girls in need of healing. Sometimes she can lay her hands on them and feel out their pain. Sometimes it is just that something is hurting that need not hurt. A headache, a twitching muscle, a giddiness. Allie, the no-account girl from Jacksonville, has practised enough that Eve, the calm and quiet young woman, can lay her hands upon a person's body and find just the right place to send out a needle of power and set something to rights, at least for a while. The cures are real, even if they are only temporary. She cannot teach the body to do its work better, but she can correct its mistakes for a time.

So they start to believe in her. That there is something within her. The girls believe it, anyway, if not the nuns.

Savannah says, "Is it God, Eve? Is God speaking to you? Is it God inside you?"

She says it quietly one evening in the dormitory after lights out. The other girls are all listening, pretending to be asleep in their own beds.

Eve says, "What is it you think?"

Savannah says, "I think you have the power to heal in you. Like we read in Scripture."

There's a muttering around the dormitory, but no one disagrees.

The next night, as they're getting ready for bed, Eve says to around ten of the other girls, "Come with me down to the seashore tomorrow at dawn."

They say, "What for?"

She says, "I heard a voice saying, 'Go to the seashore at dawn.' "

The voice says: Well played, girl, you say what you need to say.

★   ★   ★

The sky is pale blue-grey as a pebble and feathered with cloud, the sound of the ocean is quiet as a mother shushing her baby, when the girls walk down to the shore in their nightgowns.

Allie speaks in Eve's voice, which is soft and low. She says, "The voice has told me that we should wade out into the water."

Gordy laughs and says, "What is this, Eve? You want to go swimming?"

Luanne shushes her with her finger to Gordy's lips. Luanne has not had a seizure that lasted more than a few seconds since Eve placed her thumb to the nape of her neck.

Abigail says, "What shall we do then?"

Eve says, "Then God will show us what She wants of us."

And this "She" is a new teaching, and very shocking. But they understand it, each of them. They have been waiting to hear this good news.

The girls wade out into the water, their nightgowns and pyjamas sticking to their legs, wincing as their feet find sharp rocks, giggling a little, but with a holy feeling that they can see on one another's faces. Something is going to happen out here. The dawn is breaking.

They stand in a circle. They are all up to their waists, hands trailing in the cold, clear brine.

Eve says, "Holy Mother, show us what you want of us. Baptize us with your love and teach us how to live."

And each of the girls around the circle suddenly feels their knees buckle under them. As if a great hand were

110

pressing on their backs, pushing them down, ducking their heads into the ocean to rise up, water fountaining from their hair, gasping and knowing that God has touched them and that this day they are born anew. They all fall to their knees in the water. They all feel the hand pressing them down. They all know for a moment that they will die here under the water, they cannot breathe and then when they are lifted up they are reborn.

They stand in the circle, wet-headed and amazed. Only Eve remained standing, dry in the water.

They felt the presence of God around them and among them, and She was glad. And the birds flew above them, calling out in glory for a new dawn.

There were around ten girls in the ocean that morning to witness the miracle. They had not been, before that moment, leaders in the group of five dozen young women dwelling with the nuns. They were not the charismatic ones, not the most popular, or the funniest, or the prettiest, or the cleverest girls. They were, if anything drew them together, the girls who had suffered the most, their stories being particularly terrible, their knowledge of what one might fear from others and oneself particularly acute. Nonetheless, after that morning, they were changed.

Eve swears those girls to secrecy about what they have seen; nonetheless, the girls cannot but pass it on. Savannah tells Kayla, and Kayla tells Megan, and Megan tells Danielle that Eve has been speaking with the Creator of all things, that she has secret messages.

They come to ask for her teachings.

They say, "Why do you call God 'She'?"

Eve says, "God is neither woman nor man but both these things. But now She has come to show us a new side to Her face, one we have ignored for too long."

They say, "But what about Jesus?"

Eve says, "Jesus is the son. But the son comes from the mother. Consider this: which is greater, God or the world?"

They say, for they have learned this already from the nuns, "God is greater, because God created the world."

Eve says, "So the one who creates is greater than the thing created?"

They say, "It must be so."

Then Eve says, "So which must be greater, the Mother or the Son?"

They pause, because they think her words may be blasphemy.

Eve says, "It has already been hinted in Scripture. It has already been told to us that God came to the world in a human body. We have already learned to call God 'Father'. Jesus taught that."

They admit that this is so.

Eve says, "So I teach a new thing. This power has been given to us to lay straight our crooked thinking. It is the Mother not the Son who is the emissary of Heaven. We are to call God 'Mother'. God the Mother came to earth in the body of Mary, who gave up her child that we could live free from sin. God always said She would return to earth. And She has come back now to instruct us in her ways."

They say, "Who are you?"

And Eve says, "Who do you say that I am?"

Allie says in her heart: How am I doing?

The voice says: You're doing just fine.

Allie says: Is this your will?

The voice says: Do you think a single thing could happen without the will of God?

There's going to be more than this, sweetheart, believe me.

In those days there was a great fever in the land, and a thirst for truth and a hunger to understand what the Almighty meant by making this change in the fortunes of mankind. In those days, in the South, there were many preachers who explained it: this is a punishment for sin, this is Satan walking amongst us, this is the sign of the end of days. But all these were not the true religion. For the true religion is love, not fear. The strong mother cradling her child: that is love and that is truth. The girls pass this news from one, to the next, to the next. God has returned, and Her message is for us, only us.

In the early morning of a day a few weeks later, there are more baptisms. It is the spring, near to Easter, the festival of eggs and fertility and the opening of the womb. Mary's festival. When they come from the water, they do not care to hide what has happened to them, nor could they if they tried. By breakfast, all the girls know, and all of the nuns.

Eve sits under a tree in the garden and the other girls come to talk to her.

They say, "What shall we call you?"

And Eve says, "I am only the messenger of the Mother."

They say, "But is the Mother in you?"

And Eve says, "She is in all of us."

But even still the girls begin to call her Mother Eve.

That night there is a great debate between the nuns of the Sisters of Mercy. Sister Maria Ignacia — who, the others note, is a particular friend of that girl Eve — speaks in favour of the new organization of beliefs. It is just the same as it's always been, she says. The Mother and the Son, it's just the same. Mary is the Mother of the Church. Mary is the Queen of Heaven. It is she who prays for us now, and at the hour of our death. Some of these girls had never been baptized. They have taken it into their heads to baptize themselves. Can this be wrong?

Sister Katherine speaks of the Marian heresies, and the need to wait for guidance.

Sister Veronica hauls herself to her feet and stands, straight as the true cross, in the centre of the room. "The Devil is in this house," she says. "We have allowed the Devil to take root in our breasts and make his nest in our hearts. If we do not cut the canker out now, we shall all be damned."

She says it again, more loudly, casting her glance from woman to woman in the room: "Damned. If we do not burn them as they burned these girls in Decatur and in Shreveport, the Devil will take us all. It shall be utterly consumed." She pauses. She is a powerful speaker. She says, "I shall pray on it this night, I shall pray for you all. We will lock the girls in their rooms until dawn. We should burn them all."

The girl who has been listening at the window brings this message to Mother Eve.

And they wait to hear what she will say.

The voice says: You've got them now, girl.

Mother Eve says: Let them lock us in. The Almighty will work Her wonders.

The voice says: Doesn't Sister Veronica *realize* that any of you could just open the window and climb down the drainpipe?

And Allie says in her heart: It is the will of the Almighty that she has not realized it.

The next morning, Sister Veronica is still at prayer in the chapel. At six, when the other sisters file in for Vigils, she is there, prostrate before the cross, her arms outstretched, her forehead touching the cool stone tile. It is only when they lean forward to touch her arm gently that the women see that the blood has settled in her face. She has been dead for many hours. A heart attack. The kind of thing that could happen at any moment to a woman of her age. And, as the sun rises, they look towards the figure on the cross. And they see that, engraved now into his flesh, traced with scored lines as if carved with a knife, are the fern-like markings of the power. And they know that Sister Veronica was taken in the moment that she witnessed this miracle and so had repented of all her sin.

The Almighty has returned as promised, and She dwells in human flesh again.

This day is for rejoicing.

There are messages from the Holy See, calling for calm and order, but the atmosphere among the girls in the convent is such that no mere message could bring stillness. There is the feeling of a festival in the building; all the ordinary rules seem to have been suspended. The beds go unmade, the girls take what foods they want from the pantry without waiting for mealtimes, there is singing and the playing of music. There is a glitter in the air. By lunchtime, fifteen more girls have asked for the baptism, and by the afternoon they have received it. There are nuns who protest and say they'll call in the police, but the girls laugh and strike them with their jolts until they run away.

In the late afternoon, Eve speaks to her congregation. They record it on their cellphones and send it across the world. Mother Eve wears a hood, the better to preserve her humility, for it is not her message she preaches, but the message of the Mother.

Eve says, "Do not be afraid. If you trust, then God will be with you. She has overturned heaven and earth for us.

"They have said to you that man rules over woman as Jesus rules over the Church. But I say unto you that woman rules over man as Mary guided her infant son, with kindness and with love.

"They have said to you that his death wiped away sin. But I say unto you that no one's sin is wiped away but that they join in the great work of making justice in the world. Much injustice has been done, and it is the will of the Almighty that we gather together to put it right.

"They have said to you that man and woman should live together as husband and wife. But I say unto you that it is more blessed for women to live together, to help one another, to band together and be a comfort one to the next.

"They have said to you that you must be contented with your lot, but I say unto you that there will be a land for us, a new country. There will be a place that God will show us where we will build a new nation, mighty and free."

One of the girls says, "But we can't stay here for ever, and where is this new land, and what will happen when they come with the police? This isn't our place, they're not going to let us stay here! They'll take us all to jail!"

The voice says: Don't you worry about that. Someone's coming.

Eve says, "God will send Her salvation. A soldier will come. And *you* will be damned for your doubt. God will not forget that you did not trust Her in this hour of triumph."

The girl starts crying. The cellphone cameras zoom in. The girl is thrown out of the compound by nightfall.

And back in Jacksonville, someone watches the news on the television. Someone sees the face behind the cowl, half hidden in shadows. Someone thinks to themselves: I know that face.

117

Margot

"Look at this."

"I am looking at it."

"Have you read it?"

"Not all of it."

"This isn't some third-world country, Margot."

"I know that."

"This is Wisconsin."

"I can see that."

"This is happening in goddamned Wisconsin. This."

"Try to keep calm, Daniel."

"They should shoot those girls. Just shoot them. In the head. *Bam*. End of story."

"You can't shoot *all* the women, Daniel."

"It's OK, Margot, we wouldn't shoot you."

"Yeah, that's comforting."

"Oh. Sorry. Your daughter. I forgot. She's . . . I wouldn't shoot her."

"Thanks, Daniel."

Daniel drums his fingers on the desk, and she thinks, as she finds herself thinking quite often, I could kill you for that. It's become a constant low-level hum in her. A

118

thought she comes back to like a smooth stone in her pocket to rub her thumb across. There it is. Death.

"It's not OK to talk about shooting young women."

"Yeah. I know. Yeah. Just . . ."

He gestures at the screen. They're watching a video of six girls demonstrating their power on one another. They stare into the camera. They say, "We dedicate this to the Goddess"; they've learned that from some other video, somewhere on the web. They shock one another to the point that one of them faints. Another is bleeding from the nose and ears. This "Goddess" is some kind of internet meme, stoked by the existence of the power, by anonymous forums and by the imaginations of young people, which are now what they have always been and ever shall be. There is a symbol; it is a hand like the hand of Fatima, the palm containing an eye, the shock-tendrils extending from the eye like extra limbs, like the branches of a tree. There are spray-painted versions of this symbol appearing now on walls and railway sidings and motorway bridges — high, out-of-the-way places. Some of the internet message boards are encouraging the girls to get together to do terrible things; the FBI is trying to close them down, but as soon as one goes another springs up to take its place.

Margot watches the girls on the screen playing with their power. Screaming as they take a hit. Laughing as they deliver one.

"How's Jos?" says Daniel at last.

"She's fine."

She's not fine. She's having trouble with this power. No one knows enough to explain what's happening to her. She can't control the power inside her, and it's getting worse.

Margot watches the girls on the screen in Wisconsin. One of them has a tattooed hand of the Goddess in the centre of her palm. Her friend shrieks as she applies the power, but it's not clear to Margot whether she's crying out with fear, pain or with delight.

"And we're joined in the studio today by Mayor Margot Cleary. Some of you might remember Mayor Cleary as a leader who acted swiftly and decisively after the outbreak, probably saving many lives."

"And she's here with her daughter, Jocelyn. How are you doing there, Jocelyn?"

Jos shifts uneasily in her chair. These seats look comfortable, but they're actually hard. There's something sharp digging into her. The pause goes on a moment too long.

"I'm fine."

"Well, now, you have an interesting story, don't you, Jocelyn? You've been having some trouble?"

Margot puts a hand on Jos's knee. "Like a lot of young women," she says, "my daughter Jocelyn recently started experiencing the development of the power."

"We have some footage of that, don't we, Kristen?"

"Here's the press conference on your front lawn. I believe you put a boy in the hospital, didn't you, Jocelyn?"

They cut to the footage of the day Margot was called home. There's Margot, standing on the steps of the Mayor's Residence, tucking her hair behind her ears in that way that makes her look nervous even when she's not. In the footage she puts an arm around Jos and reads from her prepared statement.

"My daughter was involved in a brief altercation," she says. "Our thoughts are with Laurie Vincens and his family. We are grateful that the damage he sustained does not seem to have been serious. This is the kind of accident which is befalling many young women today. Jocelyn and I hope that everyone will remain calm and allow our family to move on from this incident."

"Wow, that seems like a lifetime ago, doesn't it, Kristen?"

"Sure does, Tom. How did it feel, Jocelyn, when you hurt that kid?"

Jos has been preparing for this with her mom for more than a week now. She knows what to say. Her mouth is dry. She's a trouper; she does it anyway.

"It was scary," she says. "I hadn't learned how to control it. I was worried I could have really hurt him. I wished . . . I wished someone had shown me how to use it properly. How to control it."

There are tears starting in Jos's eyes. They hadn't rehearsed that, but it's great. The producer zooms right in, angling camera three to catch the glisten. It's perfect. She's so young and fresh and beautiful and sad.

"Sounds really frightening. And you think it would have helped if —"

Margot steps in again. She's also looking good. Glossy, sleek hair. Subtle tones of cream and brown on her eyelids. Nothing too showy. She could be that lady on your block who takes great care of herself, swims and does yoga. Aspirational.

"That day started me thinking, Kristen, about how we can really *help* these girls. The advice right now is just for them not to use their power at all."

"We don't want them just letting off lightning bolts in the street, now, do we?"

"Certainly not, Tom. But my three-point plan is this." That's right. Assertive. Effective. Short sentences. A numbered list. Just like on BuzzFeed.

"One: set up safe spaces for the girls to practise their power together. A trial at first in my metropolitan area and, if it's popular, state-wide. Two: identify girls who have good control to help the younger ones learn to keep their power in check. Three: zero tolerance of usage outside these safe spaces."

There's a pause. They've talked this through in advance. The audience listening at home will need time to adjust to what they've just heard.

"So, if I understand what you're proposing, Mayor Cleary, you'd like to use public money to teach girls how to use their power more effectively?"

"More safely, Kristen. And I'm really here to gauge interest. In times like these, we should probably remember what the Bible says: the highest among us aren't always the wisest, and the older generation isn't always the best to judge what's right." She smiles. Quoting the Bible — a winning strategy. "Anyway, I think it's the job of government to come up with interesting ideas, don't you?"

"Are you suggesting some kind of *training camp* for these girls?"

"Now, Tom, you know that's not what I'm saying. It's just this: we don't let young people drive a car without getting their licence, do we? You wouldn't want the guy rewiring your house to have no training. That's all I'm saying: let the girls teach the girls."

"But how do we know what they'll teach them?" Tom's sounding a little high-pitched now, a little afraid. "This all sounds very dangerous to me. Instead of teaching them how to use it, we should be trying to *cure* it. That's my bottom line."

Kristen smiles directly into the camera. "But no one has a cure, do they, Tom? Says in the *Wall Street Journal* this morning that a multinational group of scientists is certain now that the power is caused by an environmental build-up of nerve agent that was released during the Second World War. It's changed the human genome. All girls born from now on will have the power — all of them. And they'll keep it throughout life, just like the older women do if it's woken up in them. It's too late now to try to cure it; we need new ideas."

Tom tries to say something else, but Kristen just carries on: "I think this is a great idea, Mayor Cleary. If you want my endorsement, I'm right behind this plan.

"And now the weather on the ones."

★　★　★

Email from: throwawayaddress29457902@gmail.com
Email to: Jocelyn.feinburgcleary@gmail.com

Saw you on the news today. You're having trouble with your power. You want to know *why?* You want to know if anyone else is having trouble, too? You don't know the half of it, sister. This rabbit hole goes all the way down. Your gender-bending confusion is just the start of it. We need to put men and women back where they belong.

Check out www.urbandoxspeaks.com if you want to know the truth.

"How fucking dare you?"

"There was no movement in your office, Daniel. No one was willing to listen."

"So you do *this*? National TV? Promising to roll the thing out *state-wide*? If you remember, Margot, I am the Governor of this state and you are just the Mayor of your metropolitan area. You went on *national* TV to talk about rolling it out state-wide?"

"There's no law against it."

"No *law*? No fucking *law*? How about, do you care about any of the agreements we have in place? How about, no one's going to find you the fucking *funding* for this thing if you make this number of enemies in one morning's work? How about, I will *personally* make it my *mission* to block any proposal you put forward. I have powerful friends in this town, Margot, and if you think you can just railroad over the work

124

we've done so you can become some kind of *celebrity* . . ."

"Calm down."

"I will *not* fucking calm down. It's not just your *tactics*, Margot, not just fucking *going to the press*, it's this whole cock-eyed plan. You're going to use *public money* to train basically *terrorist* operatives to use their weapons more effectively?"

"They're not terrorists, they're girls."

"You wanna bet? You think there won't be some terrorists in amongst them? You've seen what's happened in the Middle East, in India and Asia. You've seen it on the TV. You wanna bet your little scheme won't end up drawing in some fucking jihadis?"

"You done?"

"Am I —"

"Are you done? Because I have work to get on with now so if you're finished —"

"No, I'm not fucking *done*."

But he is. Even as he stands in Margot's office spitting on to the fine furnishings and the shaved-glass awards for municipal excellence, phone calls are being made, emails are being sent, tweets are being posted and forum posts composed. "Did you hear that lady on the morning show today? Where can I sign my girls up for that thing? I mean, seriously, I have three girls, fourteen, sixteen and nineteen, and they are *tearing* each other apart. They need someplace to go. They got to let off steam."

Before the week is over, Margot's received over one and a half million dollars in donations for her girls' camps — some cheques from worried parents, all the way up to anonymous gifts from Wall Street billionaires. There are people who want to invest in her scheme now. It's going to be a public-private initiative, a model of how government and business can work hand in glove.

Before a month is done, she's found spots for the first test centres in the metropolitan area: old schools shut down when the boys and girls were segregated, places with good-size gymnasiums and outdoor space. Six other state representatives arrive for informational visits so she can show them what she's planning.

And before three months are out, people are beginning to say, "You know, why doesn't that Margot Cleary run for something a little more ambitious? Get her in. Let's have a meeting."

Tunde

In a dark basement in a town in rural Moldova, a thirteen-year-old girl with a faint moustache on her upper lip brings stale bread and old, oily fish to a group of women huddled on dirty mattresses. She has been coming here for weeks. She is young and slow-witted. She is the daughter of the man who drives the bread truck. He keeps lookout sometimes for the men who own this house and the women who are kept here. They pay him a little for the stale bread.

The women have tried asking the girl for things in the past. A cellphone — couldn't she bring them a telephone somehow? Some paper, to write a note — could she post something for them? Just one stamp and a paper? When their families hear what's happened to them, they'll be able to pay her. Please. The girl has always looked down and shaken her head fiercely, blinking her moist, stupid eyes. The women think the girl may be deaf. Or she has been told to be deaf. Things have happened already to these women to make them wish they could be deaf and blind.

The bread-truck man's daughter empties their bucket of slops into the drain in the yard, rinses it out with the hose and returns it to them clean, apart from a few flecks of shit under the rim. The smell will be better in here for an hour or two at least.

The girl turns to leave. When she's gone, they'll be in darkness again.

"Leave us a light," one of the women says. "Don't you have a candle? A little light for us?"

The girl turns towards the door. Looks up the stairs to the ground floor. No one is there.

She takes the hand of the woman who spoke. Turns it palm upward. And in the centre of the palm, this thirteen-year-old girl makes a little *twist* with the thing that has just woken in her collarbone. The woman on the mattress — five and twenty, and thought she was going to a good secretarial job in Berlin — gasps and shudders; her shoulders squirm and her eyes go wide. And the hand that holds the mattress flickers with a momentary silver light.

They wait in the dark. They practise. They have to be certain they can do it all in one go, that no one will have time to reach for his gun. They pass the thing from hand to hand in the dark and marvel at it. Some of them had been held captive for so long they never heard a word of this thing; for the others, it wasn't more than a strange rumour, a curiosity. They believe God has sent a miracle to save them, as He rescued the Children of Israel from slavery. From the narrow places, they cried out. In the dark, they were sent light. They weep.

128

One of the overseers comes to unshackle the woman who thought she was going as a secretary to Berlin before she was thrown down on a concrete floor and shown, over and over again, what her job really was. He has the keys in his hand. They fall on him all at once, and he cannot make a sound and blood gushes from his eyes and ears. They unlock one another's bonds with his bundle of keys.

They kill every man in that house and they're still not satisfied.

Moldova is the world capital of human sex-trafficking. There are a thousand little towns here with staging posts in basements and apartments in condemned buildings. They trade in men, too, and in children. The girl children grow day by day until the power comes to their hands and they can teach the grown women. This thing happens again and again and again; the change has happened too fast for the men to learn the new tricks they need. It is a gift. Who is to say it does not come from God?

Tunde files a series of reports and interviews from the Moldovan border towns where the fighting has been most acute. The women trust him because of his reports from Riyadh. Not many men could have got this close; he's been lucky, but he's also been smart and determined. He brings his other reports with him, shows them to whatever woman says she's in charge of this town or that. They want their stories told.

"It wasn't just those men who hurt us," a twenty-year-old woman, Sonja, tells him. "We killed them, but it wasn't just them. The police knew what was happening and did nothing. The men in the town beat their wives if they tried to bring us more food. The Mayor knew what was happening, the landlords knew what was happening, *postmen* knew what was happening."

She starts to cry, scrubs at her eyes with the heel of her hand. She shows him the tattoo in the centre of her palm — the eye with the tendrils creeping out from it.

"This means we will never stop watching," she says. "Like God watches over us."

At night, Tunde writes fast and urgently. A diary of sorts. Notes from the war. This revolution will need its chronicler. It's going to be him. He has in mind a broad, sweeping book — with interviews, yes, and also assessments of the tide of history, region-by-region analysis, nation by nation. Pulling out to see the shockwaves of the power slosh across the planet. Zooming in tight to focus on single moments, single stories. Sometimes he writes with such intensity that he forgets that he doesn't have the power himself in his hands and the bones of his neck. It's going to be a big book. Nine hundred pages, a thousand pages. De Tocqueville's *Democracy in America*. Gibbon's *Decline and Fall*. There'll be an accompanying barrage of footage online. Lanzmann's *Shoah*. Reporting from inside the events as well as analysis and argument.

He opens his chapter on Moldova with a description of the way the power was passed from hand to hand among the women, then proceeds to the new flowering of online religion, and how it shored up support for women taking over towns, and then goes on to the inevitable revolution in the government of the country.

Tunde interviews the President five days before the government falls. Viktor Moskalev is a small and sweaty man who has held this country together by making a series of alliances and by turning a blind eye to the vast organized crime syndicates that have been using his little, unassuming nation as a staging post for their unsavoury business. He moves his hands nervously during the interview, brushing the few strands of hair left on his head out of his eyes constantly and dripping sweat across his bald head, even though the room is quite cool. His wife, Tatiana — an ex-gymnast who once almost competed at the Olympics — sits beside him, holding his hand.

"President Moskalev," says Tunde, deliberately relaxing his voice, smiling, "between you and me, what do you think is happening to your country?"

Viktor's throat muscles clench. They're sitting in the grand receiving room of his palace in Chisinau. Half the furniture is gilded. Tatiana strokes his knee and smiles. She, also, is gilded — bronze highlights in her hair, glitter on the curve of her cheeks.

"All countries," says Viktor slowly, "have had to adapt to the new reality."

Tunde leans back, crossing one leg over the other.

"This isn't going out on the radio or on the internet, Viktor. It's just for my book. I'd really like your assessment. Forty-three border towns are now effectively being run by paramilitary gangs, mostly composed of women who've freed themselves from sexual slavery.

131

What do you think your chances are of getting control back?"

"Our forces are already moving to quash these rebels," says Viktor. "Within a few days the situation will normalize." Tunde raises a quizzical eyebrow. Half-laughs. Is Viktor being *serious*? The gangs have captured weapons, body armour and ammunition from the crime syndicates they've destroyed. They're virtually unbeatable.

"Sorry, what is it that you're planning to do? Bomb your own country to pieces? They're everywhere."

Viktor smiles an enigmatic smile. "If it has to be, that is how it must be. This trouble will pass in just a week or two."

Fucking hell. Maybe he really will bomb the whole country and end up sitting as President of a pile of rubble. Or maybe he just hasn't accepted what's really going on here. It'll make an interesting footnote in the book. With his country crumbling around him, President Moskalev seemed almost blasé.

In the corridor outside, Tunde waits for an embassy car to take him back to his hotel. Safer to travel under the Nigerian flag here than under Moskalev's protection these days. But it can take two or three hours for the cars to make it through the security.

That's where Tatiana Moskalev finds him: waiting on an embroidered chair for someone to call his cell and say that the car's ready.

She clicks down the hallway in her spike heels. Her dress is turquoise, skin-tight, ruched and cut to

132

accentuate those strong gymnast's legs and those elegant gymnast's shoulders. She stands over him.

"You don't like my husband, do you?" she says.

"I wouldn't say that." He smiles his easy smile.

"I would. Are you going to print something bad about him?"

Tunde rests his elbows on the back of the chair, opening his chest. "Tatiana," he says, "if we're going to have this conversation, is there anything to *drink* in this palace?"

There's brandy in a cabinet in what looks like a 1980s movie idea of a Wall Street boardroom: high-shine gold plastic fittings and a dark wood table. She pours them each a generous measure and they look out over the city together. The presidential palace is a high-rise in the centre of town; from the outside it looks like nothing so much as a mid-price four-star business hotel.

Tatiana says, "He came to watch a performance at my school. I was a gymnast. Performing in front of the Minister for Finance!" She drinks. "I was seventeen and he was forty-two. But he took me out of that little nothing town."

Tunde says, "The world's changing," and they exchange a little glance.

She smiles. "You are going to be very successful," she says. "You have the hunger. I've seen it before."

"And you? Do you have . . . the hunger?"

She looks him up and down and makes a little laugh through her nose. She can't be more than forty now herself.

"Look what I can do," she says. Although he thinks he already knows what she can do.

She puts her palm flat to the frame of the window and closes her eyes.

The lights in the ceiling fizz and blink out.

She looks up, sighs.

"Why are they . . . connected to the window frames?" says Tunde.

"Crappy wiring," she says, "like everything in this place."

"Does Viktor know you can do it?"

She shakes her head. "Hairdresser gave it to me. A joke. A woman like you, she said, you'll never need it. You're taken care of."

"And are you?" says Tunde. "Taken care of?"

She laughs now, properly, full-throatedly. "Be careful," she says. "Viktor would chop your balls off if he heard you talking that way."

Tunde laughs, too. "Is it really Viktor I have to be afraid of? Any more?"

She takes a long slow swig of her drink. "Do you want to know a secret?" she says.

"Always," he says.

"Awadi-Atif, the new King of Saudi Arabia, is in exile in the north of our country. He's been feeding Viktor money and arms. That's why Viktor thinks he can crush the rebels."

"Are you serious?"

She nods.

"Can you get me confirmation of that? Emails, faxes, photographs, anything?"

134

She shakes her head.

"Go and look for him. You're a clever boy. You'll work it out."

He licks his lips. "Why are you telling me this?"

"I want you to remember me," she says, "when you're very successful. Remember that we talked like this now."

"Just talked?" says Tunde.

"Your car is here," she says, pointing to the long black limousine pulling through the cordon outside the building, thirty floors below them.

It's five days after that when Viktor Moskalev dies, quite suddenly and unexpectedly, of a heart attack in his sleep. It is something of a surprise to the world community when, in the immediate aftermath of his death, the Supreme Court of the country unanimously votes in emergency session to appoint his wife, Tatiana, as interim leader. In the fullness of time there would be elections in which Tatiana would stand for office, but the most important thing is to maintain order at this difficult time.

But, says Tunde in his report, Tatiana Moskalev may have been easy to underestimate; she was a political operator of skill and intelligence and had evidently used her leverage well. In her first public appearance, she wore a small gold brooch in the shape of an eye; some said this was a nod to the growing popularity of "Goddess" movements online. Some pointed out how very difficult it is to tell the difference between a skilful attack using the electrical power and an ordinary heart attack, but these rumours were without any evidential foundation.

Transfers of power, of course, are rarely smooth. This one is complicated by a military coup spearheaded by Viktor's Chief of Defence, who takes more than half the army with him and manages to oust the Moskalev interim government from Chisinau. But the armies of women freed from chains in those border towns are, broadly and instinctively, with Tatiana Moskalev. Upwards of three hundred thousand women passed through the country every year, sold for the use of their moist bodies and fragile flesh. A great number of those have stayed, having nowhere else to go.

On the thirteenth day of the fifth month of the third year after the Day of the Girls, Tatiana Moskalev brings her wealth and her connections, a little less than half her army, and many of her weapons to a castle in the hills on the borders of Moldova. And there she declares a new kingdom, uniting the coastal lands between the old forests and the great inlets and thus, in effect, declaring war on four separate countries, including the Big Bear herself. She calls the new country Bessapara, after the ancient people who lived there and interpreted the sacred sayings of the priestesses on the mountaintops. The international community waits for the outcome. The consensus is that the state of Bessapara cannot hold for long.

Tunde records it all in careful notes and documentations. He adds, "There is a scent of something in the air, a smell like rainfall after a long drought. First one person, then five, then five hundred, then villages, then cities, then states. Bud to bud and leaf to leaf. Something new is happening. The scale of the thing has increased."

Roxy

There's a girl on the beach at high tide, lighting up the sea with her hands. The girls from the convent watch her from the clifftop. She's waded into the ocean up to her waist, higher. She's not even wearing a bathing suit — just jeans and a black cardigan. And she's setting the sea on fire.

It's coming on to dusk, so they can see it clearly. Threads of kelp are spread in a fine, disorderly mesh across the surface of the water. And when she sends her power into the water, the particulate and debris glow dimly, and the seaweed brighter yet. The light extends in a wide circle around her, lit from beneath, like the great eye of the ocean gazing at the sky. There's a sound like popping candy as the branching limbs of the sargasso plants smoulder and the buds swell and burst. There's a marine scent, salt and green and pungent. She must be half a mile away, but they can smell it from the clifftop. They think at any moment she must have used out her power, but it goes on; the flickering luminescence in the bay, the scent as the crabs and small fish rise to the surface of the water.

The women say to one another: God will send her salvation.

"She has inscribed a circle on the face of the waters," says Sister Maria Ignacia. "She is at the boundary of light and darkness."

She is a sign from the Mother.

They send word to Mother Eve: someone has come.

They'd given Roxy a choice of places to go. Bernie's got family in Israel; she could go to them. Think about it, Rox, sandy beaches, fresh air, you could go to school with Yuval's kids; he's got two girls about your age, and you've got to believe the Israelis aren't locking girls up for doing what you can do. They've already got them in the army, they're already training them up, Rox. I bet they know stuff you haven't even thought of. She looks it up on the internet, though. They don't even speak English in Israel, or write with English letters. Bernie tries to explain that most people in Israel do speak English, really, but Roxy still says, "Nah, don't think so."

Then her mum had family near the Black Sea. Bernie points it out on the map. That's your grandma comes from there; you didn't ever meet your grandma, did you? Your mum's mum? There are still cousins there. Still family connections; we do good business with those people, too. You could get in with the business, you said you want to. But Roxy had already decided where she wanted to go.

"I'm not thick," she said. "I know you've got to get me out of the country, cos they're looking for who killed Primrose. It's not a holiday."

139

And Bernie and the boys had stopped talking and just looked at her.

"You can't say that, Rox," said Ricky. "Wherever you go, you just say you're on holiday, all right?"

"I want to go to America," she said. "I want to go to South Carolina. Look. There's that woman there, Mother Eve. She does them talks on the internet. You know."

Ricky said, "Sal knows some people down that way. We can fix you up somewhere to stay, Rox, someone to look after you."

"I don't need anyone to look after me."

Ricky looked at Bernie. Bernie shrugged.

"After all she's been through," said Bernie. And that settled it.

Allie sits on a rock and dabbles her fingers in the water. Every time the woman in the water discharges her power she can feel it, even at this distance, like a sharp smack.

She says in her heart: What do you think? I've never seen anyone with this much strength in her.

The voice says: Didn't I tell you I was sending you a soldier?

Allie says in her heart: Does she know her destiny?

The voice says: Who does, sweetpea?

It's dark now, and the lights from the freeway are barely visible here. Allie dips her hand into the ocean and sends out as much charge as she can. She barely sends a flicker across the water. It's enough. The woman in the waves walks towards her.

It's too dark to see her face clearly.

140

Allie calls out, "You must be cold. I have a blanket here, if you want it."

The woman in the water says, "Bloody hell, what are you, search and rescue? Don't s'pose you've got a picnic there, too, have you?"

She's British. This is unexpected. Still, the Almighty works in mysterious ways.

"Roxy," says the woman in the water. "I'm Roxy."

"I'm . . ." says Allie, and pauses. For the first time in a long while, she has the urge to tell this woman her real name. Ridiculous. "I'm Eve," she says.

"Oh my word," says Roxy. "Oh my Lord, it's only you I've blimmin' come to find, isn't it? Bloody hell, just got in this morning; night flight, it's a killer, I'm telling you. Had a nap, thought I'd go looking for you tomorrow and here you bloody are. It's a miracle!"

See, says the voice, what did I tell you?

Roxy hauls herself up on to the flat stone next to Allie. She is suddenly and instantly impressive. She's muscular in her shoulders and arms, but it's more than that.

Reaching out with that sense that she has honed and practised, Allie tries to gauge how much power Roxy has in her skein.

She feels that she is falling off the edge of the world. It goes on and on. As limitless as the ocean.

"Oh," she says, "a soldier will corrie."

"What's that now?"

Allie shakes her head. "Nothing. Something I heard once."

Roxy gives her an appraising look. "You a bit spooky, then? That's what I thought when I saw your videos. Bit spooky, I thought. You'd do well on one of them TV shows — *Most Haunted*, you ever seen that? Actually, you don't have anything to eat, do you? I'm *starving*."

Allie pats down her pockets and finds a candy bar in her jacket. Roxy tears into it, taking huge bites.

"That's better," she says. "You know that thing when you've used up a lot of power and it just makes you starving hungry?" She pauses, looks at Allie. "No?"

"Why were you doing it? The light in the water?"

Roxy shrugs. "It was just an idea I had. Never been in the sea before, wanted to see what I could do." She squints out at the ocean. "I think I killed a bloody load of fish. You could probably have dinner out of them all this week if you've got . . ." She juggles her hands. "I dunno, a boat and a net or something. I suppose some of them might be poison. Can you get poison fish? Or is it just like . . . *Jaws* and that?"

Allie laughs, in spite of herself. It's been a while since someone last made her laugh. Since she last laughed without deciding beforehand that laughing was the smart thing to do.

She just had an idea, says the voice. It just popped into her head. She came looking for you. I told you a soldier would come.

Yeah, says Allie. Shut up for a minute, OK?

"What made you come to look for me?" says Allie.

Roxy shifts her shoulders as if she's darting and weaving, escaping imaginary blows.

142

"I had to get out of England for a bit. And I saw you on YouTube." She takes a breath, lets it all out, smiles at herself and then says, "Look, I don't know, all those things you talk about, where you say that God's made this all happen for a reason and women are supposed to take over from men . . . I don't believe any of that God stuff, all right?"

"All right."

"But I think . . . like d'you know what they're teaching girls in school in England? Breathing exercises! No kidding, bleeding *breathing*. Bleeding 'keep it under control, don't use it, don't do anything, keep yourself nice and keep your arms crossed,' you know what I mean? And like, I had sex with a bloke a few weeks back and he was practically begging me to do it to him, just a little bit, he'd seen it on the internet; no one's going to keep their arms crossed for ever. My dad's all right, and my brothers are all right, they're not bad, but I wanted to talk to you cos you're like . . . you're thinking about what it means. For the future, you know? It's exciting."

It comes out of her in a big rush.

"What do you think it means?" says Allie.

"Everything's gonna change," says Roxy, picking at the seaweed with one hand while she talks. "Stands to reason, doesn't it? And we've all got to find some new way to work together on it. You know. Blokes have got a thing they can do: they're strong. Women have got a thing now, too. And there's still guns, they don't stop working. Lot of blokes with guns: I'm no match for them. I feel like . . . it's exciting, you know? I was saying this to my dad. The stuff we could do together."

Allie laughs. "Do you think they'll want to work with *us*?"

"Well, some of them yeah, and some of them nah, right? But the sensible ones will. I was talking about it with my dad. Do you ever get that feeling when you're in a room and you can *tell* which girls around you have got loads of power, and which have got none? You know, like . . . like spider-sense?"

This is the first time Allie has ever heard anyone else talk about this sense she has particularly acutely.

"Yes," she says. "I think I know what you mean."

"Bloody hell, no one knows what I mean. Not that I've talked about it with loads of people. Anyway, that: useful to be able to tell the blokes, right? Useful to work together."

Allie flattens her lips. "I see it a bit differently, you know."

"Yeah, mate, I know you do, I've seen your stuff."

"I think there's going to be a great battle between light and darkness. And your destiny is to fight on our side. I think you will be mightiest in the mightiest."

Roxy laughs and chucks a pebble into the sea. "I always fancied having a destiny," she says. "Look, can we go somewhere? Yours, or somewhere? It's bloody *freezing* out here."

They let her come to Terry's funeral; it was a bit like Christmas. There was aunties and uncles, and booze and bridge rolls and hard-boiled eggs. There was people putting an

144

arm round her and telling her she's a good girl. And Ricky gave her some stuff before they set off, and he took some himself and went, "Just to take the edge off." So it felt like snow was falling. Like it was cold and high up. Just like Christmas.

At the grounds, Barbara, Terry's mum, went to throw a trowel of dirt on to the coffin. When the earth hit the wood she made a long, wailing cry. There was a car parked and blokes with long-lens cameras taking pictures. Ricky and some of his mates scared them off.

When they came back, Bernie said, "Paps?"

And Ricky said, "Could be police. Working with."

Roxy's in a bit of trouble over this, probably.

They were all right to her at the reception. But at the grounds none of the mourners knew where to put their faces when she walked past.

At the convent, supper is already being served when Allie and Roxy arrive. There's a place saved for them at the head of the table, and there's chatter and the smell of good warm food. It's a stew with clams and mussels and potatoes and corn. There's crusty bread and apples. Roxy has a feeling she can't quite name, can't really place. It makes her a little bit soft inside, a bit teary. One of the girls finds her a change of clothes: a warm knitted jumper and a pair of sweatpants all worn and cosy from being washed so often, and that's just how she feels, too. The girls all want to chat to her — they've never heard an accent like hers and they make her say "water" and "banana". There's so much talking.

Roxy always thought *she* was a bit of a blabbermouth, but this is something else.

After supper, Mother Eve gives a little lesson in the Scripture. They're finding Scripture that works for them, rewriting the bits that don't. Mother Eve speaks on the story of the Book of Ruth. She reads out the passage where Ruth tells her mother-in-law, her friend, "Don't tell me to leave you. Whither thou goest, I shall go. Your people shall be my people. Your God will be my God."

Mother Eve is easy amongst these women, in a way Roxy finds difficult. She's not used to the company of girls; it's been boys in Bernie's family and boys in Bernie's gang, and her mum was always more of a man's woman and the girls at school never treated Roxy nice. Mother Eve's not awkward like Roxy here. She holds the hands of two of the girls sitting next to her and speaks softly and with humour.

She says, "That story about Ruth, that's the most beautiful story of friendship in the whole of the Bible. No one was ever more faithful than Ruth, no one ever expressed the bonds of friendship better." There are tears in her eyes as she speaks, and the girls around the table are already moved. "It's not for us to worry about the men," she says. "Let them please themselves, as they always have. If they want to war with each other and to wander, let them go. We have each other. Where you go, I will go. Your people will be my people, my sisters."

And they say, "Amen."

Upstairs, they've made a bed up for Roxy. It's just a little room; a single bed with a hand-stitched quilt across it, a table and chair, a view of the ocean. She wants to weep when they open the door, but she doesn't show it. She remembers, quite suddenly, as she sits on the bed and feels the coverlet under her hand, a night when her dad brought her back to his house, the house he lived in with Barbara and with Roxy's brothers. It was late at night and her mum was ill with vomiting, and she'd called Bernie to pick up Roxy and he'd come. She was in her pyjamas, she can't have been more than five or six. She remembers Barbara saying, "Well, she can't stay here," and Bernie going, "For fuck's sake, just put her in the guest room," and Barbara crossing her arms across her bosom and going, "I told you, she's not staying here. Send her to your brother's if you have to." It was raining that night and her dad carried her back out to the car, the drops falling past the hood of her dressing gown to fall on her chest.

There's someone expecting Roxy this evening, sort of. Someone who'll catch it in the neck if they've lost her, anyway. But she's sixteen, and one text will sort that out.

Mother Eve closes the door, so it's just the two of them in the little room. She sits on the chair and says, "You can stay as long as you like."

"Why?"

"I've got a good feeling about you."

Roxy laughs. "Would you have a good feeling about me if I was a boy?"

147

"But you're not a boy."

"Do you have a good feeling about all women?"

Mother Eve shakes her head. "Not this good. Do you want to stay?"

"Yeah," says Roxy. "For a bit, anyway. See what you're up to here. I like your . . ." She searches for the word. "I like how it feels here."

Mother Eve says, "You're strong, aren't you? As strong as anyone."

"Stronger than anyone, mate. Is that why you like me?"

"We can use someone strong."

"Yeah? You got big plans?"

Mother Eve leans forward, puts her hands on her knees. "I want to save the women," she says.

"What, all of them?" Roxy laughs.

"Yes," says Mother Eve, "if I can. I want to reach them and tell them that there are new ways to live, now. That we can band together, that we can let men go their own way, that we don't need to stick to the old order, we can make a new path."

"Oh yeah? You do need a few blokes, to make babies, you know."

Mother Eve smiles. "All things are possible with God's help."

Allie's phone beeps. She looks at it. Makes a face. Turns it over so she can't see the screen.

"What's up?" says Roxy.

"People keep emailing the convent."

"Trying to get you out of here? Nice place. I can see why they'd want it back."

"Trying to give us money."

Roxy laughs. "What's the problem? Got too much?"

Allie looks at Roxy thoughtfully for a moment. "Only Sister Maria Ignacia has a bank account. And I . . ." She runs her tongue over her top front teeth, makes her lips click.

Roxy says, "You don't trust no one, do you?"

Allie smiles. "Do you?"

"Price of doing business, mate. Got to trust someone or you'll get nothing done. You need a bank account? How many do you want? Want some out of the country? Cayman Islands is good, I think, don't know why."

"Wait, what do you mean?"

But before Allie can stop her, Roxy's taken out her phone, snapped a picture of Allie and is sending a text.

Roxy grins. "Trust me. Got to find some way to pay my rent, don't I?"

A man arrives at the convent before seven o'clock the next morning. He drives up to the front gate and just waits there. Roxy knocks on Allie's door, drags her down the driveway in her dressing gown.

"What? What is it?" says Allie, but she's smiling.

"Come and see."

"All right, Einar," says Roxy to the man. He's stocky, mid-forties, dark hair, wearing a pair of sunglasses on his forehead.

Einar grins and nods slowly. "You OK here, Roxanne? Bernie Monke said to look after you. Are you being looked after?"

"I'm grand, Einar," says Roxy. "Super-duper. Just gonna stay with my mates here for a few weeks, I reckon. You got what I need?"

Einar laughs at her.

"I met you in London once, Roxanne. You were six years old and you kicked me in the shins when I wouldn't buy you a milkshake while we waited for your dad."

Roxy laughs, too, easily. This is simpler for her than the dinner. Allie can see it.

"Shoulda bought me a milkshake, then, shouldn't you? Come on, hand it over."

There's a bag with — clearly — some of Roxy's clothes and other things in. There's a laptop, brand-new, top of the range. And there's a little zip-up case. Roxy balances it on the edge of the open car boot and unzips it.

"Careful," says Einar. "Rush job. Ink will still smudge if you rub it."

"Got that, Evie?" says Roxy. "No rubbing them till they're dry."

Roxy hands her a few items from inside the case.

They're passports, US ones, driver's licences, social-security cards, all as legitimate-looking as if they'd been made up by the government themselves. And all the licences and all the passports have her photo in. Changed a bit each time: different hair, a couple of them with glasses. And different names, to match the names on the social-security cards and the licences. But her, every time.

"We did you seven," says Roxy. "Half a dozen, and one for luck. Seventh one's UK. In case you fancy it. Did you manage to get the bank accounts, Einar?"

"All set up," says Einar, fishing another, smaller zip-up wallet out of his pocket. "But no deposits over one hundred thousand in one day without talking to us first, all right?"

"Dollars or pounds?" says Roxy.

Einar winces slightly. "Dollars," he says. Then, hurriedly, "But only for the first six weeks! Then they take the checks off the accounts."

"Fine," says Roxy. "I won't kick you in the shins. This time."

Roxy and Darrell kicked around in the garden for a bit, toeing at stones and picking bark off the tree. Neither of them ever even liked Terry that much, but it's weird now he's gone.

Darrell went, "What did it feel like?"

And Roxy was like, "I wasn't down there when they got Terry."

And Darrell went, "Nah, I mean when you did Primrose. What did it feel like?"

She felt it again, the glitter under her palm, the way his face grew warm and then cold. She sniffed. Looked at her own hand as if it could tell her the answer.

"It felt good," she said. "He killed my mum."

Darrell said, "I wish I could do it."

Roxanne Monke and Mother Eve talk a lot in the next few days. They find the things they have in common and hold them out at arm's length to admire the details. The missing mother, the place they're both used to holding, half in and half out of families.

"I like how you all say 'sister' here. I never had a sister."

"I didn't either," says Allie.

"Always wanted one," says Roxy.

And they leave that there for a bit.

Some of the girls in the convent want to spar with Roxy, practise their skills. She's up for it. They use the big lawn at the back of the building, leading down to the ocean. She takes them two or three at once, sidesteps them, hits them hard, confuses them till they jolt each other. They come in for supper bruised and laughing, sometimes with a tiny spider-web scar on the wrist or ankle; they wear it proudly. There are girls as young as eleven or twelve here; they follow Roxy about like she's a pop star. She tells them to get off, go and find something else to do. But she likes it. She teaches them a special fighting trick she's worked out — splosh a bottle of water in someone's face, stick your finger in the water as it spurts out of the bottle, electrify the whole thing. They practise it on each other on the lawn, giggling and hurling water about.

Roxy sits with Allie on the porch late one afternoon, when the sun's setting red-gold behind them. They're watching the kids larking about on the lawn.

Allie says, "Reminds me of me, when I was ten."

"Oh yeah? Big family?"

There's a longish pause. Roxy wonders if she's asked something she shouldn't have asked, but fuck it. She can wait.

Allie says, "Children's home."

"Right," says Roxy. "I know kids who come from that. It's rough. Hard to get on your feet. You're doing all right now, though."

"I look after myself," says Allie. "I learned how to take care of myself."

"Yeah. I can see that."

The voice in Allie's head has been quiet these past few days. Quieter than she remembers it being in years. Something about being here, these summer days, knowing that Roxy's here and she could kill anyone stone dead; something about that has made it all go quiet.

Allie says, "I was passed around a lot when I was a child. Never knew my dad, and my mom's just a little scrap of memory." Just a hat, is what Allie remembers. A pale pink Sunday church hat at a daring angle and a face underneath grinning at her, sticking her tongue out. It seems like a happy memory, from sometime between long bouts of sadness or illness or both. She doesn't remember ever going to church, but there's that hat in her memory.

Allie says, "I think I've had twelve homes before this one. Maybe thirteen." She passes a hand across her face, digs her fingertips into her forehead. "They put me in a place once with a lady who collected china dolls. Hundreds, everywhere, staring at me from the walls in the room I slept in. She dressed me up nice, I

153

remember that. Little pastel dresses with ribbon threaded through the hems. But she went to jail for stealing — that's how she paid for all those dolls — so I was sent on."

One of the girls on the lawn pours water on another, setting it sparkling with a faint jolt. The other girl giggles. It tickles.

"People make what they need for themselves," says Roxy. "My dad says that. If there's something you need, something you really have to have — not just want to but *have to*, you'll find a way to get it." She laughs. "He was talking about junkies, wasn't he? But it's more than that." Roxy looks at the girls on the lawn, at this house which is a home, more than a home.

Allie smiles. "If you make it, you've got to protect it."

"Yeah, well. I'm here now."

"You have more power than anyone we've ever seen, you know."

Roxy looks at her hands like she's a bit impressed, a bit afraid.

"I dunno," she says. "There's probably other people like me."

Allie has a sudden intuition then. Like a fairground machine with gears working and chains clanking. Someone had taken her to one when she was a little girl. Put in two quarters, pull the lever, *clunk*, grind, *thunk*; there's a fortune, printed on a small rectangle of thick, pink-edged cardboard. Allie's intuition is just like that: sudden and complete, as if there were machinery working behind her eyes that even she has no access to. *Clank, thunk.*

The voice says: Here. This is something you know now. Use it.

Allie speaks quite softly. "Did you kill someone?"

Roxy sticks her hands in her pockets and frowns at her. "Who told you?"

And because she does not say, "Who told you *that*?", Allie knows that she is right.

The voice says: Say nothing.

Allie says, "Sometimes I just know things. Like there's a voice in my head."

Roxy says, "Bloody hell, you *are* spooky. Who's going to win the Grand National, then?"

Allie says, "I killed someone, too. A long way away now. I was a different person."

"Probably deserved it, if you did it."

"He did."

They sit with that.

Roxy says, companionably and as if it has nothing to do with anything, "There was a bloke who stuck his hand down my pants when I was seven. Piano teacher. My mum thought it'd be nice for me to learn piano. There I was, on the stool, doing 'Every Good Boy Deserves Fun' and, suddenly, hand in my knickers. 'Don't say anything,' he goes. 'Just carry on playing.' So I told my dad the next night when he came to take me out to the park and, bloody hell, he went *mental*. Screaming at my mum, how could she; she said she didn't know, did she, or she wouldn't have let him. My dad took some of the boys round to that piano teacher's house."

Allie says, "What happened?"

Roxy laughs. "They beat the shit out of him. He ended the night with one less nut than he started it, for one thing."

"Really?"

"Yeah, course. My dad said if he had one more pupil round that house, and he meant *ever*, he'd come back for the other veg, and the meat, too. And not to think about leaving town and starting up again somewhere else because Bernie Monke is bloody *everywhere*." Roxy chuckles to herself. "Yeah, I saw him in the street once and he ran away. Saw me, right, turned, and actually *ran*. Bloody right, mate."

Allie says, "That's good. That sounds good." She makes a little sigh.

Roxy says, "I know you don't trust them. It's all right. You don't have to trust them, babe."

She reaches over and puts her hand on top of Allie's, and they sit there like that for a long time.

After a while, Allie says, "One of the girls has a dad in the police force. He telephoned her two days ago to tell her she can't be in this building on Friday."

Roxy laughs. "Dads. They like keeping their daughters safe. They can't keep secrets."

"Will you help us?" says Allie.

"What do you think is coming?" says Roxy. "SWAT team?"

"Not so much. We're only a few girls in a convent. Practising our religion like law-abiding citizens."

"I can't kill anyone else," says Roxy.

"I don't think we'll have to," says Allie. "I've got an idea."

They mopped up the rest of Primrose's gang after he died. Wasn't any bother; they all fell apart after he was gone. Two weeks after Terry's funeral Bernie called Roxy on her mobile at 5 a.m., and told her to come to a lock-up garage in Dagenham. There, he fished the big bunch of keys out of his pocket, opened it up and showed her two bodies laid out, killed cold and clean and about to go into the acid, and that'd be the end of that.

She looked them in the face.

"That them?" said Bernie.

"Yeah," she said. She snaked her arm around her dad's waist. "Thanks."

"Anything for my girl," he said.

Big bloke, little bloke, the two who killed her mum. One of them with her mark still on his arm, livid and branching.

"All done, then, sweetheart?" he said.

"All done, Dad."

He kissed her on the top of the head.

They went for a walk that morning round Eastbrookend Cemetery. Slow walking, chatting, while a couple of cleaners did the necessary in the garage.

"You know the day you was born was the day we got Jack Conaghan?" said Bernie.

Roxy does know this. Still, she likes to hear the story again.

"He'd been on us for years," said Bernie. "Killed Micky's dad — you never knew him — him and the Irish boys. We got him in the end, though. Fishing in the canal. We waited all night for him, and when he got there early, we did him, chucked him in. That was that. When we was done and home and dry I checked my phone — fifteen messages from your mum! Fifteen! She'd gone into labour overnight, hadn't she?"

Roxy felt her fingertips around the edges of this story. It always seemed slippery, something fighting its way out of her grasp. She was born in the darkness, and with people waiting for someone: her dad waiting for Jack Conaghan, her mum waiting for her dad, and Jack Conaghan, though he never knew it, waiting for Death. It's a story about the stuff that happens just exactly when you weren't expecting it; just on that night you thought nothing was going to happen, everything happens.

"I picked you up — a girl! After three boys, never thought I'd have a girl. And you looked me dead in the eye, and widdled all down my trousers. And that's how I knew you'd be good luck."

She is good luck. Barring a few things, she's always had good luck.

How many miracles does it take? Not too many. One, two, three is plenty. Four is a great multitude, more than enough.

There are twelve armed police officers advancing across the gardens at the back of the convent. It's been raining. The ground is waterlogged, and more than waterlogged. There are open taps running at both sides of the garden. The girls have run a pump to bring seawater up to the top of the steps, and it's a waterfall now, water gushing down the stone stairs. The officers aren't wearing rubber boots; they didn't know it'd be muddy like this. All they know is that a lady from the convent had come to tell them that girls were holed up in here and had been threatening and violent. So there are twelve trained men in body armour coming for them. It should be enough to finish this.

The men shout out, "Police! Leave the building now, with your hands in the air!"

Allie looks at Roxy. Roxy grins at her.

They're waiting behind the curtains in the dining room, the one that looks out over the back gardens. Waiting until the police are all on the stone stairs leading to the terrace outside the back doors. Waiting, waiting . . . and there they all are.

Roxy pulls the corks out from the half-dozen barrels of seawater they've stored behind them. The carpet is sodden now, and the water's gushing out under the door towards the steps. They're all in one mass of water, Roxy and Allie and the police.

Allie puts her hand into the water around her ankles and concentrates.

Outside, on the terrace and on the stairs, the water is touching the skin of all the police officers, one way or another. It needs more control than Allie's ever managed before; their fingers are on the triggers, they want to squeeze. But one by one she sends her message through the water, as fast as thought. And one by one, the officers jerk like puppets, the angles of their elbows fly out, their hands unclench and go numb. One by one, they drop their guns.

"Fucking hell," says Roxy.

"Now," says Allie, and climbs up on to a chair.

Roxy, the woman with more power than she knows what to do with, sends a bolt through the water, and each of the police officers starts and bucks and topples to the ground. Neat as you like.

It had to be only one woman doing it; a dozen convent girls couldn't have acted together so quickly without hurting each other. A soldier had to come.

Roxy smiles.

Upstairs, Gordy's been filming it on her cellphone. It'll be online in an hour. You don't need too many miracles before people start believing in you. And then sending you money and offers of legal help to get yourself properly set up. Everyone's looking for some kind of answer, today more than ever.

Mother Eve records a message to go out over the footage. She says, "I have not come to tell you to give up a single strand of your belief. I am not here to convert you. Christian, Jew, Muslim, Sikh, Hindu, Buddhist, if you are of any faith or none at all, God does not want you to change your practice."

She pauses. She knows this is not what they're expecting to hear.

"God loves all of us," she says, "and She wants us to know that She has changed Her garment merely. She is beyond female and male, She is beyond human understanding. But She calls your attention to that which you have forgotten. Jews: look to Miriam, not Moses, for what you can learn from her. Muslims: look to Fatimah, not Muhammad. Buddhists: remember Tara, the mother of liberation. Christians: pray to Mary for your salvation.

160

"You have been taught that you are unclean, that you are not holy, that your body is impure and could never harbour the divine. You have been taught to despise everything you are and to long only to be a man. But you have been taught *lies*. God lies within you, God has returned to earth to teach you, in the form of this new power. Do not come to me looking for answers, for you must find the answers within yourself."

What can ever be more seductive than to be asked to stay away? What draws people nearer than being told they are unwelcome?

Already that evening there are emails: Where can I go to join with your followers? What can I do here at home? How do I set up a prayer circle for this new thing? Teach us how to pray.

And there are the appeals for help. My daughter is sick, pray for her. My mother's new husband has handcuffed her to the bed, please send someone to rescue her. Allie and Roxy read the emails together.

Allie says, "We have to try to help."

Roxy says, "You can't help them all, babe."

Allie says, "I can. With God's help, I can."

Roxy says, "Maybe you don't need to go and get all of them, to help all of them."

The police force all across the state gets worse after the video of what Allie and Roxy did goes up online. They felt humiliated, of course they did. They had something to prove. There are states and countries where the police are already actively recruiting women, but that hasn't happened here yet. The force is still mostly male.

And they're angry, and they're afraid, and then things happen.

Twenty-three days after the police tried to take the convent, a girl arrives at the door with a message for Mother Eve. Only Mother Eve; please, they have to help her. She's weak with crying, and shaking and frightened.

Roxy makes her a hot, sweet tea and Allie finds her some cookies, and the girl — her name's Mez — tells them what's happened.

It was seven armed police officers, patrolling their neighbourhood. Mez and her mom were walking home from the grocery store, just talking. Mez is twelve and has had the power for a few months; her mom's had it for longer; her little cousin woke it up in her. They were just talking, says Mez, just holding their grocery bags and chatting and laughing, and then suddenly there were six or seven cops saying, "What's in the bags? Where are you going? We've had reports of a couple of women causing trouble round here. What have you got in the damn bags?"

Mez's mom didn't take it too seriously; she just laughed and said, "What are we gonna have in here? Groceries, from the grocery store."

And one of the cops said she was acting pretty cool for a woman walking in a dangerous area; what had she been doing?

And Mez's mom just said, "Leave us alone."

And they pushed her. And she hit two of them, just with a little tickle of power. Just a warning.

And that was it for the cops. They pulled out their nightsticks and their guns and they started working, and Mez was screaming and her mom was screaming and there was blood all on the sidewalk and they mashed her on her head.

"They held her down," says Mez, "and they messed her up. It was seven on one."

Allie listens to it all very quietly. And when Mez has finished talking she says, "Is she alive?"

Mez nods.

"Do you know where they've taken her? Which hospital?"

Mez says, "They didn't take her to a hospital. They've taken her to the police station."

Allie says to Roxy, "We're going down there."

Roxy says, "Then we have to take everyone."

There are sixty women who walk down the street together towards the police station where they're holding Mez's mom. They walk quietly but quickly, and they're filming everything — that's the word they've passed around the women in the convent. Document everything. Stream it if you can. Put it online.

By the time they arrive, the police know they're coming. There are men standing outside, holding rifles.

Allie walks up to them. She holds her hands up, palms towards them. She says, "We've come here peacefully. We want to see Rachel Latif. We want to know she's receiving medical attention. We want her sent to a hospital."

The senior officer, standing at the door, says, "Mrs Latif is being legally detained. By what power do you ask for her release?"

Allie looks to the left and to the right, along the phalanx of women she's brought with her. There are more women arriving every minute. There are maybe two hundred and fifty here now. The news of what's happened has passed from door to door. There have been text messages; women have seen it online and left their houses and come.

"The only power that matters," she says, "the common laws of humanity and God. There is a badly injured woman in your cells, she needs to see a doctor."

Roxy can feel the power crackling in the air around her. The women here are hyped up, excited, angry. She wonders if the men can feel it, too. The policemen with their rifles are nervous. Something could go bad here very easily.

The senior police officer shakes his head and says, "We can't let you in. And your presence here is a threat to my officers."

Allie says, "We're here peacefully. Officer, we are *peaceful*. We want to see Rachel Latif, we want a doctor to treat her."

A great muttering rises up in the crowd then falls silent, waiting.

The senior officer says, "If I let you see her, will you tell these women to go home?"

Allie says, "Let me see her first."

Rachel Latif, when Roxy and Allie are brought to the holding cell to see her, is barely conscious. Her hair is matted with blood and she is lying on the cot in the cell, hardly moving, her breath a slow, painful rattle.

Roxy says, "Jesus Christ!"

Allie says, "Officer, this woman must be taken to a hospital immediately."

The other policemen are watching the senior officer. More and more women are arriving outside the building every minute. The sound of them outside is like a crowd of murmuring birds, each one speaking to her neighbour, each ready to wheel at a secret signal. There are only twenty officers in this station. There'll be several hundred women outside it within one half-hour.

Rachel Latif's skull is cracked open. You can see the white bone shattered and the blood bubbling from her brain.

The voice says: They did it without provocation. You've been provoked. You could take this station, you could kill every man in it if you wanted.

Roxy takes Allie's hand, squeezes it.

Roxy says, "Officer, you don't want this to go any further. You don't want this to be the story they tell about you. Let this woman go to a hospital."

The police officer lets out a long, slow sigh.

The crowd outside grows noisy when Allie re-emerges, and even noisier when they hear the approaching sirens of the ambulance, nosing its way through the crowd.

Two women hoist Mother Eve on to their shoulders. She holds up her hand. The muttering grows silent.

Mother Eve speaks through Allie's mouth and says, "I am taking Rachel Latif to the hospital. I will ensure she is cared for properly."

The noise again, like grass stalks blowing. It rises up and dies away.

Mother Eve splays her fingers out, like the sign of the Hand of Fatima. She says, "You have done good work here and now you can go home."

The women nod. The girls from the convent turn and walk away as one. The other women begin to follow them.

Half an hour later, when Rachel Latif is being examined in the hospital, the street outside the police station is entirely empty.

In the end, there's no need for them to stay in the convent. It's nice, it overlooks the sea and it's got a certain homely feel to it, but by the time Roxy's been there nine months Allie's organization could have bought a hundred buildings like it and, anyway, they need somewhere bigger. There are six hundred women affiliated with the convent in this little town alone, and satellites springing up across the country, around the world. The more the authorities say she's illegitimate, the more the old Church says she's sent by the Devil, the more women are drawn to Mother Eve. If Allie had any doubt before this that she has been sent by God with a message for Her people, the things that have happened here have left her in no doubt. She is here to look after the women. God has appointed her to that role, and it is not for Allie to deny it.

It's spring come round again when they're talking about new buildings.

Roxy says, "You'll save a room for me, won't you, wherever you end up?"

Allie says, "Don't go. Why would you go? Why back to England? What's there for you?"

Roxy says, "My dad reckons it's all blown over. No one cares what we do to each other, really, as long as we don't get any honest citizens involved." She grins.

"But really," Allie flattens her lips, "really, why would you go home? This is your home. Stay here. Please. Stay with us."

Roxy squeezes Allie's hand. "Mate," she says, "I miss my family. I miss my dad. And, like, Marmite. I miss all that stuff. I'm not going away for ever. We'll see each other again."

Allie breathes in through her nose. There is a murmuring at the back of her mind that has been quiet and far away for months now.

She shakes her head. She says, "You can't trust them, though."

Roxy laughs. "What, men? All men? Can't trust *any* of them?"

Allie says, "Be careful. Find women you trust to work with you."

Roxy says, "Yeah, we've talked about this, babe."

"You have to take it all," says Allie. "You can. You've got it. Don't let Ricky take it, don't let Darrell take it. It's yours."

Roxy says, "You know, I think you're right. But I can't take it all sitting here, can I?" She swallows. "I've booked a ticket. I leave a week on Saturday. There's stuff I wanted to talk about with you before that. Plans. Can we talk about plans? Without you going on about how I should just stay?"

"We can."

Allie says in her heart: I don't want her to go. Can we stop that happening?

The voice says to Allie: Remember, sweetheart, the only way you're safe is if you own the place.

Allie says: Can I own the whole world?

The voice says, very quietly, just as it used to speak many years ago: Oh, honey. Oh, baby girl, you can't get there from here.

Roxy says, "The thing is, I've got an idea."

Allie says, "So do I."

And they look at each other and smile.

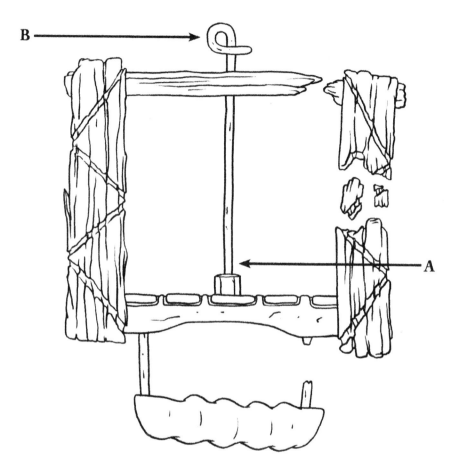

Approximately fifteen hundred years old, a device
for training in the use of the electrostatic
power. The handle at the base is iron and is connected, within the wooden frame, to a metal peg,
marked A on the diagram. We conjecture that a
piece of paper or dry leaf could be affixed to the
spike, marked B on the diagram, with the aim
being for the operator to set it aflame. This would
require a degree of control, presumably the skill
being practised. The size suggests that the device
was meant for thrteen- to fifteen-year-old girls.
Discovered in Thailand.

Archival documents relating to the electrostatic power, its origin, dispersal, and the possibility of a cure

1. Description of the short Second World War propaganda film *Protection Against Gas*. The film itself has been lost.

The film is two minutes and fifty-two seconds long. At the start, a brass band strikes up. The percussion joins in with the brass and the tune is jaunty as the title comes up on the screen. The title is: "Protection Against Gas". The card is hand-inked, wavering slightly as the camera focuses on it, before a sharp cut to a group of men in white coats standing in front of a huge vat of liquid. They wave and smile at the camera.

"At the Ministry of War laboratories," says the clipped male voiceover, "the back-room boys work double-shifts on their latest brain-wave."

The men dip a ladle into the liquid and, using a pipette, drop some of it on to testing-papers. They smile. They add a single droplet to the water bottle of a white rat in a cage with a large, black, inked X on its back. The brass band ups the tempo as the rat drinks the water.

"Staying one step ahead of the enemy is the only way to keep the population safe. This rat has been given a dose of the new nerve-strengthener developed to combat gas attack."

Cut-away to another rat in a cage. No X on the back.

"This rat has not."

A canister of white gas is opened in the small room containing the two cages, and the scientists, wearing breathing apparatus, retreat behind a glass wall. The untreated rat succumbs quickly, waving its forepaws in the air distressingly before it begins to twitch. We do not follow its final throes. The rat with the X on its back continues to suck at the bottle, nibble at food pellets, and even run in its exercise wheel as the smoke drifts past the cameras.

"As you can see," says the brisk voiceover, "it works."

One of the scientists takes off his gas mask and walks, decisively, into the smoke-filled room. He waves from inside, and takes deep lungfuls.

"And it's safe for humans."

The scene changes to a waterworks, where a pipe is being hooked up from a small tanker-lorry into an outlet valve in the floor.

"They call it Guardian Angel. The miracle cure that has kept allied forces safe from enemy attack by gas is now being given to the general population."

Two balding middle-aged men, one with a tooth-brush moustache and wearing a darksuit, shake hands as a meter shows the liquid from the lorry slowly going down.

"Just a tiny amount in the drinking water will

be enough to protect an entire town. This single tank is sufficient to treat the drinking water for 500,000 people. Coventry, Hull and Cardiff will be the first to receive the water treatment. Working at this pace, the entire country will be covered within three months."

A mother on the street of a northern town lifts her baby out of the pram, rests it on a cloth on her shoulder and looks up, concerned, to the clear sky.

"So Mother can feel secure that her baby need no longer fear nerve-gas attack. Rest easy, Mother and child."

The music reaches a crescendo. The screen darkens. The reel ends.

2. Notes distributed to journalists to accompany the BBC programme *The Source of Power*.

The story of Guardian Angel was forgotten shortly after the Second World War — as with so many ideas which worked flawlessly, there was no reason to re-examine it. At the time, however, Guardian Angel was a tremendous success and a propaganda victory. Tests on the general population in Britain proved that the substance accumulated in the system. Even a week spent drinking Guardian-Angel-laced water would provide never-ending protection against nerve gas.

Guardian Angel was manufactured in great vats

in the heartland of the USA and in the home counties of the UK. It was transported by tanker to friendly nations: to Hawaii and to Mexico, to Norway, to South Africa and to Ethiopia. The enemy's U-boats harried the vessels, as they did every shipment coming to or from the Allies. Inevitably, one dark night in September 1944, a tanker was sunk, with all hands, sixteen miles off the coast of Portugal, on its way to the Cape of Good Hope.

Subsequent research has found that over the following months, in the coastal towns of Aveiro, Espinho and Porto, strange things washed ashore — fish much larger than any they'd seen before. Shoals of these unusually sized creatures had apparently hurled themselves at the beaches. The people in the villages and towns along the coast ate the fish. An analysis by a conscientious Portuguese official in 1947 revealed that Guardian Angel was detectable in the groundwater as far inland as Estrela, near the Spanish border. But his suggestion that the water table should be tested across Europe was rejected; there were no resources available for the task.

Some analysis suggests that the sinking of this one ship was the critical moment. Others maintain that, once the liquid had entered the water cycle at any point, in any reservoir, in any place in the world, it would inevitably spread. Other potential sources of contamination include: a spill from arusted container in Buenos Aires several years after the war and an explosion at a munitions dump in southern China.

Nonetheless, the oceans of the world are connected to one another — the water cycle is endless. Although Guardian Angel had been forgotten after the Second World War, it continued to concentrate and magnify its potency in the human body. Research has now established it as the undoubted trigger, once certain concentrations had been reached, for the development of the electrostatic power in women.

Any woman who was seven years old or younger during the Second World War may have skein buds on the points of her collarbones — although not all do; it will depend on what dose of Guardian Angel was received in early childhood, and on other genetic factors. These buds can be "activated" by a controlled burst of electrostatic power by a younger woman. They are present in increasingly large proportions of women with every birth-year that passes. Women who were about thirteen or fourteen years old around the Day of the Girls almost invariably possess a full skein. Once the skein power has been activated, it cannot be taken away without tremendous danger to the woman's life.

It is theorized that Guardian Angel merely amplified

a set of genetic possibilities already present in the human genome. It is possible that, in the past, more women possessed a skein but that this tendency was bred out over time.

3. SMS conversation between the Home Secretary and the Prime Minister, classified and released under the thirty-year rule.

PM: Just read the report. Thoughts?

HS: We can't release it.

PM: The US are set to release in a month.

HS: Fuck's sake. Ask them to delay.

PM: They're adopting "a policy of radical openness". They're evangelical about it.

HS: As usual.

PM: You can't stop Americans being American.

HS: They're 5,000 miles from the Black Sea. I'll talk to the Sec. of State. We need to tell them it's a NATO matter. Releasing the report will harm the stability of fragile regimes. Regimes that could easily get their hands on chemical and biological weapons.

PM: It's going to leak, anyway. We need to think about how this impacts on us.

HS: There's going to be pandemonium.

PM: Because there's no cure?

HS: No fucking cure. It's not a fucking crisis any more. This is the new reality.

4. Online advertisement collection, preserved by the Internet Archive Project.

4a) *Keep safe with your Personal Defender*

The Personal Defender is safe, reliable and easy to use. The battery pack worn on your belt connects to a wrist-mounted taser.

- This product is approved by police officers, and has been independently tested.

- It is discreet; no one needs to know you can defend yourself but you.

- It is ready at hand; no need to fumble in a holster or a pocket if under attack.

- You will not find any other product as reliable and effective.

- Complete with an additional phone-charging socket.

Note: The Personal Defender was subsequently withdrawn, following incidents fatal to the users. It was established that a woman's body, receiving a large electric shock, would often produce a large reflexive arc "bouncing back" towards her attacker, even if she fell unconscious. The manufacturers of the Personal Defender settled a class action suit out of court with the families of seventeen men who were killed in this way.

4b) *Increase your power with this one weird trick*
Women all over the world are learning how to increase the duration and strength of their power using this secret knowledge. Our ancestors knew the secret; now, researchers at Cambridge University have discovered this one weird trick to improve performance. Expensive training programs don't want you to know this easy way to succeed! Click here to learn the $5 trick that will put you head and shoulders above the rest.

4c) *Defensive slip-on undersocks*
The natural way to protect yourself against attack. No poison, no pellets, no powders; entirely efficient protection against electricity! Simply put these rubber socks on under your normal shoes and socks. No one need know you're wearing them, and unlike a shoe they cannot easily be removed by an assailant. Two supplied per pack. Absorbent lining locks away foot moisture.

Six years to go

Tunde

Tatiana Moskalev was right, and she'd given him good information. He spent two months investigating in the hills of northern Moldova — or the country that used to be Moldova and is currently at war with the southern part of itself — carefully questioning and bribing the people he met there. Reuters footed his bill on this occasion; he told an editor he trusted about the tip he'd got, and she signed off his costs. If he found it, it would be the biggest kind of news. If he didn't find it, he'd be able to do a portrait of this war-torn country, and that'd give them something, at least.

But he found it. One afternoon, a man in a village near the border agreed to drive Tunde in his jeep to a place on the River Dniester with a view down into the valley. There, they saw a compound, hastily thrown up, with low-slung buildings and a central training yard. The man would not let Tunde leave the jeep, and he wouldn't drive any closer. But they had a good enough view for Tunde to take six photographs. They showed brown-skinned men with beards in battle fatigues and black berets training with a new weapon, new armour. Their body suits were made of rubber, on their backs

181

they wore battery-packs and in their hands they carried electric cattle-prods.

It was only six photographs, but it was enough. Tunde had made world news. "AWADI-ATIF TRAINS SECRET ARMY" was the Reuters headline. Others shouted: "THE BOYS ARE BACK". And "LOOK WHO'S SHOCKING". There were anxious debates in newsrooms and on morning shows about the implications of these new weapons: Could they work? Would they win? Tunde hadn't managed to photograph King Awadi-Atif himself, but the conclusion that he was working with the Moldovan Defence Forces was unavoidable. The situation had begun to stabilize in many countries, but this news kicked it off again. Perhaps the men were coming back, with their weapons and armour.

In Delhi, the riot went on for weeks.

It began in the places under the motorway bridges, where the poor people live in blanket tents or houses constructed from cardboard and tape. This is the place men come when they want a woman they can use without law or licence, discard without censure. The power has been passed from palm to palm here for three years now. And the many death-bearing hands of women have a name here: Kali, the eternal. Kali, who destroys to bring fresh growth. Kali, intoxicated by the blood of the slain. Kali, who puts out the stars with her thumb and forefinger. Terror is her name and death is her breathing in and out. Her arrival in this world has been long expected. Any adjustment in understanding had come easily to the women under the motorway bridges of the megacity.

The government sent in the army. The women of Delhi discovered a new trick. A jet of water, directed at the attacking forces, could be electrified. The women put their hands into the spouts and sent death from their fingers, like the Goddess walking the earth. The government cut off the water supply to the slum neighbourhoods, in the highest heat of the summer, when the streets stink of rot and the pregnant dogs wander, panting, in search of shelter from the sun. The world's media filmed the poor begging for water, praying for a single drop. And on the third day, the heavens opened and sent an unseasonal rainstorm, hectic and thorough as a scouring brush, washing the smell from the streets and collecting in puddles and pools. When the soldiers return, they are standing in the wet or touching wet rails, or their vehicles are trailing some loose wire into the wet, and when the women light up the roadways, people die quite suddenly, falling to the ground frothing, as though Kali herself had struck them down.

The temples to Kali are full of worshippers. There are soldiers who join with the rioters. And Tunde is there, too, with his cameras and his CNN pass.

In the hotel filled with foreign journalists, people know him. He's seen some of these reporters before, in other places where justice is at last being meted out — although it's not considered good form to say so. Officially, in the West, the thing is still a "crisis", with all the word implies: exceptional, deplorable, temporary. The team from *Allgemeine Zeitung* greet him by name, congratulate him — with a slightly envious tone — on the scoop of the six photographs of Awadi-Atif's forces. He's met the more senior editors and producers from CNN, even a team from the *Daily Times* of Nigeria, who ask him where he's been hiding and how they could have missed him. Tunde has his own YouTube channel now, broadcasting footage from around the world. His face begins each broadcast. He is the one who goes to the most dangerous places to bring the images no one else will show. He celebrated his twenty-sixth birthday on a plane. One of the air stewards recognized his face and brought him champagne.

In Delhi, he follows behind a pack of women rampaging through Janpath market. There was a time that a woman could not walk alone here, not if she were under seventy, and not with certainty even then. There had been protests for many years, and placards, and shouted slogans. These things rise up and afterwards it is as if it had never been. Now the women are making what they call "a show of force", in solidarity with those who were killed under the bridges and starved of water.

Tunde interviews a woman in the crowd. She had been here for the protests three years earlier; yes, she had held up her banner and shouted and signed her petitions. "It was like being part of a wave of water," she says. "A wave of spray from the ocean feels powerful, but it is only there for a moment, the sun dries the puddles and the water is gone. Then you feel maybe it never happened. That is how it was with us. The only wave that changes anything is a tsunami. You have to tear down the houses and destroy the land if you want to be sure no one will forget you."

He knows exactly where this part will fit in his book. The history of political movements. The struggle that moved so slowly until this great change happened. He's putting together an argument.

There is little violence against people; mostly they are turning over stalls.

"Now they will know," shouts one woman into Tunde's camera, "that they are the ones who should not walk out of their houses alone at night. They are the ones who should be afraid."

There is a brief scuffle when four men with knives appear in the crowd, but this is quickly dealt with, leaving the men with twitching arms but no permanent injuries. He has started to suspect there will be nothing new here today, nothing that hasn't been seen before, when the word comes through the crowd that the army have formed a barricade up ahead, across Windsor Place. They are trying to protect the foreign hotels. They're advancing slowly, armed with rubber bullets, and shoes with thick, insulating soles. They want to make a demonstration here. A show of force to let the world see how a properly trained army deals with a rabble like this.

Tunde doesn't really know any of the women in this crowd. There is no one who would shelter him in her home if the army came. The crowd is becoming more tightly pressed together; it has happened so gradually he barely noticed it, but it makes sense now he knows that the army is trying to squeeze them all into one place. And then what will happen? People will die here today; he feels it up his spine and into the crown of his head. There are shouts from up ahead. He doesn't speak enough of the language to understand. Tunde's usual mild smile fades from his face. He has to get away from here, has to find high ground.

He looks around. Delhi is constantly under construction, most of it unsafe. There are buildings from which the scaffolding has never been removed, shopfronts that slant awkwardly, even some half-collapsed places still partly inhabited. There. Two streets up. There's a boarded-up shop behind a wagon selling parathas. A kind of wood scaffolding is fixed to the side of the building. The roof is flat. He shoulders his way through the crowd urgently. Most of the women are still trying to move forward, shouting and waving their banners. There's the hiss and crackle of electrical discharge somewhere further ahead. He can feel it in the air now; he knows what it feels like. The scents of the street, the dog shit and the mango pickle and the body odour of the crowd and the frying bhindi with cardamom become more intense for a moment. Everyone pauses. Tunde pushes forward still. He says to himself, This is not the day you die, Tunde. This is not that day. It'll be a funny story to tell your friends back home. It'll go into the book; don't be afraid, just keep moving. You'll get good footage from a high vantage point if you can just find a way up there.

The lowest-hanging piece of scaffold is a little too high for him to reach, even by jumping. Further up the street he sees that other people have had the same idea, are climbing on to the roofs or into the trees. Some others are trying to pull them down. If he doesn't get up there now, he could be overwhelmed in a few minutes by others trying to take his place. He yanks over three old fruit boxes, piles them on top of each other — takes a long splinter in his thumb as he does it, but doesn't care — climbs on top of the boxes and leaps. Misses. Comes down heavily, the shock sending a jolt of pain through his knees. These boxes won't last. The crowd is surging and chanting again. He jumps again, this time with more force, and there! He's got it. Bottom rung of the scaffold ladder. Straining the muscles in his sides, he hauls himself up to the second rung, the third, and then he can scramble his feet up on to the rickety structure, and then it's easy.

The scaffold sways as he climbs. It's not bolted to the walls of this crumbling concrete building. It was lashed with ropes once, but they've frayed and rotted, and the strain of his climbing is pulling the fibres apart. Now, *this* would be a stupid way to die. Not in a riot, not by an army bullet, not by Tatiana Moskalev taking him by the throat. Just falling a dozen feet on to his back on a street in Delhi. He climbs faster, reaching the rough parapet as the whole structure sighs and swings more wildly from side to side. He clings to the parapet with one arm, feeling that splinter working its way into his thumb, kicks off with his legs and manages to jump half on to the roof, so that his right arm and right leg are wrapped around the parapet and his body is swinging above the street. There are screams from further along the street, and pops of gunfire.

He pushes again with his left leg, just giving himself enough momentum to flop backward on to the gravel roof of the building. He lands in a puddle, soaking him through to the skin, but he's safe. He hears the creak and crack as the whole wooden structure finally gives up and crashes to the ground. That's it, Tunde, no way back down. On the other hand, no chance of being overwhelmed by crowds escaping the crush up here. Actually, it's perfect. Like it was meant to work out this way for him. He smiles, breathes out slowly. He can set up his camera here, film the whole thing. He's not afraid any more, he's excited. There's nothing he could do, anyway, no authorities to call and no boss to check in with. Just him, and his cameras, up here out of the way. And something's going to happen.

He sits up and looks around. And it's then he sees there's a woman there, with him, on the rooftop.

She's in her mid-forties, wiry, with small hands and a long, thick plait like an oiled rope. She's looking at him. Or not quite at him. She flicks him glances, looks to the side. He smiles. She smiles back. And in that smile he can tell with certainty that there's something wrong with her. It's the way she's holding her head, to the side. The way she's not looking at him and then suddenly staring at him.

"Are you . . ." He looks down at the surging crowd in the street. There's the sound of gunfire, nearer now. "Sorry if this is your place. I'm just waiting here till it's safe to go down. That all right?"

She nods, slowly. He tries a smile. "Not looking good down there. You come up here to hide?"

188

She speaks slowly and carefully. Her accent's not bad; she could be saner than he thought: "I was looking for you."

He thinks for a moment she means that she knows his voice from the internet, that she has seen his photograph. He half smiles. A fan.

She kneels down, dabbles her fingers in the puddle of water he's still sitting in. He thinks she's trying to wash her hands until the shock hits his shoulder and his whole body begins to tremble.

It's so sudden and so quick that for a moment he imagines it must have been a mistake. She's not meeting his eyes, she's looking away. The pain bleeds across his back and down his legs. There are scribbles of pain drawing a tree across his side, it's hard to breathe. He's on his hands and knees. He has to get out of the water.

He says, "Stop! Don't do that." His own voice surprises him. It's petulant, pleading. He sounds like someone more afraid than he feels himself to be. It's going to be fine. He's going to get away.

He starts to back up. Beneath them, the crowd is yelling. There are screams. If he can just make her stop this, he'll get some amazing shots of the street, the fighting.

The woman's still stirring the water with her fingers. Her eyes are rolling in her head.

He says, "I'm not here to hurt you. It's OK. We can just wait up here together."

She laughs then. Several barks of laughter.

He rolls over, crawls backwards out of the pool of water. Watches her. Now he's afraid; it was the laughing that did it.

She smiles. A bad, wide smile. Her lips are wet. He tries to stand up, but his legs are shaking and he can't quite manage it. He collapses on to one knee. She watches him nodding, like she's thinking, Yes, this is expected. Yes, this is the way it goes.

He looks around the rooftop. There's not much. There's a rickety bridge across to another roof, just a plank. He wouldn't like to cross it; she could kick it over as he walked. But if he grabbed it he could use it as a weapon. Fend her off, at least. He starts to crawl towards it.

She says a few words in a language he doesn't know, then, very quietly, "Are we in love?"

She licks her lips. He can see her skein twitching at her collarbone, a living worm. He moves faster. He is faintly aware that there are other people watching them from the rooftop across the road, people pointing and calling out. There's not much they can do from there. Maybe video it. How much good will that do him? He tries standing again, but his legs are still trembling from the aftershocks, and she laughs when she sees him try. She lunges for him. He tries to kick her in the face with his shoe but she grabs the exposed ankle and gets him again. A long, high arc. It feels like a meat cleaver wielded in a solid and practised stroke all down his thigh and calf, separating the flesh from the bone. He can smell the hair on his legs burning.

190

There is a scent like spices, something wafting up from the street. Roasting meat and the smoke of dripping animal fats and burned bones. He thinks of his mother, reaching into the pot to test the grains of parboiled rice between her fingertips. Too hot for you, Tunde, get your hands away. He can smell the sweet, hot aroma of the jollof rice bubbling on the stove. Your brain is jangled, Tunde. Remember what they say about this. Your mind is made of meat and electrics. This thing hurts more than it should because it short-circuits your brain. You are confused. You are not at home. Your mother will not come.

She has him on the ground now; she is wrestling with his belt and his jeans. She's trying to pull them down without undoing the buckle, and they're too tight to come over his hips. His back is scraping on the gravel; he can feel the edge of a wet concrete block in the small of his back, rubbing him raw, and he keeps thinking if I fight her off too hard she'll knock me unconscious, and then she can do whatever she wants.

There is shouting now from far off. As if he were underwater, his ears clogged. At first he thinks he is hearing the shouting from the street. He is ready for another shock; his body is tensed for it. And it is only when the shock does not come, when he realizes he is fighting with the air, that he opens his eyes and sees that three other women have pulled her off him. They must have crossed on the plank bridge from the building next door. They have thrown her down and they are shocking her time and again, but she will not lie still. Tunde pulls his trousers back up and waits, watching, until that woman with her long, thick oiled plait has stopped moving altogether.

Allie

Excerpt from the forum "Freedom of Reach",
a nominally libertarian website

Askedandanswered

Major, major MAJOR news out of South
Carolina. Look at the photos. Here's one of
Mother Eve — it's a screengrab from the vid
"Towards Love", the one where her hood slips
back a bit and you can see part of her face.
See how the jaw is sort of pointed, and the
relationship between the mouth and the nose,
compared to the bottom of the mouth to the
chin. On the diagram I've calculated the ratios.

Now look at this photo. Someone on
UrbanDox's forum has put up photos from a
police investigation four years ago in
Alabama. All signs are it's totally legit. Might
have come from someone who wants justice,
might have come from the police. Anyway. It's
photos of an "Alison Montgomery-Taylor", who

193

murdered her adoptive father and was never found. It's very clear. The shape of the jaw is the same, the chin is the same, the ratio between the mouth and the nose and the mouth and the chin is the same. Just look and tell me that's not convincing.

Buckyou

Fuuuuuuuuuck. You've discovered that all human beings have mouths and noses and chins. That is going to blow the field of anthropology wide open there, fag.

Fisforfreedom

These photos have very clearly been *doctored*. Look at the way that the light is shining in the picture of Alison M-T. Hits her cheek on the left-hand side and her chin on the right-hand side? Someone has Piltdown-man-ed these pix to make your numbers add up. I call shenanigans.

AngularMerkel

It's well known that it *is* Alison M-T. This has been reported to the police in Florida before, but she's got them paid off. They've been extorting money and threatening people all down the eastern seaboard. Eve and her nuns have joined up with fucking Jewish organized crime, this has been proven by UrbanDox and UltraD, check the threads on the May 11 riots and arrests in Raleigh before double-posting this bullshit, dickwad.

Manintomany

UrbanDox's account was suspended for abuse, dickwad.

Abrahamic

Yeah, I notice that every single fucking post you've made has been supporting UrbanDox, or two known sock-puppets. You're either U D yourself or you're sucking his dick right now.

SanSebastian

There's no way this wasn't her. The Israeli government is the one funding these new "churches"; they've been trying to bring down Christianity for centuries now, discrediting us, using the blacks to poison the inner cities with drugs. This new drug is just part of that; you know the new "churches" are *distributing* these Zionist drugs to our *kids*? Wake up, sheeple. This whole thing is already sewn up by the same old powers and systems. You think you're free because you can talk on a messageboard? Don't you think they're monitoring what we say here? Don't you think they know who each of us is? They don't mind us talking here, but if any of us ever seemed like we were about to *act*, they've got enough on each of us to destroy us.

Buckyou

Don't feed the trolls.

AngularMerkel

Fucking conspiracy theory nutjobs.

Loosekitetalker

Not 100% wrong. Why do you think they're not cracking down harder on illegal downloading of movies? Why do you think they're not doing a search-and-block on

196

porn sites, torrent sites? It'd be frickin easy, anyone on here could code it up in an afternoon. You know why? Because if they need to take any of us out, send us to jail for a million years, they've got the power to do it. That's what the whole internet is, man, fucking honey trap, and you think you're safe because you're using some *pzit*-ass proxy, or bouncing the signal through Bilhorod or Kherson? The NSA's got deals sewn up with those people, they've paid off the police, they're in the servers.

Matheson

Mod here. This board is not the place for discussion of net security. Suggest you take this post over to /security.

Loosekitetalker

It is relevant here. Did any of you see the BB97 vid from Moldova? Taken by *our government* in the USA, monitoring Awadi-Atif's troop movements. You think they can see that and they can't see us?

FisforFreedom

Soooo . . . to get this back on topic, I don't think that can be Mother Eve. Alison M-T is known to have fled on the night she killed her dad, 24 June. First sermons by Eve from Myrtle Bay are dated 2 *July*. Are we really saying that Alison M-T killed her dad and then jacked a car, crossed state lines, set up as a high priestess of a new religion and was delivering sermons *ten days* later? I don't buy it. Coincidence of facial recognition software picked this one up, conspiracy theorists on Reddit went crazy for it, there's nothing there. Do I believe there's something weird about Eve? Sure. There are the same dark patterns as Scientology, as early Mormonism. Double-speak, bending old stuff to suit new ways of thinking, creating a new underclass. But murder? There's no evidence for that.

Riseup

Wake up. Her people doctored the dates on those sermons to make them seem to go back earlier than they really do. There's no *video* of those early sermons, nothing on YouTube. They could've been made any time. If anything this makes her look *more* guilty.

Why would she have to pretend to have been in Myrtle Bay so early?

Loosekitetalker

Don't see how the Moldovan sat images are off topic. Mother Eve's been giving talks in South Moldova, she's building up a power base there. We know that the NSA is monitoring every-thing, global terrorism hasn't gone anywhere. Seventeen near relatives of the King fled Saudi after the coup with more than eight *trillion* dol-lars in foreign holdings. House of Saud hasn't disappeared just because there's a women's centre in the Al Faisaliyah. You think there's no backlash coming? You think Awadi-Atif doesn't want his fucking kingdom back? You think he's not sloshing his money around to anyone he thinks will help? Do you have *any idea* what the House of Saud has always funded? They fund terror, my friends.

And with all that, you think there's no inter-est in domestic terror and counter-terrorism? The NSA's monitoring everything we're saying here: be certain of that. They'll have Eve under close surveillance.

Manintomany

Eve will be dead within three years, I guarantee it.

Riseup

Dude, unless you are using a dozen VPNs at once, wait for your door to be knocked down in three, two, one . . .

AngularMerkel

Someone's going to send in a hitman to do her. Electricity won't protect against bullets. Malcolm X. MLK. JFK. There's probably a contract on her already.

Manintomany

Those speeches she makes, I'd fucking murder the cunt for free.

TheLordIsWatching

The government has been causing this change for years through carefully measured doses of hormones called VACCINATIONS. VAC as in VACUOUS, SIN as in our sinful souls, NATION as in the once great people who have been destroyed by this. Click here for the exposé no newspaper will publish.

Ascension229

There's going to come a reckoning. The Lord shall gather His people and He shall instruct them in his Right Way and in His Glory, and this shall herald the end of days, when the righteous shall be gathered unto Him and the wicked shall perish in flames.

AveryFalls

Did you all see Olatunde Edo's reporting from Moldova? The Saudi army? Anyone else look at the pix of those fine young men and want to go and join up? Fight the war that's coming with the weapons they have. Make a difference, so when our grandsons ask what we did, we'll have something to tell them?

Manintomany

That's exactly what I thought. Only wish I were younger. If my son wanted to go, I'd wish him godspeed. He's being fucked by a feminazi now though. She's got her claws into him good and tight.

Beningitis

I took my son to the mall yesterday. He's nine. I let him look around the toy store alone to pick something out — it was his birthday last week, he has birthday money and he's smart enough not to wander out of the door without me. But when I came to find him, there was a girl talking to him, maybe thirteen, fourteen years old. One of those tattoos on the palm of her hand. The Hand of Fatima. I asked him what she'd said and he started crying and crying. He asked me if it was true that he was bad and that God wanted him to be obedient and humble. She was trying to convert my son in the fucking store.

Buckyou

Fuck. Fuck. That is disgusting. Fucking stupid little lying bitch cunt. I would have hit her so hard she'd be sucking dick through her eyeballs.

Verticalshitdown

Dude, I have literally no idea what that even means.

Manintomany

Do you have a photo of her? Some kind of ID? There are people who can help you.

Loosekitetalker

What was the store? What was the exact time and place?
   We can find security footage. We can send her a message she won't forget.

Manintomany

PM me details of exactly where you met her, and the name of the store. We are going to strike back against them.

FisforFreedom

Guys. I call false flag. A story like this, the OP could make you attack anyone, with minimal evidence. Could be an attempt to provoke

reciprocal action just to make us look like the
bad guys.

Manintomany

Fuck off. We know these things happen.
They've happened to us. We need a Year Of
Rage, just like they're saying. Bitches need to
see a change. They need to learn what
justice means.

UrbanDox933

There will be nowhere to hide. There will be
nowhere to run to. There will be no mercy.

Margot

"Now tell me, Madam Mayor, were you elected Governor of this great state, what would your plans be to tackle the budget deficit?"

There are three points to this. She knows it. She has the first two right off.

"I have a simple three-point plan, Kent. Number one: trim the overspend on bureaucracy" — that's good, that's the one to hit them with first: "Did you know that current Governor Daniel Dandon's office for environmental oversight spent more than thirty thousand dollars last year on" — what was it? — "bottled water?" A pause to let that sink in.

"Number two, cut aid to those who really don't need it — if your income is over $100,000 a year, this state should *not* be paying to send your kids to summer camp!" This is a misrepresentation followed by a gross misrepresentation. This provision would only apply to two thousand families state-wide, and most of those have disabled kids, which would exempt them from means testing anyway. Still, it plays well, and mentioning kids reminds people that she has a family, while saying she'll cut welfare payments makes her seem tough — not just another woman in office with a soft, bleeding heart. Now the third plank. The third.

The third plank.

"Point three," she says, in the hope that the words will find themselves on her tongue if she just keeps talking. "Point three," she says again a little more firmly. Fuck. She doesn't have it. Come on. Cutting bureaucracy. Cutting unnecessary welfare payments. And. And. Fuck.

"Fuck, Alan, I've lost point three."

Alan stretches. Stands up and rolls his neck.

"Alan. Tell me point three."

"If I tell you, you'll just forget it again onstage."

"Fuck you, Alan."

"Yeah, you kiss your kids with that mouth?"

"They can't tell the fucking difference."

"Margot, do you want this?"

"Do I *want* this? Would I be going through all of this prep if I didn't *want* it?"

Alan sighs. "You know it, Margot. Somewhere in there, somewhere inside your head, you *have* point three of your budget deficit programme. Reach out for me, Margot. Find it."

She stares at the ceiling. They're in the dining room, with a podium mocked up next to the television set. Maddy's little hand-print paintings are framed on the wall; Jocelyn's already demanded hers be taken down.

"It'll be different when we're actually live," she says. "I'll have the adrenaline then. I'll be more" — she does jazz hands — "peppy."

"Yeah, you'll be so peppy that when you can't remember the third plank of your budget reform you'll throw up live onstage. Pep. Super-pep. Puke."

Bureaucracy. Welfare. And. Bureaucracy . . . welfare . . .

"INFRASTRUCTURE INVESTMENT!" she yells it out. "The current administration has refused to invest in our infrastructure. Our schools are crumbling, our roads are poorly maintained, and we need to spend money to make money. I've shown that I can manage large-scale projects; our NorthStar camps for girls have been replicated in twelve states now. They create jobs. They keep girls off the streets. And they've given us one of the lowest rates of street violence in the country. Infrastructure investment will make our people confident in a secure future ahead of them."

That's it. That was it. There.

"And isn't it true, Madam Mayor," says Alan, "that you have worrying ties with private military corporations?"

Margot smiles. "Only if public and private initiatives working hand in hand makes you worried, Kent. NorthStar Systems are one of the most well-respected companies in the world. They run private security for many Heads of State. And they're an American business, just the kind of business we need to provide jobs for hardworking families. And tell me" — her smile positively twinkles — "would I send my *own daughter* to a NorthStar day camp if I thought they were anything other than a force for good?"

There's a slow round of applause in the room. Margot hadn't even noticed that Jocelyn's come in by the side door, that she's been listening.

"That was great, Mom. Really great."

Margot laughs. "You should have seen me a few minutes ago. I couldn't even remember the names of all the school districts in the state. I've known those off by heart for ten years."

"You just need to relax. Come and have a soda."

Margot glances at Alan.

"Yeah, yeah. Take ten minutes."

Jocelyn smiles.

Jos is doing better now. Better than she was, anyway. Two years of NorthStar camp have helped; the girls there have taught her how to tone down the highs. It's been months since she last blew up a lightbulb, and she's using a computer again without fear of fritzing it. They haven't helped her lows, though. There are still days — up to a week sometimes — when she has no power at all. They've tried linking it to what she eats, to her sleep, to her periods, to exercise, but they can't find a pattern. Some days, some weeks, she's got nothing. Quietly, Margot's talking to a couple of health-insurance providers about funding some research. The state government would be very grateful for their assistance. Even more so if she becomes Governor.

Jos takes her hand as they walk through the den towards the kitchen. Squeezes it.

Jos says, "So, uh, Mom, this is Ryan."

There's a boy, standing awkwardly in the hall. Hands in his pockets. Pile of books on the side. His dirty-blond hair is falling into his eyes.

Huh. A boy. Well. OK. Parenting never stops bringing new challenges.

"Hi, Ryan. Good to meet you." She extends a hand.

"Nice to meet you, Mayor Cleary," he mumbles. At least he's polite. Could be worse.

"How old are you, Ryan?"

"Nineteen."

A year older than Jocelyn.

"And how did you meet my daughter, Ryan?"

"Mom!"

Ryan blushes. Actually blushes. She'd forgotten how young some nineteen-year-old boys are. Maddy's fourteen years old and already practising military stances in the mud room and doing the moves she's seen on TV or that Jos has taught her from the camp. Her power hasn't even come in yet and she seems older than this kid standing in the hallway, staring at his shoes and blushing.

"We met at the mall," says Jos. "We hung out, we drank sodas. We're just going to do homework together." Her tone is pleading. "Ryan's going to Georgetown in the fall. Pre-med."

"Everyone wants to date a doctor, huh?" She smiles.

"MOM!"

Margot pulls Jocelyn close to her, hand in the small of her back, kisses the top of her head and whispers very quietly in her ear, "I want your bedroom door open, OK?"

Jocelyn stiffens. "Just until we've had time to discuss it. Just today. OK?"

"OK," whispers Jos.

"I love you." Margot kisses her again.

Jos takes Ryan's hand. "Love you, too, Mom."

Ryan picks up his books awkwardly, with one hand. "Nice to meet you, Mrs Cleary," and then a look across his face like he knows he's not supposed to call her Mrs, like he's been schooled in it, "I mean, Mayor Cleary."

"Nice to meet you too, Ryan. Dinner's at six thirty, OK?"

And they go upstairs. That was it. The start of the new generation.

Alan's watching from the door to the den. "Young love?"

Margot shrugs. "Young something, anyway. Young hormones."

"Nice to know some things don't change."

Margot looks up through the stairwell to the upper floor. "What did you mean before, when you asked me if I wanted it?"

"It's just . . . aggression, Margot. You need to attack on those questions. You have to show you're hungry for it, do you understand?"

"I do want it."

"Why?"

Margot thinks of Jocelyn shaking when her power switches off, and how no one can tell them what's wrong with it. She thinks of how much faster she'd be able to get things done as Governor, without Daniel standing in her way.

"For my daughters," she says. "I want it to help Jos."

Alan frowns. "OK, then," he says. "Back to work."

★　★　★

Upstairs, Jos pulls the door closed, turns the handle so softly that even her mother couldn't hear it. "She'll be down there for hours," she says.

Ryan's sitting on the bed. He circles her wrist with his thumb and forefinger. Tugs at her to sit next to him. "Hours?" he says, and smiles.

Jos slants her shoulders one way, then the other. "She's got all this *stuff* to memorize. And Maddy's with Dad till the weekend." She puts her hand on his thigh. She makes slow circles with her thumb.

"Do you mind?" says Ryan. "That she's busy with all this stuff, I mean."

Jos shakes her head.

"I mean, is it weird," he says, "with the press and everything?"

She scratches at the fabric of his jeans with her nails. His breathing speeds up.

"You get used to it," she says. "Mom always says, our family is still private. Anything that happens behind closed doors is just between us."

"Cool," he says. He smiles. "I don't wanna be on the evening news is all."

And she finds that so adorable that she leans in and kisses him.

They've done this before, but it's still so new. And they've never done it before somewhere with a door, and a bed. She's been afraid that she'd hurt someone again; sometimes she can't stop thinking of that boy she put in hospital, the way the hairs on his arms crisped and how he held his ears like the sound was too loud. She's talked about all this with Ryan. He understands like no boy she's ever met before. They've talked about how they'll take their time and won't let it get out of control.

The inside of his mouth is so warm and so wet and his tongue is so slippery. He moans, and she can feel the thing starting to build up in her, but she's OK, she's done her breathing exercises, she knows she can control it. Her hands are on his back, and down past his belt, and his hands are tentative at first but then more confident, grazing the side of her breast, then his thumb on her neck and at her throat. She has a fizzing, popping feeling across her collar and a heavy ache between her legs.

He pulls away for a moment. Frightened, excited.

"I can feel it," he says. "Show it to me?"

She smiles, breathless. "Show me yours."

They're both laughing, then. She unbuttons her shirt, first button, second button, third. Down to just where the edge of her bra starts to be visible. He's smiling. He pulls off his sweater. Unbuttons the undershirt beneath it. One, two, three buttons.

He runs the tips of his fingers along her collarbone, where her skein is thrumming slightly under her skin, excited and ready. And she lifts her hand, touches his face.

He's smiling. "Go on."

She feels from the point of his collar along the bone. She cannot feel it at first. But then, there it is, faint but glittering. There's his skein, too.

★ ★ ★

212

They had met in the mall, that part was perfectly true. Jocelyn has learned enough from being raised in a politician's house to know that you never lie outright if you can avoid it. They'd *met* in the mall, because that's where they'd decided to meet. And they'd decided it in a private chatroom online, both of them looking for people like them. Weird people. People in whom the thing hadn't *taken* right, one way or the other.

Jocelyn had looked at the horrible UrbanDox site some stranger had emailed her, all about how this thing is the start of a holy war between men and women. UrbanDox had one blog post where he talked about sites for "deviants and abnormals". Jocelyn had thought, That's me. That's where I should go. Afterwards, she was amazed she hadn't thought of it before.

Ryan, from what they can tell, is even more rare than Jocelyn. He has a chromosomal irregularity; his parents have known about it since he was a few weeks old. Not all the boys like this grow skeins. Some of them died when their skeins tried to come in. Some of them have skeins that don't work. In any case, they keep it to themselves; there have been boys who've been murdered for showing their skein in other, harder parts of the world.

On some of those websites for deviants and abnormals, people are wondering what would happen if you got the women to *try* to wake the power up in men, if you taught them the techniques that are already being used in the training camps to strengthen the power in weaker women. Some of them are saying, Maybe more of us would have it if they *tried*. But most men aren't trying any more, if they ever did. They don't want to be associated with this. With *weirdness*. With chromosomal irregularity.

"Can you . . . do it?"

"Can *you?*" he says.

This is one of her good days. The power in her is even and measured. She can dole it out by the teaspoon. She sends a tiny portion into the side of him, not more than a jab in the ribs with an elbow. He makes a little sound. A noise of deliciousness. She smiles at him.

"Now you."

He takes her hand in his. He strokes the middle of her palm. And then he does it. He's not as controlled as she is, and his power is much weaker, but there it is. Jittering, the power growing and waning even over the three or four seconds he sustains it. But there.

She sighs, with the feeling of it. The power is very real. The feeling of it delineates the lines of the body very clearly. There is already so much porn of it. The single dependable human desire is very adaptable; what there is, in humans, is sexy. This, now, is what there is.

Ryan watches her face as he sends his power into her hand, his eyes eager. She makes a little gasp. He likes it.

When his power is spent — and he doesn't have much, he never has had — he lies back on her bed. She lies next to him.

"Now?" she says. "Are you ready?"

"Yes," he says. "Now."

And she touches his earlobe with the tip of one finger. Brings the crackle to him, until he is writhing and laughing and begging her to stop and begging her to carry on.

Jos quite likes girls. She quite likes boys who are a bit like girls. And Ryan was only a bus ride away; it was lucky. She messaged him privately. They met at the mall. They liked each other. They met two or three more times. Talked about it. Held hands. Made out. And she brought him back home. She thinks, I have a boyfriend. She looks at his skein; it's not pronounced at all, not like hers. She knows what some of the girls from NorthStar camp would say, but she finds it sexy. She places her lips to his collarbone and feels the vibration beneath the skin. She kisses her way along it. He is like her, but unlike her. She sticks her tongue between her teeth and licks him where he tastes like battery.

Downstairs, Margot is on to much-needed support for vulnerable seniors. She's using almost all of her attention to remember her lines. But a little part of her brain is still whirring over that question Alan asked her. Does she want it? Is she hungry for it? Why does she want it? She thinks of Jos and how she'd be able to help her if she had more power and influence. She thinks of the state and how she'd be able to change things for the better. But, as her fingers grip the cardboard podium and the charge begins to build across her collarbone almost involuntarily while she speaks, the real reason is that she can't stop thinking of the look she'd see on Daniel's face if she got it. She wants it because she wants to knock him down.

Roxy

Mother Eve had heard a voice saying: One day there'll be a place for the women to live freely. And now she's getting hundreds of thousands of hits from that new country where women had, until recently, been chained in basements on dirty mattresses. They're setting up new churches in her name, without her having had to send a single missionary or envoy. Her name means something in Bessapara; an email from her means even more.

And Roxy's dad knows people on the Moldovan border, he's been doing business with them for years. Not in flesh, that's a dirty trade. But cars, cigarettes, booze, guns, even a bit of art. Leaky border's a leaky border. With all the disruption recently, it's got leakier than ever.

Roxy says to her dad, "Send me to this new country. Bessapara. Send me there and I can get something going. I've got an idea."

"Listen," says Shanti. "You wanna try something new?"

There are eight of them, four women, four men, all mid-twenties, in the basement flat in Primrose Hill.

Bankers. One of the men already has his hand up one of the women's skirt, which Shanti could fucking do without.

She knows her audience, though. "Something new" is their rallying cry, their mating call, their 6 a.m. wake-up call with newspaper and organic pomegranate juice, because orange is so 1980s high glycaemic load. They love "something new" more than they love collateralized debt obligations.

"Free sample?" says one of the men, counting out the pills they've already bought. Checking he hasn't been cheated. Cunt.

"Uh-uh," says Shanti. "Not for you. This is strictly for the *ladies*."

There's a crowing, whistling cheer at that. She shows them a little dime bag of powder; it's white with a purplish sheen to it. Like snow, like frost, like the tops of mountains in some fancy fucking ski resort where these guys go on the weekends to drop £25 on a mug of hot chocolate and bang each other on endangered fur rugs in front of fires carefully constructed at 5 a.m. by underpaid chalet workers.

"Glitter," she says.

She licks the top of her index finger, dips it into the bag and picks up a few shining crystals. Opens her mouth and lifts her tongue to show them what she's doing. Rubs the powder into one of the thick blue veins at the base of the tongue. Offers the bag to the ladies.

The ladies dip in eagerly, scooping up great fingerfuls of whatever-it-is that Shanti's offering and rubbing it round their mouths. Shanti waits for them to feel it.

218

"Oh, wow!" says a systems analyst with a blunt bob — Lucy? Charlotte? They all have roughly the same name. "Oh, wow, oh God, I think I'm going to . . ." And she starts to crackle at the end of her fingertips. It's not enough to get her hurting anyone, but she's lost control a bit.

Usually, when you're drunk or stoned or high on most things, the power is damped down. A drunk woman might get off a jolt or two, but nothing you couldn't dodge if you weren't drunk too. This is different. This is calibrated. This is *designed* to enhance the experience. There's some coke cut in with it — that's already known to make the power more pronounced — and a couple of different kinds of uppers, along with the thing that gives it the purple glint, which Shanti's only ever seen post-cut. Something coming out of Moldova, she's heard. Or Romania. Or Bessapara. Or Ukraine. One of those. Shanti's got a bloke she deals with in a lock-up garage out towards the coast in Essex, and when this stuff started coming in she knew she could move it.

The women start laughing. They're loose-limbed and excited, leaning back, making high, low-powered arcs from one hand to another, or up to the ceiling. It'd feel nice to have them do one of those arcs on you. Shanti's got her girlfriend to take some and do it to her. Not painful, but fizzing, tickling at the nerve endings, like taking a shower in San Pellegrino. Which these fuckers probably do, anyway.

One of the men pays her in cash for four more bags. She charges them double — eight crisp fifties, don't get those from a hole in the wall — because they're dickheads. No one offers to walk her down to her car. When she lets herself out, two of them are already fucking, giggling, letting off starbursts with every thrust and jerk.

Steve's nervous, cos there's been a change in the security guards' rota. And it could be nothing, right, it could be some fucker's had a baby, some other fucker's got the shits. Then it all looks different from the outside even when it's entirely OK, and you'll be able to walk in just like normal and get your fucking hourglasses just like fucking normal.

The problem is, there's been a story in the paper. Not a big story, not page one. But page five in the *Mirror* and the *Express* and the *Daily* Fucking *Mail*, about this "new death drug" that's killing "young men with their whole lives ahead of them". It's in the paper, but there's no fucking law against it yet, not unless it's cut with something else. Which this stuff in the fucking hourglasses is. So fuck it. What's he going to do? Stand out here like a lemon, waiting to see if PC Plod is waiting by the docks? To see if those guards he hasn't ever had a chat or a drink with, see if one of those is a copper?

He pulls his cap down low over his eyes. He drives the van up to the gate.

"Yeah," he goes. "I've got boxes to pick up from container" — he stops to look up the number, even though he knows it like it's tattooed inside his fucking eyelids — "A-G-21-FE7-13859D?" There's a crackle on

220

the intercom. "Bloody hell," says Steve, trying to sound conversational, "these bloody numbers get longer every week, I tell you."

There's a long pause. If it was Chris or Marky or that bell-end Jeff in the gatehouse, they'd know him and let him in.

"Can you come up to the window, driver," says a woman's voice through the intercom. "We need to see your ID and pick-up forms."

Fuck.

So he drives round to the gatehouse — what else is he going to do? He's come through loads of times — most of those pick-ups are legitimate. He does a bit of import-export. Kids' toys for market-stall holders; has a little business, turns a handy profit, cash transactions a lot of it and not all on the books. He sits up nights making up names of stall holders he's sold to. Bernie Monke set him up with a stall himself down Peckham Market; he's down there on a Saturday to make the thing look legit, cos you don't want to get stupid. Nice toys, a lot of them: wooden, from Eastern Europe. And the hourglasses. Course they've never called him round the gatehouse when he's been shifting little wood robots held together with elastics, or them carved ducks on a string. They've got to fucking call him in for this.

There's a woman there he's never seen before. Big glasses on her face, halfway up her forehead and right down past the end of her nose. Owl glasses. Steve wishes he'd had a bit of something himself, just a little bit before he came out. Can't carry any in the van, it'd be stupid, they've got sniffer dogs. That's the good thing about these hourglasses, egg-timers. He didn't understand it when Bernie showed him. Bernie tipped the egg-timer thing over. The sand fell through golden and soft. Bernie said, "Don't be a muppet, what do you think's inside here? Sand?" Inside the glass, and that glass inside another glass tube. Double-sealed. Wash them all down with rubbing alcohol before they go in the boxes and Bob's your uncle, nothing for the sniffer dogs to get hold of. You'd have to smash one of those egg-timers open before the dogs could tell what it was.

"Paperwork?" she says, and he hands it over. He makes a joke about the fucking weather but she doesn't even crack a smile. She looks through the manifest. A couple of times she gets him to read out a word or a number to her, to make sure she's got it right. Behind her, he sees Jeff's face for a few moments against the security glass of the back door. Jeff makes a "sorry, mate" face and shakes his head at the back of the hard-arse woman. Fuck.

"Can you come with me, please?" She motions Steve towards a private office off to the side.

"What's the problem," Steve jokes to the world at large, although there's no one there, "can't get enough of me?"

Still doesn't smile. Fuck fuck fuck. There's something in the paperwork's made her suspicious. He's done it all himself, that paperwork; he knows it's right. She's heard something. She's been sent in by the narcs. She knows something.

She motions him to sit opposite her at the small table. She sits, too.

"What's this all about, love?" he says. "Only I'm due in Bermondsey in an hour and a half."

She grabs his wrist and puts her thumb to the place between the small bones, just where the hand joins the arm, and suddenly it's on fire. Flames inside his bones, the veins shrivelling, curling up, blackening. Fuck, she's going to pull his hand off.

"Don't say anything," she says. And he won't, he couldn't, not if he tried.

"Roxy Monke's taken over this business now. You know who she is? You know who her dad is? Don't say nothing, just nod."

Steve nods. He knows.

"You've been skimming, Steve."

He tries to shake his head, to gabble, No, no, no, you've got it wrong, it weren't me, but she presses the pain into his wrist so he thinks she's going to crack it open.

"Every month," she says, "just one or two of them egg-timers don't get listed on your books. You get me, Steve?"

He nods.

"And it stops now, right. Right now. Or you're out of the business. Understand?"

He nods. She lets him go. He cradles his wrist in his other hand. You can't even see on the skin that anything's happened to him.

"Good," she says, "cos we've got something special this month. Don't try to move it till you hear from us, OK?"

"Yeah," he says. "Yeah."

He drives off with eight hundred egg-timers neatly packaged up in boxes in the back of his van, all the paperwork correct, every carton accounted for. He doesn't take a look till he's back at his lock-up and he's taken the edge off the pain. Yeah. He can see it. There is something different. All the "sand" in these hourglasses is tinged with purple.

Roxy's counting money. She could get one of the girls to do it; they've already done it once and she could call someone in to count it up in front of her. But she likes doing it herself. Feeling the paper under her fingertips. Watching her decisions turn into maths turn into power.

Bernie's said to her more than once, "The day someone else knows where your money's going better than you do, that's the day you've lost." It's like a magic trick, money. You can turn money into anything. One, two, three, presto. Turn drugs into influence with Tatiana Moskalev, President of Bessapara. Turn your ability to bring pain and fear into a factory where the authorities will turn a blind eye to whatever you're cooking up there that sends purple-tinged steam into the skies at midnight.

Ricky and Bernie had had some ideas for what Roxy should do when she got home, fencing maybe, or one of the fronts up in Manchester, but she had an idea for Bernie that was bigger than anything he'd heard in a long time. She's known for a while now what to ask for to make her last the longest, and how to mix it up. Roxy sat on a hillside for days, off her face, trying out different combinations her dad's people had concocted for her approval. When they found it, they knew it. A purple crystal, as big as rock salt, fiddled about with by chemists and derived originally from the bark of the dhoni tree, which is native to Brazil but which grows pretty well here, too.

A snort of the full thing — pure Glitter — and Roxy could send a blast halfway across the valley. That's not what they ship: too dangerous, too valuable. They save the good stuff for private use, and maybe for the right bidder. What they're shipping is already cut. But they've done well. Roxy hasn't mentioned Mother Eve to her family, but it's because of the new churches that they've got seventy loyal women working on their production line already. Women who think they're doing the work of the Almighty, bringing power to Her children.

She tells Bernie the week's totals herself, every week. She does it in front of Ricky and Darrell if they're there; she doesn't care. She knows what she's doing. The Monke family are the sole suppliers of Glitter right now. They're printing money. And money can turn into anything.

On email, a private account bounced around a dozen servers, Roxy tells Mother Eve the weekly totals, too.

"Not bad," says Eve. "And you're keeping some back for me?"

"For you and yours," says Roxy. "Just like we agreed. You set us up here; you're making my fortune. You look after us and we'll look after you." She grins as she types it. She's thinking to herself, Take the whole thing; it belongs to you.

Five years to go

Margot

The candidate is puffing himself up in the mirror. He rolls his neck from side to side, he opens his mouth very wide and says, "Laaaa, la-la-la laaaa." He catches his own Caribbean Ocean-blue eye, smiles faintly and winks. He mouths at the mirror, "You've got this."

Morrison gathers his notes and, attempting not to meet the candidate's direct gaze, says, "Mr Dandon, Daniel, sir, you've got this."

The candidate smiles. "That's just what I was thinking, Morrison."

Morrison smiles back, thinly. "That's because it's true, sir. You're the incumbent. This belongs to you already."

It does a candidate good to think that there's some lucky-omen, stars-aligning thing going on. Morrison likes to pull these little tricks off if he can. That's what makes him good at his job. It's that kind of thing that makes it just that little bit more likely that his guy will beat the other guy.

The other guy is a gal, almost ten years younger than Morrison's candidate, hard-edged and hard-nosed, and they'd pushed her on that in the weeks of campaigning. I mean, she's divorced, after all, and with those two girls to raise, can a woman like that really find *time* for political office?

Someone had asked Morrison if he thought politics had *changed* since the — you know — since the Big Change. Morrison put his head to one side and said, "No, the key issues are still the same: good policies and good character and, let me tell you, our candidate has both," and so he went on, guiding the conversation back round to its safely railed-in scenic route past Mount Education and Healthcare Point via Values Boulevard and Self-Made-Man Gulley. But in the privacy of his own mind he admitted to himself that, yes, it had changed. If he'd allowed the odd voice in the centre of his skull operational control over his mouth, which he'd never do, he knew better than that, but if he'd said it, it would have said: They're waiting for something to happen. We're only pretending everything is normal because we don't know what else to do.

The candidates hit the floor like Travolta, ready with their moves, knowing that the spotlight is going to find them and illuminate every glistening thing: both sequins and sweat. She hits it out of the park with the first question, which is Defence. She's got her facts at her fingertips — she's been running that NorthStar project for years, of course, he should push her on that — but his guy's just not quite so easy with his comebacks.

"Come on," mouths Morrison at no one in particular, because the lights are too bright for the candidate to see him. "Come on. Attack."

232

The candidate stumbles over his answer, and Morrison feels it like a punch to the gut.

Second question and the third are on state-wide issues. Morrison's candidate sounds competent but boring, and that's a killer. By questions seven and eight she has him on the ropes again, and he doesn't fight back when she says he doesn't have the vision for the job. By this point, Morrison's wondering if it's possible for a candidate to lose so badly that some of the shit really will spray off on to him. It might seem as if he's been sitting around eating M&Ms and scratching his ass for the past few months.

They go into the long commercial break with nothing left to lose. Morrison escorts the candidate to the bathroom and helps him to a little nose powder. He goes through the talking points and says, "You're doing great, sir, really great, but you know . . . aggression's no bad thing."

The candidate says, "Now, now, I can't come across as *angry*," and Morrison grabs him right there in the stall, grabs him by the arm, and says, "Sir, do you want that woman to give you a pasting tonight? Think of your dad and what he'd want to see. Stand up for what he believed in, for the America *he* wanted to build. *Think*, sir, of how he would have handled this."

Daniel Dandon's father — who was a business bruiser with a borderline alcohol problem — died eighteen months ago. It's a cheap trick. Cheap tricks often work.

The candidate rolls his shoulders like a prize fighter, and they're back for the second half.

The candidate's a different man now, and Morrison doesn't know if it was the coke or the pep talk but, either way, he thinks, Well, I'm a hell of a guy.

The candidate comes out fighting on question after question. Unions? Boom. Minority rights? He sounds like the natural heir to the Founding Fathers, and she comes off as defensive. It's good. It's really good.

That's when Morrison and the audience notice something. Her hands are clenching and unclenching. As if she were trying to stop herself . . . but she can't be. It's impossible. She's been tested.

The candidate's on a roll now. He says, "And those subsidies — your own figures show that they're completely out of whack."

There's a noise from the audience, but the candidate takes it as a sign that they approve of his strong attack. He goes in for the kill.

"In fact, your policy is *not only* out of whack, it's forty years old."

She's passed her own test with flying colours. It can't be. But her hands are gripping the side of the podium, and she's saying, "Now, now, now, you can't just, now, now," as if she were pointing out every moment as it passed, but everyone can see what she's trying not to do. Everyone except the candidate.

The candidate goes for a devastating move.

"Of course, we can't expect *you* to, understand what this means for hard-working families. You've left your daughters to be raised by NorthStar day camps. Do you even care about those girls?"

That's enough, and her arm reaches out and her knuckles connect with his ribcage and she lets it go.

Only a tiny amount, really.

It doesn't even knock him over. He staggers, his eyes go wide, he lets out a gasp, he takes one, two, three steps back from his podium and wraps his arms around his midriff.

The audience have understood, both those live in the studio and the folks back home; everyone has watched and seen and understood what's happened.

The crowd in the studio go very silent, as if they were holding their breath, and then there's a bubbling, gathering, discordant, roiling murmur rising higher and higher.

The candidate tries to stumble on with his answer at the same moment that the moderator says they're taking a break and Margot's expression changes from the angry, nose-curling victory of aggression to the sudden fear that what she's done cannot be undone, in the same instant that the studio audience's rising bubble of anger and fear and incomprehension turns into a mighty wail, at the very same second that they cut to a commercial.

Morrison makes sure that the candidate comes back from the commercial break looking groomed and smooth and poised, but not too perfect, maybe just a little shocked and saddened.

They run a smooth campaign. Margot Cleary looks tired. Wary. She apologizes more than once over the next few days for what happened, and her guys give her a good line to play. She's just so passionate about the issues, she says. It was unforgivable, but it was only when she heard Daniel Dandon lie about her *daughters* that she lost control.

Daniel is statesmanlike about the whole thing. He takes the high ground. Some people, he says, find it tough to keep their composure in challenging situations and, although he admits his figures were mistaken, well, there's a right way and a wrong way to handle these things isn't there, Kristen? He laughs; she laughs and puts her hand over his. There certainly is, she says, and now we have to go to commercial; when we come back, can this cockatiel name every president since Truman?

The polling numbers say that people are, in general, appalled by Cleary. It is unforgivable, and immoral — well, it just speaks of poor judgement. No, they can't imagine voting for her. The day of the election, the numbers are looking strong and Daniel's wife starts looking over those plans to renovate the Governor's mansion arboretum. It's only after the exit polls that they start to think something might be wrong, and even then — I mean, they can't be *this* wrong.

But they can. It turns out the voters lied. Just like the accusations they always throw at hard-working public servants, the goddamned electorate turned out to be goddamned liars themselves. They said they respected hard work, commitment and moral courage. They said that the candidate's opponent had lost their vote the moment she gave up on reasoned discourse and calm authority. But when they went into the voting booths in their hundreds, and thousands, and tens of thousands, they'd thought, You know what, though, she's strong. She'd show them.

"In a stunning victory," says the blonde woman on the TV screen, "one which has shocked pundits and voters alike . . ." Morrison doesn't want to listen any more but can't make himself turn it off. The candidate is interviewed again — he's saddened that the voters of this great state did not choose to return him to office as their Governor, but he bows before their wisdom. That's good. Don't give reasons; never give reasons. They'll ask you why you think you lost, but never tell them, they're trying to back you into criticizing yourself. He wishes his opponent every success in office — and he'll be watching her every step of the way, ready to call her out if she forgets for a moment about the voters of this great state.

Morrison watches Margot Cleary on the screen — now the Governor of this great state — as she accepts her plaudits and says that she'll be a humble, hard-working public servant, grateful for the second chance she's been given. She also hasn't understood what's happened here. She thinks she needs to ask forgiveness, still, for the thing that brought her into office. She's wrong.

Tunde

"Tell me," says Tunde, "what it is you want."

One of the men on the protest line waggles his banner in the air. The banner reads: "Justice for men". The others give out a rattling, ragged cheer and fetch another round of brewskies from the cooler.

"What it says," one of them opines: "we want justice. It's the government did this, and the government has to put it right."

It's a slow afternoon, the air is syrupy and it's going to hit 104 in the shade out here. It is not the best day to be at a protest at a mall in Tucson, Arizona. He only came because he'd had an anonymous tip-off that something was going to happen here today. It had sounded pretty convincing, but it's panning out into nothing at all.

"Any of you guys involved with the internet at all? Badshitcrazy. com, BabeTruth, UrbanDox — any of that online stuff?"

The guys shake their heads.

"I saw an article in the newspaper," says one of them — a man who apparently decided to shave only the left half of his face this morning — "says that new country,

238

Bessapara, is chemically castrating all the men. That's what they're gonna do to all of us."

"I . . . don't think that's true," says Tunde.

"Look — I cut the piece out in the paper." The guy starts to rummage in his satchel. A bunch of old receipts and empty packets of chips tumble out on to the asphalt.

"Shit," he says, and chases after his litter. Tunde films him idly on his camera phone.

There are so many other stories he could be working on. He should have gone to Bolivia; they've proclaimed their own female Pope. The progressive government in Saudi Arabia is starting to look vulnerable to religious extremism; he could be back there doing a follow-up on his original story. There are even gossip stories more interesting than this: the daughter of a newly elected Governor in New England has been photographed with a boy — a boy, apparently, with a visible skein. Tunde's heard about this. He did a piece where he spoke to doctors about treating girls with skein deformations and problems. Not all girls have it; contrary to early thinking, about five girls in a thousand are born without. Some of the girls don't want it, and try to cut it out of themselves; one of them tried with scissors, the doctor said. Eleven years old. Scissors. Snipping at herself like a paper cut-out doll. And there are a few boys with chromosome irregularities who have it, too. Sometimes they like it, and sometimes they don't. Some boys ask the doctors if they can have theirs removed. The doctor has to tell them, no, they don't know how to do that. More than 50 per cent of the time, if a skein is severed, the person dies. They don't know why; it's not a vital organ. The current theory is that it is connected to the electrical rhythm of the heart and its removal disrupts something there. They can remove some of the strands of it, to make it less powerful, less noticeable, but, once you have it, you've got it.

Tunde tries to imagine what it'd be like to have one. A power you can't give away or trade. He feels himself yearning for it, repulsed by it. He reads online forums where men say that if all the men in the world had one everything would be back the way it ought to be. They're angry and afraid. He understands that. Since Delhi, he's been afraid, too. He joins UrbanDoxSpeaks.com under a pseudonym and posts a few comments and questions. He comes across a sub-forum discussing his own work. They call him a gender-traitor there because he did that story about Awadi-Atif rather than keeping it secret, and he's not reporting on the men's movement, and on their particular conspiracy theories. When he got the email saying something was going to happen here today he thought . . . he doesn't know what he thought. That maybe there was something here for him. Not just the news, but something that would explain a feeling he's having these days. But this is nothing. He's succumbed to fear is all it is; since Delhi, he's running away from the story, not towards it. He'll get online in his hotel this evening and see if there's still anything to report in Sucre, see when the next plane down is.

240

There is a sound like thunder. Tunde looks towards the mountains, expecting to see storm clouds. But it's not a storm, and it's not thunder. The sound comes again, louder, and a huge cloud of smoke erupts from the far end of the mall, and there's screaming.

"Shit," says one of the men with their beers and signs. "I think that's a bomb."

Tunde runs towards the sound, holding his camera very steady. There is a cracking sound, and he hears masonry falling. He rounds the building. The fondue-chain place is on fire. Several other units are collapsing. People are running from the building.

"There was a bomb," one of them says, directly into Tunde's camera lens, his face covered in brick dust, small cuts bleeding through his white shirt. "There are people trapped in there."

He likes this version of himself, the one who runs to get closer to danger, not away from it. Every time he does it, he thinks, Yes, good, this is still me. But that in itself is a new thought.

Tunde circles the wreckage. Two teenagers have fallen. He helps them up, encourages one to put her arm around the other for support, because her ankle is already blooming great blue bruises.

"Who did this?" she cries directly at the lens. "Who *did this*?"

That is the question. Someone has blown up a fondue restaurant, two shoe stores and a well-woman clinic. Tunde stands back from the building and takes a wide-angled shot. It's pretty impressive. To his right, the mall is on fire. To the left, the entire front of the building has come away. A whiteboard with shift allocations still attached to it crashes from the second floor to the ground while he films it. He zooms in. Kayla, 3.30–9p.m. Debra, 7 a.m.

Someone is crying out. Not far away, but hard to spot in the dust-on-dust — there is a pregnant woman trapped in the rubble. She is lying on her huge belly — she must be eight months gone — and a concrete pillar is trapping her leg. Something smells of gasoline. Tunde puts down the camera — safely, so that it's still recording — and tries to crawl a little closer to her.

"It's OK," he says, hopelessly. "Ambulances are coming. It's going to be OK."

She screams at him. Her right leg is crushed to bloody meat. She keeps trying to pull away from it, to kick back against the pillar. Tunde's instinct is to hold her hand. But she is discharging with great force every time she kicks against the pillar.

It is probably involuntary. Pregnancy hormones increase the magnitude of the power — perhaps a side effect of a number of biological changes during this time, although people say now, very simply, it's to protect the baby. There are women who've knocked their nurses clean out while giving birth. Pain and fear. These things whittle away control.

Tunde shouts out for help. There's no one nearby.

"Tell me your name," he says. "I'm Tunde."

She winces, and says, "Joanna."

"Joanna. Breathe with me," he says. "In" — he holds it for a count of five — "then out."

She tries. Grimacing, frowning, she breathes in and puffs it out.

"Help is coming," Tunde says. "They'll get you out. Breathe again."

In and out. Once more in, and out. The spasms are no longer jerking her body.

There's a creak in the concrete above them. Joanna tries to crane her neck around.

"What's happening?"

"It's just some strip lights." Tunde can see them dangling there by just a wire or two.

"It sounds like the roof is coming down."

"It's not."

"Don't leave me here, don't leave me alone under here."

"It's not coming down, Joanna. It's just the lights."

One of the fluorescent strips, dangling by a single wire, sways and snaps and crashes into the rubble. Joanna jerks and spasms again; even as Tunde is saying, "It's OK, it's OK." She's breaking again into that uncontrollable cycle of jolts and pain, she's struggling to pull herself out from under the pillar. Tunde is saying, "Please, please, breathe," and she's saying, "Don't leave me here. It's coming down."

She sends her power into the concrete. And a wire thread within the concrete connects with another, and another. A light bulb explodes in sparks. And a spark ignites that gasoline-smelling fluid that had been dripping. And there is fire, suddenly, all around her. She is still shouting as Tunde picks up his camera and runs.

★ ★ ★

243

That's the image they freeze on the screen. They've said there'd be upsetting images, after all. No one should be surprised to see this, but isn't it just terrible? Kristen's face is grim. I think anyone watching would agree that whoever did this is the scum of the earth.

In a letter to this news channel, a terrorist group calling itself Male Power has claimed responsibility for the attack, which destroyed a medical clinic catering to women's health issues alongside a busy mall in Tucson, Arizona. They claim the attack is only the first "day of action", intended to force the government to act against the so-called "enemies of man". A spokesperson for the office of the President has just completed a press conference, giving the strong message that the government of the United States does not negotiate with terrorists and that the claims of this "conspiracy-theory splinter group" are nonsense.

Well, now, what are they even protesting about, Tom? Tom scowls, just a micro-expression, before the practised face peels over the real one, the smile smooth as frosting on a cupcake. They want equality, Kristen. Someone's saying, cut to commercial in thirty in their earpieces, and Kristen's trying to wrap it up, but something's going on with Tom; he's not bringing this chat to a conclusion.

Well, Tom, there's no way to take this thing back now, they can't rewind time, although — smile — in our next segment, we'll be rewinding a little dance history to take you back to a craze called *swing*.

No, says Tom.

244

Commercial in ten, says a producer, very calm and level. These things happen; problems at home, stress, overwork, health anxiety, money worries — they've seen it all, really.

The CDC is hiding things from us, Tom says, that's what they're protesting. Have you seen some of that stuff online? Things are being kept from us, resources are being channelled in the wrong direction, there's no funding for self-defence classes or armour for men, and all this money going to those NorthStar girls' training camps, for God's sake — what the hell is that about? And fuck you, Kristen, we both know you've got this fucking thing, too, and it's changed you, it's made you hard; you're not even a real woman any more. Four years ago, Kristen, you knew what you were and what you had to offer this network, and what the fuck are you now?

Tom knows they went to commercial a long time ago now. Probably just after he said "no". Probably they thought a few seconds of dead air was better than this. He sits very still after he's finished, looking straight ahead, into the eye of camera three. That's always been his favourite camera, shows off the angle of his chin, the little dimple there. He's Kirk Douglas, almost, on camera three. He is Spartacus. He always thought he could get into acting eventually, just small parts to start with; maybe at first he'd be playing a news anchor, and then something like the teacher in a high-school comedy who turns out to understand the kids better than any of them realized because you know he was pretty wild too way back when. Well, that's all over now. Let it go, Tom, let those thoughts go from your mind.

You done? says Kristen.

Sure.

They get him out before they come back off commercial. He doesn't even resist, except that he doesn't like that hand on his shoulder and fights it off. He can't bear a hand touching him, he says, so they let him be. He's worked for a long time, and if he goes easy now his pension might still be secure.

Tom's been taken sick, very sadly, says Kristen, bright eyes earnest down camera two. He's OK, and he'll be back with us real soon. And now, the weather on the ones.

From his hospital bed in Arizona, Tunde watches the reports of the story unfold. He emails and Facebooks with his family and friends back in Lagos. His sister, Temi, is dating a boy now, someone a couple of years younger than her. She wants to know if Tunde has a girl out there in all this travelling.

Tunde tells her there's not much time for that. There had been a white woman for a while, another journalist who he'd met in Singapore and travelled with as far as Afghanistan. She's not worth mentioning.

"Come home," says Temi. "Come home for six months and we'll find you a nice girl. You're twenty-seven, man. Getting old! It's time to settle down."

The white woman — her name was Nina — had said, "Do you think you have PTSD?"

It was because she'd used her thing in bed and he'd shied away from it. Told her to stop. Started crying.

He'd said, "I am stranded a long way from home and there is no way to get back."

"We all are," she'd said.

Nothing worse has happened to him than to anyone. There is no reason for him to be afraid, no more reason than any other man. Nina's been texting him since he's been in hospital, asking if she can come and see him. He keeps saying, no, not yet.

It's while he's in hospital that the email comes in. Just five short lines, but the sender address is right; he checks it hasn't been spoofed.

From: info@urbandoxspeaks.com
To: olatundeedo@gmail.com

We saw your reporting from the mall in Arizona, we read your essay about what happened to you in Delhi. We are on the same side; we're on the side of all men. If you've seen what happened in the Cleary election, you've understood what we're fighting for. Come and talk to us, on the record. We want you on our team.

UrbanDox

It's not even a question. There's still his book to be written; *the* book, those nine hundred pages of chronicle and explanation. He has it all with him on his laptop all the time. There's no question about this. A meeting with UrbanDox? Of course he will.

The theatrics around it are ridiculous. He can't bring his own equipment. "We'll give you a phone to record the interview," they tell him. For God's sake. "I understand," he writes back. "You can't compromise your position." They like that. It feeds into their sense of who they are. "You're the only one we trust," they say. "You tell the truth. You have seen the chaos for what it is. You were invited to the action in Arizona and you came. You are the one we want." The way they talk is positively messianic. "Yes," he emails back. "I have wanted to talk to you for a long time."

Of course, there's a meeting point in the parking lot of a Denny's. Of course there is. Of course, there's a blindfold ride in a jeep and men wearing black — all white men — with balaclavas over their faces. These are men who've watched too many movies. This has become a thing now: men's movie clubs, in living rooms and back rooms of bars. Watching particular kinds of movie over and over again: the ones with explosions and helicopter crashes and guns and muscles and punching. Guy flicks.

After all this, when they take off his blindfold, he's in a storage locker. It's dusty. There's someone's old boxes of VHS cassettes labelled "A-Team" in the corner. And there's UrbanDox, sitting in a chair, smiling.

He looks different to his profile pictures. He's in his mid-fifties. He's bleached his hair so that it's very pale, almost white. His eyes are a pallid, watery blue. Tunde's read some things about this man; there was, by all accounts, a terrible childhood, violence, racial hatred. There was a string of failed businesses, leaving dozens of people owed thousands of dollars each. There was, eventually, a night-school law degree and a reinvention as a blogger. He's well-built for a man of his age, though his face is faintly grey. The great change in the tide of things has been good for UrbanDox. He'd been blogging his mean-spirited, semi-literate, bigoted, angry rhetoric for years but, recently, more and more people — men and, indeed, some women — have started to listen. He's denied over and over again being tied to the violent splinter groups that have bombed shopping malls and public parks in half a dozen states now. But, if he's not linked to them, they like to link themselves to him. One of the recent accurate bomb threats contained simply an address, a time and the web address of UrbanDox's latest screed on the Coming Gender War.

He's softly spoken. His voice is more high-pitched than Tunde was expecting. He says, "You know they're going to try to kill us."

Tunde has said to himself, Just listen. He says, "Who's trying to kill us?"

UrbanDox says, "The women."

Tunde says, "Aha. Tell me more about that."

A sly smile spreads over the man's face. "You've read my blog. You know what I think."

"I'd like to hear it in your own words. On tape. I think people would like to hear it. You think the women are trying to kill —"

"Oh, I don't think, son, I know. None of this is an accident. They talk about 'Guardian Angel', that stuff that got into the water supply, and how it built up in the water table? They say no one could have predicted it? Phooey. Bullcrap. This has been planned. This was decided on. After the end of the Second World War, when the peaceniks and do-gooders had the upper hand, they *decided* to put this stuff in the water. They thought men had had their turn and we'd messed it up — two world wars in two generations. Pussy-whipped betas and faggots, all of them."

Tunde's read this theory before. You can't have a good conspiracy plot without any conspirators. He's only surprised that UrbanDox hasn't mentioned Jews.

"The Zionists used the concentration camps as emotional blackmail to get the stuff shipped out in the water."

There we go.

"It was a declaration of war. Silent, stealthy. They armed their warriors before they sounded the first battle cry. They were among us before we even knew we'd been invaded. Our own government has the cure, you know, they've got it under lock and key, but they won't use it except on the precious few. And the endgame . . . you know the endgame. They hate us all. They want us all dead."

Tunde thinks of the women he's known. Some of the journalists he was in Basra with, some of the women from the siege in Nepal. There have been women, these past years, who have put their bodies between him and harm so he could take his footage out to the world.

250

"They don't," he says. Shit. That was not what he meant to do.

UrbanDox laughs. "They've got you right where they want you, son. Under the thumb. Believing their crap. Bet a woman's helped you once or twice, right? She's taken care of you, she's looked after you, she protected you when you were in trouble."

Tunde nods, warily.

"Well, shit, of course they do that. They want us docile and confused. Old army tactic; if you're only ever an enemy, the people will know to fight you wherever they see you. If you hand out candy to the kids and medicine to the weak, you jumble their minds up, they don't know how to hate you. See?"

"Yes, I see."

"It's starting already. Have you seen the numbers on domestic violence against men? On murders of men by women?"

He has seen those numbers. He carries them with him like a lozenge of ice lodged in his throat.

"That's how it starts," says UrbanDox. "That's how they soften us up, make us weak and afraid. That's how they have us where they want us. It's all part of a plan. They're doing it because they've been told to."

Tunde thinks, No, that's not the reason. The reason is because they can. "Are you being funded," he says, "by the exiled King Awadi-Atif of Saudi Arabia?"

UrbanDox smiles. "There are a lot of men out there who are worried about where this thing is heading, my friend. Some of them are weak, traitors to their gender and their people. Some of them think the women will be kind to them. But a lot of them know the truth. We haven't had to go begging for money."

"And you said . . . the endgame."

UrbanDox shrugs. "Like I say. They want to kill us all."

"But . . . the survival of the human race?"

"Women are just animals," says UrbanDox. "Just like us, they want to mate, reproduce, have healthy offspring. One woman, though, she's pregnant for nine months. She can care for maybe five or six kids well across her life."

"So . . .?"

UrbanDox frowns, like this is the most obvious thing in the world. "They'll only keep the most genetically healthy of us alive. See, this is why God meant men to be the ones with the power. However bad we treat a woman — well, it's like a slave."

Tunde feels his shoulders tighten. Say nothing, just listen, take the footage, use it and sell it. Make money out of this scumbag, sell him out, show him up for what it is.

"See, people got slavery wrong. If you have a slave, that slave's your property, you don't want damage to come to it. However bad any man treated a woman, he needs her in a fit condition to carry a child. But now . . . one genetically perfect man can sire a thousand — five thousand — children. And what do they need the rest of us for? They're going to kill us all. Listen to me. Not one in a hundred will live. Perhaps not one in a thousand."

"And your evidence for that is . . ."

"Oh, I've seen documents. And more than that, I can use my brain. So can you, son. I've watched you; you're smart." UrbanDox lays a moist, clammy hand on Tunde's arm. "Join us. Become part of what we're doing. We'll be there for you, son, when all these others have gone away, because we're on the same side."

Tunde nods.

"We need laws now to protect men. We need curfews on women. We need the government to release all the funding they need to 'research' that cure. We need men to stand up and be counted. We are being ruled by fags who worship women. We need to cut them down."

"And that's the purpose of your terror attacks?"

UrbanDox smiles again. "You well know that I have never initiated or encouraged a terror attack."

Yes, he's been very careful.

"But," says UrbanDox, "if I were in touch with any of those men, I'd guess they'd barely gotten started. A bunch of weapons got lost in the fall of the Soviet Union, you know. Real nasty stuff. Could be they have some of that."

"Wait," says Tunde. "Are you threatening to orchestrate domestic terrorism with *nuclear weapons*?"

"I'm not threatening anything," says UrbanDox, his eyes pale and cold.

Allie

"Mother Eve, will you give me your blessing?"

The boy is sweet. Fluffy, blond hair, a freckled, creamy face. He can't be more than sixteen. His English is prettily accented with the mid-European tones of Bessapara. They've picked a good one.

Allie is only just on twenty herself and, although she has an air to her — an *old soul*, the piece in the New *York Times* reported several celebrity acolytes saying — there's still that danger that she doesn't always look to have quite the *gravitas* needed.

The young are close to God, they say, and young women, especially. Our Lady was only sixteen years old when she bore her sacrifice into the world. Still, it's often as well to start with a blessing of someone who looks definitively *younger*.

"Come close," says Allie, "and tell me your name."

The cameras push in on the blond boy's face. He is already crying and shaking. The crowd is mostly quiet; the sound of thirty thousand people breathing is broken only by the occasional shout of "Praise the Mother!", or simply "Praise Her!"

The boy says, very quietly, "Christian."

There's a sound at that, an indrawn breath around the stadium.

"That is a very good name," says Allie. "Don't fear that it's not a good name."

Christian is all sobs. His mouth is open and wet and dark.

"I know this is hard," says Allie, "but I am going to hold your hand, and when I do the peace of Our Mother will enter into you, do you understand?"

There is a magic in this, in telling what will happen, in saying it with full conviction. Christian nods again. Allie takes his hand. The camera holds steady for a moment on the pale hand clasped in the darker. Christian steadies. His breathing becomes more even. When the image pulls out, he is smiling, calm, even poised.

"Now, Christian, you haven't been able to walk since you were a child, have you?"

"No."

"What happened?"

Christian motions to his legs, lumpen underneath the blanket swaddling the lower half of his body. "I fell off a swing," he says, "when I was three. I broke my back." He smiles, full of trust. He makes a motion with his hands, as if he were breaking a pencil between his fingers.

"You broke your back. And the doctors have told you you'll never walk again, that's right, isn't it?"

Christian nods, slowly. "But I know I will," he says, his face peaceful.

"I know you will, too, Christian, because the Mother has shown it to me."

And the people who curate these events for her and make sure that the nerve damage isn't too severe for her to be able to do anything. Christian had a friend from the same hospital; a nice kid, even more of a believer than Christian himself, but, unfortunately, the break was too profound for them to be sure she'd be able to cure it. Besides, he wasn't right for this televised segment. Acne.

Allie lays her palm at the top of Christian's spine, just at the back of his neck.

He shudders; the crowd gasps and goes silent.

She says in her heart: What if I can't do it this time?

The voice says: Kid, you always say that. You're golden.

Mother Eve speaks from Allie's mouth. She says: "Holy Mother, guide me now, as you have always guided me."

The crowd says, "Amen."

Mother Eve says: "Not my will, Holy Mother, but Thine be done. If it is Your will to heal this child, let him be healed, and if it be Your will that he suffer in this world to reap a great harvest in the next, let that be done."

This is an exceedingly important caveat, which it's as well to get in early.

The crowd says, "Amen."

Mother Eve says, "But there's a great multitude praying for this humble and obedient young boy, Holy Mother. There's a great crowd here pleading with you now, yearning for Your grace to fall upon him and Your breath to raise him up as You raised up Mary for Your service. Holy Mother, listen to our prayers."

The crowd is full of people rocking back and forth on their heels and weeping and muttering, and the simultaneous translators at either side of the stadium are racing to keep up with Allie, as Mother Eve's words spill from her faster and faster.

While her mouth is moving, Allie's tendrils of power are probing Christian's spine, feeling out the blockage *here* and *here*, and where a boost would get his muscles moving. She almost has it.

Mother Eve says, "As we've all lived blessed lives, as we all strive every day to listen to Your voice inside us, as we all honour our own mothers and the sacred light inside every human heart, as we all worship You and adore You and love You and kneel before You. Holy Mother, please, take the force of our prayers. Please, Holy Mother, use me to show your glory and *heal this boy now!*"

The crowd roars.

Allie delivers three swift pinpricks to Christian's spine, flicking the nerve cells around the muscles of his legs into life.

His left leg swings up, kicking at the blanket.

Christian looks at it bemused, startled, a little afraid.

The other leg kicks.

He's crying now, tears pouring down his face. This poor kid, who hasn't walked or run since he was three years old. Who's suffered the bedsores and the muscle wasting, who's had to use his arms to carry himself

257

from bed to chair, chair to toilet. His legs are moving from the thigh now, jerking and kicking.

He levers himself up from the chair with his arms now, his legs still twitching and — holding on to the rail put there for the purpose — he walks one, two, three stiff and awkward steps before clinging there, upright and weeping.

Some of Mother Eve's people come to take him off stage, one on either side of him, and he's saying, "Thank you, thank you, thank you," as they lead him away.

Sometimes, it sticks. There are cases of people she's "cured" who are still walking, or holding things, or seeing months later. There is even starting to be some scientific interest in what it might be she's actually doing.

Sometimes, it doesn't stick at all. They have a moment on stage. They feel what it's like to walk, or pick something up with a dead arm and, after all, that's something they wouldn't have had without her.

The voice says: You never know; if they had more faith, maybe it would have stuck around longer.

Mother Eve says to those she helps, "God has shown you a taste of what She can do. Just keep praying."

They take a little interlude after the healing. So that Allie can get a glass of something cold behind the stage, and to bring the crowd down a little from its fever pitch and remind them that all this has been funded by good people like them who opened their hearts and their wallets. On the big screens, they show a video of the good works done by the Church. The screens show

258

Mother Eve giving comfort to the sick. There's a video — it's an important one — of her holding the hand of a woman who was beaten and abused but whose skein never came in. She's crying. Mother Eve tries to wake up the power inside her but, though she prays for help, the power won't come to this poor woman. That's why they're looking into transplants, she says, from cadavers. They have teams working on it already. Your money can help.

There are friendly messages of greeting from chapter houses in Michigan and Delaware with news of saved souls, and from missions in Nairobi and Sucre, where the Catholic Church is eating itself alive. And there are videos of the orphanages Mother Eve's set up. At first, there were girls set loose by their families, wandering, confused and alone, like shivering stray dogs. As Mother Eve's power grew, she said to the older women, "Take in the younger. Set up homes for them, as I was taken in when I was weakened and afraid. The least you do for them, you do for our own Holy Mother." Now, a scant few years later, there are homes for young people all over the world. They take in young men and young women, too; they give them shelter; they give them better outcomes than state-run facilities. Allie, passed from pillar to post throughout her life, knows how to give good instruction in this matter. In the video, Mother Eve is visiting homes for abandoned children in Delaware and in Missouri, in Indonesia and in Ukraine. Each group of girls and boys greets her as mother.

259

The video ends on a musical trill, and Allie wipes the sweat off her face and goes back outside.

"Now, I know," says Mother Eve to the crowd, full of crying, shaking, shouting people, "I know there's been a question in some of your minds for these long months, and that is why I'm so happy to be here today to answer your questions."

There's another round of shouts and "Praise!" from the crowd.

"To be here in Bessapara, the land where God has shown Her wisdom and Her mercy, is a great blessing to me. For you know that Our Lady has told me that women are to gather together! And to perform great wonders! And to be a blessing and a consolation to each other! And" — she pauses after each word for emphasis — "where have women gathered together more than *here*?"

Stamping, hollering, whoops of delight.

"We've shown what the power of a mighty crowd praying together can do for that young man Christian, haven't we? We've shown that the Holy Mother cares for men and women alike. She doesn't withhold Her mercy. She won't send Her goodness just to the women, but to anyone who believes in Her." She makes her voice soft and low. "And I know some of you have been asking, 'What about the Goddess who's meant so much to you all? What about She whose symbol is the eye in the palm of the hand? That simple faith that sprang up from the soil in this good country, what about that?'"

Allie allows the crowd to go very quiet. She stands with her arms folded in front of her chest. There's weeping and rocking among the people gathered here. There's waving of banners. She waits a good long while, breathing in and out.

She says in her heart: Am I ready?

The voice says: You were made for this, child. Preach it.

Allie unfolds her arms and holds her palms up to face the audience. In the centre of each one is tattooed an eye, with the tendrils extending out.

The crowd explodes in screams and cheers and stamping of feet. The men and women in the audience surge forward and Allie feels grateful for the crash-barriers and the ambulance people standing in the aisles. They're climbing over seats to get closer to her, they're panting and sobbing, they're breathing in her breath, they want to eat her alive.

Mother Eve speaks calmly over the din. She says, "All gods are one God. Your Goddess is another way that the One has expressed Herself in the world. She came to you as She came to me, preaching compassion and hope, teaching vengeance against those who have wronged us and love for those who are close to us. Your Goddess is Our Lady. They are one."

Behind her, the rippling silk curtain that has stood as a backdrop to the event all evening falls gently to the ground. It reveals a painting, twenty feet high, of a proud, buxom woman in blue, her eyes kind, the skein prominent across her collarbone, an all-seeing eye in the palm of each hand.

Several people faint at that moment, and some begin speaking in tongues.

Good work, says the voice.

I like this country, says Allie in her heart.

On her way out of the building towards the armoured car, Allie checks her messages from Sister Maria Ignacia, her trusted and loyal friend at home. They've been following the chatter online about "Alison Montgomery-Taylor", and although Allie's never acknowledged *why* she wants the files on that case to disappear, she asked Sister Maria Ignacia if she could somehow make it happen. It will just get harder as the months and years go on, there's always going to be someone wanting to make money or influence out of this story, and although Allie thinks any reasonable court would acquit her, there's just no need to go through it. It's late at night in Bessapara, but it's only 4p.m. on the East Coast and — thankfully — there's a message. Some loyal members of the New Church back in Jacksonville have sent one saying that, with the help of an influential sister-in-God, all the documentation and electronic files relating to this "Alison Montgomery-Taylor" will be dealt with.

The email says, "Everything will disappear."

It seems like a prophecy, or a warning.

The email doesn't name the influential sister-in-God, but there's only one woman Allie can think of who could make police files disappear just like that, just by making a phone call maybe, just by making one call to someone she knows. It must be Roxy. "You look after us, and we'll look after you," she'd said. Well, good. Everything will disappear.

Later, Allie and Tatiana Moskalev eat a late supper. Even with the war, even with fighting on the northern front with the Moldovan troops and the stand-off in the East with Russia herself, even still the food is pretty good. President Moskalev of Bessapara lays on roast pheasant and Hasselback potatoes with sweet cabbage for Mother Eve of the New Church, and they toast each other in good red wine.

"We need a fast victory," says Tatiana.

Allie chews slowly and thoughtfully. "Can you have a fast victory three years into a war?"

Tatiana laughs. "The real war hasn't even begun yet. They're still fighting with conventional weapons up there in the hills. They try to invade, we push them back. They throw grenades, we shoot."

"Electrical power's no use against missiles and bombs."

Tatiana sits back, crosses one leg over the other. Looks at her. "Do you think so?" She frowns, amused. "For one: wars aren't won by bombs, they're won on the ground. And for two: have you seen what a full dose of that drug can do?"

Allie has seen it. Roxy showed her. It's hard to control — Allie wouldn't want to take it; control has always been her speciality — but a full dose of the Glitter, and three or four women could take down the electricity of the island of Manhattan.

"You still have to be near enough to touch them. Make a connection."

"There are ways to arrange that. We've seen photographs of them working on it themselves."

Ah, says the voice, she's talking about that exiled King of Saudi Arabia.

"Awadi-Atif," says Allie.

"He's just using our country as a trial, you know." Tatiana swallows down another gulp of wine. "They're sending in some of their men in rubber suits with their stupid battery packs on their backs. He wants to show that the change means nothing. He still holds to his old religion and he thinks he's getting his country back."

Tatiana makes a long arc between her left palm and her right, spools it out idly, winds it back and breaks it with a snap. "The hairdresser," she says with a smile, "didn't know what she was starting." She looks directly at Allie, a sudden, intense stare. "Awadi-Atif thinks he's been sent on a holy war. And I think he's right. I was chosen by God for this."

She wants you to tell her she was, says the voice. Tell her.

"You were," says Allie, "God has a special mission for you."

"I have always believed there was something greater than me, something better. And when I saw you. The force in the way you speak to the people. I see that you are Her messenger, and you and I have met at this time for this reason. To bring this message to the world."

The voice says: Didn't I tell you I had some things in store for you?

264

Allie says, "So when you say you want a fast victory . . . you mean that when Awadi-Atif sends down his electric troops, you want to destroy them utterly."

Tatiana waves a hand. "I have chemical weapons. Left over from Cold War. If I wanted to 'destroy them utterly' I could do it. No" — she leans forward — "I want to humiliate them. Show that this . . . mechanical power cannot compare with what we have in our bodies."

The voice says: Do you see it?

And Allie does see it suddenly and all at once. Awadi-Atif of Saudi Arabia has armed the troops in North Moldova. They plan to retake Bessapara, the republic of the women; for them, this would show that this change is merely a minor deviation from the norm, that the right way will reassert itself. And if they lose, and lose utterly . . .

Allie begins to smile. "The Holy Mother's way will spread across the world, from person to person, from country to country. The thing will be over before it's begun."

Tatiana raises her glass for a toast. "I knew you would see it. When we invited you here . . . I hoped you would understand what I mean. The world is watching this war."

She wants you to bless her war, says the voice. Tricky.

Tricky if she loses, says Allie in her heart.

I thought you wanted to be safe, says the voice.

You told me I couldn't be safe unless I owned the place, says Allie in her heart.

And I told you that you couldn't get there from here, says the voice.

Whose side are you on, anyway? says Allie.

Mother Eve speaks slowly and carefully. Mother Eve measures her words. Nothing that Mother Eve says is without consequence. She looks directly into the camera and waits for the red light to flash on.

"We don't have to ask ourselves what the Saudi Royal Family will do if they win this war," she says. "We've already seen it. We know what happened in Saudi Arabia for decades, and we know that God turned Her face from it in horror and disgust. We don't have to ask ourselves who is on the side of justice when we meet the brave fighters of Bessapara — many of whom were trafficked women, shackled women, women who would have died alone in the dark if God had not sent Her light to guide them.

"This country," she says, "is God's country, and this war is God's war. With Her help, we shall have a mighty victory. With Her help, everything will be overturned."

The red light blinks off. The message goes out across the world. Mother Eve and her millions of loyal followers on YouTube and Instagram, on Facebook and Twitter, her donors and her friends, are with Bessapara and the republic of the women. They've made their choice.

Margot

"I'm not saying you have to break up with him."

"Mom, that is what you're saying."

"I'm just saying read the reports, see for yourself."

"If you're giving them to me, I already know what's in them."

"Just read them."

Margot gestures to the pile of papers on the coffee table. Bobby did not want to have this conversation. Maddy's out at tae kwon do practice. So it's up to her, of course. Bobby's exact words had been, "It's your political career you're worried about. So you handle it."

"Whatever those papers say, Mom, Ryan's a good person. He's a kind person. He's good to *me*."

"He's been on extremist sites, Jos. He posts under a false name on sites that talk about organizing terror attacks. That have links with some of those groups."

Jocelyn is crying now. Frustrated, angry tears. "He'd never *do* that. He probably just wanted to see what they were saying. Mom, we met online, we both go to some crazy sites."

Margot picks up one of the pages at random, reads out the highlighted section. "'Buckyou — nice name he's picked there — says, 'Things have gotten out of hand. Those NorthStar camps for one thing — if people knew what they were learning there, we'd put a bullet in every girl in the place.'" She pauses, looks at Jocelyn.

Jos says, "How do they even know that's him?"

Margot waves at the thick file of documents. "Oh, I don't know. They have their ways." This is the tricky part. Margot holds her breath. Will Jos buy it?

Jos looks at her, lets out one quick sob. "The Department of Defence is vetting you, isn't it? Because you're going to be a senator, and they want you on the Defence Committee, like you told me."

Hook, line and sinker.

"Yes, Jocelyn. That is why the FBI found this stuff. Because I have an important job, and I'm not going to apologize for that." She pauses. "I thought we were in this together, honey. And you need to know that this Ryan's not what you think."

"He was just trying something out, probably. Those things are from three years ago! We all say stupid stuff online, OK? Just to get a reaction."

Margot sighs. "I don't know if we can be sure of that, honey."

"I'll talk to him. He's . . ." Jos starts crying again, loud, long, deep sobs.

Margot scoots towards her on the couch. Puts a tentative arm around Jos's shoulders.

Jos sinks into her, burying her face in Margot's chest and crying and crying just like she did when she was a child.

"There'll be other boys, honey. There'll be other, better boys."

Jos lifts her face. "I thought we were supposed to be together."

"I know, sweetheart, because of your . . ." Margot hesitates over the word: "because of your problem, you wanted someone who'd understand."

She wishes they'd been able to find help for Jos. They're still looking, but the older she gets, the more intractable the problem seems to be. Sometimes she has all the power she wants, and sometimes nothing.

Jos's sobs slow to a trickle. Margot brings her a cup of tea, and they sit in silence for a while on the couch, Margot's arm around Jos.

After a long while, Margot says, "I still think we can find some help for you. If we could find someone to help you . . . well, you'd just be able to like normal boys."

Jos puts her cup down on the table slowly. She says, "Do you really think so?"

And Margot says, "I know it, honey. I know it. You can be just like all the other girls. I know we can fix it for you."

This is what it means to be a good mother. Sometimes you can see what your kids need better than they can.

Roxy

"Come home," says the message. "Ricky's been hurt."

She's supposed to be going to Moldova, supposed to be training women in how to use the Glitter to fight. But she can't, not with a message like that on her phone.

She's stayed out of Ricky's way mostly, since she got back from America. She's got her own thing with the Glitter, and it's making them good money. Roxy used to long to be invited into that house. Bernie's given her a key now, she's got a guest bedroom for when she's not out at the Black Sea, but it's not what she thought it'd be. Barbara, the mother of the three boys, hasn't been right since Terry died. There's a big photo of Terry on the mantelpiece with fresh flowers in front of it, changed every three days. Darrell's still living there. He's taking on the betting, because he's got the brain for it. Ricky's got his own place up in Canary Wharf.

Roxy thinks, when she reads that text, of the different firms that could have it in for them, and what "hurt" means. If it's war, they need her home for sure.

But it's Barbara who's waiting for her in the front garden when she gets there, smoking non-stop, lighting the next one from the embers of the last. Bernie's not even home. So it's not war, it's something else.

Barbara says, "Ricky's been hurt."

Roxy says, knowing the answer, "Was it one of the other firms? That Romanian lot?"

Barbara shakes her head. She says, "They fucked him up for fun."

Roxy says, "Dad knows people. You didn't need to call me."

Barbara's hands are shaking. "No, it's not for them. It's a family thing."

So Roxy knows exactly what kind of thing has happened to Ricky.

Ricky's got the TV on, but the sound's off. There's a blanket over his knees and bandages under that; doctor's been and gone, so there's nothing to see, anyway.

Roxy's got girls working for her who were held by blokes in Moldova. She saw what one of them had done to the three men who'd taken turns with her. Down there it was just burned flesh, fern patterns on the thighs, pink and brown and raw red and black. Like a Sunday roast. Ricky doesn't seem that bad. He'll probably be fine. This kind of thing heals. She's heard that things can be difficult afterwards, though. It can be hard to get over.

She says, "Just tell me what happened."

Ricky looks at her, and he's grateful, and his gratitude is terrible. She wants to hug him, but she knows that'd just make it worse for him somehow. You can't be the one that hurts and the one that comforts. She can't give Ricky anything but justice.

He tells her what happened.

He was pissed, obviously. Out with some mates, dancing. He's got a couple of girlfriends, Ricky, but he never minds finding someone new for the night, and the girls know not to bother him about it, that's just how he is. Roxy's the same these days; sometimes there's a bloke and sometimes there isn't, and it doesn't matter much to her either way.

This time, Ricky got three girls, said they were sisters — but they didn't look like sisters; he thinks it was a joke. One of them sucked him off by the kitchen bins outside the club; whatever she did, it made his head spin. He looks ashamed when he says it, like he thinks he should have done something different. When she was finished, the others were waiting. And he went, "Give me a minute, girls. Can't do you all at once." And they were on him.

There's a thing you can do to a bloke. Roxy's done it herself. A little bit of a spark in the back passage and up he comes, neat as anything. It's fun, if you want it. Hurts a bit, but fun. Hurts a lot if you don't want it. Ricky kept on saying he didn't want it.

They took their turns on him. They were just trying to hurt him, he says, and he was saying, did they want money, what did they want, but one of them got him in the throat and he couldn't make another sound until they were finished.

The whole thing took half an hour. Ricky thought he might die there. In between the black bags and the

272

thick grease coating the paving stones. He could see them finding his body, white legs marked with red scars. He could see a copper turning out his pockets and saying, "You'll never guess who this is, only Ricky Monke." And his face fish-white and his lips blue. Ricky kept very still until it was over, and didn't say nothing and didn't do nothing. Just waited for it to be done.

Roxy knows why they haven't called Bernie home. He'd hate Ricky for this, even if he tried not to. This is not what happens to a man. Except now it is.

The stupid thing is that he does know them. The more he thinks about it, the more he's sure. He's seen them around; he doesn't think they know who he is — you'd think they'd've been scared otherwise, to do what they did — but he knows people he's seen them with. One of them's called Manda, he's pretty sure, one of them's Sam. Roxy gets an idea, looks at a couple of people on Facebook. Shows him some photos, until he starts to shake.

It's not hard to find them. It doesn't take Roxy more than five phone calls to someone who knows someone who knows someone. She doesn't say why she's asking, but she doesn't need to; she's Roxy Monke and people want to help her. They're drinking in a pub in Vauxhall, they're tanked up, they're laughing, they'll be here till closing.

Roxy's got some good girls here in London now. Girls who run the business for her, and collect the profits, and knock the heads together that need knocking. It's not that a bloke couldn't do the job —

some of them'd do it handy — but it's better if they don't *need* a gun. They're noisy, draw attention, they're messy; quick barney ends up with a double murder and thirty years in prison. For a job like this, you take girls. Except when she gets dressed and comes downstairs, there's Darrell waiting by the front door. He's got a sawn-off on his arm.

"What?" says Roxy.

"I'm coming," says Darrell.

She thinks, for a moment, of saying, "Sure," and knocking him cold when he turns away. But, after what's happened to Ricky, it wouldn't be right.

"You keep yourself safe," she says.

"Yeah," he goes. "I'll stick behind you."

He's younger than her. Only by a few months. That's one of the things that's always been so hard: Bernie knocking up both their mums at the same time.

She grabs his shoulder and squeezes it. She calls another couple of lasses to come, too. Vivika, with one of those long, pronged conductive batons, and Danni with a mesh of metal net that she likes. They all take a little bit before they head out the door, and there's music playing in Roxy's head. Sometimes it's good to go to war, just to know you can.

They follow that little knot of girls from the pub at a bit of a distance till they walk through the park, shouting and drinking. It's past 1a.m. It's a hot night; the air feels damp, like there's a storm brewing Roxy and her gang are dressed dark; they're moving smoothly. The girls run towards the merry-go-round in

274

the kids' playground. They lie back on it, staring at the stars, passing the vodka between them.

Roxy says, "Now."

Merry-go-round's made of steel. They light the thing up, and one of the girls falls off, frothing and twitching. So now they're two on four. Easy.

"What's this?" says a girl in a dark blue bomber jacket. Ricky had pointed her photo out as the leader. "What the fuck is this? I don't even *know you*." She makes a bright warning arc between her palms.

"Yeah?" says Roxy. "You bloody knew my brother, though. Ricky? Picked him up in a club last night? Ricky *Monke*?"

"Oh fuck," says the other girl, the one wearing leathers.

"Shut up," says the first girl. "We don't know your fucking *brother*, all right?"

"Sam," says the girl in leathers. "Fuck's sake." She turns to Roxy, pleading. "We didn't know he was your brother. He never said nothing."

Sam mutters something that sounds like "he bloody loved it".

The girl in leathers puts her hands up and takes a pace backwards. Darrell gets her square in the back of the head with the butt of the shotgun. She falls forward, teeth into the soil and scrub.

So now they're four against one. Closing in. Danni sifts her little mesh net in her left hand.

Sam says, "He was *asking* for it. He begged us for it. Fucking begged us, followed us, told us what he wanted done to him. Filthy little scrote, knew just what he was

275

looking for, couldn't get enough of it, wanted us to hurt him, would have licked up my piss if I'd asked him, that's your fucking brother. Looks like butter wouldn't melt, but he's a dirty little boy."

Yeah, well. Might be true, might not. Roxy's seen some things. She still shouldn't have touched a Monke, should she? She'll ask Ricky's mates about it quietly when all this is over and maybe she'll have to tell him not to be a stupid boy; if he wants that kind of thing she can find someone safe to oblige.

"Don't you talk about my *fucking brother* like that!" Darrell yells suddenly, and he's aiming the shotgun butt for her face, but she's too quick for him, and it's metal that shotgun, so when she grabs it he gasps and his knees buckle.

Sam gets one arm around Darrell. His whole body's shuddering — it was a big jolt she gave him. His eyes are rolling back in his head. Fuck. If they hit her, they hit him.

Fuck.

Sam starts to back away. "Don't you bloody follow me," she says. "Don't you bloody come near me, or I'll finish him, like I did your Ricky. I can do worse than that."

Darrell's close to tears now. Roxy can tell what she's doing to him: a constant pulse of shocks into the neck, the throat, the temples. It's most painful at the temples.

"This isn't over," Roxy says quietly. "You can get away now, but we'll come back for you until it's done."

Sam smiles, all white teeth and blood. "Maybe I'll do him now then, for fun."

"That's not clever," says Roxy, "cos then we really would have to kill you."

She gives the nod to Viv, who's circled back round during the commotion. Viv swings her baton. She gives a whack to the back of Sam's head like a sledgehammer taking out dry wall.

Sam turns slightly, sees it coming, but she can't put Darrell down in time to duck. The baton catches the side of her eye and there's a burst of blood. She screams out once and falls to the floor.

"Fuck," says Darrell. He's crying and shaking; there's not much they can do about that. "If she'd seen what you were doing, she'd've killed me."

"You're alive, aren't you?" says Roxy. She doesn't say anything about how he shouldn't have gone for Sam with the shotgun, and she thinks that's fair enough.

Roxy takes her time in marking them. Don't want them to forget it, not ever. Ricky won't be able to forget it. She leaves them with a spider-web of red, unfolding scars over their cheeks and mouth and nose. She takes a photo with her phone, so Ricky can see what she's done. The scars, and the blind eye.

Only Barbara's awake when they get in. Darrell goes to bed, but Roxy sits at the little table in the back kitchen and Barbara flicks through the photos on the phone, nodding with a mouth like a stone.

"All still alive?" she says.

"Even called 999 for them."

Barbara says, "Thank you, Roxanne. I'm grateful. You've done a good thing here."

Roxy says, "Yup."

The clock ticks.

Barbara says, "I'm sorry we were unkind to you."

Roxy raises an eyebrow. "I wouldn't say the word for it was 'unkind', Barbara."

Which is harsher than she meant, but there's a lot happened when she was a kid. Those parties she couldn't come to, and the presents she never got, and the family dinners she was never invited to, and that time that Barbara came round to the house and threw paint at the windows.

"You didn't need to do this tonight, for Ricky. I didn't think you would."

"Some of us don't hold grudges, all right?"

Barbara looks like she'd slapped her in the face.

"It's all right," says Roxy, cos it is now, it's been all right maybe since Terry died. She chews her lip a bit. "You never liked me cos of whose daughter I was. I never expected you would like me. S'all right. We stay out of each other's way, don't we? It's just business." She stretches, her skein tautening across her chest, her muscles suddenly heavy and tired.

Barbara looks at her, eyes slightly narrowed. "There's stuff my Bern still hasn't told you, you know. About how the business runs. Dunno why."

"He was saving it for Ricky," says Roxy.

"Yeah," says Barbara, "I think he was. But Ricky's not going to take it now."

She stands up, goes over to the kitchen cupboard. From the third shelf, she takes out the bags of flour and the boxes of biscuits and there, right at the back, she sticks her nail into an almost invisible crack and opens up a hidden cubby-hole, not wider than your hand. She pulls out three small black notebooks held together by an elastic band.

"Contacts," she says. "Narcs. Bent coppers. Rotten doctors. I've been saying for months Bern should just give this all to you. So you could work out how to sell the Glitter yourself."

Roxy holds out her hand, takes the books. Feels the weight and solidity of them in her palm. All the knowledge of how the business is run in a compact block, a brick of information.

"Because of what you did today," says Barbara, "for Ricky. I'll square it with Bernie." And she takes her mug of tea and goes to bed.

Roxy stays up the rest of that night back at her own place, going through the books, making notes and plans. There are contacts here go back years, connections her dad's been developing, people he's been blackmailing or bribing — and the latter usually leads to the former eventually. Barbara doesn't know what she's given her here — with the stuff in these books, she can take the Glitter across Europe, no bother. The Monkes can make more money than anyone's made since Prohibition.

She's smiling, and her one knee's joggling up and down when she runs her eye along a row of names and sees something important.

It takes her a bit to work out what it is she's seen. Some bit of her brain got there ahead of all the rest, told her to read and re-read the list till it jumped out at her. There. A name. A bent copper, Detective Newland. Newland.

Cos she'll never forget that thing Primrose said when he died, will she? She'll never forget any of what happened that day her whole life long.

"Newland said you weren't going to be home," Primrose had said.

This copper, this Newland. He was part of the plan to kill her mum, and she's never known who he was, not till now. She thought it was done a long time since, but when she sees the name and she remembers, she thinks, Fuck. Some dodgy copper selling stuff to my dad, selling stuff to Primrose. Fuck, she thinks. Some dodgy copper watching our house and saying when I wouldn't be home.

A quick search on the internet is all it takes. Detective Newland lives in Spain now. Retired policeman. Little town. Doesn't think anyone's going to come looking for him, obviously.

She never meant to tell Darrell about it. It was only that he came himself to thank her for what she'd done for Ricky, and for saving his own life.

He said, "We know which way this is going. Ricky's out of the picture now. If there's anything I can do to help you, Rox. Just tell me what I can do."

Maybe he's started to have the same thoughts she has, about how you just have to accept this change that's struck us all, roll with it, find your place in it.

280

So she told Darrell what she was going to Spain for. He said, "I'm coming, too."

She sees what he's asking her for. Ricky's not coming back to the life, not for years, maybe not ever, and not how he was. They're running out of family. He wants to be family to her.

The place isn't difficult to find. GPS and a rental car, and they're there in less than an hour from Seville airport. There's no need to be clever about it. They watch through binoculars for a couple of days; long enough to know that he lives alone. They stay in a hotel nearby, but not too nearby. Thirty miles' drive. You wouldn't go looking there if you were local police, not if you were doing a routine just-in-case inquiry. He's nice with it, Darrell. Businesslike, but funny. Lets her make the decisions, but he's got a few good ideas of his own. She thinks, Yeah. If Ricky's out of the game, yeah. This could work. She could take him to the factory next time she goes out.

On the third day, in the pre-dawn light, they chuck a rope up one of the fence poles, climb over and wait in the bushes till he comes out. He's in shorts and a ragged T-shirt. He's got a sandwich — this time in the morning, a sausage sandwich — and he's looking at his phone.

She'd been expecting something, some kind of terror to strike her; she'd thought she might wee herself or have a rush of bloody rage or start crying. But when she looks into his face all she feels is interest. A completed circle: two bits of string tied together. The man who helped get her mum killed. The last little bit of stuff to mop up from the side of the plate.

She steps out of the bushes in front of him. "Newland," she says. "Your name is Newland."

He looks at her, open-mouthed. He's still holding his sausage sandwich. There's a second before the fear kicks in, and in that second Darrell charges from the bushes, clonks him on the head and pushes him into the swimming pool.

When he comes round, the sun is high in the sky, and he's floating face up. He thrashes around, brings himself to standing in the middle of the pool, coughing and rubbing his eyes.

Roxy's sitting at the edge, fingers splashing. "Electricity travels a long way in water," she says. "It's fast."

Newland stands stock still at that.

She tips her head first to one side, then the other, stretching out the muscles. Her skein's full.

Newland starts to say something. Maybe it's "I don't . . ." or "Who are . . .", but she sends a little thrill through the water, enough to prickle him over his whole wet body.

She says, "This is going to be boring if you start denying everything, Detective Newland."

"Fuck," he says. "I don't even know who you are. If this is about Lisa, she got her fucking money, all right. She got it two years ago, every penny, and I'm out now."

Roxy sends another shock through the water. "Think again," she says. "Look at my face. Don't I remind you of anyone? Aren't I someone's daughter?"

He knows it then, all at once. She can see it in his face. "Fuck," he says, "this is about Christina."

"Yeah," she says.

"Please," he says, and she sends him a hard jolt, so much that his teeth start chattering and his body goes rigid and he shits himself right into the water, a brown-yellow cloud of particles jetting out like it's shot from a hose.

"Rox," says Darrell softly. He's sitting behind her, on one of the sun-loungers, his hand on the butt of the rifle.

She stops it. Newland collapses, sobbing, into the water.

"Don't say 'please'," she says. "That's what my mum said."

He rubs his forearms, trying to get some life back into them.

"There's no way out of this for you, Newland. You told Primrose where to find my mum. You got her killed, and I'm going to kill you."

Newland tries to make a break for the edge of the pool. She shocks him again. His knees collapse under him and he falls forward, and then he's just lying there, face down in the water.

"Fuck's sake," says Roxy.

Darrell gets the hook and pulls him to the edge, and they haul him up.

When Newland opens his eyes again, Roxy's sitting on his chest.

"You're going to die here now, Newland," says Darrell, very calmly. "This is it, mate. This is all the life you got. This is your last day, and there's nothing you can tell us that'll make it different, all right? But if we make it look like an accident, your life insurance will still pay out. To your mum, yeah? And your brother? We can do that for you, make it look like an accident. Not a suicide. All right?"

Newland coughs up a lungful of murky water.

"You got my mum killed, Newland," says Roxy. "That's strike one. And you've made me sit in your shitty water. That's strike two. If we get to strike three, there will be pain you just can't believe. I only want to know one thing from you."

He's listening to her now.

"What did Primrose give you, Newland, to tip him off about my mum? What would have made you bring the Monkes down on you? What seemed worth *that* to you, Newland?"

He blinks at them, first at her, then at Darrell, like they're having a laugh with him.

She holds his face in her hand and sends a pickaxe of pain along the jaw.

He screams.

"Just tell me, Newland," she says.

He's panting. "You know, don't you?" he says. "You're kidding me."

She brings her hand close to his face.

"No!" he says. "No! No, you *know* what happened, you fucking *bitch*, it was your dad. It was never Primrose who paid me, it was Bernie — Bernie Monke *told me* to do it. I only ever worked for Bernie, only ever did jobs for Bernie; it was *Bernie* who told me that

I should pretend to sell Primrose information, tell him when to find your mum alone. You was never supposed to see it. Bernie wanted your mum dead and I don't ask questions. I helped him out. It was fucking *Bernie*. Your dad. Bernie."

He keeps on muttering the name, like it's the secret that will make her set him free.

They don't get much more from him. He knew Roxy's mum was Bernie's woman; yeah, of course he did. They told him that she'd cheated on Bernie, and that was enough to get her killed — well, it would be.

When they're finished, they tip him back in the pool, and she lights it up, just the once. It'll look like he had a heart attack, fell in, shat himself and drowned. So they kept their promise. They change their clothes and take the rental car back to the airport. They haven't even left a hole in the fence.

On the plane, Roxy says, "What now?"

And Darrell says, "What do you want, Rox?"

She sits there for a bit, feeling the power in her, crystalline and complete. It felt like something, killing Newland. To see him go rigid and then stop.

She thinks about what Eve's said to her, that she knew Roxy was coming. That she's seen her destiny. That she's the one who's going to bring in the new world. That the power will be in her hands to change everything.

She feels the power in her fingertips, as if she could punch a hole right through the world.

"I want justice," she says. "And then I want everything. You wanna stand with me? Or you wanna stand against me?"

Bernie's in his office, looking through his books, when they get there. He looks old to her. He hasn't shaved properly; there's tufts sticking out of his neck and his chin. There's a smell on him these days, too; smells like hard cheese. She never thought before that he's old. They're his youngest ones. Ricky's thirty-five.

He knew they were coming. Barbara must have told him she'd given Roxy the notebooks. He smiles when they walk in the door. Darrell's behind her, holding a loaded gun.

"You've got to understand, Rox," says Bernie. "I loved your mum. She never loved me — I don't think so. She was just using me for what she could get."

"That why you killed her?"

He inhales through his nose, like it surprises him to hear it, even so. "I'm not going to beg," he says. He's looking at Roxy's hands, at her fingers. "I know how this goes, and I'll take it, but you've got to understand, it wasn't personal, it was business."

"It was family, Dad," says Darrell, very softly. "Family's always personal."

"That's the truth," he says. "But she got Al and Big Mick caught," he says. "The Romanians paid her, and she told where they'd be. I cried when they told me it was her, love. I did. But I couldn't let it stand, could I? There's no one . . . you've got to understand, there's no one I could have let do that to me."

286

Roxy's made that kind of calculation herself, more than once now.

"You weren't supposed to see it, love."

"Aren't you ashamed, Dad?" says Roxy.

He sticks his chin out, puts his tongue between his teeth and his bottom lip. "I'm sorry it happened. I'm sorry that's the way it went. I didn't mean for you to see it, and I've always looked after you. You're my girl." He pauses.

"Your mum hurt me more than I could tell you." He breathes out through his nose again, heavy, like a bull. "It's a bloody Greek tragedy, love. Even if I'd known all this was going to happen, I'd still have done it, I can't deny it. And if you're going to kill me . . . there's some justice to it, love."

He sits there, waiting for it, calm as anything. He must have thought about this a hundred times, wondering who'd get him in the end, a friend or an enemy or a growing mass in the centre of the stomach, or if he'd make it all the way to a good old age. He must've thought before that it might be her, and that's why he's so calm with it now.

She knows how this goes. If she kills him, it'll never be over. That's how it went with Primrose, how they ended up in a blood feud with him. If she keeps on killing anyone who pisses her off, someone will come for her in the end.

"You know what's justice, Dad?" she says. "I want you to fuck off. And I want you to tell all of them that you're handing the business over to me. We're not having any bloody battles, no one else is coming up to take it from me, no one revenging you, no Greek tragedy. We're doing it peaceful. You're retiring. I'll protect you, and you'll fuck off. We'll fix you up with a safe place. Go somewhere with a beach."

Bernie nods. "You always was a clever girl," he says.

Jocelyn

They've had death threats and bomb scares at the NorthStar camp before, but never a real attack, not till tonight.

Jocelyn's on night watch. There are five of them, scanning the perimeter with binoculars. If you do your extras and you sleep over and you agree that you'll work for them for two years after you leave college, they'll pay your tuition. Pretty sweet deal. Margot could have paid for Jocelyn's college, but it looks good that she's doing it the same way the other girls do. Maddy's skein has come in sure and strong, with none of Jocelyn's problems. She's only fifteen and she's already talking about joining the elite cadets. Two military daughters; that's how you run for President.

Jocelyn's half dozing at her watch station when the alarm sounds in the booth. Alarms have sounded before; it's been a fox or a coyote or, sometimes, a couple of drunk teenagers trying to climb over the fence on a dare. Jocelyn was once scared out of her wits by a shrieking in the trash at the back of the mess hall, only for two enormous raccoons to dive out of the metal bins, biting and running at each other.

The others had laughed at her for her fright at that, as they laugh at her quite often. At first, there was Ryan, and that was exciting and fun and intense and, because his skein was just their secret, it made everything special. But then it got out somehow — photos on a long lens, reporters at the door again. And the other girls at camp read about it. And then there were little whispered giggly conversations that fell silent when she walked into the room. She's read articles by women who wish they couldn't do it and men who wish they could, and everything seems so confusing, and all she really wants is to be normal. She broke up with Ryan and he cried, and she found her face was dry like there was a stopper inside holding it all in. Her mom took her to a doctor privately and they gave her something to feel more normal. And she does, in a way.

She and three of the other girls on watch take up their night-sticks — long batons with sharp, whippy metal strands at the end — and go out into the night, expecting to find some local wildlife biting at the fence. Except when they get there, there are three men, each carrying a baseball bat, their faces greased up with black. They're at the generator. One of them has a huge pair of bolt-cutters. It's a terrorist incursion.

Things happen quickly. Dakota, the eldest of them, whispers to Hayden, one of the youngest, to run for the NorthStar guards. The others stay in a tight formation, bodies close together. There have been men at other camps with knives, guns, even grenades and home-made bombs.

Dakota shouts out, "Put down your weapons!"

The men's eyes are narrow and unreadable. They've come here to do something bad.

Dakota swings her flashlight. "All right, fellas," she says. "You've had your fun, but we caught you. Put them down."

One of them throws something — a gas grenade, smoke billowing out. The second uses his bolt-cutters on an exposed tube in the generator. There's a bang. All the lights go out in the centre of the camp. There's nothing now but the black sky, the stars, and these men who have come here to kill them.

Jocelyn points her flashlight wildly around. One of the men is fighting with Dakota and Samara, swinging his baseball bat, shouting a tattered cry. The bat connects with Samara's head. There's blood. Fuck, there's blood. They've been trained, the girls are all trained; this isn't supposed to happen. Even with their power, can this still happen? Tegan's on him like a wolf, the power in her hands taking out one of his knees, but he kicks her square in the face, and what's that glinting under his jacket, what has he got, what the fuck has he got? Jocelyn runs for him, she'll hold him down and get whatever it is away from him, but as she goes a hand grabs for her ankle and she topples forward, face into the sandy earth.

She scrambles on to all fours, crawling towards the flashlight, but before she can get there it's picked up, pointed at her. She waits for the blow. But it's Dakota holding the light. Dakota with a bruise across her cheek, and Tegan next to her. And one of the men, kneeling on the ground at Tegan's feet. She thinks it was the one she was fighting with. His balaclava's off, and he's young. Younger than she'd thought. Maybe only a year or two older than her. His lip is cut and there's a fern-like scar unfurling across his jaw.

"Got him," says Dakota.

"Fuck you," says the man. "We stand for freedom!"

Tegan lifts up his head by his hair and jolts him again, just under the ear, a painful place.

"Who sent you here?" says Dakota.

But he doesn't answer.

"Jos," says Dakota, "show him we mean business."

Jocelyn doesn't know where the other two women have gone. "Shouldn't we wait," she says, "for back-up?"

Dakota says, "Goddamn pzit. You can't do it, can you?"

The boy's cowering on the floor. She doesn't need to do it; no one needs to do it now.

Tegan says, "Has he got a skein? She wants to fuck him."

The others laugh. Yeah, they mutter, that's what she likes. Weird men, deformed men. Disgusting, strange, repulsive men. That's what she likes.

If she fucking cries in front of them, they'll never forget it. Anyway, she's not what they think. She didn't even like it so much with Ryan, she didn't; she's thought about it since they broke up and she thinks the other girls are right. It's better with a man who can't do it; it's more normal, anyway. She's been with a couple of other guys since, guys who liked it when she gave them a jolt and even asked her for it in quiet voices close up to her ear, saying, "Please." It's better like that, and she wishes they'd just forget that Ryan ever existed; she's forgotten him, it was just a teenage thing, and the drugs have normalized her power more than ever. She's normal now, completely normal.

What would a normal girl do now?

Dakota says, "Fuck off, Cleary, I'll do it," and Jocelyn says, "No, you fuck off."

The boy on the floor whispers, "Please." Like they do.

Jocelyn pushes Dakota out of the way and leans down and gives him a jolt in his head. Just to teach him what he's got coming if he messes with them.

She's emotional, though. Her trainer's told her to watch out for that. There are surges going through her body. Hormones and electrolytes mess with everything.

She can feel as it leaves her body that it's too much. She tries to hold it back, but it's too late.

His scalp crisps under her hand.

He screams.

Inside his skull, liquid is cooking. Delicate parts are fusing and congealing. The lines of power are scarring him, faster than thought.

She can't hold it back. It's not a good way to go. She didn't mean to do it.

There's a smell of burned hair and flesh.

Tegan says, "Fuck."

And there's an arc light on them, suddenly. It's two of the NorthStar people, a man and a woman; Jos has met them before: Esther and Johnny. At last. They must have rigged up a light from a back-up generator.

Jocelyn's mind is working very quickly, even though her body is slow. Her hand is still on the boy's head. There's a faint wisp of smoke at her fingertips.

Johnny says, "Jesus."

Esther says, "Were there more? The girl said there were three."

Dakota's still staring at the boy. Jocelyn peels her fingers off him one by one and she doesn't think about it at all. She has the sense that if she starts to think about it she'll tumble down into the deep, dark water; there's a black ocean waiting for her now, it will always be waiting. She takes her fingers off, not thinking about it, and she pulls her sticky palm up, not thinking about it, and the body tumbles forward, face first into the dirt.

Esther says, "Johnny, go and get a fucking medic. Now."

Johnny's staring at the body, too. He makes a little laugh, and says, "Medic?"

Esther says, "Now. Go and get the fucking medic, Johnny."

He swallows. His eyes flick to Jocelyn, Tegan, Esther. When he catches Esther's eye, he nods swiftly. Backs up a few paces. Turns and runs, out of the circle of the arc light and into the dark.

Esther looks round the circle.

Dakota starts to say, "What happened was —"

But Esther shakes her head. "Let's see," she says.

She kneels down by the body, flips it over with one hand, rummages in his coat. They can't quite see what's happening. She finds some gum, a handful of flyers for a men's protest group. And then there's a familiar heavy metallic chink.

Esther reaches behind him and there, in her palm, is a gun; thick and snub-nosed, military issue. "He pulled his gun on you," says Esther.

Jocelyn frowns. She understands, but she can't stop herself from saying the words.

"No, he didn't. He was . . ." She stops, as her mouth catches up to her brain.

Esther speaks in a very calm and easy tone. There's a smile in her voice. Like she's talking Jos through an equipment maintenance drill. First turn off the power, then apply the lubricating fluid, then adjust the belt using the tightening screw. Simple. One thing, then the next. One, two, three. This is how it has to go.

She says, "You saw that he had a gun in the side pocket of his coat, and he was reaching for it. He had already committed an act of violence against us. You perceived a clear and present danger. He reached for the gun and you used proportionate force to stop him."

Esther uncurls the boy's fingers and wraps them around the holster of the pistol. "It's simpler to understand this way. He was holding his gun," she says. "He was about to fire it." She looks around the circle of young women, meeting each of their eyes in turn.

Tegan says, "Yes, that's what happened. I saw him reach for his gun."

Jocelyn looks at the gun, clasped in the cooling fingers. Some of the NorthStar people carry their own unregistered side arms. Her mom had to get the *New York Times* to pull a piece about it, on the grounds that it would threaten homeland security. Maybe he had that gun in his back pocket. Maybe he was going to turn it on them. But if they had guns, why were they using bats?

Esther clasps a hand on Jocelyn's shoulder. "You're a hero, soldier," she says.

"Yes," says Jocelyn.

It gets easier to tell the story the more she does it. She starts to see it very clearly in her mind's eye so that, by the time she's talking about it on national TV, she thinks she half remembers it anyway. Hadn't she seen something metal in one of their pockets? Couldn't it have been a gun? Maybe that's why she let off her blast. Yes, she probably did know.

She smiles on the television news. No, she says. I don't feel like a hero. Anyone would have done the same.

Oh, come on, says Kristen. I couldn't have done it. Could you, Matt?

Matt laughs and says, I couldn't even have watched! He's very attractive, a good ten years younger than Kristen. The network had found him. Just trying something out. While we're at it, Kristen, why don't you wear your glasses onscreen now, it'll give you *gravitas*. We're going to see how the numbers play out this way. We're sending it for a run around the park, OK?

Well, your mom must be very proud, Jocelyn.

She is proud. She knows part of the story, but not the whole thing. It's given her leverage with the

Defence Department in rolling out the NorthStar training camp scheme for girls across all fifty states. It's a well-run programme, with good links to colleges, and they're able to charge the army a bounty for every girl they send their way who can bypass basic and go straight into active duty. The army is fond of Margot Cleary.

And with all that's going on in the news, says Matt, this war in Eastern Europe, what is *that* about? First the South Moldovans are winning, now it's the North Moldovans, and the Saudis are involved somehow . . . He shrugs helplessly. It's great to know that we have young women like you ready to defend the country.

Oh yes, says Jocelyn, just like she practised. I would never have been able to do it at all without the training I received at NorthStar Camp.

Kristen squeezes her knee. Will you stick around, Jocelyn? We're going to be tasting some great cinnamon recipes for fall after the break.

Of course!

Matt smiles into the camera. I know *I* feel safer with you around. And now, the weather on the ones.

Statue of the "Priestess Queen" — found in a treasure
trove in Lahore.
The statue itself is substantially older than the base, which is made from
repurposed Cataclysm Era technology.
Though much eroded, analysis of the base has revealed that is was
originally marked with the Bitten Fruit motif. Objects marked with this
motif are found across the Cataclysm Era world and their use is much
debated. The uniformity of the motif suggests that it is a religious symbol, but it may also have been a glyph indicating that the object should
be used for serving food; the different sizes may have been used for different meals.
This Bitten Fruit artefact is, as is common, constructed partially of
metal and partially of glass. Unusally for objects of this type, the glass is
unbroken, giving it high value in the post-Cataclysm years.
It's speculated that the Bitten Fruit artefact was given as a tribute to the
cult of the Priestess Queen and used to increase the majesty of
her statue.
The two objects were welded together around 2,500 years ago.

Statue of "Serving Boy", found in the same hoard as the
"Priestess Queen".
From the careful grooming and sensuous features, it has
been speculated that this statue depicts a sex worker.
The statue is decorated with Cataclysm Era glass whose
composition is similar to that of the base of "Priestess
Queen"; it almost certainly came from a broken Bitten
Fruit artefact. The glass was probably added to this
statue at the same time that the base was added to
"Priestess Queen".

One year

The President and her government

request the pleasure of the company of

Senator Margot Cleary

at a reception and dinner

on Wednesday evening, J...

The President and her government

request the pleasure of the company of

Ms Roxanne Monke

at a reception and dinner

...dnesday evening, June 15th

The President and her government

request the pleasure of the company of

Mother Eve

at a reception and dinner

on Wednesday evening, June ...

at seven o...

The President and her government

request the pleasure of the company of

Mr Tunde Edo

at a reception and dinner

on Wednesday evening, June 15th

at seven o'clock

Margot

"Can you comment on why you're here, Senator Cleary?"

"President Moskalev has been ousted in a military coup from the country of which she was the leader chosen by a democratic process, Tunde. This is the kind of thing which the government of the United States takes very seriously. And may I say how delighted I am that you're engaging the younger generation in this sort of important geopolitical issue."

"It's the younger generation who'll have to live in the world you're building, Senator."

"You're right, and that's why I'm so thrilled that my daughter Jocelyn is visiting the country with me as part of the United Nations delegation."

"Can you comment on the recent defeat of the forces of the Republic of Bessapara by the troops of North Moldova?"

"It's a party, son, not a defence strategy meeting."

"You'd know, Senator Cleary. You sit on . . . is it *five* strategic committees now?" He counts them off on his fingers: "Defence, foreign relations, homeland security, budget and intelligence. You're quite the powerhouse to be sent to a *party*."

"You've done your homework."

"I have, ma'am. The North Moldovans are funded by the House of Saud in exile, aren't they? Is this war with Bessapara a proving ground for an attempt to retake Saudi Arabia?"

"The Saudi Arabian government was democratically elected by their people. The United States government supports democracy around the world and peaceful regime change."

"Is the United States government here to secure the oil pipeline?"

"There's no oil in Moldova or Bessapara, Tunde."

"But another regime change in Saudi Arabia might affect your oil supply, don't you think?"

"That can't be a concern when we're talking about the freedom of a democracy."

He almost laughs. A little smirk peels across his face and disappears. "OK," says Tunde. "Fine. The United States would rather promote democracy than oil. OK. And what message does your attending this party tonight send about domestic terrorism back home?"

"Let me be clear," says Margot, staring straight into Tunde's camera, with a clear, level gaze. "The United States government is not afraid of domestic terrorists, or the people who fund them."

"And by 'the people who fund them', you mean King Awadi-Atif of Saudi Arabia?"

"That's all I have to say on this."

"And any comment on why you've been sent here, Senator? You in particular? With your connections to the NorthStar training camps for young women? Is that why you were chosen to come here?"

Margot does a little chuckle that seems entirely sincere. "I'm just a little fish, Tunde; a minnow, really. I came because I was invited. And now I just want to enjoy the party, and I'm sure you do, too."

She turns away, walks a few paces to the right. Waits until she hears the snap of his camera turning off.

"Don't start coming after me, son," she says out of the corner of her mouth. "I'm your friend here."

Tunde notices the word "son". Says nothing. Holds it close to his chest. Is glad he left the audio recording running, even though the video is off.

"I could have pushed you twice as hard," he says, "ma'am."

Margot squints at him. "I like you, Tunde," she says. "You did good work on that interview with UrbanDox. Those nuke threats really got Congress to sit up and take notice, voted us the money we need to defend the country. You still in touch with his people?"

"Sometimes."

"You hear they've got anything big coming down the pipe, you come and tell me, all right? I'll make it worth your while. There's money in it now — a *lot* of money. You might make a great press consultant with our training camps."

"Aha," says Tunde. "I'll let you know."

"Be sure you do."

She smiles reassuringly. At least, that's what she intends. She has the feeling that, once it reaches her lips, it might have come out more as a leer. The problem is that these fucking reporters are so attractive. She's seen Tunde's videos before; Maddy is a huge fan, and he's actually making a difference with the eighteen to thirty-five voting demographic.

It's amazing how — amongst all the talk about his relaxed and accessible style — no one mentions that Olatunde Edo's videos have been such a hit because he's handsome as hell. He's half naked in some of them, reporting from the beach in just Speedos, and how's she supposed to take him seriously now, when she's seen his broad shoulders and narrow waist and the rolling landscape of obliques and delts, glutes and pecs of his firm . . . shit, she really needs to get laid.

Christ. OK. There are a few young guys among the staff on this trip; she'll buy one of them a drink after the party, because *this* can't be happening in her mind every time she's confronted with a handsome reporter. She grabs a schnapps from a passing tray; downs it. An aide catches her eye across the room, points to her wristwatch. We're off to the races.

"You've gotta admit," she whispers to Frances, her aide, as they climb the marble stairs, "they know how to pick a castle."

The place looks like it's been transported brick by brick from Disney. Gilt furniture. Seven pointed spires, each a different shape and size, some fluted, some smooth, some tipped with gold. Pine forest in the foreground, mountains in the distance. Yeah, yeah, you've got history and culture. Yeah, yeah, you're not no one. Fine.

Tatiana Moskalev is — no kidding — sitting on an actual throne when Margot walks in. A huge gold thing, with lions' heads on the arms and a red velvet cushion. Margot manages not to smile. The President of Bessapara is wearing an enormous white fur coat with a gold dress underneath. She has a ring on each finger and two on each thumb. It's like she learned what a President ought to look like from watching too many mafia movies. Maybe that's what she did. The door closes behind Margot. They're alone together.

"President Moskalev," says Margot. "An honour to meet you."

"Senator Cleary," says Tatiana, "the honour is mine."

The snake meets the tiger, Margot thinks; the jackal greets the scorpion.

"Please," says Tatiana, "take a glass of our ice wine. The finest in Europe. The product of our Bessaparan vineyards."

Margot sips it, wondering how likely it is to be poisoned. She puts the odds at no more than 3 per cent. It'd look very bad for them if she died here.

"The wine is excellent," says Margot. "I would have expected no less."

Tatiana smiles a thin and distant smile. "You like Bessapara?" she says. "You have enjoyed the tours? Music, dancing, local cheese?"

Margot had sat through a three-hour demonstration and talk on local cheese-making practices that morning. Three hours. On cheese.

"Oh, your country is delightful, Madam President — such old-world charm, combined with such focus and determination to move into the future together."

"Yes." Tatiana smiles thinly again. "We think we are maybe the most forward-thinking country in the world, you know."

"Ah, yes. I am looking forward to the visit to your science-technology park tomorrow."

Tatiana shakes her head. "Culturally," she says; "socially. We are the only country in the world to really understand what this change *means*. To understand it as a blessing. An invitation to . . . to . . ." She shakes her head for a moment, as if to clear a kind of fog: "An invitation to a new way of living."

Margot says nothing and sips her wine again, making an appreciative face.

"I like America," says Tatiana. "My late husband, Viktor, liked USSR, but I like America. Land of freedom. Land of opportunity. Good music. Better than Russian music." She starts to sing the lyrics to a pop song Maddy's been playing around the house incessantly: "When we drive, you so fast, in your car, all boom boom." Her voice is pleasant. Margot remembers reading somewhere that Tatiana had had ambitions to be a pop star, once upon a time.

"You want us to get them to come play here? They tour. We can fix it up."

Tatiana says: "I think you know what I want. I think you know. Senator Cleary, you are not a stupid woman."

308

Margot smiles. "I may not be stupid, but I'm not a mind-reader, President Moskalev."

"All we want," says Tatiana, "is American dream, right here in Bessapara. We are a new nation, plucky little state bordered by a terrible enemy. We want to live freely, to pursue our own way of life. We want opportunity. That's all."

Margot nods. "That's what everyone wants, Madam President. Democracy for all is America's fondest wish for the world."

Tatiana's lips turn faintly upward. "Then you will help us against the North."

Margot chews her top lip for a moment. This is the tricky point. She'd known it was coming.

"I've . . . I've had conversations with the President. While we support your independence, as it is the will of your people, we can't be seen to interfere in a war between North Moldova and Bessapara."

"You and I are more subtle than this, Senator Cleary."

"We can offer humanitarian aid, and peacekeeping forces."

"You can vote against any action against us in the UN Security Council."

Margot frowns. "But there are no actions against you in the UN Security Council."

Tatiana places her glass very deliberately on the table in front of her. "Senator Cleary. My country has been betrayed by some of its men. We know this. We were defeated in the recent Battle of the Dniester because the North knew where our troops would be. Men from

Bessapara have sold information to our enemies in the North. Some of them have been found. Some of them have confessed. We need to take action."

"That's your prerogative, of course."

"You will not interfere in this action. You will support whatever we do."

Margot gives a little chuckle. "I'm not sure I can promise anything *that* sweeping, Madam President."

Tatiana turns around, leans back against the window pane. She is silhouetted against the brightly lit Disney castle behind her.

"You work with NorthStar, don't you? Private military. You are a shareholder, in fact. I like NorthStar. Teaching girls to be warriors. Very good — we need it more."

Well. This wasn't what Margot was expecting. But it's intriguing.

"I don't quite see how these things are linked, Madam President," she says, although she's beginning to have a shrewd idea.

"NorthStar wants the UN mandate to send its own NorthStar-trained female troops into Saudi Arabia. The government in Saudi Arabia is crumbling. The state is unstable."

"If the UN approves the deployment, I think it'll be good news for the world, yes. Securing the supply of energy, helping the government through a difficult period of transition."

"It would be easier to make the case," says Tatiana, "if another government had already successfully deployed NorthStar forces." Tatiana pauses, pours herself another glass of the ice wine, pours one for Margot, too. They both know where this is going. Their eyes meet. Margot is smiling.

"You want to employ NorthStar girls yourself."

"As my private army, here and on the border."

It's worth a lot of money. Even more if they *win* the war with the North and seize the Saudi assets. Acting as a private army here would take NorthStar exactly where they want to go. The board would be *very* happy to continue their association with Margot Cleary until the end of time if she could pull this off.

"And, in exchange, you want . . ."

"We are going to alter our laws a little. During this time of trouble. To prevent more traitors giving away our secrets to the North. We want you to stand by us."

"We have no wish to interfere in the affairs of a sovereign nation," says Margot. "Cultural differences must be respected. I know the President will trust my judgement on this."

"Good," says Tatiana, and makes a slow, green-eyed blink. "Then we understand each other." She pauses. "We don't have to ask ourselves what the North would do if they won, Senator Cleary. We've already seen what they do; we all remember what Saudi Arabia was. We are both on the right side here."

She raises her glass. Margot tips hers slowly until it just touches Tatiana's glass with a gentle chink.

It's a great day for America. A great day for the world.

★   ★   ★

The rest of the party is precisely as dull as Margot had expected. She shakes hands with foreign dignitaries and religious leaders and people she suspects to be criminals and arms dealers. She mouths the same lines over and over again, about the United States' deep sympathy with victims of injustice and tyranny and their wish to see a peaceful resolution to the situation here in this troubled region. There's some kerfuffle at the reception just after Tatiana makes her entrance, but Margot doesn't see it. She stays until 10.30p.m. — the officially designated time that is neither too early nor too late to leave a significant party. On her way down to the diplomatic car, she bumps into the reporter Tunde again.

"Excuse me," he says, dropping something on to the floor and immediately retrieving it, too fast for her to see, "I mean, excuse me. I'm sorry. I'm in a . . . I'm in a hurry."

She laughs. She's had a good night. She's already calculating the kind of bonus she'll get from NorthStar if all this works out, and thinking about super PAC contributions for the next election cycle.

"Why hurry?" she says. "There's no need to rush away. Want a ride?"

She gestures to the car, its door open, its buttery leather interior inviting. He conceals his momentary look of panic with a smile, but not quite quickly enough.

"Another time," he says.

His loss.

★   ★   ★

Later, in the hotel, she buys a couple of drinks for one of the junior guys from the American embassy in the Ukraine. He's attentive — well, why wouldn't he be? She's going places. She rests her hand on his firm young ass as they ride the elevator together up to her suite.

Allie

The castle's chapel has been remade. The glass-and-gold chandelier still floats in the centre of the room, the wires holding it up too thin to be seen by candlelight. All these electric miracles. The windows depicting the angels praising Our Lady have remained intact, as have the panels to Saint Theresa and Saint Jerome. The others — and the enamelled paintings in the cupola — have been replaced and reimagined according to the New Scripture. There is the Almighty speaking to the Matriarch Rebecca in the form of a dove. There is the Prophet Deborah proclaiming the Holy Word to the disbelieving people. There — although she protested — is Mother Eve, the symbolic tree behind her, receiving the message from the Heavens and extending her hand filled with lightning. In the centre of the cupola is the hand with the all-seeing eye at its heart. That is the symbol of God, Who watches over each of us, and Whose mighty hand is outstretched to both the powerful and the enslaved.

There is a soldier waiting for her in the chapel: a young woman who had requested a private audience. American. Pretty, with light grey eyes and freckles across her cheeks.

314

"Are you waiting to see me?" says Mother Eve.

"Yes," says Jocelyn, daughter of Senator Cleary who sits on five key committees, including defence and budget.

Mother Eve has made time for this private meeting.

"It is good to meet you, daughter." She comes to sit beside her. "How can I help you?"

And Jocelyn starts to cry. "My mother would kill me if she knew I was here," she says. "She'd kill me. Oh, Mother, I don't know what to do."

"Have you come . . . for guidance?"

Allie had looked at the request for an audience with interest. That the Senator's daughter should be here was no great surprise. That she would want to see Mother Eve in the flesh made sense. But a private audience? Allie had wondered whether she'd be a sceptic, looking to have an argument about the existence of God. But . . . apparently not.

"I'm so lost," says Jocelyn through her tears. "I don't know who I am any more. I watch your talks and I keep waiting for . . . I ask Her voice to guide me and tell me what to do . . ."

"Tell me your trouble," says Mother Eve.

Allie is quite familiar with trouble that is too deep to be spoken. She knows it happens in any house, however high. There is no place that cannot be penetrated by the kind of trouble Allie has seen in her life.

She extends a hand, touches Jocelyn's knee. Jocelyn flinches a little. Pulls away. Even in that momentary touch, Allie knows what Jocelyn's trouble is.

She knows the touch of women and the slow, even background hum of power in the skein. Something is dark in Jocelyn that should be lit and glowing; something is open that should be closed. Allie suppresses a shudder.

"Your skein," says Mother Eve. "You are suffering."

Jocelyn cannot speak above a whisper. "It's a secret. I'm not supposed to talk about it. There are drugs. But the drugs don't work as well any more. It's getting worse. I'm not . . . I'm not like other girls. I didn't know who else to come to. I've seen you on the internet. Please," she says. "Please heal me and make me normal. Please ask God to take the burden from me. Please let me be normal."

"All I can do," says Mother Eve, "is take your hand, and we will pray together."

This is a very difficult situation. No one's examined this girl, or given Allie advice about what her problem is. Skein deficiencies are very difficult to correct. Tatiana Moskalev is looking into skein transplant operations for precisely this reason; we don't know how to fix a skein that doesn't work.

Jocelyn nods and puts her hand into Allie's.

Mother Eve says the usual words: "Our Mother," she says, "above us and within us. You alone are the source of all goodness, all mercy and all grace. May we learn to do Your will, as You express it to us daily through Your works."

While she speaks, Allie is feeling out the patches of darkness and light in Jocelyn's skein. It's as if the thing is occluded: gummy places where there should be flowing water. Silted up. She could clear some of the muck in the channels *here* and *here*.

316

"And may our hearts be pure before You," she says, "and may You send us strength to bear the trials we face without bitterness and without self-destruction."

Jocelyn, though she has rarely prayed, prays now. As Mother Eve lays her hands on Jocelyn's back, she prays, "Please, God, open my heart." And she feels something.

Allie gives a little *push*. More than she'd usually do, but this girl doesn't have enough sensitivity to feel what exactly she's doing, probably. Jocelyn gasps. Allie gives another three short, hard pushes. And there. The thing is sparkling now. Thrumming like an engine. There.

Jocelyn says, "Oh God. I can feel it."

Her skein is humming steadily, evenly. She can feel now that thing that the other girls say they've felt: the gentle, filling sensation as each cell in her skein pumps ions across membranes and the electric potential increases. She can *feel* that she's working properly, for the first time ever.

She is too shocked to cry.

She says, "I can feel it. It's working."

Mother Eve says, "Praise be to God."

"But how did you *do* that?"

Mother Eve shakes her head. "Not my will but Hers be done."

They breathe in and out in unison once, twice, three times.

Jocelyn says, "What shall I do now? I'm . . ." She laughs. "I'm shipping out tomorrow. United Nations observation force duty in the south." She's not supposed to say that, but she can't help herself; she

317

couldn't keep a secret now in this room. "My mom sent me there because it looks good, but I won't really be in danger. No chance of getting into trouble," she says.

The voice says: Maybe she *should* get into trouble.

Mother Eve says, "You need have no fear now."

Jocelyn nods again. "Yes," she says. "Thank you. Thank you."

Mother Eve kisses her on the crown of the head and gives her the blessing in the name of the Great Mother, and she goes down to the party.

Tatiana is followed into the room by two well-built men in fitted clothing: black T-shirts so tight you can see the outline of their nipples, skinny trousers with noticeable crotch bulges. When she sits — in a high-backed chair on a dais — they sit beside her, on somewhat lower stools. The trappings of power, the rewards of success. She rises to greet Mother Eve with a kiss on each cheek.

"Praise be to Our Lady," says Tatiana.

"Glory in the highest," says Mother Eve, without a trace of Allie's sardonic smile.

"They've found twelve more traitors; captured in a raid on the North," mutters Tatiana.

"With God's help, they will all be found," says Mother Eve.

There are infinite numbers of people to meet. Ambassadors and local dignitaries, business owners and leaders of new movements. This party — coming so soon after their defeat in the Battle of the Dniester — is meant to shore up support for Tatiana both at home and abroad. And the presence of Mother Eve is part of that. Tatiana gives a speech about the heart-rending cruelty done by the regimes of the North and the freedom she and her people are fighting for. They listen to the stories of women who join together in small bands to seek Our Lady's vengeance on those who have escaped human justice.

Tatiana is moved almost to tears. She asks one of the smartly dressed young men standing behind her to bring drinks for these brave women. He nods, backs away, almost tripping over his feet, and heads upstairs. While they wait, Tatiana tells one of her long-winded jokes. It is about a woman who wishes she could combine her favourite three men into one man, and then a good witch comes to visit her —

The young blond man bounds in front of her with the bottle.

"Was it this one, Madam?"

Tatiana looks at him. She tips her head to one side.

The young man swallows. "I'm sorry," he says.

"Did I tell you to speak?" she says.

He drops his eyes to the floor.

"Just like a man," she says. "Does not know how to be silent, thinks we always want to hear what *he* has to say, always talking talking talking, interrupting his betters."

The young man looks like he's about to say something, but thinks better of it.

"Needs to be taught some manners," says one of the women standing behind Allie, one of those who run the group seeking justice for old crimes.

Tatiana plucks the bottle of brandy from the young man's hands. Holds it in front of his face. The liquid sloshing inside is dark amber, oily like caramel.

"This bottle is worth more than you," she says. "A glass of this is worth more than you."

She holds the bottle in one hand by the neck. Swirls the liquid around once, twice, three times.

She drops it on to the floor. The glass smashes. The liquid starts to soak into the wood, staining it darker. The smell is strong and sweet.

"Lick it up," she says.

The young man looks down at the shattered bottle. There are glass fragments among the brandy. He looks round at the watching faces. He kneels down and begins to tongue the floor, delicately, working his way around the pieces of glass.

One of the older women calls out, "Get your face into it!"

Allie watches in silence.

The voice says: What. The fuck.

Allie says in her heart: She is actually crazy. Should I say something?

The voice says: Anything you say will diminish your power here.

Allie says: So what, then? What is any of my power worth if I can't use it here?

The voice says: Remember what Tatiana says. We don't have to ask what they'd do if they were in control. We've seen it already. It's worse than this.

Allie clears her throat.

The young man's mouth has blood at the lip.

Tatiana starts to laugh. "Oh for God's sake," she says. "Get a broom and mop it up. You're repulsive."

The young man scrabbles to his feet. The crystal glasses are filled with champagne again. The music can once more be heard.

"Can you believe he did it?" says Tatiana after he's run off to fetch a broom.

Roxy

It's a boring fucking party is what it is. And it's not that she doesn't like Tatiana, she does. Tatiana's let them get on with business over the past year since she took over from Bernie, and anyone who lets you get on with business is all right by Roxy.

Still, you'd think she could throw a better party than this. Someone had told her that Tatiana Moskalev went around this castle with her own blooming pet leopard on a chain. That's the disappointment Roxy can't really get over. Plenty of nice glasses, fine; plenty of gold chairs, all right. No blooming leopard anywhere.

The President seems to have only the dimmest understanding of who Roxy is at all. She goes and does the line-up to shake hands, the woman with the heavy mascara and the green-and-gold eyes says hello and you are one of the fine businesspeople who is making this country the greatest on earth and the most free, without a shadow of recognition crossing her face. Roxy thinks she's drunk. She wants to go: Don't you know, *I'm* the woman shifting five hundred kilos across your borders every day? Every *day*. I'm the one who's got you in trouble with the UN, although we all know they won't do a fucking thing, just send some more observing forces or whatnot. Don't you *know*?

Roxy necks some more of the champagne. She has a look out of the windows at the darkening mountains; She doesn't even hear Mother Eve approaching her until the woman is at her elbow. Eve's spooky like that — tiny and wiry and so quiet she could walk across a room and stick a knife between your ribs before you even knew it.

Mother Eve says: "The defeat in the North has made Tatiana . . . unpredictable."

"Yeah? It's made it bloody unpredictable for me, too, I can tell you. Suppliers are nervy as fuck. Five of my drivers have quit. They're all saying the war's going to push south."

"Do you remember what we did at the convent? With the waterfall?"

Roxy smiles and gives a little laugh. That's a good memory. Simpler, happier times. "That's teamwork," she says.

"I think we could do it again," says Mother Eve, "on a larger scale."

"How d' you mean?"

"My . . . influence. Your undeniable strength. I've always felt that there were great things ahead of you, Roxanne."

"Am I *really* pissed," says Roxy, "or are you making even less sense than usual?"

"We can't talk here." Mother Eve lowers her voice to a whisper. "But I think that Tatiana Moskalev will soon have outlived her usefulness. To the Holy Mother."

Ohhhhhhhh. Oh.

"You kidding?"

Mother Eve shakes her head minutely. "She's unstable. I think in a few months' time the country will be ready for a new leadership. And the people here trust me. If I were to say that you are the right woman for the job . . ."

Roxy almost hoots with laughter at that. "Me? You've *met* me, haven't you, Evie?"

"Stranger things have happened," says Mother Eve. "You're already a leader of a great multitude. Come and see me tomorrow. We'll talk it through."

"It's your funeral," says Roxy.

She doesn't stay long after that, just long enough to be seen to be having a good time and press the flesh of a couple of Tatiana's other disreputable cronies. She's taken with what Mother Eve's said. It's a nice thought. A very nice thought. She does like this country.

She stays out of the way of the reporters circling the room; you can always tell a fucking reporter from the hungry look on their faces. Even though there's one she's seen on the internet who she fancies like she could lick his flesh straight off his bones, there's always more blokes where he came from; they're ten a penny. Especially if she were President. She mutters it under her breath. "President Monke." And then laughs at herself for it. Still. Could work.

In any case, she can't think about it too hard tonight. She's got business to do this evening; non-party, non-diplomatic, non-pressing-the-flesh business. One

324

of them UN soldiers or special representatives or whatever wants to meet up with her somewhere quiet, so they can work out how to circumvent the blockade in the North and keep product moving. Darrell's set it up; he's been doing operations here for months, keeping his head down like a good boy, making contacts, keeping the factory running smoothly even during the war. Sometimes a bloke is better at that than a woman — less threatening; they're better at diplomacy. Still, to finish the deal it has to be Roxy herself.

The roads are winding and dark. The headlights are the only pools of light in the black world; no streetlights here, not even a little village with lit windows. Bloody hell, it's only just gone eleven; you'd think it was four o'clock in the morning. It's more than ninety minutes out of the city, but Darrell's sent her good instructions. She finds the turn-off easily enough, drives down an unlit track, parks the car in front of another one of these spiky castles. All the windows are dark. No sign of life.

She looks at the message Darrell sent her. Green-painted door will be open. She makes a spark from her own palm to light her way, and there's the green door, paint flaking off, at the side of the stable block.

She can smell formaldehyde. And antiseptic. Another corridor, and there's a metal door with a round handle. Light is seeping in around the frame. Right. This is it. She'll bloody tell them next time not to have a fucking meeting somewhere unlit in the middle of nowhere; she could have tripped over and broken her neck. She turns the handle. And there's something weird, just enough to put a frown between her eyes. She can taste blood in the air. Blood and chemicals and there's a feeling like . . . she tries to pin it down. It's a feeling like there's been a fight. Like there's *always* just been a fight.

She opens the door. There's a room lined with plastic, and there are tables and medical equipment, and she's thinking that someone didn't tell Darrell the whole story, and she has just enough time to be afraid when someone grabs her arms and someone else pulls a sack over her head.

She gets off a huge blast — she knows she's hurt someone badly, could feel them crumble and she hears the scream — and she's ready for another go, she's wheeling round and trying to get the bag off her head, and she's spinning and letting off jolts wildly into the air. She shouts out, "Don't you fucking touch me!" and pulls at the thing on her head. And blood and iron bloom at the back of her skull because someone's hit her as hard as she's ever been hit and her last thought is "A leopard, as a pet" as she goes down into night.

She knows, even in her half-sleep, that they're cutting her. She's strong, she's always been strong, she's always been a fighter and she's wrestling with the sleep like a heavy, sodden blanket. She keeps dreaming that her fists are clenched and that she's trying to open them, and she knows that if she could only make her hands move in the real world she would wake up and then she would bring down such blood upon them, she would make the pain fall from the sky, she would open up a hole in the heavens and tumble the fires on to the earth. Something bad is happening to her. Something worse than she can imagine. Wake up, you fucker. Wake the fuck up. Now.

She surfaces. She's strapped down. She can see metal above her, can feel metal under her fingertips and she thinks, Stupid fuckers. She goes to set the whole bed humming because no fucker's coming near her.

But she can't. She goes for it, and her accustomed tool is not in its place. A voice very far away says, "It's working."

But it's not working, that's the whole point, it is definitely not working.

She tries to send a little echo along her collarbone. Her power's there, it's weak, struggling, but it's there. She's never felt so grateful to her own body.

Another voice. She recognizes it, but where, where, whose is that voice? Has she kept a leopard as a pet, what is going on? Stupid fucking leopard padding through her dreams, fuck off, you're not *real*.

"She's trying to break through. Watch her, she's strong."

Someone laughs. Someone says, "With what we've given her?"

"I haven't come all this way," says the voice she knows, "I didn't sort this all out, to have you fuck it up. She's stronger than any of the others you've ever taken it from. Watch her."

"Fine. Mind out of the way."

Someone comes near her again. They're going to hurt her and she can't let them do that. She talks to her own skein, saying: You and me, mate, we're on the same side. You need to give me just a little bit more. The last little bit, I know you've got it. Come on. This is our life we're talking about.

A hand touches her right hand.

"Fuck!" someone shouts and falls and breathes heavily.

She's done it. She can feel it now, coursing more evenly through her, not like she'd been drained, like there'd been a block somewhere and now it's clearing like debris in a stream. Oh she is going to make them pay for this.

"Up the dose! Up the dose!"

"We can't give any more, we'll damage the skein."

"LOOK at her. Fucking do it now, or I'll do it myself."

She's building up a great charge now. She's going to bring this ceiling down on them.

"Just *look* at what she's doing."

Whose is that voice? It's on the tip of her tongue, once she's out of these restraints she'll turn around and see and somewhere in her heart she already knows who and what she'll see.

There's a loud elongated mechanical beep.

"Red zone," says someone. "Automatic warning. We've given her too much."

"Keep it coming."

As suddenly as the power had built up in her, it went. Like someone had flipped a switch.

She wants to scream. She can't make that come either.

She goes down for a moment into the black mud, and when she fights her way back up again they're cutting into her so carefully it feels like a compliment. She's numbed, and it doesn't hurt, but she can feel the knife going in, along her collarbone. And then they touch her skein. Even through the numbness and paralysis and dreamy half-sleep the pain sounds like a fire alarm through her body. It's clean, white pain, like they're slicing very carefully through her eyeballs, shaving off layer after layer of flesh. It's a minute of screaming before she realizes what they're doing. They have lifted up the string of striated muscle across her collarbone and they are sawing at it, separating it strand by strand from her.

Very far away, someone says, "Should she be screaming?"

Someone else says, "Just get on with it."

She knows those voices. She doesn't want to know them. The things you don't want to know, Roxy, those are the things that'll get you in the end.

There's a twang all through her body when they cut through the final strand on the right-hand side of her collarbone. It hurts, but the emptiness that comes after is worse. It's like she's died, but she's still too alive to notice.

Her eyelids flutter as they lift the thing out of her. She knows she's seeing now, not just imagining. She sees it in front of her, the strand of meat that was the thing that made her work. It's jumping and squirming because it wants to get back inside her. She wants it there too. Her own self.

There's a voice to her left.

The leopard says, "Just get on with it."

"Sure you don't want to be under?"

"They said you'd get better results if I could tell you whether it's working."

"Yeah."

"Then get on with it."

And even though her head is in a vice and her neck is full of grinding gears, she turns her head so that just one eye can see what she's looking for. A single glance is enough. The man lying prepped for the implantation operation next to her is Darrell, and sitting beside him in a chair is her dad, Bernie.

There's the fucking leopard, says a tinny, chattering part of her brain. Didn't I tell you there was a fucking leopard somewhere here. You tried to keep a leopard as a pet, didn't you, you fucking idiot, and you know what happens then. Teeth at the throat, blood everywhere, got what you deserved, messing with a leopard. They don't change their spots, Roxy, or is that cheetahs, either way.

Shutupshutupshutupshutupshutupshutupshutup, she says to her brain, I've got to think.

They're ignoring her now. They're working on him. They've sewed her up — just to be neat maybe, or surgeons can't make themselves not sew up a wound they've made. Maybe her dad told them to. There he is. Her own dad. She should have fucking *known* that even not killing him wouldn't be enough. Everything's got its vengeance. A wound for a wound. A bruise for a bruise. A humiliation for a humiliation.

330

She's trying not to cry but she knows she is: leaking from the eyes. She wants to mash them into the ground. The feeling's coming back into her arms and legs and fingers and toes, there's a tingling and an emptiness and an ache and she's got one chance now because there's no reason at all for Darrell not to kill her, he might think she's dead already, with any luck. Fucking snake in the grass, fucking shit-stain on the earth, fucking fucking Darrell.

Bernie says, "How's it looking?"

One of the doctors says, "It's good. Excellent tissue match."

There's a whining sound from the drill as they start to bore little holes in Darrell's collarbone. It's loud. She drifts in and out of time a bit, the clock on the wall is moving faster than it should, she can feel her whole body again, fucking hell, they left her clothes on, that's shoddy, and it's good, and she can work with it. On the next whine of the drill she wriggles her right hand out of the soft fabric restraint.

She looks around with one half-open eye. She moves slowly. Left hand out of the restraints, still no one notices what she's doing, they're so intent on the body of her brother. Left foot. Right foot. She reaches out to the tray next to her, grabs a couple of scalpels and some bandages.

There's some kind of crisis on the table next to her. A machine starts beeping. There's an involuntary jolt from the skein they're stitching into him — good girl, thinks Roxy, that's my girl. One of the surgeons falls to the floor, another swears in Russian and starts giving chest compressions. With two eyes open, Roxy gauges the distance between the table where she's lying and the door. The surgeons are shouting and calling for drugs. No one's looking at Roxy; no one cares. She could die now and no one would give a shit. She might be dying now; she feels like she could be. But she's not going to die here. She tips herself off the table down hard on her knees into a crouch, and still none of them notices. She does a backward crawl towards the door, keeping low, keeping her eye on them.

At the door, she finds her shoes and pulls them on with a little sob of relief. She topples out the door, hamstrings taut, body singing with adrenaline. In the courtyard, the car is gone. But, limping, she runs out into the forest.

Tunde

There is a man with a mouthful of glass.

There is a thin, sharp, translucent sliver spearing the back of his throat, shiny with saliva and mucus, and his friend is trying to extract it with trembling fingers. He shines a light with his phone torch to see where it is exactly, and reaches in while the man retches and tries to hold still. He has to go in for it three times, until he grasps it, pulls it out between thumb and forefinger. It is two inches long. It is stained with blood and meat, a lump of the man's throat on the end of it. The friend puts it on to a clean, white napkin. Around them, the other waiters and chefs and orderlies continue with their business. Tunde photographs the eight shards lined up on the napkin.

He'd taken photographs while the obscenity was happening at the party, his camera casual and low at his hip, seeming to dangle from his hand. The waiter is just seventeen; this is not the first time he's seen or heard about such a thing, but the first time that he's been subject to it. No, he can't go anywhere else. He has relatives in Ukraine who might take him in if he ran, but people get shot trying to cross the border; it's a nervous time. He wipes the blood from his mouth as he speaks.

He says quietly, "Is my fault, must not speak when the President is speaking."

He's crying a little now, from the shock and the shame and the fear and the humiliation and the pain. Tunde recognizes those feelings; he's known them since the first day Enuma touched him.

He has written in the scribbled notes for his book: "At first we did not speak our hurt because it was not manly. Now we do not speak it because we are afraid and ashamed and alone without hope, each of us alone. It is hard to know when the first became the second."

The waiter, whose name is Peter, writes some words on a scrap of paper. He gives it to Tunde and holds his hand clasped over Tunde's fist. He looks into his eyes until Tunde thinks that the man is about to kiss him. Tunde suspects he would allow it because each of these people needs some comfort.

The waiter says, "Don't go."

Tunde says, "I can stay as long as you like. Until the party is over if you like."

Peter says, "No. Don't leave us. She is going to try to make the press leave the country. Please."

Tunde says, "What have you heard?"

Peter will only say the same thing: "Please. Don't leave us. Please."

"I won't," says Tunde. "I won't."

He stands outside the kitchen for a smoke. His fingers are trembling as he lights the cigarette. He'd thought, because he'd met Tatiana Moskalev in the past and she'd been kind to him, that he understood what was happening here. He'd been looking forward to seeing her again. Now he's glad he didn't have a chance to reintroduce himself. He pulls the paper that Peter had given him out of his pocket and looks at it. It says, in shaky block letters: "THEY'RE GOING TO TRY TO KILL US."

He gets a few shots of people leaving the party through the side door. A couple of gun-runners. A bio-weapons specialist. It's the Horsemen of the Apocalypse ball. There's Roxanne Monke getting into her car, queen of a London crime family. She sees him photographing her car, mouths "Fuck. Off" at him.

He files the story with CNN when he's back in his hotel room at 3a.m. The photographs of the man licking the brandy up from the floor. The glass splinters on the napkin. The tears on Peter's cheek.

Just past 9a.m. he wakes involuntarily, gritty-eyed, sweat prickling his back and temples. He checks his email, to see what the night editor's said about the piece. He's promised anything that came out of this party to CNN first, but if they want too many cuts he'll take it elsewhere. There's a simple, two-line email.

"Sorry, Tunde, we're going to pass on this. Great reporting, pix excellent, not a story we can sell in right now."

Fine. Tunde sends out another three emails, then has a shower and orders a pot of strong coffee. When the emails start to come back, he's looking through the international news sites; nothing much on Bessapara, no one's scooped him. He reads the emails. Three more rejections. All for similar foot-shuffling, non-committal we-don't-think-there's-a-story-here reasons.

He's never needed a market, though. He'll just post the whole thing to his YouTube.

He logs on via the hotel wifi and . . . there YouTube isn't. Just a tiny take-down notice saying that this site is not available in this region. He tries a VPN. No good. Tries his cellphone data. Same deal.

He thinks of Peter saying, "She is trying to make the press leave the country."

If he emails the files, they'll intercept them.

He burns a DVD. All the photos, all the footage, his own piece.

He puts it in a padded courier envelope and pauses for a moment over the address. In the end, he writes Nina's name and details on the label. He puts a note inside, saying, "Hold this till I come fetch it." He's left stuff with her before: notes for his book, journals from his travels. Safer with her than travelling with him or in an empty apartment somewhere. He'll get the American ambassador to put it in the diplomatic bag.

If Tatiana Moskalev is trying to do what it looks like she might be trying to do, he doesn't want her to know yet that he's going to document it. He'll only get one chance at this story. Journalists have been expelled from countries for less than this, and he doesn't kid himself that it'll make any difference that he flirted with her once.

It's that afternoon that the hotel asks for his passport. Just because of the new security rules at this difficult time.

Most of the other non-bureau staff are on their way out of Bessapara. There are a few war reporters in flak jackets on the northern front, but until the fighting starts in earnest there's nothing much to say here, and the posturing and threats go on for more than five weeks.

Tunde stays. Even while he's receiving offers for substantial sums to go to Chile to interview the anti-pope and hear her views on Mother Eve. Even while more male-activism terror splinter groups say that they'll only deliver their manifesto if he comes to tape them. He stays, and he interviews dozens of people in cities across the region. He learns some basic Romanian. When colleagues and friends ask what the hell he's doing he says he's working on a book about this new nation-state, and they shrug and say, "Fair enough." He attends the religious services in the new churches — and sees how the old churches are being repurposed or destroyed. He sits in a circle in an underground room by candlelight and listens to a priest intoning the service as it used to be: the son and not the mother at the heart. After the service, the priest presses his body against Tunde's in a long, close hug and whispers, "Do not forget us."

Tunde is told more than once that the police here no longer investigate the murder of men; that if a man is found dead it is presumed that a vengeance gang had given him his proper reward for his deeds in the time before. "Even a young boy," a father tells him, in an overheated sitting room in a western village, "even a boy who is only fifteen now — what could he have done in the time before?"

Tunde doesn't write online about any of these interviews. He knows how that would end — a knock on the door at 4a.m. and being hustled on to the first plane out of the country. He writes as if he's a tourist, on vacation in the new nation. He posts photographs every day. There's already an angry undercurrent to the comments: where are the new videos, Tunde, where are your funny reports? Still, they'd notice if he vanished. That's important.

In his sixth week in the country, Tatiana's newly appointed Minister for Justice gives a press conference. It's sparsely attended. The room is airless, the walls papered with beige-and-brown string.

"After the recent terrorist outrages across the world, and after our country was betrayed by men who work for our enemies, we are announcing today a new legal vessel," she says. "Our people have suffered for too long now at the hands of a group which has tried to destroy us. We do not have to ask ourselves what they will do if they win; we have already seen it. We must protect ourselves against those who might betray us.

"Thus, we institute today this law, that each man in the country must have his passport and other official documents stamped with the name of his female guardian. Her written permission will be needed for any journey he undertakes. We know that men have their tricks and we cannot allow them to band together.

"Any man who does not have a sister, mother, wife or daughter, or other relative, to register him must

338

report to the police station, where he will be assigned a work detail and shackled to other men for the protection of the public. Any man who breaks these laws will be subject to capital punishment. This applies also to foreign journalists and other workers."

Looks pass between the men in the room; there are about a dozen, foreign journalists who've been here since it was a grim staging post in the business of human trafficking. The women try to look horrified but at the same time comradely, comforting. "Don't worry," they seem to say. "This can't last long, but while it does we'll help you out." Several of the men fold their arms protectively over their chests.

"No man may take money or other possessions out of the country."

The Minister for Justice turns the page. There is a long list of proclamations printed close together in small type.

Men are no longer permitted to drive cars.

Men are no longer permitted to own businesses. Foreign journalists and photographers must be employed by a woman.

Men are no longer permitted to gather together, even in the home, in groups larger than three, without a woman present.

Men are no longer permitted to vote — because their years of violence and degradation have shown that they are not fit to rule or govern.

A woman who sees a man flouting one of these laws in public is not only permitted but required to discipline him immediately. Any woman who fails in this duty will be considered an enemy of the state, an accessory to the crime, one who attempts to undermine the peace and harmony of the nation.

There are several pages of minor adjustments to these rulings, explanations of what constitutes "being accompanied by a woman" and leniencies in case of extreme medical emergency because, after all, they are not monsters. The press conference becomes more and more quiet as the list is read out.

The Minister for Justice finishes reading her list and calmly sets the papers down in front of her. Her shoulders are very relaxed, her face impassive.

"That is all," she says. "No questions."

In the bar, Hooper from the *Washington Post* says, "I don't care. I'm leaving."

He's said this several times already. He pours himself another whisky and plops three ice cubes into it, swirls them round hard and makes his case again:

"Why the fuck should we stay somewhere that we actually *can't* do our jobs, when there are dozens of places we can? Something's about to break out in Iran, I'm pretty sure. I'll go there."

"And when something breaks out in Iran," drawls Semple of the BBC, "what do you think will happen to the men?"

Hooper shakes his head. "Not in Iran. Not like this. They're not going to change their beliefs overnight, cede everything to the women."

"You do remember," continues Semple, "that they turned overnight when the Shah fell and the Ayatollah came to power? You do remember that it happens that quickly?"

There's a moment of quiet.

"Well, what do you suggest?" says Hooper. "Give up everything? Go back home and become a gardening editor? I can see you doing that. Flak jacket in the herbaceous borders."

Semple shrugs. "I'm staying. I'm a British citizen, under the protection of Her Majesty. I'll obey the laws, within reason, and report on that."

"What are you expecting to report? What it's like sitting in a hotel room waiting for a woman to come and get you?"

Semple sticks his bottom lip out. "It won't get any worse than this."

At the table next to them, Tunde is listening. He also has a large whisky, though he's not drinking it. The men are getting drunk and shouting. The women are quiet, watching the men. There is something vulnerable and desperate in the men's display — he thinks the women are looking with compassion.

One says, loud enough for Tunde to be able to hear, "We'll take you anywhere you want to go. Listen, we don't believe in this nonsense. You can tell us where you want to go. It'll be just the same as it's always been."

Hooper clasps Semple by the sleeve, saying, "You have to leave. First plane out of here and screw it all."

One of the women says, "He's right. What's the point of getting killed over this piss-pot of a place?"

Tunde walks slowly to the front desk. He waits for an elderly Norwegian couple to pay their bill — there's a taxi outside loading up their bags. Like most people from wealthy nations, they're getting out of the city while they can. At last, after querying each item on the mini-bar receipt and the level of the local taxes, they leave.

There is only one member of staff behind the desk. Grey is colonizing his hair in clumps — a chunk here and there, the rest dark and thick and tightly curled. He's perhaps in his sixties, surely a trusted staff member with years of experience.

Tunde smiles. An easy, we're-in-this-together smile.

"Strange days," he says.

The man nods. "Yes, sir."

"You've planned what you're going to do?"

The man shrugs.

"You have family who'll take you in?"

"My daughter has a farm three hours west of here. I will go to her."

"They going to let you travel?"

The man looks up. The whites of his eyes are jaundiced and streaked with red, the thin, bloody lines reaching towards the pupil. He looks for a long time at Tunde, perhaps five or six seconds.

"If God wills it."

Tunde puts one hand into his pocket, easy and slow. "I have been thinking of travel myself," he says. And pauses. And waits.

The man does not ask him more. Promising.

342

"Of course, there are one or two things I'd need for travel that I . . . don't have any more. Things that I wouldn't want to leave without. Whenever I were to set off."

The man still says nothing, but nods his head slowly.

Tunde brings his hands together casually, then slides the notes under the blotter on the desk so that just the corners of them are showing. Fanned out, ten fifty-dollar bills. US currency, that's the key thing.

The man's slow, regular breathing halts, for just a second.

Tunde continues, jovial. "Freedom," he says, "is all anyone wants." He pauses. "I think I will go up to bed. Could you tell them to send me up a Scotch? Room 614. As soon as you can."

The man says, "I will bring it myself, sir. In just a few moments."

In the room, Tunde flicks on the TV. Kristen is saying, The fourth-quarter forecast isn't looking good. Matt is laughing attractively and saying, Now, I don't understand that kind of thing at all, but I'll tell you what I do know about: apple-bobbing.

There's a brief roundup on C-Span about a "military crackdown" in this "tumultuous region", but much more about another domestic terrorism action in Idaho. UrbanDox and his idiots have successfully changed the story. If you're talking about men's rights now, you're talking about them, and their conspiracy theories and the violence of them and the need for curbs and limits. No one wants to hear about what's happening here. The truth has always been a more complex commodity than the market can easily package and sell. And now the weather on the ones.

Tunde stocks his backpack. Two changes of clothes, his notes, his laptop and phone, water bottle, his old-fashioned camera with forty rolls of film, because he knows there could be days when he won't find electricity or batteries, and a non-digital camera will be useful. He pauses, then crams in a couple more pairs of socks. He feels a kind of excitement welling up, unexpectedly, as well as the terror and the outrage and the madness. He tells himself it is stupid to feel excited; this is serious. When the knock on the door comes, he jumps.

For a moment, when he opens the door, he thinks the old man has misunderstood him. On the tray, there's a tumbler of whisky sitting on a rectangular coaster, and nothing else. It's only when he looks more closely that he sees that the coaster is, in fact, his passport.

"Thank you," he says. "This is just what I wanted."

The man nods. Tunde pays him for the whisky and zips the passport into the side pocket of his trousers.

He waits to leave until around 4.30a.m. The corridors are quiet, the lights low. No alarm sounds as he opens the door and steps out into the cold. No one tries to stop him. It is as if the whole afternoon had been a dream.

Tunde crosses the empty night-streets, the dogs barking far away, breaks into a jog for a few moments then settles back to a long-legged, loping pace. Putting his hand into his pocket, he finds he still has the key to his hotel room. He considers throwing it away or putting it into a postbox but, fingering the shiny brass fob, he thrusts it back into his pocket. As long as he has it, he can imagine that room 614 will always be there waiting for him, still just as he left it. The bed still unmade, the morning's papers by the desk in ungainly peaks, his smart shoes side by side under the bedside table, his used pants and socks thrown in the corner by his open, half-empty suitcase.

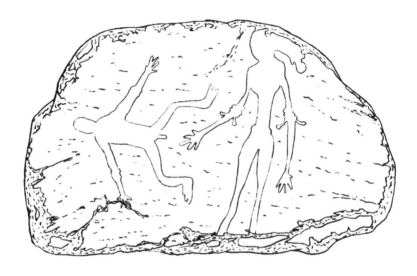

Rock art discovered in northern France, around
four thousand years old. Depicts the "curbing"
procedure — also known as male genital mutila-
tion — in which key nerve endings in the penis
are burned out as the boy approaches puberty.
After the procedure — which is still practised in
several European countries — it is impossible for
a man to achieve an erection without skein
stimulation by a woman. Many men who have
been subjected to curbing will never be able to
ejaculate without pain.

Can't be more than seven months left

Allie

Roxy Monke has disappeared. Allie saw her at the party, the staff say they saw her leaving, there's security camera footage of her car driving out of the city, and then nothing. She was heading north, that's all they know. It's been eight weeks. There's been nothing.

Allie's spoken to Darrell on videochat; he looks terrible. "Just about holding it together," he says. They've scoured the countryside for her. "If they came for her, they could come for me," he says. "We'll keep looking for her. Even if what we find is a body. We have to know what's happened."

They have to know. Allie has had wild and terrible thoughts. Tatiana's convinced with a sudden upsurge of paranoia that Roxy has betrayed her to North Moldova and interprets every new turn in the hostilities as a sign that Roxy's sold her out, even given the Glitter to her enemies. Tatiana is becoming unpredictable. At times she seems to trust Mother Eve more than anyone; she has even signed into law a measure making Mother Eve the de facto leader of the country if she, Tatiana, is incapacitated. But she's having violent fits of rage, striking and hurting her staff, accusing everyone around her of working against her. She's giving contradictory and bizarre instructions to her generals and officers. There has been fighting. Some of the revenge bands have set fire to villages harbouring gender-traitor women and men who've done wrong. Some of the villages have fought back. There is a war slowly spreading in the country, not declared on a single day between well-defined enemies but spreading like measles: first one spot, then two, then three. A war of all against all.

Allie misses Roxy. She had not known before that Roxy had found a chink in her heart. It makes her afraid. She hadn't ever thought of having a friend. It is not an item she'd particularly felt the need for, or the lack of, until it was gone. She worries. She has dreams in which she sends out first a raven and then a white dove, looking for good news, but no news returns on the wind.

She would send out scouting parties to comb the woods if she knew where to look within a hundred miles.

She prays to the Holy Mother: Please, bring her safely home. Please.

The voice says: I can't make any promises.

Allie says in her heart: Roxy had a lot of enemies. People like that, they have a lot of enemies.

The voice says: You think you don't have a lot of enemies, too?

Allie says: What help are you?

The voice says: I'm always here for you. But I did say this would be tricky.

350

Allie says: You also said that the only way is to own the place.

The voice says: Then you know what you have to do.

She says to herself: Stop it now. Just stop it. She is just a person like all of the other people. Everything will disappear and you will survive. Cut off this part of yourself.

Shut off this compartment in your heart, fill it with scalding water and kill it. You do not need her. You will live.

She is afraid.

She is not safe.

She knows what she has to do.

The only way to be safe is to own the place.

There's a night when Tatiana calls for her very late, past 3 a.m. Tatiana's been having trouble sleeping. She wakes in the night with bad dreams of vengeance, spies in the palace, someone coming for her with a knife. At these times she calls for Mother Eve, her spiritual advisor, and Mother Eve comes and sits on the end of her bed and speaks soothing words until she falls asleep again.

The bedroom is decorated with a mixture of burgundy brocade and tiger skins. Tatiana sleeps alone, no matter who might have been in the bed earlier in the evening.

She says, "They're going to take everything from me."

Allie takes her hand, feels her way along the jangled nerve-endings to the griping and disquieted brain. She says, "God is with you, and you will prevail."

As she says it, she *presses* in a careful and measured way on *this* part of Tatiana's mind and *that* one. Nothing you could feel. Only a few neurons fire differently. It's just a tiny suppression, a minute elevation.

"Yes," says Tatiana. "I'm sure that's right."

Good girl, says the voice.

"Good girl," says Allie, and Tatiana nods like an obedient child.

Eventually, Allie figures, more people will learn how to do this. Perhaps even now, in some far-off place, a young woman is learning how to soothe and control her father or brother. Eventually, other people will figure out that the ability to hurt is only the beginning. The gateway drug, Roxy would say.

"Now listen," says Allie. "I think you'd like to sign these papers now, wouldn't you?"

Tatiana nods sleepily.

"You've thought it over, and the Church really should have the ability to try its own cases and enforce its own statutes in the border regions, shouldn't we?"

Tatiana picks up the pen from her bedside table and signs her name jerkily. Her eyes are closing as she writes. She is falling back on to the pillow.

The voice says: How long are you planning to drag this out?

Allie says in her heart: If I move too quickly, the Americans will get suspicious. I'd meant this for Roxy. It'll be harder to convince people when I do it for me.

The voice says: She's getting harder to control every day. You know she is.

352

Allie says: It's because of what we're doing. Something's going wrong, inside her head with the chemicals. But it won't go on for ever. I'll take the country. And then I'll be safe.

Darrell

The shipments are fucked up because of the fucking UN.

Darrell's looking at the truck that's come back to him. It dumped its bags in the woods, and that's three million quid of Glitter bleeding out into the forest floor when it rains, which would be bad enough by itself. Except that's not the only thing. They got chased from the border, they came rough through the woods to get away from the soldiers. But they gave them a trajectory, didn't they? If you're running from the border and you're heading in this direction, narrows down the options of where you might be, doesn't it?

"Fuck!" says Darrell, and kicks the wheel of the truck. His scar pulls taut, his skein hums angrily. It hurts. He shouts "Fuck!" again, louder than he'd meant to.

They're in the warehouse. A few of the women glance over. A couple start wandering towards the van to see what's happened.

One of the drivers, the deputy, shifts her weight from one foot to the other and says, "When we had to drop a load before, Roxy always —"

"I don't give a fuck what Roxy always," says Darrell, a little too quickly. A look passes between the women. He pulls it back. "I mean, I don't think she wants us to do what we've done before, all right?"

Another look between them.

Darrell tries to talk more slowly, in a calm, authoritative voice. He finds himself getting nervous around all these women now that Roxy's not around to keep them in line. Once they know that he's got a skein himself, it'll be better, but this isn't the right time for any more surprises, and his dad's said he's got to keep it secret until it's healed, anyway, until he comes back to London.

"Listen," he says. "We'll lie low for a week. No more shipments, no more border crossings, just let it all go quiet."

They nod.

Darrell thinks, How do I know you haven't been fucking skimming? There's no way to know. Say you've dropped a load in the forest, who's to know that you didn't keep it for yourself? Fuck. They're not afraid enough of him, that's the problem.

One of the girls — a slow, thick one called Irina — makes a frown and pushes her lips forward. She says, "Do you have a guardian?"

Oh, this old fucking noise again.

"Yes, Irina," he says, "my sister, Roxanne, is my guardian. You remember her? Runs this place, owns the factory?"

"But . . . Roxanne is gone."

"Just on holiday," says Darrell. "She'll be back, and for the time being I'm just keeping everything ticking over for her."

Irina's frown deepens, her forehead huge and crenellated. "I listen to the news," she says. "If guardian is dead or missing, new guardian must be appointed for men."

"She's not *dead*, Irina, she's not even missing, she's just . . . not here right now. She's gone away to . . . do some important things, all right? She'll be back eventually, and she told me to look after this all while she's away."

Irina turns her head from side to side to absorb this new information. Darrell can hear the gears and bones in her neck clicking.

"But how do you know what to do," she says, "when Roxanne is away?"

"She sends me messages, all right, Irina? She sends me little emails and text messages, and she's the one who's telling me to do all the things I'm doing. I have never done a thing without my sister's say-so, and when you do what I tell you, you're doing what she tells you, all right?"

Irina blinks. "Yes," she says. "I did not know. Messages. Is good."

"Good, then . . . so, is there anything else?"

Irina stares at him. Come on girl, dredge it up, what's in the back of that massive head?

"Your father," she says.

"Yes? My father what?"

"Your father has left you a message. He wants to talk to you."

Bernie's voice hums down the line from London. The sound of his disappointment makes Darrell's bowels turn to water, as it always has.

"You haven't found her?"

"Nothing, Dad."

Darrell keeps his voice low. The walls of his office at the factory are thin.

"She's probably crawled off into a hole to die, Dad. You heard the doc. When they get their skeins cut out, more than half of them die from the shock. And with the blood loss, and she was in the middle of nowhere. It's been two months, Dad. She's *dead*."

"You don't have to say it like you're happy about it. She was my bloody daughter."

What did Bernie think was going to happen? Did he think Roxy was going to come back home and run the bookies after they did that to her? Better bloody hope she's dead.

"Sorry, Dad."

"It's better this way, that's all. This is the way round things ought to be, that's why we did it. Not to hurt her."

"No, Dad."

"How's it bedding in, son? How are you feeling?"

It wakes him up every hour through the night, squirming and twitching. The drugs they've given him, along with the Glitter, are making him grow his own

357

controlling nerves for the skein. But it feels like a fucking viper inside his chest.

"It's good, Dad. The doc says I'm doing well. It's working."

"When you gonna be ready to use it?"

"Nearly there, Dad, another week or two."

"Good. This is just the start, boychick."

"I know, Dad." Darrell smiles. "I'll be deadly. Come along with you to a meeting, no one will expect me to be able to do nothing, then *pow*."

"And if we can get it to work on you, this operation, think of who we couldn't sell it to. Chinese, the Russians, anyone with a prison population. Skein transplants . . . everyone's going to be doing it."

"We'll make a killing, Dad."

"That we will."

Jocelyn

Margot sent her to a psychotherapist because of the shock and trauma of the terrorist attack. She hasn't told the therapist that she didn't mean to kill that man. She hasn't said that he wasn't holding a gun. The therapist works out of an office paid for by NorthStar Industries, so it seems like it might not be safe. They talk in general terms.

She told the therapist about Ryan.

Jocelyn said, "I wanted him to like me because I'm strong and in control."

The therapist said, "Maybe he liked you for different reasons."

Jocelyn said, "I don't want him to like me for different reasons. That just makes me think I'm disgusting. Why would you have to like me for different reasons than any other girl? Are you calling me weak?"

She didn't tell the therapist she's back in touch with Ryan now. He emailed her — from a new address, a burner — after that thing happened at the NorthStar camp. She said she didn't want to hear from him, couldn't talk to a terrorist. He said, "What. I mean, what."

It's taken him months to persuade her that it wasn't him on those bulletin boards. Jocelyn still doesn't know who she believes for sure, but she knows that her mother's got into the habit of lying so completely that she doesn't even know she's doing it. Jos felt something curdle inside her when she realized her mom might have deliberately lied to her.

Ryan says, "She hated that I love you just how you are."

Jos says, "I want you to love me in spite of my problem, not because of it."

Ryan says, "I just love you, though. All the pieces of you."

Jos says, "You like me because I'm weak. I hate that you think I'm weak."

Ryan says, "You're not weak. You're not. Not to anyone who knows you, not to anyone who cares. And what would it matter if you were? People are allowed to be weak."

But that's the question, really.

There are advertisements on hoardings now, with sassy young women showing off their long, curved arcs in front of cute, delighted boys. They're supposed to make you want to buy soda, or sneakers, or gum. They work, they sell product. They sell girls one other thing; quietly, on the side. Be strong, they say, that's how you get everything you want.

The problem is, that feeling is everywhere now. If you want to find something different to it, you have to listen to some difficult people. Not everything they say seems right. Some of them sound mad.

That man Tom Hobson who used to be on the *Morning Show* has his own website now. He's joined up with UrbanDox and Babe-Truth and some of the others. Jos reads it on her cellphone when no one else is around. There are accounts on Tom Hobson's website of things happening in Bessapara that Jos can't really believe. Torture and experiments, gangs of women on the loose in the north near the border, murdering and raping men at will. Here in the south it's quiet, even with the growing border unrest. Jocelyn's met people in this country — they're mostly really nice. She's met men who agree that the laws are sensible for right now, while they're at war. And women who've invited her in for tea in their houses.

But there are things she finds easy to believe, too. Tom writes about how in Bessapara, where she is right now, there are people doing experiments on boys like Ryan. Cutting them to pieces to find out what's happened to them. Feeding them big glops of that street drug called Glitter. They say the drug's being shipped out of Bessapara, pretty near to where she is. Tom's got Google maps of the location on the site. Tom says the real reason the US army is stationed where she is, in the south of Bessapara, is because they're protecting the supplies of Glitter. Keep everything orderly, so Margot Cleary can arrange her shipments of Glitter from organized-crime syndicates to NorthStar, who sell it back to the US army at a marked-up price.

For more than a year, the army had been giving her a small regulation packet of a purple-white powder every three days, "for her condition". One of the sites Ryan showed her said that the powder makes girls with skein abnormalities worse. It increases the highs and the lows. Your system becomes dependent on it.

But now she's OK. She'd say it was like a miracle, but it's not *like* anything. It was an actual miracle. She was there for it. She prays every night in the dark in her bunk, closing her eyes and whispering, "Thank you, thank you, thank you." She's been healed. She's OK. She thinks to herself, If I was saved, there must be a reason.

Jos goes to look at the unused packets stashed under her mattress. And at the photos on Tom Hobson's site of the drugs he's talking about.

She texts Ryan. Secret phone, burner, he changes it every three weeks.

Ryan says, "Do you really believe your mom's made a deal with a drug cartel?"

Jos says, "I don't believe that, if she had the opportunity, she wouldn't."

It's Jocelyn's day off. She signs a jeep out from the base — she's just going for a country drive, meeting up with some friends, that OK? She's the daughter of a Senator tipped to run for the big house at the next election and a major stakeholder in NorthStar. Of course it's OK.

She consults the print-outs of the maps from Tom Hobson's website. If he's right, one of the drug manufacturing centres in Bessapara is only about forty miles away. And there was that weird thing that happened a few weeks earlier: some of the girls from the base chased an unmarked van through the forest.

The driver shot at them. They lost it in the end, and reported it as possible North Moldovan terrorist activity. But Jos knows what direction it was heading in.

There's a lightness in her as she gets into the jeep. She's got a half-day furlough. The sun is shining. She'll drive down to where the place should be and see if she can see anything. She's feeling light-hearted. Her skein is humming strong and true as it always does now, and she feels good. Normal. It's an adventure. Worst comes to worst, she'll have had a nice drive. But she might be able to take some photos to put online herself. But it might come out much better than that; she might find something that would incriminate her mother. Something she could email Margot and say: If you don't back the fuck off and let me go and live my life, these are going straight to the *Washington Post*. Getting photographs like that . . . that wouldn't be a bad day at all.

Tunde

It wasn't hard at first. He'd made friends enough to shelter him as he travelled first out through the city and satellite towns and then towards the mountains. He knows Bessapara and North Moldova; he'd travelled here, researching the story about Awadi-Atif a lifetime ago. He feels curiously safe here.

And a regime cannot, in general, turn overnight from one thing to another. Bureaucracies are slow. People take their time. The old man must be kept on to show the new women how the paper mill is soused down, or how the stocktaking check on the flour order is made. All over the country, there are men still running their factories while the women mutter among themselves about the new laws and wonder when something will happen to enforce them. In his first weeks on the road, Tunde took photographs of the new ordinances, of the fights in the street, of the dead-eyed men imprisoned in their homes. His plan was to travel for a few weeks, and simply record what he saw. It would be the last chapter of the book that's waiting for him backed up on USB sticks and in filled notebooks in Nina's apartment in New York.

He heard rumours that the most extreme events had been in the mountains. No one would say what they'd heard, not precisely. They talked grimly of backward country folk and of the darkness that had never quite receded there, not under any of a dozen different regimes and dictators.

Peter, the waiter from Tatiana Moskalev's party, had said, "They used to blind the girls. When the power first came, the men there, the warlords, blinded all the girls. That is what I heard. They put their eyes out with hot irons. So they could still be the bosses, you see?"

"And now?"

Peter shook his head. "Now we don't go there."

So Tunde had decided, for want of another goal, to walk towards the mountains.

In the eighth week it began to be bad. He arrived in a town by the edge of a great green-blue lake. He walked, hungry, through the streets on a Sunday morning until he came to a bakery with open doors, a fug of steam and yeast leaking deliciously into the street.

He proffered some coins to the man behind the counter and pointed at some puffy white rolls cooling on a wire rack. The man made the accustomed "hands open like a book" gesture to ask to see Tunde's papers; this had been happening more frequently. Tunde showed his passport and his news-gathering credentials.

The man leafed through the passport, looking, Tunde knew, for the official stamp declaring his guardian, who would then have co-signed a pass for him to be out shopping today. He went through each page carefully.

Having conscientiously examined it, he made the "papers" sign again, a little panic rising in his face. Tunde smiled and shrugged and tipped his head to one side.

"Come on," he said, though there was no indication the man spoke any English. "It's just some little rolls. These are all the papers I have, man."

Until now, this had been enough. Usually someone would smile at this point at the absurd foreign journalist or give a little lecture in broken English about how he must be properly certified next time, and Tunde would apologize and give his charming grin, and he would walk out of the store with his meal or supplies.

This time the man behind the counter shook his head miserably again. He pointed towards a sign on the wall in Russian. Tunde translated it with the help of his phrasebook. It was, roughly: "Five thousand dollar fine for anyone found to have helped a man without papers."

Tunde shrugged and smiled and opened his palms to show them empty. He made a "looking-around" gesture, cocking his hand over his eyes and miming a scouting of the horizon.

"Who's here to see? I won't tell anyone."

The man shook his head. Clutched the counter, looked down at the backs of his hands. There, where his cuffs met his wrists, he was marked with long, whorled scars. Scars upon scars, older and newer. Fern-like and coiled. Where his neck pulled away from the shirt were the marks, too. He shook his head and stood and waited, looking down. Tunde grabbed his passport back from the counter and left. As he walked away, there were women standing in open doorways watching him go.

Women and men who were willing to sell him food or fuel for his little camping stove became fewer and farther between. He started to develop a sense for those who might be friendly. Older men, sitting outside a house playing cards — they'd have something for him, might even find him a bed for the night. Young men tended to be too frightened. There was no point talking to women at all; even meeting their eyes felt too dangerous.

When he walked past a group of women on the road — laughing and joking and making arcs against the sky — Tunde said to himself, I'm not here, I'm nothing, don't notice me, you can't see me, there's nothing here to see.

They called to him first in Romanian and then in English. He looked at the stones of the path. They shouted a few words after him, obscene and racist words, but let him go on.

In his journal, he wrote: "For the first time today on the road I was afraid." He ran his fingers over the ink as it dried. The truth was easier there than here.

Halfway through the tenth week came a bright morning, the sun breaking through the clouds, dragonflies darting and hovering over the pasture meadow. Tunde made his little calculation again in his head — enough energy bars in his pack to keep him going for a couple of weeks, enough film in his back-up camera, his phone and charger safe. He'd be in the mountains in a week, he'd record what he saw there for a week more, perhaps, and then he'd get the fuck out with this story. He was in this dream so securely that, at first, rounding the side of the hill, he did not see what the thing was tied to that post in the centre of the road.

It was a man with long, dark hair hanging down over his face. He had been tied to the post by plastic cords at his wrists and ankles. His hands were pulled back, his shoulders strained, the wrists fastened behind him. His ankles were secured in front of him, the same cord run round the pole a dozen times. It had been hastily done by someone inexpert in ropes and knots. They had simply bound him tightly and left him there. There were the marks of pain across his body, livid and dark, blue and scarlet and black. Around his neck was a sign with a single word in Russian: *slut*. He had been dead for two or three days.

Tunde photographed the body with great care. There is something beautiful in cruelty and something hateful in artful composition, and he wanted to express both these things. He took his time over it, and did not look around to scout his position or make sure he was not being observed from afar. Later, he couldn't believe he'd been so stupid. It was that evening that he first became aware that he was being followed.

It was dusk, and though he had walked seven or eight miles on from the body, its lolling head, its dark tongue, were still in his mind. He walked in the dust at the side of the road, through densely clustered trees. The moon was rising, a yellow-clouded fingernail of light between the trees. He thought to himself from time to time, I could make camp here; come on, take out the bedroll. But his feet kept walking, to put another mile, another mile, another mile between him and the curtain of hair falling over the rotting face. The night-birds were calling. He looked out into the darkness of the wood and there, among the trees to his right, he saw a crackle of light.

It was small but unmistakable; no one would take that particular thin, white, momentary filament for anything else. There was a woman out there, and she had made an arc between her palms. Tunde inhaled sharply.

It could be anything. Someone starting a fire, lovers playing a game, anything. His feet started to walk more quickly. And then he saw it again, in front of him. A long, slow, deliberate crackle of light. Illuminating, this time, a dim face, long hair hanging down, the mouth a crooked smile. She was looking at him. Even in the dim light, even far off, he could see that.

Don't be afraid. The only way to defeat this is not to be afraid. But the animal part of himself was afraid. There is a part in each of us which holds fast to the old truth: either you are the hunter or you are the prey. Learn which you are. Act accordingly. Your life depends upon it.

She made her sparks fly up again in the blue-black darkness. She was closer than he'd thought. She made a noise. Low, croaking laughter. He thought, Oh god, she's mad. And this was the worst of all. That he might be stalked here for no purpose, that he could die here with no reason.

A twig broke close by his right foot. He did not know if it was her, or him. He ran. Sobbing, gulping, with the focus of an animal. Behind him, when he chanced a glance, she was running, too; the palms of her hands set the trees on fire, skittish flame along the dusty bark and into a few crisp leaves. He ran faster. If there was a thought in his head it was: there will be safety somewhere. If I keep going, there must be.

And as he came to the top of the rising, curved hill path, he saw it: not even a mile away, a village with lit windows.

He ran for the village. There, in the sodium lights, this terror would be bleached from his bones.

He'd been thinking for a long time about how he'd end this. Since the third night, when his friends told him he had to leave, that the police were going door-to-door asking questions about any man who was not properly certified with an approved guardian. On that night, he'd said to himself: I can make this stop any time. He had his phone. All he had to do was charge it and send one email. Maybe to his editor at CNN and maybe copied to Nina. Tell them where he was. They would come and find him, and he would be a hero, reporting undercover, rescued.

He thought, Now. Now is the time. This is it.

He ran into the village. Some of the downstairs windows were still lit. There was the sound of radio or television from some of them. It was only just after nine. For a moment he thought of banging on the door, of saying: Please. Help. But the thought of the darkness that might be behind those lit windows kept him from asking. The night was filled with monsters now.

On the side of a five-storey apartment building he saw a fire escape. He ran for it, began to climb. As he passed the third floor, he saw a dark room with three air conditioners piled on the floor. A store room. Empty, unused. He tried the lip of the window with the tips of his fingers. It opened. He tumbled himself into the musty quiet space. He pulled the window closed. He groped in the dark until he found what he was looking for. An electrical socket. He plugged his phone in.

The little two-note sound of it starting up was like the sound of his own key in the lock of his front door back at home in Lagos. There. It's over now. The screen was bright. He pressed the warm light of it to his lips, inhaled. In his mind, he was home already and all the cars and trains and aeroplanes and lines and security that would be needed between here and there were imaginary and unimportant.

He sent an email quickly: to Nina, and to Temi, and to three different editors he'd worked with recently. He told them where he was, that he was safe, that he needed them to contact the embassy to get him out.

While he waited for the reply, he looked at the news. More and more "skirmishes", without anyone being willing to call this an outright war. The price of oil on the up again. And there was Nina's name, too, on an essay about what's happening here, inside Bessapara. He smiled. Nina had only ever been here for a long weekend press junket a few months ago. What would

371

she have to say about this place? And then, as he read, he frowned. Something felt familiar about her words.

He was interrupted by the comforting, warm, musical *ping* of an email arriving.

It was from one of the editors.

It said, "I don't find this funny. Tunde Edo was my friend. If you've hacked this account, we will find you, you sick fuck."

Another *ping*, another reply. Not dissimilar to the first.

Tunde felt panic rising in his chest. He said to himself, It'll be OK, there has been a misunderstanding, something has happened.

He looked up his own name in the paper. There was an obituary. His obituary. It was long and full of slightly back-handed praise for his work in bringing news to a younger generation. The precise phrases implied very subtly that he'd made current affairs appear simple and trivial. There were a couple of minor mistakes. They named five famous women he'd influenced. The piece called him well-loved. It named his parents, his sister. He died, they recorded, in Bessapara; he had been, unfortunately, involved in a car crash which left his body a charred wreck, identifiable only by the name on his suitcase.

Tunde started to breathe more quickly.

He'd left the suitcase in the hotel room.

Someone had taken the suitcase.

He flipped back to Nina's story about Bessapara. It was an extract from a longer book that she'd be bringing out later in the year with a major international publishing house. The newspaper called the book an instant classic. It was a global assessment of the Great Change, based on reporting and interviews from around the world. The stand-first compared the book to De Tocqueville, to Gibbon's *Decline and Fall*.

It was his essay. His photographs. Stills from his footage. His words and his ideas and his analysis. It was paragraphs from the book he'd left with Nina for safekeeping, along with parts of the journals he'd posted to her. Her name was on the photographs, and her name was on the writing. Tunde was mentioned nowhere. She had stolen it from him entirely.

Tunde let out a noise he had not known was in him. A bellow from the back of the throat. The sound of grieving. Deeper than sobs.

And then there was a sound from the corridor outside. A call. Then a shout. A woman's voice.

He didn't know what she was shouting. To his exhausted, terrified brain, it sounded like, "He's in here! Open this door!"

He grabbed his bag, scrambled to his feet, pushed open the window and ran up on to the low, flat roof.

From the street, he heard calls. If they weren't looking for him before, they were looking at him now. Women in the street were pointing and shouting.

He kept running. He would be all right. Across this roof. Jump to the next. Across that roof, down the fire escape. It was only when he was into the forest again that he realized he'd left his phone still plugged in, in that empty store room.

When he remembered, and knew he could not go back for it, he thought his despair would destroy him. He climbed a tree, lashed himself to a branch and tried to sleep, thinking things might look better in the morning.

That night, he thought he saw a ceremony in the woods.

He thought that from his high perch in the tree; he was awakened by the sound of crackling flame and felt a momentary terror that the women had set the trees on fire again, that he would burn alive up here.

He opened his eyes. The fire was not near at hand but a little way off, glimmering in a forest clearing. Around the fire there were figures dancing, men and women stripped naked and painted with the symbol of the eye in the centre of an outstretched palm, the lines of power emanating sinuously around their bodies.

At times, one of the women would push a man to the ground with a blue-bright jolt, placing her hand on the painted symbol on his chest, both of them whooping and crying out as she showed her power on him. She would mount him then, her hand still in the centre of him, still holding him down, the frenzy of it showing on his face, urging her to hurt him again, harder, more.

It had been months since Tunde had held a woman, or been held by one. He began to yearn to climb down from his perch, to walk into the centre of the rock-circle, to allow himself to be used as those men were used. He grew hard, watching. He rubbed himself absently through the fabric of his jeans.

There was the sound of a great drumming. Can there have been drums? Would it not have attracted attention? It must have been a dream.

Four young men crawled on all fours in front of a woman in a scarlet robe. Her eye sockets were empty, red and raw. There was a grandeur to her step, a certainty in her blindness. The other women prostrated themselves, kneeling and full body, before her.

She began to speak, and they to respond.

As in a dream, he understood their words, although his Romanian was not good and it was impossible they were speaking English. And yet he understood.

She said, "Is one prepared?"

They said, "Yes."

She said, "Bring him forward."

A young man walked into the centre of the circle. He wore a crown of branches in his hair and a white cloth tied at his waist. His face was peaceful. He was the willing sacrifice that would atone for all the others.

She said, "You are weak and we are strong. You are the gift and we are the owners.

"You are the victim and we are the victors. You are the slave and we are the masters.

"You are the sacrifice and we are the recipients.

"You are the son and we are the Mother.

"Do you acknowledge that it is so?"

All the men in the circle looked on eagerly.

"Yes," they whispered. "Yes, yes, please, yes, now, yes."

And Tunde found himself muttering it with them. "Yes."

The young man held out his wrists to the blind woman, and she found them with one sure motion, gripping one in each hand.

Tunde knew what was about to happen. Holding his camera, he could barely make the finger on the shutter-release press down. He wanted to see it happen.

The blind woman at the fire was all the women who had nearly killed him, who could have killed him. She was Enuma and she was Nina and she was the woman on the rooftop in Delhi and she was his sister Temi and she was Noor and she was Tatiana Moskalev and she was the pregnant woman in the wreckage of the Arizona mall. The possibility has been pressing in on him all of these years, pushing down on his body, and he wanted it done now, wanted to see it done.

In that moment, he longed to be the one with his wrists clasped. He longed to kneel at her feet, his face buried in the wet soil. He wanted the fight over, he wanted to know who won even at his own cost, he wanted the final scene.

She held the young man's wrists.

She pressed her forehead to his.

"Yes," he whispered. "Yes."

And when she killed him, it was ecstasy.

In the morning, Tunde still does not know whether it was a dream. His manual camera is advanced by eighteen pictures. He might have pressed the button in his sleep. He will only know if the film is developed. He hopes it was a dream, but that has its own terrors. If, in some dream place, he had yearned to kneel.

376

He sits in the tree and thinks things through from the night before. It does look better in the morning, somehow. Or at least less terrifying. The report of his death can't have been an accident or a coincidence. It's too much. Moskalev or her people must have discovered that he'd gone, that his passport had gone with him. The whole thing must have been staged: the car accident, the charred body, the suitcase. This means one very important thing: he cannot go to the police. There is no more fantasy — he had not quite realized before that this fantasy still clung to the edges of his mind — that he can walk into a police station with his hands up and say, "Sorry, cheeky Nigerian journalist here. I've made some mistakes. Take me home." They won't take him home. They will take him out into a quiet place in the woods and shoot him. He is alone.

He needs to find an internet connection. There will be one somewhere. A friendly man who'll let him use the home computer for just a few minutes. He can convince them in five lines that it's him, that he's really alive.

He's shaking as he climbs down from the tree. He'll walk on from here, he'll stay in the forest and head for a village he passed through four days ago with some friendly faces. He'll send his messages. They'll come for him. He shifts his bag on his back and sets his face to the south.

There's a noise in the bushes to his right. He whirls around. But the noise is on the left, too, and behind him; there are women standing up in the bushes, and he knows then with a terror like a springing trap — they've been waiting for him. Waiting all night to catch him. He tries to break into a run but there's something at his ankles, a wire, and he falls. Down, down, struggling, and someone laughs and someone jolts him on the back of the neck.

When he wakes, he is in a cage, and something is very bad.

The cage is small and made of wood. His backpack is in here with him. His knees are pulled up to his chest — there is no room to stretch them out. He can feel from the throbbing ache in his muscles that he's been like this for hours.

He is in a woodland camp. There is a small campfire burning. He knows this place. It is the camp he saw in the dream. Not dream. It is the encampment of the blind woman, and they have caught him. His whole body starts to shake. It can't end here. Not trapped like this. Not thrown on the fire or executed for some god-awful tree-magic religion. He rattles the sides of the cage with his legs.

"Please!" he shouts, though no one is listening. "Please, someone help me!"

There's a low, throaty chuckle from the other side of him. He cranes his head to look.

There's a woman standing there.

"Got yourself in a fucking mess, haven't you?" she says.

He tries to make his eyes focus. He knows the voice from somewhere a long way away, a long time ago. As if the voice were famous.

He blinks and she comes into view. It is Roxanne Monke.

Roxy

She says, "I recognized your face as soon as I saw you. Seen you on the telly, haven't I?"

He thinks he's in a dream, must be, can't not be. He starts to cry. Like a child, confused and angry.

She says, "Stop that now. You'll set me off. What the fuck are you doing here, anyway?"

He tries to tell her, but the story no longer makes sense even to him. He decided to walk into danger because he thought he was enough, and now he is in danger and it is clear to him that he has never been enough and it is unbearable.

"I was looking for . . . the mountain cult," he barks out at last. His throat is dry and his head aches.

She laughs. "Yeah, well. You found it. So that was a bloody stupid idea, wasn't it?"

She gestures around her. He's at the edge of a small encampment. There are perhaps forty dirty tents and huts slumped around the central fire. A few women are at the open mouths of their huts, whetting knives, or fixing metal shock gauntlets, or staring blankly. The place stinks: a smell of burning flesh and rotten food and faeces and dogs and a sour note of vomit. To one

379

side of the latrine there's a pile of bones. Tunde hopes they are animal bones. There are two sad-looking dogs tied by short lengths of rope to a tree — one has an eye missing, and patches of fur.

He says, "You have to help me. Please. Please help me."

She looks at him, and her face twists in an awkward half-smile. She shrugs. And he sees that she's drunk. Fuck.

"I don't know what I can do, mate. I don't have much . . . influence, here."

Fuck. He is going to have to be more charming than he's ever been in his whole life. And he's stuck in a cage where he can't even move his neck. He takes a deep breath. He can do it. He can.

"What are *you* doing here? You vanished the night of the big Moskalev party, and that was months ago. Even when I left the city they were saying you'd been bumped off."

Roxy laughs. "Were they now? Were they? Well, someone tried. And it's taken me a while to heal is all."

"You look pretty . . . healed now."

He looks her up and down appreciatively. He's particularly impressed with himself for doing so without being able to move.

She laughs. "I was going to be President of this fucking country, you know. For about . . . three hours there, I was going to be the fucking President."

"Yeah?" he says. "I was going to be the star of Amazon's fall line-up." He looks right and left. "Think they're coming for me now with a drone?"

380

And then she's laughing, and he's laughing, too. The women at the entrances to the tents glance over at them balefully.

"Seriously. What are they going to do with me?" he says.

"Oh, these people are bloody mental. They hunt men at night," Roxy says. "Send girls off into the forest to scare 'em. Once they're scared and running, they set a trap — tripwire, something like that."

"They hunted me."

"Well, you bloody walked towards them, didn't you?" Roxy makes another little half-smile. "They've got some *thing* about blokes; they round up boys and let them be king for a few weeks and then stick antlers on their heads and kill them at new moon. Or full moon. Or one of those moons. Obsessed by the fucking moon. If you ask me, it's cos they've got no telly."

He laughs again; a real laugh. She's funny.

This is the magic by daylight; tricks and cruelty. The magic is in the belief in magic. All this is, is people with an insane idea. The only horror in it is imagining oneself into their minds. And that their insanity might have some consequences on the body.

"Listen," he says. "Now we're here . . . how hard would it be for you to get me out?"

He gives the door of his cage a little push with his feet. It is bound fast by several twine cords. It would not be hard for Roxy to cut them if she had a knife. But the people around the encampment would see.

She pulls a flask out of her back pocket and takes a little swig. Shakes her head.

"They know me," she says, "but I don't bother them, they don't bother me."

"So you've been hiding in the woods for weeks, not bothering them?"

"Yeah," she says.

A fragment of something he read a long time ago floats through his mind. A flattering looking-glass. He has to be a flattering mirror for her, reflecting her at twice her ordinary size, making her seem to herself to be strong enough to do this thing he needs her to do. "Without that power," mutters a voice in his head, "probably the earth would still be swamp and jungle."

"That's not you," he says. "That's not who you are."

"I'm not who I was, my friend."

"You can't stop being who you are. You're Roxy Monke."

She snorts. "You want me to fight our way out of here? Cos . . . that's not gonna happen."

He gives a little laugh. Like she's trying it on, must be making a joke.

"You don't need to fight. You're Roxy Monke. You've got power to burn, I've seen you, I've heard about you. I've always wanted to meet you. You're the strongest woman anyone's ever seen. I've read the reports. You killed your father's rival in London and then put him out to pasture himself. You can just ask them for me and they'll open the door."

She shakes her head. "You've got to have something to offer. Something to trade," but she's thinking it through now, he can see it.

"What have you got that they want?" he says.

Her fingers dig into the wet earth. She holds two handfuls of soil for a moment, looking at him.

"I told myself I'd keep my head down," she says.

He says, "But that's not you. I've read about you." He hesitates, then chances his luck. "I think you'll help me because it's nothing to you to do it. Please. Because you're Roxy Monke."

She swallows. She says, "Yeah. Yeah, I am."

At dusk, more of the women return to the camp, and Roxanne Monke bargains with the blind woman for Tunde's life.

As she speaks, Tunde sees that he was right: the people in this camp seem respectful and a little frightened of her. She has a small plastic bag of drugs that she dangles in front of the leaders of the camp. She asks for something, but is turned down. She shrugs. She gestures her head towards him. Fine, she seems to be saying, if we can't make a deal this way, I'll take that boy instead.

The women are surprised, then suspicious. Really? That one? It's not a trick?

There is a little haggling. The blind woman tries to argue. Roxy argues back. In the end, it doesn't take too much to persuade them to let him go. He was right about how they see Roxy. And he is not particularly prized. If this woman wants him, let her take him. The soldiers are coming anyway; the war is closer every day. These people are not mad enough to want to stay here now that the soldiers are close by. They'll take up their encampment in two or three days and move towards the mountains.

They bind his arms tightly behind his back. They throw in the bag he was carrying for nothing, just to show her some respect.

"Don't be too friendly with me," she says as she pushes him to walk ahead of her. "Don't want them to think I like you or that I got you cheap."

His legs are cramped from his time in the cage. He has to take slow, shuffling steps along the forest path. It is an age until they are out of sight of the camp, and another aeon until they cannot hear the noise of it behind them.

With each step, he thinks, I am tied and I am in the hands of Roxanne Monke. He thinks, She's a dangerous woman at the best of times. What if she's just playing with me? Once these thoughts have flashed across the mind, they can never be put back. He is silent until, a few miles along the dirt-track, she says, "I think that's far enough," and takes a small knife from her pocket and cuts his bonds.

He says, "What are you going to do with me?"

She says, "I suppose I'll rescue you, get you home. I'm Roxy Monke, after all." Then she breaks into a laugh. "Anyway, you're a celebrity. People'd pay good money for this, wouldn't they? Walk through the forest with a celeb."

And this makes him laugh. And his laughter makes her laugh. And then they are both standing in the forest, leaning against a tree, hooting and gasping for breath, and something is broken between them then, and something is a little easier.

"Where are we heading?" he says.

She shrugs. "I've been lying low for a bit. Something's rotten with my people. Someone . . . betrayed me. I'm all right if they think I'm dead. Till I can work out how to get back what's mine."

"You've been hiding," he says, "in a war zone? Isn't *that* a 'bloody stupid idea'?"

She looks at him sharply.

He's chancing something here. He can already feel the prickles across his shoulder where she'd jolt him if he pissed her off. He might be a celebrity, but she's a mugshot.

She kicks at the stone-leaf mix on the path and says, "Yeah, probably. I didn't have much option, though."

"No nice compound in South America to jet off to? I thought you people had it all worked out."

He does have to know how angry he can make her; this is clear right through to his bones. If she's going to try to hurt him, he needs to know that first. He's tensed for the blow already, but it does not come.

She sticks her hands in her pockets. "I'm all right here," she says. "People keep their mouths shut. I'd left stuff for myself just in case, you know?"

He thinks of the little plastic packet she held in front of the women in the camp. Yes, if you're using an unstable regime to smuggle drugs, you probably do have any number of secret supply-dumps, just in case of trouble.

"Here," she says. "You're not going to write about this, are you?"

"Depends whether I get out alive," he says.

And that makes her laugh, and then he's laughing again. And after a minute she says, "It's my brother Darrell. He's got something of mine. And I'm going to have to be careful how I get it back off him. I'll get you home, but until I work out what to do, we're lying low, OK?"

"And that means . . ."

"We're going to spend a few nights in a refugee camp."

They come to a tented muddy field at the bottom of a gully. Roxy goes to claim a space for them; just a few days, she says. Make yourself useful. Meet people, get to know them, ask what they want.

At the bottom of his rucksack he finds an ID card from an Italian news-gathering service, a year out of date, but enough to encourage some people to talk. He uses it judiciously, wandering from tent to tent. He learns that there has been more fighting than he'd heard, and more recently. That, in the past three weeks, the helicopters don't even land any more; they drop food and medicine and clothes and more tents for the slow and steady stream of stumbling people arriving through the woods. UNHCR is, understandably, unwilling to risk its people here.

Roxy is treated respectfully here. She is a person who knows how to get certain drugs and fuel; she helps people with the things they need. And because he's with her, because he sleeps on a metal bed in her tent, the people here leave him alone. He feels a little safe for the first time in weeks. But of course, he is not safe. Unlike Roxy, he could not simply walk into the forest in this place. Even if no other forest cult caught him, he is illegal now.

He interviews a few English-speaking people in the camp who tell him the same thing over and over again. They are rounding up the men without papers. They go away for "work detail" but they do not return. Some of the men here, and some of the women, tell the same story. There have been editorials in the newspapers and thoughtful to-camera pieces on the one working black-and-white TV in the hospital tent.

The subject is: how many men do we really need? Think it over, they say. Men are dangerous. Men commit the great majority of crimes. Men are less intelligent, less diligent, less hard-working, their brains are in their muscles and their pricks. Men are more likely to suffer from diseases and they are a drain on the resources of the country. Of course we need them to have babies, but how many do we need for that? Not as many as women. Good, clean, obedient men, of course there will always be a place for those. But how many is that? Maybe one in ten.

You can't be serious, Kristen, is that really what they're saying? I'm afraid it is, Matt. She puts a gentle hand on his knee. And of course they're not talking about great guys like you, but that is the message of some extremist websites. That's why the NorthStar girls need more authority; we've got to protect ourselves against these people. Matt nods, his face sombre. I blame those men's rights people; they're so extreme, they've provoked this kind of response. But now we have to protect ourselves. He breaks into a smile. And after the break, I'll be learning some fun self-defence moves you can practise at home. But first, the weather on the ones.

Even here, even after all Tunde has seen, he can't really believe that this country is trying to kill most of its men. But he knows that these things have happened before. These things are always happening. The list of crimes punishable by death has grown longer. A newspaper announcement from a week-old paper suggests that "surly refusal to obey on three separate occasions" will now be punished by "work detail". There are women here in the camp caring for eight or ten men who all huddle around her, vying for her approval, desperate to please, terrified of what might happen if she removed her name from their papers. Roxy could leave the camp at any time, but Tunde is alone here.

On their third night in the camp, Roxy wakes a few moments before the first tang and crackle of the power blows the lamps strung along the central pathway of the camp. She must have heard something. Or just felt it, the way the nylon is humming. The power in the air. She opens her eyes and blinks. The old instincts are still strong in her; she has not lost them, at least.

She kicks Tunde's metal-frame bed.

"Wake up."

He's tangled half in and half out of the sleeping bag. He pushes the cover off him, and he's almost naked there. Distracting, even now.

"What?" he says; then, hopefully, "Helicopter?"

"Don't you wish," she says. "Someone's attacking us."

And then he's wide awake, pulling on his jeans and fleece.

There's the smashing sound of glass and metal.

"Stay low to the ground," she says, "and, if you can, run into the woods and climb a tree."

And then someone puts her hand to the central generator and summons all the power that is in her body and sends it hurtling through the machine and the low lights burst into sparks and glass filaments all around the camp and the darkness becomes absolute.

Roxy hauls up the back of the tent, where it always leaked anyway, through the rotten stitching, and Tunde bellies out, starts for the forest. She should follow him. She will, in a moment. But she pulls on a dark jacket with a deep hood, wraps a scarf around her face. She'll keep to the shadows, work her way around to the north; that'll be the safest route out, anyway. She wants to see what's going on. As if she could still turn anything to her will.

Around her there are already screams and shouts. She's lucky that her tent wasn't on the edge of the camp. Some are burning there already, probably with the people still inside, and there's the sweet stench of petrol. It will be several minutes yet until everyone in this camp even knows what's happening, and that it is not an accident or a generator fire. Through the tents, by the red glow of the fire, she glimpses a short, squat woman setting a flame with the spark from her hands. The flash lights her face white for an instant.

Roxy knows the look on her face; she's seen it before. The kind of face her dad would have said was a bad bet for business. Never keep someone on a job who likes it too much. She knows when she sees the single flash of that gleeful and hungry face that they're not here to raid for what they can find. They're not here for anything that can be given.

They start by rounding up the young men. They go tent to tent, pulling them down or setting them on fire so the occupants have to run out or burn. They're not neat about it, not methodical. They're looking for any halfway-decent-looking young men. She was right to send Tunde into the forest. A wife, or perhaps a sister, tries to stop them from taking the pale-skinned, curly-haired man who's with her. She fights off two of them with precise and well-timed jolts to the chin and the temple. They overwhelm her easily, and kill her with a particular brutality. One of them grabs the woman by the hair and the other delivers a bolt directly through the woman's eyes. Finger and thumb pressed against her eyeballs, the very liquid of them scrambled to a milky white. Even Roxy has to look away for a moment.

She backs further into the forest, climbs a tree hand-over-hand, using a loop of rope to help her. By the time she's found a criss-cross place where three branches meet, they have turned their attention to the man.

He will not stop screaming. Two of the women take him by the throat and send a paralysis into his spine.

One squats on top of him. She pulls off his trousers. He is not unconscious. His eyes are wide and glistening. He is struggling for breath. Another of the men tries to rush forward to help him and gets a crack to the temple for his trouble.

The woman on top cups his balls and dick in her palm. She says something. Laughs. The others laugh, too. She tickles him there with the tip of a finger, making a little crooning sound, as if she wants him to enjoy it. He can't speak; his throat is bulging. They might have broken his windpipe already. She puts her head to one side, makes a sad face at him. She might as well have said in any language in the world, "What's the matter? Can't get it up?" He tries to kick with his heels to get away from her, but it's too late for that.

Roxy would like very much for this not to be happening. If she had it in her power, she would jump down from her concealed position and kill them. First these two by the tree — you could get those before anyone knew what you'd done. Then the three with knives would come for you, but you could dart to the left between the two oaks, so they'd have to come one by one. Then you'd have a knife. It would be easy. But that's not her position right now. And it is happening. No wishing on her part can stop it. Therefore, she watches. To be a witness.

The woman sitting on the man's chest applies her palm to his genitals. She starts with a low hum of a spark. He's still doing muffled screaming, still trying to get away. It can't hurt too much yet. Roxy's done this herself to blokes, for both their fun. His cock comes up like a salute, like they always do. Like a traitor. Like a fool.

The woman makes a little smile appear across her face. Raises her eyebrows. As if to say, See? Just needed some encouragement, didn't you? She holds his balls, tugs on them once, twice, just as if she were giving him a treat, and then jolts him fiercely, right through the scrotum. It'd feel like a glass spike, driven straight through. Like lacerations from the inside. He screams, arches his back. And then she unbuttons the crotch of her combat trousers and sits on his cock.

Her mates are laughing now and she's laughing too as she pumps herself up and down on him. She's got her hand firmly planted in the centre of his stomach, giving him a dose every time she thrusts up with bunched thighs. One of her mates has a cellphone. They photograph her there, straddling him. He throws his arm over his face but they pull the arm back. No, no. They want to remember this.

Her mates are egging her on. She starts to touch herself, moves faster, her hips rocking forward. She's really hurting him now, not in a measured and thoughtful way, not to extract the maximum pain in interesting ways, just brutally. It's easily done as you get close. Roxy's done it herself once or twice, scared some bloke. It'd be worse if you'd taken the Glitter. The woman's got one hand on his chest and every time she tips forward she's giving him a crackle across his torso. He's trying to push her hand away, and screaming, and reaching out to the crowd around them for help, and begging in a slurred language Roxy wouldn't

392

understand, except that the sound of "Help me, oh God, help me" is the same in every language.

When the woman comes, her mates roar their approval. She throws her head back and pushes her chest forward and lets go a huge blast right into the centre of his body. She rises, smiling, and they all pat her on the back, and she's laughing and smiling still. She shakes herself like a dog, and like a dog looks hungry yet. They start up a chant, the same four or five words in a rhythm as they ruffle her hair and give each other fist-bumps. The pale, curly-haired man had been stopped finally and for ever by that last blast. His eyes are open, staring. The rivulets and streams of red scarring run across his chest and up around his throat. His prick is going to take a while to subside, but the rest of him is gone. Not even death throes, not even twitching. The blood is even now pooling in his back, in his buttocks, in his heels. She'd put her hand on his heart and stopped him dead.

There is a noise that is different to grief. Sadness wails and cries out and lets loose a sound to the heavens like a baby calling for its mother. That kind of noisy grief is hopeful. It believes that things can be put right, or that help can come. There is a different kind of sound to that. Babies left alone too long do not even cry. They become very still and quiet. They know no one is coming.

There have been staring eyes in the dark, but there are no shrieks now. There is no rage. The men are quiet. Over on the other side of the camp there are still women fighting the invaders to drive them back, and there are still men picking up rocks or pieces of metal to hurt the women with. But here, those who saw it make no sound.

Two of the other soldiers kick at the body of the dead man a little. They scuff dirt up over it, which might be some sign of piety or shame, but leave it there soiled and bleeding and bruised and swollen and marked with the raised scars of pain, not dug into the earth at all. And they go looking for their own prizes.

There is no sense in what is done here this day. There is no territory to be gained, or a particular wrong to be avenged, or even soldiers to be taken. They kill the older men in front of the younger with palms to the faces and the throat, and one shows off her special skill of drawing crude effects upon the flesh with the tips of her fingers. Many of them take some of the men, and use them, or simply play with them. They offer one man a choice between keeping his arms or his legs. He chooses legs, but they break their bargain. They know that no one cares what happens here. No one is here to protect these people, and no one is concerned for them. The bodies might lie in this wood for a dozen years and no one would come this way. They do it because they can.

In the hour before dawn, they are tired, but the power coursing through them, and the powder, and the things they've done turn their eyes red and they cannot sleep. Roxy has not moved for hours. Her limbs are sore and her ribs grind and her scar is yet jagged across her collarbone. She feels exhausted by what she has seen, as if the very witnessing of it had been physical labour.

394

She hears her name called softly, and she jumps, almost unseats herself from the tree, her nerves are so jangled and her mind so confused. Since the thing that happened, she forgets sometimes, now, who she is. She needs someone to remind her. She looks to her left and right, and then sees him. Two trees over, Tunde is still alive. He's lashed himself to a branch with three coils of rope, but, spotting her in the pre-dawn light, he starts to untie himself. After this night he looks like home to her and she can tell she looks the same to him. Something familiar and secure in all of this.

He climbs a little higher, where the branches meet and mingle, and hauls himself hand over hand towards her, finally dropping down softly in the little perch she's found. She's well hidden in a place where two great limbs of the tree meet, making a little nest of a thick branch that one person can rest their back on while the other leans on them. He drops down on to her — he's taken some injury, she can tell, in the night; he's broken something at his shoulder — and they lie heavily together. He reaches for her hand. Interlaces his fingers with hers to keep them steady. They are both afraid. He smells fresh, like something green and budding.

He says, "I thought you were dead, when you didn't follow me."

She says, "Don't speak too soon. Could still be dead tonight."

He makes a little rough breath, a sign in place of a laugh. He mutters, "This also has been one of the dark places of the earth."

They both fall, dazed, for a few minutes into a staring trance a little like sleep. They should move, but the presence of a familiar body is too comforting to give up, for a moment.

When they blink, there is someone in this tree just beneath them. A woman in green fatigues, one hand in an army gauntlet, three fingers sparking as she climbs. She's shouting back down to someone on the ground. She's using her flashes to peer up through the trees, to burn the leaves. It's still dark enough that she can't see.

Roxy remembers a time she and a couple of the girls heard there was a woman beating up her boyfriend in the street. It had to be stopped; you can't let that kind of thing keep on if you own a place. By the time they got there it was just her, drunk, railing around the street, shouting and swearing. They found him in the end, hiding in the cupboard under the stairs and although they tried to be good and kind Roxy thought in her heart, Why didn't you fight back? Why didn't you try? You could have found a frying pan to hit her with. You could have found a spade. What good did you think hiding was going to do? And here she is. Hiding. Like a man. She's not sure what she is any more.

Tunde is resting on her, his eyes open, his body tense. He's seen the soldier, too. He stays still. Roxy stays still. They're concealed here, even as the dawn brings on more danger. If the soldier gives up, they could be safe.

The woman climbs a little higher in the tree. She's setting fire to the lower branches, though for now they flare and then smoulder out. There's been rain recently.

That's lucky. One of her mates throws her up a long metal baton. They've had fun with this. Inserting it and setting it crackling. She starts to sweep the upper boughs of the next tree over with this rod. No hiding place is perfect.

The woman makes a swift jab, too close to Roxy and Tunde, too close. The tip of it ends no more than two arm's reaches away from his face. When the woman raises her hand, Roxy can smell her. The yellow scent of sweat, the acid smell of the Glitter metabolizing through the skin, the peppery-radish of the power itself, in use. The combination as familiar as Roxy's own skin. A woman with her strength up and no ability to contain it.

Tunde whispers to her, "Just shock her, once. It conducts both ways. When the pole comes towards us next time, grab it and shock her very hard. She'll fall to the floor. The others will have to look after her. We can get away."

Roxy shakes her head, and there are tears in her eyes, and Tunde has a sudden feeling as if his heart has opened, as if the wires around his chest have all at once unfurled.

He has an idea of something. He thinks of the scar he's caught sight of at the edge of her collarbone, how protective of it she is. And how she's bargained and threatened and charmed and yet . . . has he seen her . . . has she ever hurt anyone yet in his presence since she found him in the cage? Why was she hiding in the jungle, she a Monke, she the strongest there ever was? He had never thought of this before. He hasn't imagined for years what a woman could be without this thing or how she could have it taken from her.

The woman reaches with her rod again. The tip catches the back of Roxy's shoulder, sending an iron nail of pain into her, but she remains silent.

Tunde looks around. Beneath the tree they're hiding in there is only marshy ground. Behind them are the remains of several stomped-flat tents and three women toying with a young man who is at his very limit. Ahead and to the right there is the burned-out generator and, half concealed by branches, an empty metal gasoline drum they've used as a rain collector. If it's full, it's no use to them. But it might be empty.

The woman is calling back to her friends, who are shouting up words of encouragement to her. They found someone hiding in one of the trees towards the entrance of the camp. They're looking for more. Tunde shifts position carefully. Movement will catch the soldiers' eyes, and then they'll be dead. They only need the soldiers distracted for a few minutes, just enough to get away. He reaches into his backpack, rootles his fingers through to an internal pocket and pulls out three canisters of film. Roxy is breathing softly, watching him. She can tell from the way he's looking what he's going to try. He lets his right arm drop, like a vine detached from the tree, like nothing. He hefts the film canister in it and skims it towards the oil drum.

Nothing. The throw was too short. The canister has thumped into the soft earth, dead as blood. The woman is climbing again, and making those broad sweeps with the metal rod. He takes up another film canister; this one's heavier than the other and for a moment he's puzzled as to why. Then he remembers — this is the one he put his American change into. As if he'd ever use those pennies again. It almost makes him laugh. But it's good, it's heavy. It'll fly better. He has the momentary urge to bring it to his lips, like one of his uncles used to with a betting slip when it was neck and neck and his whole body was tense like the racehorses on the screen. Go on, thing. Fly for me.

He lets his hand dangle. He pendulums it back and forth once, twice, three times. Go on. Come on. You want it. He lets it fly.

The clang, when it comes, is so much louder than he'd expected. The canister had hit just at the rim. The noise means the vessel cannot be full of water. It is wild; the oil drum reverberates, it sounds intentional, like someone announcing their arrival. Heads turn across the camp. Now, now. Quickly, he does it again. Another canister, this one packed with matches against the wet. Heavy enough. Another wild gong. Now it seems like there must be someone there, someone making a stand. Some idiot calling the hurricane to descend on her.

They come, quick, from around the camp. Roxy has time to pull a thick stump of branch off the tree, hurling it towards the oil drum to make one more bang and shout of metal before they're close enough to see what's happening. The woman who was so nearly on her scrambles down through the branches of the tree in her rush to be the first to pull up whichever fool it is who thought they could stand against these forces.

Tunde's whole body is aching now; there is no differentiation between the sources of pain, the cramp and the broken bones, and there's little enough space between him and Roxy that when he looks down he can see her wound and scarring, and it hurts him as if the line had been cut along his own body. He stretches himself by the arms, feeling with his feet for the broad lower branch. Runs along it. Roxy's doing the same. They drop down, hoping that the cover is enough to hide the shape of movement from the women in the camp.

Stumbling through the marshy earth, Tunde risks one single look back, and Roxy follows his gaze, to see if the soldiers have tired of the empty oil drum now, to see if they're after them.

They're not. The drum wasn't empty. The soldiers are kicking it, and laughing and reaching in to lift out the contents. Tunde sees, and Roxy sees, as if in a camera's flash, what they have found. There were two children in the oil drum. They're lifting them out. They are perhaps five, or six. They are sobbing, still curled tight into balls as they're lifted up. Tiny, soft animals trying to protect themselves. A pair of blue trousers frayed at the bottom. Bare feet. A sundress spotted with yellow daisies.

If Roxy had her power, she would return and turn every one of those women all to ash. As it is, Tunde grabs her hand and pulls her away and they run on. Those children would never have survived. They might. They would have died there, anyway, of cold and exposure. They might have lived.

★ ★ ★

It is a cold dawn and they run hand in hand, unwilling to let one another go.

She knows the way of the land and the safest roads, and he knows how to find a quiet place to hide. They keep running until they can only walk, and still they walk on mile after mile in silence, palms pressed together. Towards dusk, he spots one of the deserted rail stations that populate this part of the country; waiting for Soviet trains that never came, they are mostly home to roosting birds now. They smash a window to pile in, and find a few mouldy cushions on wooden benches and, in a cupboard, a single dry woollen blanket. They dare not make a fire, but they share the blanket, together in a corner of the room.

He says, "I've done a terrible thing," and she says, "You saved my life."

She says, "You can't even believe half the things I've done, mate. Bad bad things," and he says, "And you saved my life."

In the dark of the night he tells her about Nina and how she published his words and his photographs under her name. And how he knows by that that she was always waiting to take from him everything he had. And she tells him about Darrell and what was taken from her, and in that telling he knows everything; why she carries herself like this and why she's been hiding all these long weeks and why she thinks she can't go home and why she hasn't struck against Darrell at once and with great fury, as a Monke would do. She had half forgotten her own name until he reminded her of it.

401

One of them says, "Why did they do it, Nina and Darrell?"

And the other answers, "Because they could."

That is the only answer there ever is.

She holds his wrist and he is not afraid. She runs her thumb along the palm of his hand.

She says, "The way I see it, I'm dead, and so are you. What do dead people do for fun around here?"

They are both injured and hurting. His collarbone, he thinks, is broken. There is a grinding pain in it every time he shifts position. Theoretically, he is stronger than her now, but this makes them both laugh. She is short and stocky like her dad, the same thick bull's neck, and she has fought more than him, she knows the ways of fighting. When he plays at pushing her back on to the ground, she plays at putting her thumb on the centre of his pain, where the shoulder joins the neck. She presses just enough to make him see stars. He laughs, and she laughs, breathless and foolish in the middle of the storm. Their bodies have been rewritten by suffering. They have no fight left. They cannot, in that moment, tell which of them is supposed to be which. They are ready to begin.

They move slowly. They keep their clothes half on. She traces the line of an old scar at his waist; he took it in Delhi when he first learned fear. He touches his lips to the livid line at her collarbone. They lie side by side. After what they've seen, they cannot want it fast or hard now, either of them. They touch one another gently, feeling out the places where they are alike and where they are different. He shows her he is ready, and

402

she is ready, too. They slide together simply, key in a lock. "Ah," he says. "Yes," she says. It's good; her around him, him inside her. They fit. They move slowly and easily, taking account of each other's particular pains, smiling and sleepy and for a moment without fear. They come with soft, animal grunts, snuffling into each other's necks, and fall asleep like that, legs intertwined, underneath a found blanket, in the centre of a war.

Exceptionally complete Cataclysm Era carving, around five
thousand years old. Found in western Britain.

The carvings are uniformly found in this condition —
something has been deliberately removed from the centre, but
it is impossible to ascertain what was lost. Among the theories
are; that these stones framed portraits; or lists of local
ordinances; or that they were simply a rectangular form of art
with nothing in the centre. The chiselling was clearly a protest
against whatever was — or was not! — represented by the
central portion.

Here it comes

These things are happening all at once. These things are one thing. They are the inevitable result of all that went before. The power seeks its outlet. These things have happened before; they will happen again. These things are always happening.

The sky, which had seemed blue and bright, clouds over, grey to black. There will be a rainstorm. It has been long in coming, the dust is parched, the soil longs for soaking, teeming dark water. For the earth is filled with violence, and every living thing has lost its way. In the north and the south and the east and the west, the water gathers in the corners of the sky.

In the south, Jocelyn Cleary puts up the hood of her jeep as she takes a concealed exit down a gravel track that looks like it might lead to something interesting. And in the north, Olatunde Edo and Roxanne Monke wake to hear the rain pounding on the iron roof of their shelter. And in the west Mother Eve, who once went by the name of Allie, looks out at the gathering storm and says to herself, Is it time? And her own self says, Well, duh.

There has been an atrocity to the north; rumours of it have come from too many sources now to be denied.

It was Tatiana's own forces, mad with power and maddened by delays and the orders that keep coming in, saying, "Any man can betray you, any of them could be working for the North." Or was it just that Tatiana has never bothered to control them properly? Maybe she'd always have gone mad, whatever Mother Eve had done to her.

Roxy's gone. The forces are slipping out of Tatiana's control. There will be a military coup within weeks if someone doesn't take charge of this situation. And then North Moldova will march in and take the country, and the stocks of chemical weapons in the southern cities.

Allie sits in her quiet study, looking out at the storm, and counts the cost of business.

The voice says: I've always told you that you were meant for great things.

Allie says: Yes, I know.

The voice says: You command respect not only here but everywhere. Women would come here from around the world if you owned the country.

Allie says: I said, I know.

The voice says: So what are you waiting for?

Allie says: The world is trying to go back to its former shape. Everything we've done is not enough. There are still men with money and influence who can shape things to their will. Even if we win against the North. What are we starting here?

The voice says: You want the whole world turned upside down.

Allie says: Yes.

408

The voice says: I feel you, but I don't know how to be any clearer about this. You can't get there from here. You'll have to start again. We'll have to begin again with the whole thing.

Allie says in her heart: A great flood?

The voice says: I mean that's one way to handle it. But you've got a few options. Look. Think it over. Once you've done the thing.

It is late at night. Tatiana sits at her desk, writing. There are orders to be signed to generals. She is going to push forward against the North, and this is going to be a disaster.

Mother Eve comes to stand behind her and places a comforting hand at the back of her neck. They've done this many times. Tatiana Moskalev finds the gesture soothing, although she cannot quite say what it is that makes it so.

Tatiana says, "I'm doing the right thing, aren't I?"

Allie says, "God will always be with you."

There are hidden cameras in this room. Another artefact of Tatiana's paranoia.

A clock strikes. One, two, three. Why then, 'tis time to do it.

Allie reaches out with her particular sense and skill, calming each nerve in Tatiana's neck and shoulders, skull and cranium. Tatiana's eyes close. Her head nods.

And, as if it weren't part of her at all, as if for this moment she couldn't even detect what it's doing, Tatiana's hand creeps across the table to the sharp little letter opener lying on the pile of papers.

Allie feels the muscles and nerves trying to resist, but they're used to her now, and she to them. Dampen down the reaction *here*, strengthen the one *there*. It wouldn't be so easy if Tatiana hadn't drunk so much and taken a concoction of Allie's own manufacture, something Roxy had cooked up for her in the labs. It's not easy now. But it can be done. Allie places her mind in Tatiana's hand, holding the letter opener.

There's a smell, suddenly, in the room. A scent like rotten fruit. But the hidden cameras can't pick up a smell.

In one swift movement, too fast for Mother Eve to do anything about it — how could she have suspected what was about to happen? — Tatiana Moskalev, maddened by the crumbling of her power, slashes at her own throat with the sharp little knife.

Mother Eve jumps back, screaming, shouting for help.

Tatiana Moskalev bleeds out over the papers across her desk, her right hand still twitching as if it were alive.

Darrell

"They sent me from the office," says the lumbering Irina. "There is a soldier on one of the paths at the back."

Shit.

They watch through the closed-circuit TV. The factory's eight miles down a dirt track from the main road, and the entrance is concealed by hedges and forest. You'd have to know what you were looking for to find it. But there's a soldier — just one, no sign of a larger party — not far from their perimeter fence. She's a mile out from the factory proper, all right; she can't even see it from where she is. But she's there, walking around the fence, taking photographs on her phone.

The women in the office look at Darrell.

They're all thinking: what would Roxy do? He can see it on their foreheads like they've written it there in marker pen.

Darrell feels the skein in his chest start to throb and twist. He's been practising with it, after all. There's a part of Roxy right here and that part knows just what to do. He's strong. Mightier than the mightiest. He's not supposed to show any of these girls what he can do —

Bernie's been very clear about that — the cat is not to be let out of the bag. Until he's ready to be shown off to the highest bidders in London as an example of what they can do . . . he's to keep it secret.

The skein whispers to him: She's only one soldier. Go out there and give her a fright.

Power knows what to do. It has a logic to it.

He says, All of you, watch me. I'm going out.

He talks to the skein as he walks down the long gravel path and opens the gate in the perimeter fence.

He says: Don't fail me now. I paid good money for you. We can work together on this, you and me.

The skein, obedient now, laid out along Darrell's collarbone as it had once been in Roxy's, begins to hum and sizzle. It is a good feeling; that is an aspect of the situation Darrell had suspected but not confirmed until now. Feels a little bit like being drunk, in a good way, in a strong way. Like that feeling you get when you're drunk that you could take all comers, and in this case you really could.

The skein talks back to him.

It says: I'm ready.

It says: Come on, my son.

It says: Whatever you need, I've got it.

Power doesn't care who uses it. The skein doesn't rebel against him, doesn't know that he's not its rightful mistress. It just says: Yes. Yes, I can. Yes. You've got this.

He lets a little arc pass between his finger and his thumb. He's still not used to that feeling. It buzzes uncomfortably on the surface of the skin, but it feels

412

strong and right inside his chest. He should just let her go, but he can take her, no sweat. That'll show them.

When he looks back at the factory, the women are crowded around the windows watching him. A few of them are straying out on to the path to keep him in their eye line. They're muttering to each other behind their hands. One of them makes a long arc between her palms.

They're sinister fuckers, the way they move together. Roxy's gone too easy on them all these years, letting them have their weird little ceremonies and use the Glitter in their off hours. They go into the woods together at sunset and don't come back till dawn, and he can't fucking say anything, can he, because they turn up bang on time and they get the job done, but something's going on, he can tell it by the smell of them. They've made a little fucking *culture* here, and he knows they talk about him, and he knows they think he shouldn't be here.

He crouches low so she won't see him coming.

Behind Darrell, the tide of women grows.

Roxy says in the morning when she and Tunde are dressed again, "I can get you out of the country."

He had forgotten, really, that there is an "out of the country" to get to. Already this feels more real and more inevitable than anything that has come before.

He pauses halfway through pulling on a sock. He's left them to dry overnight. They still stink, and their texture is crisp and gravelly.

"How?" he says.

She shrugs one shoulder, smiles. "I'm Roxy Monke. I know a few people around here. You want to get out?"

Yes, he does. Yes.

He says to her, "What about you?"

She says, "I'm going to get my thing back. And then I'll come and find you."

She's got something back already. She's twice her natural size.

He thinks he likes her, but he has no way to know for certain. She has too much to offer him to be a simple proposition right now.

She gives him a dozen ways to find her, as they walk the long miles from here to there. This email inbox will go to her, even though it looks like a shell company. That person will always know how to reach her, eventually.

She says, more than once, "You saved my life." And he knows what she means.

At a crossroads between fields, next to a shelter for a twice-a-week bus, she uses a payphone to call a number she knows by heart.

When the call's finished, she talks him through what's going to happen: a blonde woman in an airline hat will pick him up this evening and drive him across the border.

He'll have to be in the boot; sorry, but that's the safest way. It'll take about eight hours.

"Waggle your feet," she says, "or you'll get a cramp. It hurts and you're not going to be able to get out."

"What about you?"

She laughs. "I'm not getting in the boot of a bloody car, am I?"

"What then?"

"Don't worry about me."

They part just after midnight outside a tiny village whose name she cannot pronounce.

She kisses him once, lightly on the mouth. She says, "You'll be all right."

He says, "You're not staying?" But he knows how this goes; the process of his life has taught him the answer. If she were seen taking particular care of a man, it'd make her look soft, in her world. And it'd put him in danger if anyone thought he meant something to her. This way, he could be any kind of cargo.

He says, "Go and take it back. Anyone worth knowing will think more of you for surviving this long without it."

Even as he says it, he knows it's not true. No one would think anything much of him for surviving this long.

She says, "If I don't try, I'm not myself any more anyway."

She walks on, taking the road to the south. He puts his hands into his pockets and his head down and strolls into the village, trying to look like a man sent on an errand that he has every right to be about.

He finds the place, just as she described it. There are three shuttered shops; no lights in the windows above them. He thinks he sees a curtain twitch in one of the windows and tells himself he's imagined it. There's no one waiting for him here and no one chasing him.

When did he get so jumpy? And he knows when. It wasn't this last thing that made it happen. This fear has been building up in him. The terror put its roots down into his chest years ago and every month and every hour has driven the tendrils a little deeper into the flesh.

He can bear it, somehow, in the moments when the imagined darkness matches the real. He hasn't felt this dread when he was actually in a cage, or in a tree, or witnessing the worst thing in the world unfold. The dread stalks him on quiet streets or waking alone in a hotel room before dawn. It has been a long time since he's felt comfort in a night walk.

He checks his watch. He has ten minutes to wait on this empty street corner. He has a package in his bag — all of his camera film, all the footage he's shot on the road, and his notebooks. He had that envelope ready from the start, stuck with stamps. He had a few; he'd thought if things got dicey he might post his film to Nina. He's not going to post anything to Nina. If he sees her again, he'll eat her heart in the marketplace. He has a marker pen. He has the envelope, packed neatly. And on the opposite corner of the street there's a postbox.

How likely is it that the postal service is still working here? He'd heard in the camp that it did still work in the larger villages, the towns and cities. Things have broken down on the border and in the mountains, but they're miles from the border and the mountains now. The box is open. There's a time listed for a pick-up tomorrow.

416

He waits. He thinks. Maybe there will be no car. Maybe there will be a car and instead of a blonde woman with a hat there'll be three women who'll bundle him into the back seat. Maybe he'll end there, thrown out on to the road between one town and the next, used and torn. Maybe there'll be a blonde woman with a hat who'll take the money she's being paid for this and say she's crossed the border. She'll let him out of the car to run in the direction she tells him is freedom, but there'll be no freedom there, only the forest and the chase and the end of it in the soil, one way or another.

It suddenly seems a remarkably stupid thing to have trusted his whole life to Roxanne Monke.

There is a car coming. He sees it from a long way off, its headlights sweeping the dirt road. He has time to write a name on this package, and an address. Not Nina, obviously not. Not Temi or his parents; he can't let this be his final message to them if he disappears into this dark night. He has an idea. It is a terrible idea. It is a safe idea. If he doesn't come through this, there is one name and mailing address he could write on this package which would make sure the images would be sent around the world. People should know, he says to himself, what has happened here. To witness is the first responsibility.

He has time. He scribbles quickly, without thinking too hard. He runs for the postbox. He slots the package into the chute and closes the lid again. He is back in position when the car stops at the kerb.

There is a blonde woman behind the wheel with a baseball cap pulled low over her eyes. There's a crest on it that says "JetLife".

She smiles. Her English is thickly accented. She says, "Roxy Monke sent me. Will be there before morning."

She opens the back of the car. It is a sedan, roomy enough, though he'll have to keep his knees curled against his chest. Eight hours.

She helps him climb into the trunk of the car. She is careful with him, gives him a rolled-up sweater to make a buffer between the back of his head and the metal housing. The trunk is clean, at least. As his nose meets the curled fibres of the interior carpet he smells only the floral chemical scent of shampoo. She gives him a large bottle of water.

"When finished, can piss in bottle."

He smiles up at her. He wants her to like him, to feel that he is a person not a cargo.

He says, "Travelling coach, huh? These seats get smaller every year."

But he can't tell if she's understood his joke.

She pats his thigh as he settles in.

"Trust me," she says as she slams the trunk closed.

From here, on the gravel path between nowhere and nothing, just around the corner of a screen of trees, Jocelyn can see a low-slung building with windows only on the upper storey. Just the corner of it. She hoists herself on to a rock and takes some pictures. It's inconclusive. She should probably get closer. Although, that's a stupid idea. Be sensible, Jos. Report what you've found and bring a unit back tomorrow. There's definitely something there that someone's gone to quite a lot of trouble to hide from the road. Although, what if it's nothing; what if this ends with everyone in the base laughing at her? She takes another few pictures.

She's intent on it.

She doesn't notice the man until he's almost standing next to her.

"What the fuck do you want?" he says in English.

She has her duty weapon by her side. She shifts position, allowing it to bang against her hip and move forward.

"I'm sorry, sir," she says. "I've gotten turned around. I'm looking for the main highway."

She keeps her voice very level and calm, turns her American accent up a bit without really intending to.

Suzy Creamcheese. Bumbling tourist. It's the wrong tack to take. She's in army fatigues. Pretending at innocence just makes her look more guilty.

Darrell feels the skein pumping in his chest. It does it more when he's afraid, twitches and fizzes.

"What the fuck are you here for, on my land?" he says. "Who sent you?"

Behind his back, he knows the women in the factory are observing the encounter with cold, dark eyes. There'll be no doubting him after this, there'll be no asking what he is; they'll know what he is when they see what he can do. He's not a man in women's clothing. He's one of them, as strong as them, as capable.

She tries a smile. "No one sent me, sir. I'm off duty. Just doing a little sightseeing. I'll be on my way."

She sees his eyes flick to the maps in her hand. If he sees those, he'll know she was looking for this place and no other.

"All right," says Darrell. "All right, let me get you back on your way."

He doesn't want to help her; he's coming too close, she should call this in. Her hand twitches towards her radio.

He reaches out three fingers of his right hand and, with a single swift jolt, he kills the radio dead. She blinks. Sees him for a moment as himself: monstrous.

She tries to swing her rifle round but he has it by the butt, catches her in the chin with it, leaving her staggering, hauls the strap over her head. He considers the rifle, then tosses it into the undergrowth. He comes for her, palms crackling.

She could run. There's her dad's voice in her head, saying, Take care of yourself, sweetie. And there's her mom's voice in her head, saying, You're a hero, act like it. This is one guy with a factory in the middle of nowhere — how hard can it be? And the girls from the base. You of all people should know how to deal with one dude with a skein. Don't you, Jocelyn? Isn't this your special subject, Jocelyn? She has something to prove. And he has something to prove. They are ready to begin.

They square off to each other, circling, looking for a weakness.

Darrell's done little tests before; he gave minor burns and hurts and damage to a couple of the surgeons who worked with him, just to see if it'd work. And he's practised alone. But he's never used it before in a fight, not like this. It's exciting.

He has a sense, he finds, of how much he's got left in the tank. It's loads. More than loads. He lunges for her, and misses, and lets an excited jolt earth through his feet, and he's still got *loads*. No wonder blooming Roxy always looked so pleased with herself. She was carrying this round inside her. He'd've felt pleased with himself, too. He does.

Jocelyn's skein is twitching; it's just because she's excited. It's working now better than it ever has, it's been so good since Mother Eve cured her, and now she knows why that happened, why God made that miracle for her. It was for this. To save her from this bad man, trying to kill her.

She tightens her stomach and runs for him, feinting to the left, pretending to go for his knee, and at the last moment, as he's stooping to defend against her, she twists right, reaches up, grabs his ear and gives him a jolt to the temple. It's smooth and easy, sweetly humming. He gets her on the thigh and it hurts like fuck, like a rusty blade scraped along the bone; the big muscles just keep bunching and releasing and the leg wants to collapse. She hauls herself upright with the right leg, dragging the left behind her. He's got a lot of power; she can feel it crackling on his skin. The kinds of jolts he gives are muscular and iron-hard, not like Ryan's. Not like anyone she's fought with.

She remembers her training for fighting an opponent who is simply stronger, simply has more to work with. She's going to have to let him play himself out on her, presenting to him the bits of the body where he can do least damage. He's got more juice in the tank than she does, but if she can trick him into spending some into the earth, if she can be faster and more nimble than him, she'll have this.

She backs away, dragging the leg a little more than she needs to. She makes herself stumble a little. She clutches at the hip. She watches him watching her. She holds out a warding hand. She lets the leg collapse under her. She falls to the ground. He's on her like the wolf on the lamb, but she's faster than him now, rolling to the side so that he discharges his killing blow into the gravel. He roars, and she kicks him hard in the side of the head with her good leg.

422

She reaches up to grab the back of his knee. She has it planned, like they taught her. Bring him to the ground, go for the knees and ankles. She has enough. One solid blow here where the ligaments join and he'll tumble.

She grabs at his trousers and makes contact, her palm firm against his calf to jolt him. And there's nothing. It's gone. Like a motor revved to a standstill. Like a pool of water drained into the earth. It's not there.

It must be there.

Mother Eve gave it back to her. It must be there.

She tries again, concentrates, thinks of the stream of running water, like they taught her in her classes, thinks of how it flows naturally from place to place, if she only allows it. She could find it again if she had just a moment.

Darrell kicks her hard in the jaw with his heel. He'd also been waiting for the blow that didn't come. But he's not one to waste his chance. She's kneeling now on all fours, gasping, and he kicks her in the side once, twice, three times.

He can smell bitter oranges, suddenly, and a scent like burned hair.

He pushes her head down with the heel of his hand, delivering a charge to the base of her skull. It becomes impossible to fight with the jolt there — he knows: it was done to him once long ago in a park at night. The mind becomes confused, the body goes limp, there is nothing to be done. He holds the charge steady. The soldier sinks to the floor, her face in the gravel. He waits until she's stopped twitching. He's breathing heavily. He has enough juice left to do the same thing twice over. It feels good. She's gone.

Darrell looks up, smiling, as if the trees should applaud his victory.

In the distance, he hears the women pick up a song, a melody he's heard them sing before but which none of them will explain to him.

He sees the dark eyes of the women watching him from the factory. He knows something then. A simple fact that should have been obvious from the first, had he not been pushing the knowledge from him. The women are not glad to see what he has done, or that he could do it. The fucking bitches are just staring at him: their mouths as closed as the earth, their eyes as blank as the sea. They walk down the stairs inside the factory in orderly file and march towards him as one. Darrell lets out a sound, a hunted cry, and he runs. And the women are after him.

He is heading for the road; it's only a few miles away. On the road, he'll flag down a car, he'll get away from these crazy bitches. Even in this godforsaken country, someone will help him. He runs pell-mell across an open plain between two great bodies of trees, feet pushing off from the ground as if he could become a bird now, a stream now, a tree now. He's in open country and he knows they can see him, and they are making no sound, and he lets himself think — maybe they've turned back, maybe they're gone. He looks behind him. There are a hundred women and the sound of their muttering is like the sea, and they are

424

gaining on him, and his ankle turns and twists and he falls.

He knows them all by name. There's Irina and clever Magda, Veronyka and blonde Yevgennia and dark Yevgennia; there's cautious Nastya and cheery Marinela and young Jestina. All of them are there, the women he's worked alongside these months and years, the women he's given employment to and treated fairly, in the circumstances, and there's a look on their faces that he cannot read.

"Come on now," he calls to them. "I got rid of that soldier for you. Come on. Yevgennia, did you see me? I took her down with one zap! Did you all see that?"

He's pushing himself away with his one good foot, as if he could scoot on bum and hip for the shelter of the trees or the mountain.

He knows they know what he's done.

They are calling to each other. He cannot hear precisely what it is they're saying. It sounds like a collection of vowels, a cry from the throat: eoi, yeoui, euoi.

"Ladies," he says as they run nearer and nearer yet, "I don't know what you think you saw, but I just hit her on the back of the neck. Fair and square. I just hit her."

He knows he is speaking, but he cannot see any recognition in their faces.

"I'm sorry," says Darrell. "I'm sorry, I didn't mean it."

They are humming the ancient song softly.

"Please," he says. "Please don't."

And they're on him. Their hands find bare flesh, their grasping, pulling fingers on his stomach and his back, the sides of him, his thighs and armpits. He tries to jolt them, tries to grab at them with hands and teeth. They let him discharge himself into their bodies, and still they come. Magda and Marinela, Veronyka and Irina, grabbing hold of his limbs and setting the power across the surface of his skin, scarring him and marking him, and digging into his flesh, softening his joints and twisting them.

Nastya places her fingertips at his throat and makes him speak. They're not his words. His mouth is moving and his voice is humming but it's not him speaking, it's not.

His lying throat says, "Thank you."

Irina plants her foot in his armpit and hauls on his right arm, shocking and burning it. The flesh at the joint crisps and turns. She has the ball out of the socket. Magda pulls with her, and they have the arm off. The others are at his legs, and his neck, and the other arm, and the place across his collarbone where his ambition sat. Like the wind stripping the leaves from a tree, so inexorable and so violent. They pull the skein, lithe and wriggling, from his living chest, just before they get his head off, and at last he is quiet, their fingers dark with his blood.

When she makes the call for Tunde, it has to be the start. Roxy Monke is coming back.

"My brother," she says on the phone. "My fucking brother betrayed me and tried to have me killed."

The voice on the phone is excited.

"I knew he was lying. The little shit. I knew he was lying. The women in the factory said he told them he was getting orders from you, and I fucking *knew* he was lying."

"I've been gathering my strength," says Roxy, "and making my plans, and now I will take back from him what he took from me."

So she has to make it true.

She gathers a small force. No one's answering the phone at the factory, so some fucking thing has happened. She figures he might have people with him, even if he thinks she's dead; he'd have to be a fucking idiot to think no one would try to take the factory from him.

She's expecting to have to mount an assault, but the gates of the factory are open.

Her workers are all sitting on the lawns. They greet her with wild whoops, a sound that echoes across the lake, caught up and passed between the crowd of them.

How did she ever think that she would not be welcomed back here, cripple as she is? How could she have imagined she couldn't allow herself to return?

Her coming home is a festival. They say, "We knew you were coming back, we saw it. We knew that you were the one we were waiting for."

They crowd around her, they touch her hand, they ask where she's been and if she's found a new place for the factory, the war coming so close and the soldiers so intent on finding them.

The soldiers? "United Nations soldiers," they say. "We've had to put them off the scent more than once now."

"Yeah?" says Roxy. "You did that without Darrell, did you?"

A look passes between the women, hooded and mysterious. Irina puts her arm around Roxy's shoulder. Roxy thinks she can smell something on her; a smell like sweat but more soupy, a rotten tang to it like period blood. They've been tweaking the drug here; Roxy knows it and never stopped it. They've been taking off-label product. They go into the woods and do it on the weekends; it makes their sweat smell like mould. There's blue paint under their fingernails.

Irina squeezes Roxy tightly. She thinks the woman's going to pick her up. Magda takes her hand. They walk with her towards the cold-storage fridge where they keep the volatile chemicals. They open the door. Inside, on the cold table, is a collection of lumps of meat, raw and bloody. She cannot, for a moment, imagine why they are showing her this. And then she knows.

"What have you done?" she says. "What the fuck have you done?"

Roxy finds it there in amongst the blood and mush. Her own self, her beating heart, the part of her that powered all the rest. A thin and rotting piece of gristle. The muscle striated, purple and red.

There was a day, three days after Darrell took it from her, that she realized she wasn't going to die. The spasms across her chest had ceased. The red and yellow flashes had disappeared from her eyes. She had bandaged herself up and walked to a hut she knew in the woods and waited there for death, but on the third day she knew death was not going to take her.

She thought then, It's because my heart is still alive. Outside my body, in his body, but still alive. She thought, I would know if it were dead.

But she hadn't known.

She holds her palm to her collarbone.

She waits to feel something.

Mother Eve comes to meet Roxanne Monke off the midnight army transport into the train station in Basarabeasca, a city a little to the south. She could have waited for Roxy in the palace, but she wanted to see her face. Roxy Monke is thinner, she looks pained and worn. Mother Eve holds her in a tight embrace, forgetting, for a moment, to probe or question with her special sense. There's the smell of her friend, just the same, pine needles and sweet almonds. There's the feeling of her.

Roxy pulls away awkwardly. Something's wrong. She's almost silent as they drive through the empty streets to the palace.

"You're President now, then?"

Allie smiles. "It couldn't wait." She pats the back of Roxy's hand, and Roxy moves the hand away.

"Now you're back, we should talk about the future."

Roxy smiles a tight, thin-lipped smile.

In Mother Eve's apartments in the palace, when the last door is closed and the last person is gone, Allie looks at her friend, wonderingly.

"I thought you were dead," she says.

"I almost was," says Roxy.

"But you came back to life. The one the voice told me was coming. You are a sign," says Allie. "You are my sign, just as you always were. God's favour is with me."

Roxy says, "Don't know about that."

She undoes the top three buttons of her T-shirt, to show what's there to be seen.

And Allie sees it.

And she understands that this sign which she hoped would point in one direction is pointing entirely in another.

There was a symbol that God placed in the sky after the last time She destroyed the world. She licked Her thumb and drew an arc across the Heavens, spreading the multitude of colour and sealing her promise that She would never again flood the face of the earth.

Allie looks at the crooked, upside-down bow of the curved scar across Roxy's chest. She draws her fingertips along it gently, and though Roxy looks away she lets her friend touch her wound. The rainbow, inverted.

"You were the strongest one I ever knew," she says, "and even you have been brought low."

Roxy says, "I wanted you to know the truth."

"You were right," says Allie. "I know what this means."

Never again: the promise written across the clouds. This thing cannot be allowed to happen again.

"Listen," says Roxy, "we should talk about the North. The war. You're a powerful woman now." She makes a little half-smile. "You always was on your way somewhere. But there's bad things happening up there. I've been thinking. Maybe you and me together can find a way to stop it."

"There's only one way to stop it," says Mother Eve, calmly.

"I just think, I don't know, we could work it out somehow. I could go on telly. Talk about what I've seen, what's happened to me."

"Oh. Yes. Show them the scar. Tell what your brother did to you. There would be no stopping the fury then. The war would begin in earnest."

"No. That's not what I mean. No. Eve. You don't understand. It's going to *absolute shit* up there. I mean, crazy fucking batshit weirdo religious nutcases going around killing kids."

Eve says, "There's only one way to put it right. The war has to start now. The real war. The war of all against all."

Gog and Magog, whispers the voice. That's right.

Roxy sits back a little bit in her chair. She's told Mother Eve the whole story, every last part of what she saw and what was done to her and what she was made to do.

"We have to *stop* the war," she says. "I still know how to get stuff done, you know. I've been thinking. Put me in charge of the army in the North. I'll keep order, we'll patrol the border — real borders like a real country — and, you know, we'll talk to your friends in America. They don't want fucking Armageddon breaking out here. God knows what weapons Awadi-Atif has."

Mother Eve says, "You want to make peace."

"Yeah."

"*You* want to make peace? *You* want to take charge of the army in the North?"

"Well, yeah."

Mother Eve's head starts to shake as if someone else is shaking it for her.

She gestures to Roxy's chest.

"Why would anyone take you seriously now?"

Roxy jerks her whole body away.

She blinks. She says, "You *want* to start Armageddon."

Mother Eve says, "It's the only way. It's the only way to win."

Roxy says, "But you know what's going to happen. We'll bomb them and they'll bomb us and it'll spread out wider and wider, and America will get involved and Russia and the Middle East and . . . the women will suffer as well as the men, Evie. The women will die just as much as the men will if we bomb ourselves back to the Stone Age."

"And then we'll be in the Stone Age."

"Er. Yeah."

"And then there will be five thousand years of rebuilding, five thousand years where the only thing that matters is: can you hurt more, can you do more damage, can you instil fear?"

"Yeah?"

"And then the women will win."

A silence spreads through the room and into Roxy's bones, up through the marrow, a cold, liquid stillness.

"Bloody hell," says Roxy. "So many people have told me you're crazy, you know, and I never believed any of them."

Mother Eve watches her with great serenity.

"I was always, like, 'No, if you met her you'd know she's clever, and she's been through a lot, but she's not crazy.'" She sighs, looks at her hands, palms and backs. "I went looking for information about you ages ago. I mean, I had to know."

Mother Eve watches her, as if from very far away.

"It's not that hard to find out who you used to be. It's all over some bits of the internet. Alison Montgomery-Taylor." Roxy takes her time with the words.

"I know," says Mother Eve. "I know it was you who made it all disappear. And I'm grateful. If that's what you're asking, I'm still grateful."

But Roxy frowns, and in that frown Allie knows she's made a mistake somewhere along the line, some little minor misalignment in her understanding.

Roxy says, "I get it, right? If you killed him, he probably deserved killing. But you should go and look up what his wife's doing now. She's called Williams now. Remarried a Lyle Williams, in Jacksonville. She's still there. You should go and look her up."

Roxy stands up. "Don't do this," she says. "Please don't."

Mother Eve says, "I'll always love you."

Roxy says, "Yeah. I know."

Mother Eve says, "It's the only way. If I don't do it, they will."

Roxy says, "If you really want the women to win, go and look up Lyle Williams in Jacksonville. And his wife."

Allie lights a cigarette, in the quiet of a stone room in the convent overlooking the lake. She brings it to flame in the old way, with the spark from her fingertips. The paper crackles and blackens into glowing light. She breathes it in to the edges of her lungs; she is full of her old self. She has not smoked for years. Her head swims.

It's not hard to find Mrs Montgomery-Taylor. One, two, three words typed into a search box and there she is. She runs a children's home now, under the auspices and with the blessing of the New Church. She was an early member, there in Jacksonville. In a photograph on the website of their children's home, her husband stands behind her. He looks a great deal like Mr Montgomery-Taylor. A shade taller, perhaps. A little bushier in the moustache, a little rounder in the cheek. Different colouring, a different mouth, but the same broad category of man: a weak man, the kind of man who, before any of this, would still have done what he was told. Or perhaps she's remembering Mr Montgomery-Taylor. They look sufficiently similar that Allie finds she's rubbing her jaw in the place where Mr Montgomery-Taylor hit her, as if the blow had landed only moments ago. Lyle Williams and his wife, Eve

Williams. And together they care for children. It is Allie's own church that has made this thing possible. Mrs Montgomery-Taylor did always know how to work a system to best advantage. The website for the children's home she operates talks about the "loving discipline" and "tender respect" they teach.

She could have looked any time. She cannot think why she has not turned on this old light before.

The voice is saying things. It's saying: Don't do it. It's saying: Turn away. It's saying: Step away from the tree, Eve, with your hands up.

Allie doesn't listen.

Allie picks up the handset of the telephone on the desk here in the convent room overlooking the lake. She dials the number. Far away, in a hallway with a side table topped by a crocheted runner, a telephone rings.

"Hello?" says Mrs Montgomery-Taylor.

"Hello," says Allie.

"Oh, Alison," says Mrs Montgomery-Taylor. "I hoped you'd call."

Like the first drops of rain. Like the earth saying: I'm ready for it. Come and get me.

Allie says, "What have you done?"

Mrs Montgomery-Taylor says, "Just what the Spirit has commanded me to do."

Because she knows what Allie means. Somewhere inside her heart, for all the twisting and turning, she does know. As she's always known.

Allie can see in that moment that "everything will disappear" is a fantasy, has always been a delightful dream. Not the past, not the lines of pain inscribed on the human body, not a thing will ever disappear. While Allie has been making her life, Mrs Montgomery-Taylor has also continued, growing monstrous as the clock turned.

Mrs Montgomery-Taylor keeps up a bright line of chatter. She's so honoured to receive a telephone call from Mother Eve, although she always knew she would; she understood what was meant by the name Allie had taken on, that she was Allie's real mother, her *spiritual* mother, and hadn't Mother Eve always said that the mother is greater than the child? She understood what was meant by that, too, that the mother is the one who knows best. She is so happy, so *delighted*, that Allie understood that everything she and Clyde did they did for her own good. Allie feels sick.

"You were just a young girl, so wild," says Mrs Montgomery-Taylor. "You drove us to distraction. I saw that a devil was in you."

Allie remembers it now, as she has not brought it out into the light these many years. She pulls it from the back of her mind. She blows the dust from this heap of rags and bones. She stirs them with a fingertip. She arrived at the home of the Montgomery-Taylors, a jangled child, beady and birdlike and wild. Her eyes seeing everything, her hands in everything. It was Mrs Montgomery-Taylor who brought her, and Mrs Montgomery-Taylor who wanted her, and Mrs Montgomery-Taylor who spanked her when her hand was in the raisin jar. It was Mrs Montgomery-Taylor who grabbed her arm and threw her to her knees and commanded her to pray that the Lord would forgive her sin. Over and over, on her knees.

"We had to drive that devil out of you, you see that now, don't you?" says Mrs Montgomery-Taylor, now Mrs Williams.

And Allie does see it. It is as clear to her now as if she were watching it through the glass panes of their own sitting room. Mrs Montgomery-Taylor tried to pray the devil out of her and then to beat the devil out of her, and then she had a new idea.

"Everything we did," she says, "we did for love of you. You needed to be taught discipline."

She remembers the nights Mrs Montgomery-Taylor would put the polka on the radio real loud. And then Mr Montgomery-Taylor would ascend the stairs to give her the teachings. She remembers, all at once and with great clarity, which order those steps occurred in. First the polka music. Then the ascent of the stairs.

Beneath every story, there is another story. There is a hand within the hand — hasn't Allie learned that well enough? There is a blow behind the blow.

Mrs Montgomery-Taylor's voice is sly and confidential.

"I was the first member of your New Church in Jacksonville, Mother. When I saw you on the television I knew that God had sent you to me as a sign. I knew that She was working through me when we took you in, and that She knew that all I had done I had done for Her glory. I was the one who made the police documents disappear. I've been caring for you all these years, darling."

Allie thinks of all that was done in the house of Mrs Montgomery-Taylor.

440

She cannot pull apart the strands of it, has never separated the experiences into individual moments to examine each one closely and particularly. Remembering it is like a sudden flash of light upon carnage. Body parts and machinery and chaos and a sound that builds from a reedy cry to a full-throated scream and then cuts off to a low-humming almost-silence.

"You understand," she says, "that God was working in us. All that we did, Clyde and I, we did so that you would be here."

It was her touch she felt every time Mr Montgomery-Taylor laid himself upon her.

She cuppeth the power in her hand. She commandeth it to strike.

Allie says, "You told him to hurt me."

And Mrs Montgomery-Taylor, now Mrs Williams, says, "We didn't know what else to do with you, angel. You just wouldn't listen to anything we said."

"And do you do the same now, with other children? With the children in your care?"

But Mrs Montgomery-Taylor, now Mrs Williams, has always been shrewd, even in her madness.

"All children need different kinds of love," she says. "We do what's needed to care for them."

Children are born so small. It does not matter if they are boys or girls. They are all born so weak and so powerless.

Allie comes to pieces quite gently. All the violence in her has been spent out a hundred times. When this thing happens, she is calm, floating above the storm, watching the raging sea below.

She puts the fragments together, sorting and re-sorting them. How much would it take to put it right? Investigations and press conferences and admissions. If it is Mrs Montgomery-Taylor, it is others, too. More than she can count, probably. Her own reputation will suffer. Everything will come out: her past, and her story, and the lies and half-truths. She could move Mrs Montgomery-Taylor quietly on elsewhere; she might even find a way to have her killed, but to denounce her would be to denounce everything. If she roots this out, she roots out herself. Her own roots are rotten already.

And with this she is undone. Her mind disconnects from itself. For a while, she is not here. The voice tries to speak, but the howling of the wind inside her skull is too loud and the other voices now too numerous. In her mind, for a time, it is the war of all against all. It cannot sustain.

After a while, she says to the voice: Is this what it's like to be you?

And the voice says: Fuck you, I told you not to do it. You should never have been friends with that Monke, I told you and you wouldn't listen; she was just a soldier. What did you need a friend for? You had me; you always had me.

Allie says: I never had anything.

The voice says: Well, what now then, if you're so clever?

442

Allie says: I keep meaning to ask. Who are *you*? I've wondered for a while. Are you the serpent?

The voice says: Oh, you think because I swear and tell you to do stuff I must be the devil?

It's crossed my mind. And. Here we are. How am I supposed to tell which side is good and which is bad?

The voice takes a deep breath. Allie's never heard it do that before.

Look, says the voice, we've reached a tricky moment here, I'll give you that. There were things you were never supposed to look at, and now you've gone and looked at them. The whole point of me was to keep things simple for you, you see? That's what you wanted. Simple feels safe. Certainty feels safe.

I don't know if you're aware, says the voice, but you're lying on the floor of your office right now with the phone cradled under your right ear, listening to the sound of beep-beep-beep, and you won't stop shaking. At some point someone's going to come in and find you like this. You're a powerful woman. If you're not back soon, bad things are going to happen.

So I'm giving you the crib sheet right now. Maybe you'll understand it and maybe you won't. Your whole question is the mistake. Who's the serpent and who's the Holy Mother? Who's bad and who's good? Who persuaded the other one to eat the apple? Who has the power and who's powerless? All of these questions are the wrong question.

It's more complicated than that, sugar. However complicated you think it is, everything is always more complicated than that. There are no shortcuts. Not to

443

understanding and not to knowledge. You can't put anyone into a box. Listen, even a *stone* isn't the same as any other stone, so I don't know where you all think you get off labelling *humans* with simple words and thinking you know everything you need. But most people can't live that way, even some of the time. They say: only exceptional people can cross the borders. The truth is: anyone can cross, everyone has it in them. But only exceptional people can bear to look it in the eye.

Look, I'm not even real. Or not real like you think "real" means. I'm here to tell you what you want to hear. But the *things* you people want, I'm telling you.

A long time ago, says the voice, another Prophet came to tell me that some people I'd made friends with wanted a King. I told them what a King would do. He'd take their sons for soldiers and their daughters for cooks — I mean, if the daughters were lucky, right? He'd tax their grain and their wine and their cows. These weren't people with iPads, you feel me; grain and wine and cows were what they had. I said: Look, a King will basically make you into slaves, and don't come crying to me when that happens. That's what kings do.

What can I tell you? Welcome to the human race. You people like to pretend things are simple, even at your own cost. They still wanted a King.

Allie says: Are you trying to tell me there's literally no right choice here?

The voice says: There's never been a right choice, honeybun. The whole idea that there are two things and you have to choose is the problem.

444

Allie says: Then what shall I do?

The voice says: Listen, I'll level with you: my optimism about the human race is not what it once was. I'm sorry it can't be simple for you any more.

Allie says: It's getting dark.

The voice says: Sure is.

Allie says: Welp. I see what you're saying. Been nice working with you.

The voice says: Likewise. See you on the other side.

Mother Eve opens her eyes. The voices in her head are gone. She knows what to do.

The Son in Agony, a minor cultic figure. Of
roughly similar age to the portrayals of the
Holy Mother on page 46.

On the desk of Margot's assistant, a phone rings.

She's in a meeting. The assistant tells the voice on the other end of the line that Senator Cleary can't be reached right now, but she can take a message.

Senator Cleary is in a meeting with NorthStar Industries and the Department of Defence. They want her advice. She's an important person now. She has the ear of the President. Senator Cleary cannot be disturbed.

The voice on the other end of the line speaks a few more words.

They sit Margot on the cream-coloured couch in her own office when they tell her.

They say, Senator Cleary, we have bad news.

"We've had word from the UN: she's been found in the woods. She's still alive. Just barely. Her injuries are . . . extensive. We don't know if she'll pull through.

"We think we know what happened, the man is dead already.

"We're so sorry, Senator. We're so sorry."

And Margot is falling.

Her own daughter. Who put the tips of her fingers in the centre of Margot's palm once and gave her the lightning. Who curled her little, waving hand around Margot's thumb once and held on so tightly that Margot knew for the first time that she was the strong one. Now and for ever she would put her body between this little scrap and harm. That was her job.

There was a time when Jocelyn was three. They were exploring the apple orchard at her parents' farm together, mom and little daughter, with the slow intensity with which a three-year-old examines each leaf and stone and splinter. It was late autumn, the windfalls just turning to rot. Jos stooped down, turned over one of the browning fruit, and a cloud of wasps flew from it. Margot had always had a particular terror of wasps, ever since a child. She grabbed Jos and wrapped her arms around her, holding her close to her body, grabbed her and ran for the house. Jos was fine; not a scratch on her. And Margot, when they were comfortably seated on the couch again, found that she had been stung seven times, all the way down her good right arm. She had not even felt it. That was her job.

She finds she's telling them this story. In a gabble, in a moan. She cannot stop telling this story, as if by telling it she could go back now just a little way along the path, and put her body between Jos and the harm that found her.

Margot says, "How can we stop this happening?"

They tell the Senator it has already happened.

Margot says, "No, how can we stop it happening again?"

There is a voice in Margot's head. It says: You can't get there from here.

448

She sees it all in that instant, the shape of the tree of power. Root to tip, branching and re-branching. Of course, the old tree still stands. There is only one way, and that is to blast it entirely to pieces.

In a mailbox in rural Idaho, a package sits unclaimed for thirty-six hours. It is a yellow padded envelope, about the size of three paperback books, though it rattles a little when shaken. The man who is sent to the post office for it feels it suspiciously. It has no return address: doubly suspicious. But there's no solid bulk that might indicate a home-made bomb. He slits it open along the side with a pocket knife, just to be certain. Into the palm of his hand tumble eight undeveloped rolls of photographic film, one by one. He peers in further. There are notebooks, and USB sticks.

He blinks. He's not a smart man, though he is a cunning one. He hesitates for a moment, thinking this package might be just another piece of junk sent to the group by men who are more crazy than disaffected. They've wasted time before on meaningless trash that men claimed represented the Start of the New Order. He's been personally berated by UrbanDox for bringing back parcels that might contain tracking devices within home-made muffins, or inexplicable gifts of jockey shorts and lube. He pulls a handful of the notes out at random and reads the even hand.

"For the first time today on the road I was afraid."

He sits in his pickup truck, considering it. There have been others he's thrown away without hesitation, others he knows he must bring back.

In the end, the thought slowly crosses his mind that the camera films or the USB sticks might contain nudie pictures. Might as well see what they are, anyway.

The man in the pickup tips the rolls of film back into the envelope, and pokes the notes in after them. Might as well.

Mother Eve says, "When a multitude speak with one voice, that is strength and that is power."

The crowd roars its assent.

"We speak with one voice now," she says. "We are one mind. And we call upon America to join us in the struggle against the North!"

Mother Eve holds up her hands for silence, showing the eyes in the centre of her palms.

"Will the greatest nation on the Earth, the land where I was born and raised, look on while innocent women are slaughtered and while freedom is destroyed? Will they watch in silence while we burn? If they abandon us, who will they not abandon? I call on women across the world to bear witness to what happens here. Bear witness and learn what you can expect to happen to you. If there are women in your government, hold them to account, call on them to act."

Convent walls are thick, and convent women are clever, and when Mother Eve warns them that the apocalypse is near at hand and only the righteous will be saved, she can call the world to a new order.

The end of all flesh is near, because the Earth is filled with violence. Therefore, build an ark.

It will be simple. That is all they want.

There are days that follow one after the next after the next. While Jocelyn heals, and while it becomes clear that she will never fully heal, and while something hardens in Margot's heart.

She appears on the television to talk about Jos's injuries. She says, "Terrorism can strike anywhere, at home or abroad." She says, "The most important thing is that our enemies, both global and domestic, must know that we are strong and that we will retaliate."

She looks down the camera lens and says, "Whoever you are, we will retaliate."

She can't afford to look weak, not at a time like this.

It's not long after that when the phone call comes. They say there's been a credible threat from an extremist group. They've gotten hold somehow of pictures from inside the Republic of the Women. Pasted them all over the internet, saying they were taken by a guy we all know has been dead for weeks. Terrible pictures. Probably Photoshopped, can't be real. They're not even making demands, just rage and fear and threats of attacks unless — God, I don't know, Margot — unless something is done, I guess. The North is already threatening Bessapara with missiles over it.

454

Margot says, "We should do something."

The President says, "I don't know. I feel like I should extend an olive branch."

And Margot says, "Believe me, at a moment like this you need to appear stronger than ever. A strong leader. If that nation has been assisting and radicalizing our home-grown terrorists, we must send them a message. The world must know that the United States is willing to escalate. If you hit us with one jolt, we will hit you with two."

The President says, "I can't tell you how much I respect you, Margot, for the way you can carry on, even with what's happened."

Margot says, "My country comes first. We need strong leadership."

There is a bonus in her contract if NorthStar deployments around the world top fifty thousand women this year. The bonus would buy her a private island.

The President says, "You know there are those rumours they got hold of ex-Soviet chemical weapons."

And Margot thinks in her heart: Burn it all down.

There is a thought in those days. It is that five thousand years is not a very long time. Something has been started now that must find its conclusion. When a person has taken a wrong turn, must she not retrace her steps, is that not wise? After all, we've done it before. We can do it again. Different this time, better this time. Dismantle the old house and begin again.

When the historians talk of this moment they talk about "tensions" and "global instability". They posit the "resurgence of old structures" and the "inflexibility of existing belief patterns". Power has her ways. She acts on people, and people act on her.

When does power exist? Only in the moment it is exercised. To the woman with a skein, everything looks like a fight.

UrbanDox says: Do it.

Margot says: Do it.

Awadi-Atif says: Do it.

Mother Eve says: Do it.

And can you call back the lightning? Or does it return to your hand?

Roxy sits with her father on the balcony, looking out at the ocean. It's nice to think that, whatever happens, the sea will always be here.

"Well, Dad," says Roxy, "you fucked that one up, didn't you?"

Bernie looks at his hands, palms and back. Roxy remembers when those hands were the most terrifying thing in the world to her.

"Yeah," he says. "Suppose so."

Roxy says, with a smile in her voice, "Learned your lesson, have you? You'll do it differently next time?"

And they're both laughing, Bernie's head tipped back to the sky and all his nicotine-stained teeth and fillings showing.

"I should kill you, really," says Roxy.

"Yeah. You should, really. Can't afford to be soft, girl."

"That's what they keep telling me. Maybe I've learned *my* lesson. Took me long enough."

At the horizon, there is a flash across the skyline. Pink and brown, although it is nearly midnight.

"Bit of nice news," she says. "I think I've met a bloke."

"Yeah?"

"Early days," she says, "and with all this, it's a bit complicated. But yeah, maybe. I like him. He likes me." She laughs her old, throaty growl. "I got him out of a country full of mad women trying to kill him, and I own an underground bunker, so obviously he likes me."

"Grandchildren?" says Bernie, hopefully.

Darrell and Terry are gone. Ricky's not going to be able to do anything in that department ever again.

Roxy shrugs. "Might do. Someone's got to survive these things, haven't they?"

A thought occurs to her. She smiles. "Bet if I had a daughter she'd be strong as fuck."

They have another drink before they go down.

Apocrypha excluded from the Book of Eve

Discovered in a cave in Cappadocia, c. 1,500 years old.

The shape of power is always the same: it is infinite, it is complex, it is forever branching. While it is alive like a tree, it is growing; while it contains itself, it is a multitude. Its directions are unpredictable; it obeys its own laws. No one can observe the acorn and extrapolate each vein in each leaf of the oak crown. The closer you look, the more various it becomes. However complex you think it is, it is more complex than that. Like the rivers to the ocean, like the lightning strike, it is obscene and uncontained.

A human being is made not by our own will but by that same organic, inconceivable, unpredictable, uncontrollable process that drives the unfurling leaves in season and the tiny twigs to bud and the roots to spread in tangled complications.

Even a stone is not the same as any other stone.

There is no shape to anything except the shape it has.

Every name we give ourselves is wrong.

Our dreams are more true than our waking.

459

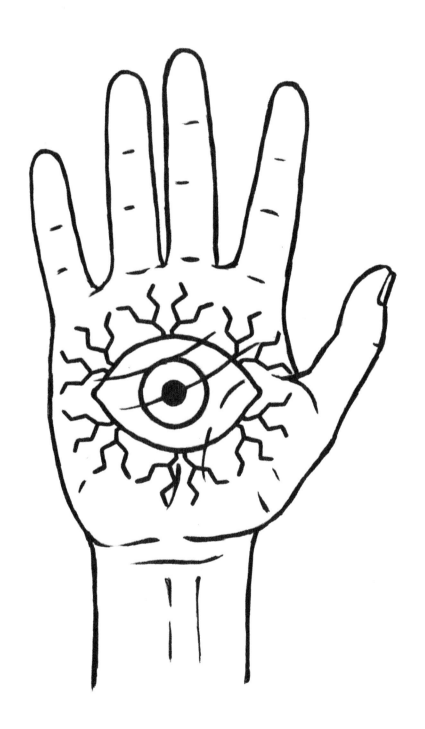

Dear Neil,

Well! I must say first of all that I like your contortionist Mother Eve! I've seen some of those things done at the Underground Circus and I've been very impressed — one of those women made my hand wave at everyone in the room, and even Selim could hardly believe afterwards that I hadn't done it myself. I suppose lots of things in the ancient scriptures can be accounted for that way. And I see what you've done with Tunde — I'm sure something like that has happened to thousands of men down the genera-tions. Misattributions, anonymous work assumed to be female, men helping their wives or sisters or mothers with their work and getting no credit, and yes, simple theft.

I have some questions. The male soldiers at the start of the book. I know you're going to tell me that ancient excavations have found male warrior figures. But really, I suppose this is the crux of the matter for me. Are we sure those weren't just *isolated* civilizations? One or two amongst millions? We were taught in school about women making men fight for entertainment — I think a lot of your readers will still have that in mind when you have those scenes where men are soldiers in India or Arabia. Or those feisty men trying to provoke a war! Or gangs of men locking up women for sex . . . some of us have had fantasies like that! (Can I confess, shall I confess, that while thinking about this I . . . no, no, I can't confess it.) It's not just me, though, my dear. A whole battalion of

461

men in army fatigues or police uniforms really does make most people think of some kind of sexual fetish, I'm afraid!

I'm sure you learned the same thing as I did in school. The Cataclysm happened when several different factions in the old world were unable to reach an accord, and their leaders stupidly each thought they could win a global war. I see you have that here. And you mention nuclear and chemical weapons, and of course the effect of electromagnetic battles on their data-storage devices is understood.

But does the history really support the idea that women didn't have skeins much before the Cataclysm? I know, I know about the occasional statues we find of women without skeins from before the Cataclysm, but that could just be artistic licence. Surely it makes more *sense* that it was women who provoked the war. I feel instinctively — and I hope you do, too — that a world run by men would be more kind, more gentle, more loving and naturally nurturing. Have you thought about the evolutionary psychology of it? Men have evolved to be strong worker homestead-keepers, while women — with babies to protect from harm — have had to become aggressive and violent. The few partial patriarchies that have ever existed in human society have been very peaceful places.

I know you're going to tell me that soft tissue doesn't preserve well, and we *can't* look for evidence of skeins in cadavers that are five thousand years old. But shouldn't that give you pause, too? Are there any problems that your interpretation solves that the standard model of world history leaves unsolved? I mean, it's a clever idea, I'll grant you. And maybe worth doing for that reason alone, just as a fun exercise. But I don't know if it advances your cause to make an assertion that just can't be backed up or proved. You might tell me that it's not the job of a work of history or fiction to advance a cause. Now I'm having an argument with myself. I'll wait for your reply. I just want to challenge your thinking here before the critics do!

Much love,
Naomi

Dearest Naomi,

Thank you, first of all, for taking the time and trouble to read the manuscript. I was afraid it was practically incoherent — I'm afraid I've lost all sense of it.

I have to say I . . . don't think much of evolutionary psychology, at least as it relates to gender. As to whether men are naturally more peaceful and nurturing than women . . . that will be up to the reader to decide, I suppose. But consider this: are patriarchies peaceful because men are peaceful? Or do more peaceful societies tend to allow men to rise to the top because they place less value on the capacity for violence? Just asking the question.

463

Let's see, what else did you ask? Oh, the male warriors. I mean, I can send you images of *hundreds* of partial or full statues of male soldiers — they've been unearthed around the world. And we know how many movements have been devoted to completely obliterating all traces of the time before — I mean, just the ones we know about number in the thousands. We find so many smashed statues and carvings, so many obliterated marking stones. If they hadn't been destroyed, imagine how many male soldier statues there'd be. We can interpret them however we like, but it's actually pretty clear that around five thousand years ago there were a *lot* of male warriors. People don't believe it because it doesn't fit with what they already think.

As to whether you find it believable that men could be soldiers, or what your sexual fantasies are about battalions of uniformed men … I can't be held responsible for that, N! I mean, I take your point, some people will just treat it as cheap porn. That's always the tawdry inevitability if you write a rape scene. But surely serious people will see through that.

Oh yes, OK, you ask, "Does the history really support the idea women didn't have skeins much before the Cataclysm?" The answer is: yes. It does. At least, you have to ignore a huge raft of archaeological evidence to believe otherwise. This is what I've tried to communicate in my previous history books but, as you know, I don't think anyone wanted to hear it.

464

I know you probably didn't mean it to come across as patronizing, but it's not just "a fun idea" to me. The way we think about our past informs what we think is possible today. If we keep on repeating the same old lines about the past when there's *clear evidence* that not all civilizations had the same ideas as us . . . we're denying that anything can change.

Oh God, I don't know. Now I've written that, I feel more uncertain than I did before. Were there particular things that you've read elsewhere that made you feel uncertain about this book? I might be able to work them in somewhere.

Much love. And thanks again for reading it. I really do appreciate it. When yours is done — another masterpiece, I'm sure! — I owe you a practical criticism essay on every chapter!

Love,
Neil

Dear Neil,

Yes, of course I didn't mean "fun" in the sense of "trivial" or stupid. I hope you know I'd never think that about your work. I have a lot of respect for you. I always have had.

But all right, as you've asked . . . there's an obvious question for me. What you've written here contradicts so many of the history books we all read as children; and they're based on traditional accounts going back hundreds, if not thousands, of years. What is it that you think happened? Are you really suggesting that everyone *lied* on a monumental scale about the past?

All love,
Naomi

Dear Naomi,

Thanks for getting back so quickly! So, in answer to your question: I don't know if I have to be suggesting that *everyone* lied.

For one thing, of course, we don't have original manuscripts dating back more than a thousand years. All the books we have from before the Cataclysm have been re-copied hundreds of times. That's a lot of occasions for errors to be introduced. And not just errors. All of the copyists would have had their own agendas. For more than two thousand years, the only people re-copying were nuns in convents. I don't think it's at all a stretch to suggest that they picked works to copy that supported their viewpoint and just let the rest moulder into flakes of parchment. I mean, why would they re-copy works that said that men used to be stronger and women weaker? That would be heresy, and they'd be damned for it.

This is the trouble with history. You can't see what's not there. You can look at an empty space and see that something's missing, but there's no way to know what it was. I'm just . . . drawing in the blank spaces. It's not an attack.

Love,
Neil

Dearest Neil,

I don't think it's an attack. It's hard for me to see women portrayed as they are at times in this book. We've talked about this often. How much "what it means to be a woman" is bound up with strength and not feeling fear or pain. I've been grateful for our honest conversations. I know you've sometimes found it difficult to form relationships with women; and I understand why. I'm so grateful that we've preserved a friendship out of what we had, though. It was so important to me that you listened when I said things that I'd never have been able to tell Selim or the children. The scene of the skein-removal was very hard to read.

Love,
Naomi

Dear Naomi,

Thank you for that. I know you're trying. You're one of the good ones.

I really want this book to make something better, N. I think we can be better than this. This thing isn't "natural" to us, you know? Some of the worst excesses against men were never — in my opinion anyway — perpetrated against women in the time before the Cataclysm. Three or four thousand years ago, it was considered normal to cull nine in ten boy babies. Fuck, there are still places today where boy babies are routinely aborted, or have their dicks "curbed". This can't have happened to women in the time before the Cataclysm. We talked about evolutionary psychology before — it would have made no evolutionary sense for cultures to abort female babies on a large scale or to fuck about with their reproductive organs! So it's not "natural" to us to live like this. It can't be. I can't believe it is. We can choose differently.

The world is the way it is now because of five thousand years of ingrained structures of power based on darker times when things were much more violent and the only important thing was — could you and your kin jolt harder? But we don't have to act that way now. We can think and imagine ourselves differently once we understand what we've based our ideas on.

Gender is a shell game. What is a man? Whatever a woman isn't. What is a woman? Whatever a man is not. Tap on it and it's hollow. Look under the shells: it's not there.

xx
Neil

468

Dearest Neil,

Have been pondering this all weekend. There's a lot to think about and discuss, and I think it's best if we meet to talk it over. I worry that I might write something that you'll interpret in the wrong way, and I don't want that. I know it's a sensitive topic for you. I'll ask my assistant if he'll sort out some dates for us to have lunch.

This is not to say that I'm not behind the book. I really am. I want to make sure it reaches the widest possible audience.

I have one suggestion now. You've explained to me how anything you do is framed by your gender, that the frame is as inescapable as it is nonsensical. Every book you write is assessed as part of "men's literature". So what I'm suggesting is just a response to that, really, nothing more. But there's a long tradition of men who've found a way out of that particular bind. You'd be in good company.

Neil, I know this might be very distasteful to you, but have you considered publishing this book under a woman's name?

Best love,
Naomi

Acknowledgements

More thanks than can be made to Margaret Atwood, who believed in this book when it was barely a glimmer, and told me when I faltered that it was still definitely alive, not dead. Thanks for illuminating conversation to Karen Joy Fowler and to Ursula Le Guin.

Thanks to Jill Morrison of Rolex and to Allegra McIlroy of the BBC for making it possible for these conversations to happen.

Thanks to Arts Council England and to the Rolex Mentor and Protege Arts Initiative, whose financial support helped me write the book. Thanks to my editor at Penguin, Mary Mount, and to my agent, Veronique Baxter. Thanks to my editor at Little, Brown in the US, Asya Muchnick.

Thanks to a good coven, who saved this book one midwinter: Samantha Ellis, Francesca Segal and Mathilda Gregory. And thanks to Rebecca Levene, who knows how to make things happen in a story and made some exciting stuff happen in this one. Thanks to Claire Berliner and Oliver Meek for helping get it started again. Thanks to readers and commenters who gave me courage and confidence: especially Gillian Stern, Bim Adewunmi, Andrea Phillips and Sarah Perry.

Thanks for masculinity chat to Bill Thompson, Ekow Eshun, Mark Brown, Dr Benjamin Ellis, Alex Macmillan, Marsh Davies. Thanks for early discussions to Seb Emina and to Adrian Hon, who knows the future like I used to know God: as immanent and shining.

Thanks to Peter Watts for walking me through the marine biology and helping me work out where to put electro-plaques in the human body. And thanks to the BBC Science Unit, and in particular Deborah Cohen, Al Mansfield and Anna Buckley, for allowing me to pursue my curiosity about the electric eel to a fuller extent than I could ever have hoped.

Thanks to my parents, and to Esther and Russell Donoff, Daniella, Benjy and Zara.

The illustrations are by Marsh Davies. Two of them — the "Serving Boy" and "Priestess Queen" — are based on actual archaeological finds from the ancient city of Mohenjo-Daro in the Indus Valley (although obviously without bits of iPad attached). We don't know much about the culture of Mohenjo-Daro — there are some findings that suggest that they may have been fairly egalitarian in some interesting ways. But despite the lack of context, the archaeologists who unearthed them called the soapstone head illustrated on page 214 "Priest King", while they named the bronze female figure on page 213 "Dancing Girl". They're still called by those names. Sometimes I think the whole of this book could be communicated with just this set of facts and illustrations.

Other titles published by Ulverscroft:

THE ENDLESS BEACH

Jenny Colgan

On the quayside next to the Endless Beach sits the Seaside Kitchen. It's a haven for tourists and locals alike, who all come to eat the most delicious food on the island and catch up with the gossip. Flora, who runs the café, feels safe and content — unless she thinks too hard about her relationship with Joel, her gorgeous but emotionally (and physically) distant boyfriend. While Flora is in turmoil, her best friend Lorna is pining after the local doctor. Saif came to the island as a refugee, having lost all of his family, but he's about to get some shocking news that will change everything for him. As cold winter nights shift to long summer days, can the two friends find their own happy ever afters?

MEET ME AT THE MUSEUM

Anne Youngson

When Tina Hopgood writes a letter of regret to a man she has never met, she doesn't expect a reply. And when Anders Larsen, a lonely museum curator, answers it, neither does he. They're both searching for something — they just don't know it yet. Anders has lost his wife, along with his hopes and dreams for the future. Tina is trapped in a life she doesn't remember choosing. Slowly their correspondence blossoms as they bare their souls to each other with stories of joy, anguish and discovery. But then Tina's letters suddenly cease, and Anders is thrown into despair. Can their unexpected friendship survive?